MW00337046

Praise for *No Thru Road*

(2nd Edition)

In her debut mystery novel, Linda M. Vogt evokes a multitude of emotions with clean, spare prose. The suspense gradually ramps up all the way to the climactic end. Best of all, who can resist Duffy the Dog? Not me!

~Jessie Chandler, award-winning author of the Shay O'Hanlon Caper Series

Linda Vogt's debut novel, *No Thru Road*, immerses readers into the quirky world of Galiano Island, BC, where every villager becomes suspect. Vogt's dynamic duo, Riley Logan and Marie Wells, are intrepid and endearing, and with Riley's trusty dog, Duffy, they stumble into the intrigue of a Patagonia-wearing heroine, Kit, involved in a smoldering environmental vs. commercial clash threatening the island. Solving the murder of a well-connected and beloved villager uncovers personal history for Riley and a strength she didn't know she had. Readers will delight in this charming and layered tale.

~Kate Gray, poet, writing coach, and award-winning author of Carry the Sky

A friend gave me this book to read. I really enjoyed it! Love the witty banter between Riley and Marie. I appreciated their long-time friendship and kindness toward each other. The plot kept my interest, and I was surprised in the end. The island, scenery, and islanders were perfectly described, and I could easily picture everything. Kudos for a lovely beach read. Perfect road trip book!

~Sara Rishforth, author of Adventures in Dating *and* After We Met

No Thru Road

By

Linda M. Vogt

Launch Point Press

Portland, Oregon

2017

A Launch Point Press Trade Paperback Original

ISBN 978-1-63304-200-1

SECOND EDITION
First Printing, 2017

Editing: Lori L. Lake
Copyediting: Luca Hart
Proofreading: Judy M. Kerr
Book format/typeset: Patty Schramm
Cover design: Sandy Knowles

Published by:
Launch Point Press

Portland, Oregon

www.LaunchPointPress.com

Printed in the United States of America

My life is rich with a circle of fine friends who helped make this book a reality. I dedicate this second edition of *No Thru Road* to them, with grateful thanks.

Acknowledgments

I have always been a writer, but this is my first time as a novelist. I like how it sounds: an author! I would not have gotten here without the support of Lori L. Lake. Her guidance, encouragement and enthusiastic cheerleading of my work has taken me from freelance feature writer and college journalism instructor to published author, and I am ever grateful.

I have many dear friends who listen, offer ideas, read first drafts, listen some more, and encourage me to be a better writer. For this book, fourteen of those friends met monthly to read the manuscript aloud and offer feedback. This made the story so much better! They also dressed as characters from the novel and surprised me on my birthday. Wow. I'm so lucky to have them! Thank you Carol E., Lark, Kate, Cheryl, Ellen, Kath, Beverly, Carol T., Gwenlyn, Carol D., Gail, Quince, Sue, and René.

When the first edition of this book came out, I took great delight in the many friends, family members, and former students who read the book and told me they liked it. Many of you said you love the characters and especially appreciate the sweet friendship between Riley and Marie. This is happy-making. Thank you to all of you who took a chance on a new author!

Lastly, my thanks to Launch Point Press for giving this book a new life. I'm thrilled to work with friends who make writing and publishing a delightful experience.

Linda M. Vogt
June 2017

Chapter One

RILEY LOGAN LEANED AGAINST the car door in the early morning sunshine and scanned the crowd. The ferry line stretched on and on, but she and Marie had made reservations so there was no worry. The B.C. Ferry people were highly organized even in June, the start of their busiest season.

"I'm little, but I'm old," Riley said.

Marie looked at her, puzzled. "What did you say?"

"I said, I'm little, but I'm old."

"That's what I thought you said. I guess the more accurate question, Oh Reporter Best Friend of Mine, would be why did you say that?"

Riley smiled and gazed off across Georgia Strait. The scene this morning in mid-June was so familiar: in the ferry line at Tsawwassen, headed for Galiano Island with all the other tourists, were kayakers, bikers and island residents. Most of the cars had license plates from British Columbia. Once in a while, a Washington State plate popped up, and even more seldom, the blue-with-a-green-fir-tree plate of Oregon.

The wind was cool at nine o'clock, and Riley pulled her fleece jacket collar around her. She loved the mingling of familiar smells—the salty ocean and the faint aroma of coffee coming from the ferry landing café.

The water was choppy blue, and the ferry dock was chaotic with activity. People hurried to the shops for coffee, for something from the new crepe stand, or strolled through the outdoor market buying gifts and souvenirs from artisans and local vendors. Some exchanged currency at the ATM, pocketing colorful Canadian twenty-dollar bills.

"Hello? Riley? Are you there?" Marie nudged her friend back to the conversation.

"Oh. Sorry, Marie. It's what Dill says in *To Kill a Mockingbird*. He comes to Maycomb to stay with his aunt for the summer, and he's in the backyard. Scout and Jem see him from their tree, and they ask him how old he is and he says, 'Seven!' and then he says, 'I'm little, but I'm old.' Don't you remember?"

"I do, but I still don't know why you're thinking about it."

"I guess because I'm thirty-five, which isn't all that young. And I'm only five-foot-two. And Scout and Jem and Dill were always having adventures, and I always have adventures on Galiano. And I'm going to my aunt's, even though she's no longer there. It makes perfect sense to me."

Marie shook her head. "It does, I guess, if one is privy to your strange and wonderful train of thought. But you know, even after almost thirty years of friendship, I'm not sure I can say that I always follow it. Be right back. Gotta go get us some coffee."

"Excellent. Duffy and I will wait here."

"Shall I get her a cookie or something?"

"You know she prefers chicken. Dark meat. Breast meat is too dry."

"That dog eats better than I do."

"I know. I think she's pretty proud of that fact."

Marie headed across the eight lanes of parked cars. Riley opened her passenger side door and sat with Duffy on her lap, soaking in the sunshine. Ah, British Columbia, she thought. I love it here.

A man and a child of perhaps five approached hand in hand. They stopped when the little girl spotted Duffy in Riley's lap.

"Look, Daddy, a puppy!" the girl said.

"What kind of a dog is that?" the dad asked.

Riley was used to the question because people always asked it whenever she took Duffy out in public.

"She's a Jack Russell terrier/toy poodle cross," she would say. "Small body, big spirit."

It was the truth. Duffy was fifteen pounds of pure, exuberant spunk. She was devoted to Riley and took her job as protector very seriously. She slept when Riley did, ate when she did, and loved to relax and hang out at home. She was especially fond of long walks, which did them both good.

The little girl petted the blond curly hair on Duffy's head. Then, finished with her Duffy visit, she tugged her dad's hand and they left.

"Bye," Riley called after them, then she saw Marie weaving her way between the cars.

She still looks good, Riley thought. Marie Wells was Riley's age. Her hair was a rich, dark brown and her green eyes were bright. She'd been divorced for three years and owned a popular art gallery in Ashland. A fanatic about exercise, she'd managed to keep her 130-pound self fit by walking every day. Some days, Riley took a break from her job at the Ashland Daily Tidings to walk with Marie, but she wasn't as devoted to the exercise routine. They'd been friends since the first grade, and though their lives were radically different, they loved each other like sisters. Neither one had a sister—maybe that was why they'd remained close. But they didn't look alike. Riley's hair was blonde, short and wavy, with a touch of Irish setter red.

Marie stood by Riley through two long-term relationships and was there each time things broke down. "What's up with you lesbians?" she'd ask. "How come you don't stay together?"

Riley always had an answer ready, and Marie knew what it would be. "Because we fall in love, get together, break up, and then remain friends the rest of our lives. "Not like you straight people. Divorce. Unfriendliness. Estrangement. What's up with you straight people?" This conversation always helped them through the break-ups of those romantic relationships. Then they moved on.

Riley watched Marie and thought about the day ahead of them

on Galiano Island. The ferry ride from Tsawwassen, BC, would be short—less than an hour—so they'd arrive by mid-morning and be settled into the Cliffhouse by noon. That was the easy part. The hard part would be staying there without Aunt Joan.

Marie was back with the coffee.

"Extra hot, one cream." She set two familiar green-and-white cups on the hood of the Subaru. She opened the back and pulled out two camp chairs, unfolded them and set them up next to the car. "Can you believe they have a Starbucks here now, right on the ferry dock? In Canada? America! We're everywhere."

"At least it's not McDonald's."

"Yay for that. Doesn't the air smell fresh here, though? Let's sit in the sun for a while. They won't start loading for at least another forty-five minutes."

They were early because Marie was always early. Riley depended on her for that. In college, Marie was the one who made sure they got to their eight o'clock class on time. Riley hated eight o'clock classes, but sometimes they were a necessity, so she had always been grateful that Marie was an early bird.

"Check it out," Marie said, gazing past Riley toward the snack bar. "Wow. Even I would look twice at her."

Riley followed Marie's gaze and spotted a tall, strikingly beautiful woman in a plum-colored fleece jacket and faded blue jeans. Riley guessed her to be in her early thirties. She had short dark brown hair and wore a faded blue baseball cap, on backwards.

"Hmm. I think she wants to meet me," Riley said. "I'd better go over there and make sure she's okay. She seems a little lost."

"Oh, sure she does. Not. That's a woman who probably always knows where she's going and what she wants. She's our first character. Let's see. I think her name is Chris. But I'll call her Patagonia Woman. P.W. for short."

Marie and Riley loved to name people they didn't know, and then make up stories about them.

"Right-o, and I think she wants me."

"In your dreams."

The woman glanced their way, and then strolled toward her car, carrying a Starbucks cup. She walked confidently, as though she was sure of herself. She got into a green Volkswagen Bug three rows away. A classic yellow Schwinn bicycle hung on a rack on the back.

"P.W. has a classy ride and a practical, classic bike," Riley said. "That's a good sign. And I like the way she moves—like an athlete. I think we're going to get along fine."

"You have such a rich fantasy life."

"Yes, isn't it wonderful?" Riley sipped her coffee and thought some more about the day ahead of them. She wasn't sure yet what she would do with the Cliffhouse—keep it, sell it, or rent it out—but the first task was to collect and box up some of Aunt Joan's things.

The death had happened suddenly, this loss of her only aunt. The call came at home, in Ashland, in the middle of the night from Ruth, Joan's longtime friend on the island. It appeared that Joan had a heart attack. Riley was stunned and sad, and Marie was the first person she'd called. Marie arrived at Riley's door ten minutes later, even though it was four o'clock in the morning. She remembered exactly what Marie said to her: "She was seventy-six years old, and you were the dearest niece she could ever hope for." Marie always knew what to say to comfort her, and Riley knew she was right about her Aunt Joan. But life wouldn't be the same.

"Daydreaming again? P.W.?" Marie asked.

"Not this time. I was thinking about the night Aunt Joan died."

"Are you all right?"

"I think so. It's hard, going to Galiano for the first time without her there."

"We'll do it together. Wherever I am, there's always Pooh, remember?"

"Now we're both thinking about great literature."

"Indeed, we are. Hey, too bad this isn't a longer trip because maybe then you'd get invited to that dark-haired buff girl's stateroom."

"Very funny. You know this ferry doesn't have staterooms."

"I figured you'd find a way."

"This is a business trip. I'm not looking for love. I have work to do, and so do you."

"Never stopped you before."

Riley knew she was right, but resisted the temptation to agree. Sparring was more fun. "Nope, I'm not gonna go there. I'm here to take care of Aunt Joan's affairs, and that's all. No foolin' around."

Marie laughed. "That'll be the day. You always take time to fool around."

The car in front of them started up, and Riley and Marie jumped up to fold and stow the camp chairs back into the Subaru.

"Time to move out, I guess." Riley headed for the driver's side. "All aboard."

Riley drove slowly as the cars snaked their way toward the ramp of the three-level ferry. Once parked on the car deck, she lowered the front windows a couple inches. Riley took Duffy off her lap and set her down on the passenger seat. "You get to stay here, Duffy. You have to guard the car."

Duffy cocked her head to the side and gave her the "I know you're leaving me here again" look. It was very familiar.

"It's not for long. They don't allow dogs up on the passenger deck. It's not called a dog deck, you see." Riley liked to explain things to Duffy and assumed that she understood every word. Duffy never gave her cause to think otherwise.

Riley locked the Subaru and she and Marie scooted through narrow passageways between cars toward the stairway. They climbed the steps to the passenger deck, wandered through the ferry lounges, and found two seats by the window. Riley pulled out a Tess Gerritsen mystery and lost herself in the adventures of Rizzoli and Isles. Marie headed for the gift shop and came back with the *Vancouver Sun*.

They'd been reading for about ten minutes when P.W. appeared, walking through the lounge, talking on an iPhone. She stopped near them to peruse a rack of brochures advertising island food, lodging and adventure options. Riley heard her one-way conversation.

"Yes, I'll be there in less than an hour," she said. "Will you be able to meet me at the landing?"

Riley pretended to read and strained to listen.

"That's okay, I can find it. No, I didn't get that information, but I did get the minutes from a planning meeting with a lot details about the Bodega Ridge acreage." The woman had a black spiral notebook in her right hand and juggled to hold the phone between her head and shoulder as she leafed through it.

"No, I didn't list all the names here, but I know they're in the copy of the minutes. What? Yeah. Of course, I brought them."

The woman turned her back on Riley as she moved toward the other end of the brochure rack. Riley noticed that a balding man seated near P.W. appeared to be listening, too. So did a hippie woman in a tie-dyed T-shirt. Guess this is the most interesting thing happening on the ferry, Riley thought. She could barely hear P.W. but then the woman turned.

"Yeah, I'm ready," she said. "Brought the bike and lots of kayaking gear. Should be fun. Oh, yeah. I will. See you there, Michael."

Patagonia Woman tapped the phone to end the call and smiled at the balding man.

"Don't you love iPhones?" she said to him as she stowed the phone in her green daypack.

He smiled weakly and went back to reading the *Sun*.

P.W. went around the corner and disappeared up the steps to the sundeck. Riley watched her go, and Marie seemed to notice.

"Want to go outside and get some air?" Marie asked as she put down the newspaper, smiling in that knowing way that comes from years of friendship.

"Sounds good." They gathered their things and went out into the sun and wind. Galiano Island was visible now, a long, dark green mass on the horizon, covered with trees and surrounded by gray water. Riley still thrilled to see it, even though she'd been here too many times to count.

A horn blasted above them and Riley jumped. "Jesus H. Christ— that was loud! It'd be nice if they'd warn us before they blast us off the deck with that thing."

"They did, but you weren't paying attention. I think you're a little jumpy. What does the 'H' stand for, anyway? And how come you keep scanning the crowd? Looking for someone?"

"She's probably going to Salt Spring, anyway." Over Marie's shoulder, Riley eyed the line of people headed for the car deck. "Fat chance she'll get off at Galiano. The 'H'?"

"In Jesus's name. I've been listening to you say that for over twenty years, and you never told me what the 'H' stands for."

"I have no idea. I never thought about it," Riley said, still scanning the crowd that had gathered now on the bow. "Probably it stands for 'holy.' Or 'heavenly,' or something like that. Don't you think?" Riley was distracted again because Patagonia Woman had appeared, car keys in hand.

"Oh, this is getting more interesting by the moment," Marie said. "I think she's going your way, baby. Galiano, here we come."

Chapter Two

THE BALDING MAN STOWED his *Vancouver Sun* and stood to stretch. He picked up a *Galiano Highlights* brochure from the rack in front of him and made his way to the stairs. The woman with the iPhone was ahead, going down the aft stairway toward Car Deck 2. Good, he thought. That's where I'm parked, too. How convenient.

He kept the woman in view as he made his way down the crowded steps. Once on the car deck, it would be easy to lose sight of her since the vehicles were packed in so tightly. And he didn't want her to know he was following. That would be very bad. Besides, it might turn out to be nothing. But he couldn't take that chance.

She ducked between a black Ford Explorer and a motor home, and for a moment he couldn't see her. He shoved past an overweight woman carrying a crying toddler. "Sorry," he mumbled.

There she was, next to a green Volkswagen Bug.

He pretended to dig in his jacket pocket for his keys as he watched. He knew he had the right person, because he'd waited outside that Tsawwassen motel most of the night and followed her to the ferry landing. He wouldn't have gone to the trouble, but since he got paid by the hour, it was money in his pocket.

The woman sauntered to the back of the VW to the bike rack. She undid the straps of a leather satchel attached behind the seat of her yellow classic bike and transferred some things from her daypack—water bottle, sunscreen, black spiral notebook—to the satchel.

Excellent, he thought. That has the notes in it. I need to see those.

The woman tossed the daypack on the passenger seat and got into her car.

He scurried past the VW to his black Honda Civic. He saw the VW in his rearview mirror, four cars back. No problem, he thought. She'll be easy to follow once we get on the island.

THE FERRY STAGING AREA was jammed with tourists as Riley and Marie drove off the dock. The 17-mile-long island had only two grocery stores, one service station, a bakery and a restaurant, and business owners counted on summer profits to last through the winter.

Riley asked, "Shall we stop and get a few groceries before we head to the Cliffhouse? Do you remember where the grocery store is?"

Marie was driving and shot a sideways glance at her friend. "Of course I do. I was here three years ago, remember?"

Riley did remember. They'd had a grand two weeks that summer, relaxing at the Cliffhouse, fishing, hiking, reading mystery novels, and laughing at all of Aunt Joan's stories. She recalled it as one of their best vacations.

"Of course you remember. Sure. Let's stop for a few things." They rounded the curve and saw the grocery. The green Volkswagen was parked in front.

"It's P.W. You are destined to meet!" Marie smiled at Riley, who was slinking down in her seat.

"I'm not sure I'm ready to meet Ms. Patagonia. I didn't wash my hair this morning."

"You look stunning. Walk in there and wow her. She won't know what hit her when she sees your bright smile headed her way."

Riley wasn't amused. She stayed hunkered down. "Really. I don't think now is the time. Let's buy some milk and fruit and get the heck out of here."

As Marie got out of the Subaru, P.W. emerged from the store carrying a sack of groceries, a six-pack of mineral water and a bag of ice.

"Excuse me," the woman said to Marie. "Have you been here before? I'm trying to find Ridge Road."

"Oh, sure, we know our way around. If you take a right at the first intersection, you'll be on Ridge Road. The island's only seventeen miles long, so it's not too hard to find anything."

"I'm looking for the kayak and adventure school."

"It's about eight miles down, on the left. There's a green and white sign. You can't miss it." Riley got out of the car and smiled at the woman, but didn't say anything.

"Cool," the woman said simply as she pulled her keys from her jacket pocket, unlocked the VW and stashed her groceries in the car. "By the way, my name's Kit." She came to the driver's side of the Subaru and extended her hand.

Marie shook it firmly. "I'm Marie, and this is my friend Riley. Nice to meet you. Here on vacation?"

"I wish. No, I'm here to teach kayaking to teenagers. How about you?"

"We came to take care of some business," Marie said, glancing at Riley expectantly.

"My aunt passed away," Riley said, finally breaking her silence. "I'm managing her estate. We're here to pack up her things."

"Interesting," Kit said. "Sorry about your aunt." With that, she turned toward her car.

Marie said, "That's quite a classic bike you have there. Reminds me of one I had when I was a kid."

"Thanks," Kit said. "It was my mom's. Don't know how long she'd had, it but she used to ride it around the neighborhood for some exercise. Thought it might come in handy here on the island."

"I bet it will," Marie said. "Maybe we'll see you ride by someday."

"Could happen. Hope so."

"Uh, see you around, maybe," Riley said. Boy, did that sound stupid, she thought. This woman probably thinks I'm a geek.

Kit waved a goodbye and started up the VW.

Marie headed for the grocery. "Come on, Casanova. Gotta shop."

Riley threw Marie a disapproving glance. "You are relentless."

"I know. That's one of the reasons you love me."

"HEY, RILEY! HALF OF Friday is going to be gone before you come down from there."

Riley rolled over in her cozy double bed and put a pillow over her head. She sneaked a peek at the clock. It was 8 a.m. Why did she have to have a best friend whose idea of midmorning was eight o'clock?

"I don't smell the coffee yet. Can't get up 'til I smell the coffee."

"I'll turn it on, my little morning glory. That gives you another ten minutes to enjoy the view up there."

Riley lay in the double bed and stared up at the ceiling. She was always amazed and amused at what her Aunt Joan had created. The bedroom was octagonal, and the roof was supported by rough-hewn logs that came together in the center and were nailed together with 8-inch, thick spikes. Her aunt's longtime friend, Patrick, had helped her build the Cliffhouse nearly twenty-five years earlier using trees on the island as timber and figuring out what to build as he went along. The result was a rustic yet comfortable home with sweeping views of the water.

Riley sat up in bed, arranged three pillows behind her, and gazed out at the morning sun on bright whitecaps. From the upstairs bedroom, water was all you could see. The Cliffhouse, perched high on a bluff with only the channel far below for a front yard, was aptly named. Aunt Joan had loved the seclusion of the place. The bedroom was up a flight of narrow stairs and its crowning glory was a clawfoot bathtub. While soaking, you could watch the boats going by in the channel.

There was movement under the down comforter near the foot of the bed. Riley watched as a soft lump of something moved slowly toward her. Duffy poked her nose out, and two brown eyes and a blond curly head emerged.

"Good morning, Little Sunshine. Did you sleep well?"

This question was their morning ritual. Duffy's answer was to do a loooong, slow stretch and sometimes a little dog yawn. Then she plopped into her relaxed pose again and closed her eyes.

"Not a morning dog, are you? We're perfect for each other."

The aroma of strong coffee wafted up the stairs and Riley breathed it in.

"What would I have to do to get you to bring me a cup up here, my dear best friend in all the world?" Riley said to the top of the stairs.

No reply.

"Are you there, Marie?"

Still no reply.

"Is this a trick to get me to come down? Come on. I know you're down there somewhere."

"Yes, it's a trick," Marie finally said from the bottom of the stairs. "I wanted to see if you'd get up before nine. Guess not."

"Ha ha. I'm laughing at that one."

"Okay, I'm bringing the coffee. But only because this is our first morning here, and I'm such a nice person."

"You're the best. I don't care what anybody says."

"Ha ha. I'm laughing at that one."

Moments later, Marie climbed the steep steps to the bedroom. She carried a silver coffee carafe, a mug, and a blueberry muffin on a white plate.

"This is my idea of heaven," Riley said. "I think I'm in love."

"Of course you are. How could you not be? I'm wonderful."

"That you are."

Marie handed her the muffin plate and set the coffee on the dresser.

Riley reached for the Thermos. "Marry me."

"We could get married here in Canada—or back at home now, since it's legal, but I think it would ruin our friendship."

"You're right. And that would be a tragedy."

Marie headed back down the steep stairs, and Riley poured her first cup of French roast, breathing in that wake-me-up-coffee-aroma she loved so much. Duffy watched her, then hopped down off the bed to start her day. This morning she was on ant patrol.

This often happened at the Cliffhouse, where various bugs made their home year-round and only moved over slightly for the humans they encountered. For Duffy, they were a glorious game. The sow bugs weren't as challenging because they were slow and solid and easy prey. The ants, however, were different. They could move quickly if they wanted to, and Duffy found pouncing on one extremely satisfying.

Duffy kept busy patrolling while Riley sipped her coffee and gazed out onto Trincomali Channel. Directly in front of the Cliffhouse were two islands, plopped about halfway between Galiano and Salt Spring Islands. They were both flat and low to the water. The one on the left reminded Riley of that drawing in *The Little Prince*—the one that looked like a hat, but was really a snake that had swallowed something. She wondered what it was. A rat? A mouse? Riley couldn't remember.

This morning the islands were a soft green and provided contrast to the navy blue of the choppy water. The wind had blown all night, and the fir boughs outside the bedroom had clawed and beckoned, their scratchy sounds finding their way into Riley's dreams.

Ant patrol completed, Duffy carefully positioned herself in the sun that came streaming in the picture window early in the mornings. For her, the sun was pure heaven and all she needed to declare this a fine morning.

Riley knew that she and her dog weren't so different. For Riley, the sun and the water made it a fine morning. And she loved the always incredible sight of an eagle soaring right by the Cliffhouse windows. This morning, the eagle had been a young one—still brown all over, and no white on the head. But the eagle's soar and the strength and the grandeur were unmistakable. Aunt Joan had taught Riley a lot about these majestic birds, and seeing one now reminded her why she had come to the Cliffhouse.

Each time she thought about her aunt, Riley got a fresh dose of grief and a longing she couldn't quite describe. For Riley, Aunt Joan had been home. Warmth. Unconditional love. I miss her, she thought. Every day.

Riley poured more coffee from the metal carafe and watched Duffy, who was lying full-bodied in the patch of sunlight. Life is good if you're a dog.

Riley's aunt had loved Duffy, too. She was the only dog ever invited to stay at the Cliffhouse, and Riley knew that was a significant concession on her aunt's part.

"This dog is the funniest little creature I have ever seen," Riley remembered Aunt Joan saying. And she had been right. Duffy made Riley laugh, and that could only be good for a person. Riley liked to think of her as a fifteen-pound bundle of dog therapy.

"You're the best dog ever," Riley said. Duffy put her head down on her front paws and closed her eyes. A moment later, she was up on all fours, growling softly at another ant invading her space.

"You crack me up."

"Are you talking to the dog, or to me?" Marie stood at the top of the stairs again, still in her red and blue cat pajamas, running her hand through her stand-up, morning hair.

"Good morning, Best Friend. I didn't hear you coming up."

"Can't hear much above the terrible and frightening sound of Duffy's growl, can you?"

"Nope, I guess I can't. Did you sleep well?"

"It was another good sleep, except, of course, for the tree scratching at my window. That could scare a person if she didn't know what it was."

"No kidding. Me, too."

They were quiet as they gazed out at the Galiano morning.

"What shall we do first today?" Marie asked.

"Drink coffee, of course. Then we'll tackle some projects. No hurry, though. We have two weeks."

They both smiled at that thought, and Duffy got up to follow another ant.

AFTER BREAKFAST, RILEY AND Marie went through the house methodically to see what was there and began creating a list of Aunt Joan's things. The Cliffhouse was long and narrow, with decks on each end, and a kitchen, living room and bedroom on the main level. And everywhere were things that make up a life. They found colorful souvenirs of her aunt's many trips, magazines in neatly categorized stacks, and, of course, books. Aunt Joan loved books.

Riley was packing some of those books in the living room when Marie came in with a thick file of papers.

"What do you think we should do with these notes?" she asked. "They seem to be part of your aunt's writing files."

"Let's have a look. Maybe she was working on another novel."

Aunt Joan had been a mystery buff and had tried her hand at writing one herself. The novel had never been published, but Riley had read it and thought it decent enough. Mostly, she'd been impressed that her aunt would attempt such a daunting task. When she asked her about it, Aunt Joan said she was inspired by Jane Rule, the well-known lesbian novelist who wrote *Desert of the Heart* and had lived with her partner on Galiano Island.

"Wow. This is pretty interesting stuff." Riley leafed through the hand-written pages. "It appears my aunt was taking notes for a new mystery. There's lots of stuff here about the Graham family. They are the ones who first settled Galiano. Aunt Joan took me to see their home once. It's a historical site now, up at the north end of the island."

"Anything creepy, weird or kinky there? I love it when I can read personal things about families."

"I don't think my aunt was into creepy, weird or kinky. I can't believe you would suggest that."

"We don't know all about your dear Aunt Joan. Maybe she had stories to tell. Maybe she knew some things about this island after sixty years living here."

"Yeah, maybe. But let's leave out kinky."

"If you say so. Look. Here's something. It's a photocopy of a newspaper story about a drowning in 1949. The headline says, 'Tragedy hits Graham family.' Listen to this."

A freak windstorm on the Trincomali Channel is considered the cause of a tragic accident Sunday night off the north end of Galiano Island. The two children from the Graham family are missing and presumed drowned; their nanny, Katherine Irene Taylor, survived but was hospitalized for hypothermia.

According to Galiano Sheriff James Carver, the children—Emily, age 8 and William, age 2—were in the care of Miss Taylor on a picnic outing on Wallace Island. They were on their way back in the Grahams' twelve-foot rowboat when high winds developed suddenly, and the boat swamped about one hundred yards from the Galiano shore. The children were presumably pulled under by strong currents.

Local volunteers searched through the night for the bodies, but found nothing.

The Graham family was unavailable for comment. Matthew Graham and his wife, Ella, have no other children.

Marie handed Riley the photocopy, which she tucked back into the file. "Come to think of it, I remember Aunt Joan telling me about that incident. The drowning happened long before I was born, but I remember as a child hearing Aunt Joan talk about it with Patrick and Ruth, her best friends here. The loss of those children shook up the entire island community."

"Did they ever find the bodies?"

"I don't think so. The tragedy was also the end of the Graham family's influence on Galiano. Mrs. Graham died in the early nineties, and Matthew Graham was moved to a care facility in Vancouver a couple years ago. I think he has Alzheimer's disease. Doesn't know anybody anymore. My aunt knew the Grahams and the nanny. I remember her telling me that Katherine never was the same after the accident."

"Who would be? That's got to be about the worst thing that can happen to a person."

"No kidding. Everyone blamed Katherine for the accident, even though she was only seventeen when it happened, and there probably wasn't much she could do. People still talk about her as though it was her fault."

"That's terrible. The poor young woman couldn't do anything to help those kids in that kind of a storm, and people still blame her. You'd think they'd let it go. I wonder what happened to her."

"I always wondered, too. I guess she moved to the mainland soon after the accident and started a new life. People here were too hard on her."

"What a shame."

"No one knew what happened to her after that. I asked Aunt Joan once, but she didn't want to talk about it. It's odd that she saved this newspaper story."

"It's another Galiano mystery," Marie said. "And you know how you love mysteries."

BY LATE AFTERNOON, RILEY and Marie had packed eighteen boxes of books, four boxes of files and notes, and several more of Aunt Joan's collections of precious things: Hummel figurines, colorful ceramic animals, miniature tea sets, and lots of Pooh characters. Aunt Joan had loved *Winnie the Pooh* stories and had read them to Riley throughout her childhood.

"What are you going to do with these?" Marie asked, wrapping yet another Piglet in tissue paper.

"I certainly can't get rid of them. They *are* Aunt Joan, to me. I'll find a place for them at my house."

"I knew you were going to say that. Where do you think you'll put them?"

"There's always room for Pooh. You know that."

"I thought it was 'There's always room for Jell-O.'"

Riley smiled and turned to finish packing the last shelf of books, popped open a Diet Pepsi and sprawled onto the couch in the living room. The wind had picked up, and she could see that the sailboats were moving along at a good clip on the channel.

"What say we get out of here for a while?" she said to Marie. "It's only a couple of hours until sunset. Want to go get a bite of dinner and then go sightseeing?"

"What do you have in mind?"

"How about we eat at the deli, and then go over to Bluff Park and watch the Canadian ferries come through that narrow channel? I always loved doing that when I was a kid. Boat watching was one of the outings my aunt and I did together."

"Sounds good to me. I'm ready for some fresh air and a change of scenery. We got a lot done today, don't you think?"

"We certainly put a dent in it, as Aunt Joan used to say. Come on, let's do the tourist thing."

Chapter Three

"THE PEOPLE OF GALIANO Island welcome you to Bluff Park," a faded green sign read. Its white letters were chipped. "We take pride in this beautiful area, and ask you to help us preserve it."

"If they take so much pride in it, why don't they repaint that sign?" Marie asked as she squinted in the fading light to read the map on the back of the island brochure. "Are you sure we're going the right way?"

Riley was concentrating on maneuvering the Subaru on the narrow gravel road and not knocking Duffy off her lap.

"It's the right way, Marie. I've been here many times."

"But where's the bluff these people are so excited about?"

"It's just up ahead." Riley peered through the window at the growing dark. All she saw in the dim light was a thick forest of tall firs. No branches grew down low. The trunks were bare until about twenty feet up, where fir boughs created a thick canopy, shutting out the light that tried to filter through.

Marie checked the door on her side to make sure it was locked. "This road is creeping me out. It looks like a good place for ax murderers."

"You're edgy because of that story about the Graham children. But that was over sixty years ago, remember? Besides, what ax murderer would go to all the trouble of riding the ferry for an hour from the mainland to get to Galiano, then drive this bumpy gravel road to come out here and kill someone?"

"Good point. Too creepy even for ax murderers. Besides, we have the mighty and buff Duffy to protect us!"

"Indeed, we do." Ever alert on Riley's lap, Duffy peered intently out the driver-side window.

Riley drove slowly through the darkening woods, urging the Subaru up a steep incline.

"Look! There's some light up ahead," Marie said. "I can see blue sky. I think there really is a bluff."

Riley steered the Subaru from the darkness onto an empty graveled parking area. She parked as far away as she could from the cliff, remembering the sheer drop-off from the bluff. With no guardrail, she took no chances.

"Hey, check it out! I can see the water." Marie was out of the car in a flash, heading toward the edge of the bluff.

"Slow down, girlfriend. It's quite a drop-off there." Riley clipped Duffy's leash to her collar and let her hop out of the car.

If Marie was worried about the drop-off, she didn't show it. She walked to the edge, looked down, turned toward Riley and grinned.

"It's a fantastic view. I can see three other islands from here. Lots of fishing boats, too. And check out that sunset!"

"Don't go any closer to the cliff, okay? You enjoy the view for me. Duffy and I will go nose around a little and I'll take some pictures."

Riley got her camera from the back seat and headed for the trail that led from the back of the parking lot. It curved down through the trees, and she saw light at the end of the path. From previous visits over the years, she recalled another viewpoint up ahead where the path turned.

"Be right back," she shouted over her shoulder. "Don't leave without me."

"I won't. You have the car keys."

"Good point."

Walking slowly in the low light with Duffy pulling at the leash, Riley headed down the trail and took in the beauty of the island. Orange sunlight sparkled on bright blue water, boats bobbed on the channel, islands stood green and silent in the distance. The air smelled of salt water, and a cool breeze came up from the sea. The only noise was the muffled rumble of the outboard motor on a fishing boat far below.

This place is a bit of heaven, Riley thought. No wonder Aunt Joan loved it.

As she neared the end of the trail, Riley saw a twenty-foot section of guardrail at the edge. She approached the rail slowly. She was not fond of heights, but her curiosity nudged her on. Peeking over, she saw a sheer rock cliff that plunged down into dark blue water. Rays from the sunset flickered on the surface, sending beams of yellow dancing on the rocks. Across the channel, Salt Spring Island lay peacefully in the evening light, its green shores soft above the water.

"Sit, Duffy." Duffy was capable of following that basic instruction, and this evening she was willing to do so. She hated being on the leash, but in her dog-wise way, she seemed to understand when it was necessary. She sat, and Riley let go of the leash. She stayed.

"Good girl!"

Riley found a good angle, balanced her camera on a wide place on the rail to steady it, and took a photograph of the sunset. The sky was turning soft lavender.

She took one more look at the sun as it slipped into the water, then tucked the camera back into the case, picked up Duffy's leash and made her way carefully back up the gravel trail. With the sun down, once the path entered the trees, she found it hard to see.

This is getting to be what Marie would call spooky, she thought. Time to hurry.

She picked up her pace and soon reached the parking lot.

She called Marie's name.

No answer.

"Marie. Are you there?"

Still no answer. Riley crossed the parking lot and approached the bluff where Marie had been standing. The lookout point was empty; Marie's daypack lay on the ground.

Her heart thumping faster, Riley shouted Marie's name again.

"Stay calm," she said aloud. "She's got to be here somewhere."

Riley stood silently in the growing dark and strained to listen for any sound of Marie. She heard the crunch of footsteps on gravel behind her. Duffy heard it too and began to bark.

Relieved, she whirled around.

The man coming toward her wore a heavy-knit brown and white sweater. His hair was dark, his beard flecked with gray, and he seemed about Riley's height. He squinted at her through thick glasses.

"I heard you shouting," he said in a low voice. "Is something wrong?"

Riley's heart was racing now, and she tried to forget Marie's comments about ax murderers. Who was this strange little man? She thought maybe she'd seen him before on Galiano, but she couldn't be sure. And the Subaru was still the only car in the parking lot. Where did he come from?

"I was calling to my friend. She took a walk, I guess. It's getting dark and I thought we should get going." Duffy was pulling at her leash now and barking louder and faster. "Quiet, Duffy!" Riley didn't want to aggravate this strange person, but she did feel safer with Duffy there to protect her.

"I saw her." He didn't offer any other information.

"Where?"

"She took a steep trail that starts about there." He pointed toward where Marie had stood.

Riley tugged on Duffy's leash and moved quickly to the spot and peered over. Marie was sitting below on a narrow ledge. She was watching a B.C. ferry pass through the channel.

"What in the hell are you doing down there?" Riley shouted. "You scared me to death! Didn't you hear me calling you?"

Marie looked up. "I can't hear much from down here when those ferries are passing by. Sorry I frightened you. I know you don't like heights, but I think you'd better come down here."

"You've got to be kidding. There's no way I'm climbing down that narrow trail."

"I'm not kidding, Riley. I found something."

She held up a twisted piece of bright yellow metal. "It's part of a bicycle fender. It looks like it could be part of that yellow bicycle we saw on the back of Kit's car."

Riley strained to see, but in the fading light, she could barely make out what Marie was holding. Then she remembered the man standing behind her and turned to tell him she'd found Marie.

The gravel parking lot was empty, except for the Subaru.

"THIS IS REALLY FREAKING me out," Riley said. "If that's part of Kit's bicycle, how did it get here? And where is Kit? I think you'd better come up. We need to get out of here."

"What do you think we should do?" Marie asked as she made her way carefully up the narrow path.

"First of all, we need to find out who that peculiar man is. Maybe he saw something."

"What man?"

"The one in the parking lot. Didn't you see him?"

Marie looked at her best friend as if she was off her rocker.

"Oh, well of course you didn't see him. You were already down there. He appeared as I was calling for you. Dark hair, beard, thick glasses, brown and white sweater. Why would he be out here, no car in sight?"

"Another unanswered question. I think we'd better go before he comes back to murder us with his ax. And we're taking this evidence with us."

Marie clutched the yellow fender as though it were buried treasure.

Riley opened the driver-side door of the Subaru and Duffy jumped into the front seat.

Marie got in. "Lock the doors, won't you? No telling who might be lurking nearby, ready to pounce on two naïve tourist girls. And now we have to drive back through those creepy woods."

Riley backed the car out and headed down the narrow gravel lane. Dusk had swallowed the light, and the trees were black against the deep dark of the forest. They were both relieved to come to the paved main road. Duffy remained ever vigilant on Riley's lap.

BACK AT THE CLIFFHOUSE, Riley used the wall phone to dial the number of the kayak school, not sure what she would say.

"Gulf Island Kayak School," a male voice answered.

"Uh, hello. I'm wondering if I could talk with one of your instructors, Kit." Riley realized she didn't know Patagonia Woman's last name.

"Oh, you want Kit Powell. Yeah, she'll be teaching the beginning kayak course. But she's not here right now. I could take a message."

Sure, Riley thought, like I'd leave a message asking, are you okay, or have you been brutally murdered. "No, there's no message," she said. "But do you know when she'll be back?"

"Classes don't start until Monday evening, and until then she has some free time. I think she went exploring. She wants to acquaint herself with the island. Probably be back later tonight."

"Maybe I'll call back then. Thanks anyway." She hung up the phone.

Marie was waiting to hear the update.

"They don't know where she is," Riley said. "Big surprise."

"What are we going to do?"

"We're going to find that mysterious man. I think he knows something."

"Tonight?"

"I'm too creeped out to go tonight. It's a relief to feel safe here at the house. Let's go in the morning."

"You don't have to talk me into that. Are our doors locked?"

Chapter Four

SOFT PEACH-COLORED LIGHT greeted Riley when she awoke at 7:15 a.m. For some reason, she felt wide awake and ready to start solving today's mysteries. Duffy, asleep under the comforter at the foot of the bed, peeked out and opened one eye to look at Riley; she seemed confused at the fact that Riley was stirring so early.

"I know, little Duffy, this isn't how we usually do things. But I have a lot on my mind, so I guess you're going to have to get up early with me."

Duffy was not impressed. But she jumped off the bed as soon as Riley's feet found her slippers.

Getting down the steep stairs from the bedroom was challenging, and even more so if one was trying to be quiet. The rough stairs creaked with each step. Marie had stayed up late the night before and was still asleep in the downstairs bedroom. Riley didn't want to wake her.

Riley turned on the coffeepot and savored the aroma of that brewing wake-up call. She always thought the most clearly right after coffee and up until lunch. Those morning hours were her most creative time. She liked having a pen and pad nearby because writing things down helped her ponder the possibilities.

A gentle breeze sent the water lapping softly onto the rocks below. Gulls were making their morning journeys past the deck. On the water, weekend sailors motored past, eager to get an early start on the day. Riley hoped they had lots of fuel for those motors because the slight morning breeze might be all they got today.

Riley sat in the soft leather chair in the living room, still looking out onto the water, and put her feet up on the ottoman. She set her coffee on the end table. Duffy hopped up next to her, snuggled into the soft chair and closed her eyes.

Riley opened her spiral notebook and began a list.

1. Go into town—identity of Little Bearded Man?
2. Ask around about Kit. Did anyone see her yesterday? Today?
3. Call the RCMP constable, Paul Snow. Any reports of stolen bicycles or vehicles?
4. Check with woman at post office (seems to know everyone).
5. Drive up to kayak school and ask about Kit.

Marie wandered in as Riley was finishing her list.

"You're up early." Marie stifled a yawn. "What's the deal?"

"I don't know. I woke up and started thinking about everything and couldn't get back to sleep. Thought I'd make some coffee and make one of my famous lists."

"Okay, I'm ready for duty as soon as I have a cup. Where to begin?"

"With breakfast. Then on to sleuthing."

"My kind of vacation day. Good food, intrigue and a dash of danger."

"Very funny. Let's hope it's a small dash."

FROM WHERE HE SAT on a weathered chair at the southeast corner of the deck of his log house, Jonathan MacAlister saw the mammoth B.C. ferries as they eased slowly into the landing. He liked to watch the ferries come in—not because he was happy to see the tourists, because he could do without them—but because he thrilled at the sight of those powerful and magnificent ships.

Some mornings, he liked to watch through binoculars as the cars drove off the dock or up and down the main road below his house. He paid attention to the license plates: B.C. and Alberta, most often, and now and then Washington, USA. Rarely did he see anything else, but this morning his gaze followed the path of a dark green Subaru with Oregon plates as it headed toward the Day Market, the same car he'd seen the night before at Bluff Park. Those two women again. The short-haired one he had recognized as Joan's niece. Joan had displayed several photos of her out at the Cliffhouse.

They must be up to no good, he thought, coming here to go through Joan's things. Probably trying to get everything they could out of her house and land. Opportunists, just like all those land developers always trying to build on this island and turn it into a circus. He despised those people, too. No good, any of them.

Jonathan checked his Timex wristwatch. 8:49. Though he didn't want to, he knew it was time to head down the hill and open up shop. People would be waiting, probably. They usually were. Pesky tourists.

He went back inside, returned the binoculars to the kitchen table, picked up his knitted brown and white sweater off the chair and took the back door out. He trudged down the worn path down to the main road where the kiosk, about the size of a cargo van, awaited him. He unlocked the door in the back and went in. He had a padded chair there and enough room to move around. Good thing it was only for three hours a day.

Unlatching it, Jonathan pulled the wooden-framed sliding door all the way to the right, letting in the bright morning sun. He sat, relieved that no one waited on the other side, and took out the Dean Koontz novel he had started the night before and began to read, shifting his thick glasses so that the bifocals were in the right place.

When he heard the crunch of feet on gravel outside the kiosk, he looked up, annoyed to be disturbed.

"Good morning," a blonde woman said. She was dressed in sandals, red shorts and a white sleeveless blouse. "Glad to see you're open."

In a weary voice he said, "Galiano Visitors' Bureau. How can I help you?"

"MAYBE WE SHOULD START at the constable's office, if there is one," Riley said as she drove down the main road toward the ferry dock. This morning, Duffy had decided to sit on Marie's lap in the car.

"What are we going to tell him?" Marie said. "That we think some crazed killer murdered this cute dyke that you've been lusting over? That we found her bicycle, twisted and destroyed, at Bluff Park? Think about it. We're going to sound loony."

"You're right. Let's start at the post office. We'll be casual."

Riley pulled into the gravel lot in front of the Day Market. The post office counter was inside, conveniently located next to the dairy case.

Marie said, "Leave the car running. Duffy and I will wait. I'm going to cruise for the oldies station while you're gone."

Inside, the aged postmistress stood sorting letters slowly at a tall table, her back to the counter. She had gray hair pulled into a scruffy ponytail held with a hand-knitted barrette.

Riley cleared her throat. The woman turned around.

"Yes?" She peered at Riley over half-glasses.

"Hi. Do you have a minute to talk to me?"

"Hello, Riley. Is there something you need?"

Somewhat surprised that the woman remembered her name, Riley got flustered. But then she remembered that Aunt Joan had known everyone here, and therefore everyone knew her niece.

"My friend and I are here to take care of Aunt Joan's things, and on the ferry yesterday we met someone. She teaches at the kayak school, and I guess she took off for a couple days in her VW bug or on her bike. I wondered if maybe she had come by here yesterday or today. We're not sure where she was headed, and we need to get a message to her. We thought maybe she'd checked in here for her mail."

"Nope. Haven't seen anyone come up in a VW, or on a bike." The woman turned and resumed sorting the letters.

Riley tried to think of what else to ask. "Uh, maybe you could tell me where to find another islander. I don't know his name, but I think maybe he'd know where she might have gone. He's about sixty, thick glasses, brown and white sweater."

Still sorting the mail, the woman said, "That would be Jonathan. Go see him at the Galiano Visitors' Bureau."

"Thanks. I appreciate your time."

"Uh-huh." A long pause. "Your Aunt Joan was a good person."

Riley considered that one of the nicest things any islander had said to her.

"Goodbye and thanks again." Riley let the door swing shut.

As Riley got in the car, Marie asked, "What did you find out?"

"I think we can find Jonathan."

"Who the heck is Jonathan, and why do we want to find him?"

"Brown and white sweater man. Get ready for an island experience!"

AS THE POST OFFICE lady had said, Jonathan was tucked into the kiosk, his eyes peering at a book through thick glasses. As Riley headed his way, he didn't look up, even though he must have heard her coming. He was still wearing that sweater.

"Good morning," Riley said.

Jonathan carefully placed a bookmark in the pages of the paperback, placed it on a stool beside him, took off his glasses, and at last met Riley's gaze. "How can I help you?"

"Hello. My name is Riley. I'm Joan Walker's niece."

Jonathan continued the steady gaze. "I know. How can I help you?"

Riley wondered how he knew, since she didn't recall ever meeting him with her aunt, and the first she'd seen of him was last night at Bluff Park. She blundered boldly on.

"I'm wondering if you might know anything about the whereabouts of one of the kayak school teachers. Her name's Kit. She arrived here a few days ago, and we'd like to talk to her. Seems she left yesterday on her bike, and no one knows where she went."

"And why is it you think I might know? I've never even met this girl."

"I thought that since you run this visitor kiosk near the ferry, you might have seen her or have information that would be helpful."

"I don't." He looked past Riley, apparently to see who was in the car with her. "Anything else I can do for you?"

Riley knew when she was being dismissed. She felt like she was in the third grade again.

"Yes, maybe there is. Can you tell me who I could talk to at the kayak school? Who's in charge up there? Maybe they know something more."

"That would be Michael Barsotti. Italian. He runs the place."

"Thank you very much."

"Uh-huh. Have a nice day." These two sentences were uttered with no inflection.

Riley backed away from the kiosk and waved, but Jonathan was already putting his bi-focals on to return to his book.

Thanks so much for being so helpful, Riley thought. Wow. The tourist bureau! I wonder if he treats all the visitors like that.

Marie was sitting in the Subaru with the windows down and Duffy asleep on her lap. She was humming along to "Ferry 'Cross the Mersey". The station came from Victoria. Marie hummed slightly off-key, which never seemed to bother her, but drove Riley crazy. It was, however, endearing.

"Well? What did he say?" Marie asked, turning down the radio.

"He said, 'Have a nice day.'" Riley imitated Jonathan's

monosyllabic delivery. "Buckle up. We're going to the Gulf Island Kayak School."

EVEN THE MOST UNAWARE tourist couldn't miss the Kayak School turnoff. Marked by a green and white sign shaped like a kayak, it read Gulf Island Kayak School (GIKS). Riley turned left onto the narrow gravel drive and headed down through the trees.

"And exactly what do you think you're going to say to these people?" Marie asked as the Kayak School building came into sight. "Hello. My name is Riley, and I've been lusting after that cute dyke teacher, Kit. I'm worried about her. Do you know where she went? Is that what you're going to say?"

"Very funny, Marie. Of course not. I'm going to ask around a bit and try to meet the director, Michael. Maybe he'll know something, and we can quit worrying."

"That would be excellent. I might want to do something the next few days besides run all over the island like amateur detectives, thrashing through the bushes to find Patagonia Woman. I don't care how cute she is. Maybe I'd like to read a book or get a tan. What about that?"

Riley pulled the car into a slot next to the Kayak School office. "You're kind of grumpy this morning, aren't you? Did you forget to drink your coffee?"

"No, that's not it at all. Must be the island air. Makes me agitated."

"How about you agitate yourself right out of the car and up those steps? I need your moral support for this one."

"Okay, but only because I love you."

"I know you do. You're the best. Really."

"Knock it off, Riley. I already said I'd go in with you."

"Right. Let's go. Duffy, you stay."

Duffy looked disappointed, which, of course, always made Riley feel guilty.

"It's not for long, I promise."

Six narrow wooden steps led up to the main office. The entire building looked as though someone had created it from several singlewide trailers. They were patched together at the corners to form a horseshoe-shaped tin building reminding Riley of a Girl Scout camp she'd gone to when she was a young teen. All those buildings had been tin, too, and the rain at night sounded as though the goddesses were drumming on the roof. Or gods. Or whatever.

"Riley!" Marie, waiting behind her, whispered her name sounding cranky. "Knock on the door, for heaven's sake!"

Riley pulled herself back from the nostalgic trip to Girl Scout camp. What a crush she'd had on her counselor, Miss Waterfall.

"Oh, yeah, sure. Sorry. Got distracted." Riley knocked lightly.

A male voice said, "Come on in. It's unlocked."

They stepped inside the cramped office. Kayak paddles, lifejackets and various straps were stacked high on both the beat-up wooden desks. A thin, graying, dark-haired man looked up from a computer. He appeared busy, but his eyes were friendly.

"Hi. Are you Michael?" Riley asked.

The man laughed, deep and throaty. "Oh, my goodness, no. I wouldn't even want to try to be Michael."

Riley and Marie exchanged a quizzical glance.

"My name's Riley, and this is my friend Marie. Do you know where we could find Michael?"

"Did you want to sign up for a kayak course? I could help you with that. I'm Robert Burrows. I manage the office."

"No, we're not here to sign up. Actually, we met one of your instructors. Her name's Kit, and we wondered if we might talk to her. We called earlier to ask about her."

"Oh, yes, Kit. Right. Her course begins Monday night. Seems like a nice girl."

"Do you know where we might find her? Does she have a cabin here or something?"

Robert laughed, deep again. "Oh, no. We don't have cabins for staff. I wish we did! It would be nice to get away from these little mons—I mean these young adventurers once in a while. Nope. No cabins, only single rooms, side-by side. Like those." Robert pointed out the back window of the office toward the tin buildings. The doors were numbered—Room 1, Room 2, etc.—and were spaced about ten feet apart.

"I see," Riley said. "Would she be here in her room?"

"Doubt it. I haven't seen any movement all day. But Michael might know."

"Is he here?"

"Don't know. But you could check downstairs in the equipment room. That's where he usually is. Take those stairs to the left, and it's the first door on your right."

Riley thanked him, and she and Marie headed downstairs.

"That didn't get us too far, did it?" Marie said. "Man. It's hard to get information out of these people."

"No kidding. It seems as though everyone's in cahoots with everyone else to give out Absolutely No Information to anyone who's not an islander. This is not going to be easy."

"Maybe Michael will be the exception. We can hope."

The equipment room door was painted bright blue. Faint pounding sounds came from inside.

"I'm thinking that's Michael making that noise," Riley said as she rapped on the door.

"Yeah?" a deep voice said. "What is it now?"

The voice was impatient and somewhat cross. Riley resisted the urge to run back up the stairs, go home, and lie in the lounge chair in the sun while drinking a beer.

"Uh, we're looking for Michael," she said through the door.

"I'm him."

"So much for his command of the English language," Marie whispered. "May we come in?" she said, a little louder.

"Guess so. No one's stoppin' you."

Marie rolled her eyes as Riley turned the doorknob.

The room was bathed in bad fluorescent light. A dark-haired, muscular man sat beside a red two-person kayak, making an adjustment to the rudder. He looked up, seemed puzzled, and then his eyes locked on Marie. He stood and walked toward his visitors.

Michael was tall—at least six feet. He wore a bright red golf shirt with the collar up. His biceps pushed tight at the fabric of his sleeves. He had on faded, torn Levi's and bright white Nike athletic shoes. His eyes were dark, and they were still on Marie.

"How may I help you?" he asked rather formally. "I'm Michael Barsotti."

"Nice to meet you." Riley wondered if the man would ever glance her way. He did, but briefly. "I'm Riley Logan, and this is my friend, Marie Wells."

"Pleased. What brings you here?"

"We're trying to catch up with one of your teachers," Marie said. Michael was still staring at her. "Her name is Kit."

Michael said nothing.

"Would you happen to know where she is?" Riley asked, hoping to get him out of his Marie-trance.

Michael turned toward Riley then and spoke softly. "I haven't seen her since last night. I think she wanted to see some of the island before her course starts tomorrow. Don't know where she went."

Unsure how to proceed, Riley searched Marie's face for a clue, an idea, an indication of what she thought should come next. Since Michael seemed to be most interested in her (and Riley was getting worried about how interested) it seemed as though Marie should call the shots on this part of their investigative efforts.

Marie finally spoke. "Do you know Kit well?"

Michael smiled at her. "Not well, but I'm the one who hired her. I liked her style and her sense of adventure. After this first kayak trip, we're going to work together on a documentary film about the island."

Now we're getting somewhere, Riley thought. You go, girl!

"What kind of documentary?" Marie asked, moving closer to Michael.

"It's about the age-old conflict here: development versus environmentalism. The island people against the loggers and the wealthy developers. There's always a new battle for some piece of the island and always a new story to tell. We thought it was time to put something together to be broadcast by the BBC. I got a grant to do it." Michael stopped, looked from Riley to Marie, then asked, "Why do you want to talk to her?"

Marie said, "Truth is, we're worried about her."

"Why's that?"

"Up at Bluff Park last night, we found a part of a fender that looked like it came from her yellow bicycle. We're worried."

"Is she a friend of yours?" Michael put down his screwdriver on a workbench and turned to face them.

"No, actually, she's not," Riley said. "We met her on the ferry coming over."

"I haven't seen her since last night. She dumped her stuff in Room Two, took her backpack and mentioned she'd be back in time for the Monday night opening session. I figured she was off exploring the island."

"She could be," Marie said. "But why did we find a part of her bike?"

Michael brushed dust off the front of his shirt. "Good question. But, then, this island is full of questions, isn't it?"

Marie reached out to shake Michael's hand. "That it is. Thanks, and it's nice to meet you, Michael. We won't take any more of your time."

"My pleasure. I hope I see you again."

Riley also shook his hand, but she still wasn't sure what to think about this handsome Italian.

Chapter Five

"THAT WASN'T ESPECIALLY SATISFYING," Marie said as they turned back onto the main road.

"Satisfying is what he had on his mind," Riley said. "Only it didn't have to do with the conversation. It had to do with you. Wow. Was he ever checking you out!"

"He was not," Marie said, blushing. "He was just being friendly."

"Uh-huh. Friendly like the spider to the fly."

"Besides, I've never gone for the dark muscular type."

"There's always a first time, as they say. I think we'll be hearing from Michael sometime soon. He seems to like you, and he's an interesting guy who cares a lot about this island. I hope he doesn't make people mad with this film he's creating. Developers are investing a lot of money in the Bodega Ridge development, and they might not appreciate his efforts."

"I'm not sure he likes me, but I agree with you that he may be stirring up trouble with that film. Not our problem, though. Where to now, Sherlock?"

"We didn't make too much progress on the Kit search, but I have an idea about how to get more information out of Michael about the film project, and maybe that would lead us to Kit—or at least tell us more about her. Maybe I could tell him I'm working on a freelance article for a magazine—about environmentalists versus developers in the Northwest. It would add an interesting element to include B.C., don't you think?"

"But you're not working on an article, are you?"

"No, but Michael doesn't know that. Could be just the ticket to get him to open up."

"Very clever, my friend, the sleuth."

"Thanks for that. Now let's drive down to the campground and ask around. Maybe Kit did stay there last night. I don't know where else to look."

"Sounds like a plan."

Marie always said that: sounds like a plan. Riley felt comforted and safe and at home hearing something Marie had been saying for twenty years.

They drove the four miles of narrow road slowly, watching for any sight of the green VW. At the entrance to the one campground on the island, the sign offered "Overnight sites and day-use area for picnicking. Please register with Camp Host in Site 2."

Pulling up to campsite number two, Riley and Marie were greeted by a white-haired, perky woman in worn blue jeans and a yellow sweatshirt that read "World's Greatest Grandma." She approached the car, and Riley opened the window.

"May I help you?" the woman asked, smiling broadly.

Riley thought, that's the warmest welcome we've gotten on the island. This woman must be from somewhere else.

"I hope you can," Riley said. "We're trying to find a friend. Her name is Kit, and she might have come in last night, driving a green VW bug. Did she camp here?"

"We did have one young woman show up here about nine o'clock. She needed a tent site, so I sent her down to number seventeen. Didn't see her leave yet today, so maybe she's still around. It's been busy, though, so I guess I might have missed her."

Riley put the Subaru into reverse. "Thanks. We'll go check it out."

"If you find her, would you ask her to come back up and register? She said she would last night, but she didn't come back."

"We will. Thanks again."

Marie noted the campsite numbers as they headed down the narrow one-way road. "Do you think we're going to find her sitting there singing camp songs to herself? Somehow I don't think Kit's hanging out, waiting for us to show up."

"Maybe not. But if we can find her campsite, there might be a clue. She can't vanish, even on this wacky little island."

"Can't she? It's happened before."

Riley slowed in front of campsite seventeen. "Don't start spooking me again. Look, there's a blue dome tent. Maybe she's sleeping peacefully inside. I better go check it out."

Marie smiled at her friend. "Maybe you better go crawl in with her and interrogate her."

"Great idea." Riley parked the car. "You and Duffy wait here."

"Like hell I will. I don't trust you alone with her."

"Why, Marie. What do you think I am?"

"Somewhat star struck. And you know I'm right, so don't try to deny it."

"Okay, come with me then. You think you know everything."

Marie got out of the car.

The blue dome tent was zipped up tight. "Anybody there?" Riley called as they meandered toward the campsite. "Kit? Are you in there?"

No answer.

"Do you think we should invade her privacy?" Marie asked as they drew near the nylon tent. "God, what if she's dead in there?"

"Oh, for heaven's sake, Marie, don't be so dramatic! You read way too many mysteries."

"Maybe, but you have to admit this is strange. Where could she be?"

"The only way we'll find out anything is to check out that tent. You go first."

"No way. You're the one who wants her, so to speak. *You* first."

At the entrance to the tent, Riley wondered if maybe she should knock, then felt ridiculous for the thought. She unzipped the door opening slowly, peeking in. The light was dim and she could barely make out what was inside.

"There's no one here," she said, relieved. "Just an empty sleeping bag, a backpack and some clothes."

"Excellent. Clues!" Marie glanced around the campground to see if anyone was watching them. In site number eighteen, a young mother was sitting by the fire, holding a toddler on her lap. She was facing away from them. "Coast is clear. Go on in."

"Oh, sure, like I'm the one who has to do the breaking and entering of a dome tent," Riley said. "That probably carries a mandatory two-year sentence in Canada."

"What a wuss! I'll go in if you won't."

"I'm going, I'm going," Riley finished unzipping the tent and crawled through the narrow opening. "Wait right there."

Marie did.

Inside, Riley pushed a sleeping bag out of the way to see what else was stashed there. She found a few food items—graham crackers, low-fat potato chips, bottled water. Kit's clothes were stuffed into a bright blue Nike backpack. A pair of running shoes had white socks rolled up in them.

"There's not much here."

Marie waited outside the tent. "Keep looking. It's our only hope."

Riley shoved the bag to the side and noticed a paperback book. "Hey, I think I might have something here. A lead!"

"And why do you think that?"

"Because I'm an excellent detective."

"Sure you are. Especially when you can break into someone's tent and go through her things."

Riley picked up the book. "It's a kayak book for the Canadian San Juan Islands." She noticed a corner of one page turned down and opened the guidebook. "She's marked the page for Wallace Island Marine Park. Maybe that's where she went this morning."

"Great! You are an excellent detective after all. I bow to your expertise."

Riley replaced the book where she found it and backed out of the tent. "Let's go drop Duffy off at the Cliffhouse and then see what's happening over at Spanish Hills Marina. They rent boats and kayaks there. I have a feeling this part of the adventure has just begun."

THE LITTLE MARINA WAS bustling with summer kayakers and tourists who wanted to be kayakers. Riley nudged the Subaru into a narrow space between two madrona trees, and they got out of the car.

"There's the rental place," Marie said. "If she went to Wallace Island, I bet she left from there."

"Let's check it out."

As they neared the wooden structure, a young man in shorts and a bright green windbreaker staggered out carrying four kayak paddles and an armload of lifejackets.

"Excuse me," Riley said, "are you the owner here?"

The man laughed and turned around. "I wish. If I were, maybe I'd make enough to survive. No, I'm the kayak teacher. Name's Sam Olson. Did you want a lesson?"

"Hi, Sam. I'm Riley Logan, and this is my friend, Marie. We may want a lesson, but first we were hoping you might have some information. We're looking for a friend who might have rented a kayak here this morning. Her name's Kit. Have you seen her?"

"Yes, I did. She was here before daybreak—our first customer. She rented a bright blue single and paddled off toward Wallace Island."

"Wow. Really? What would she be doing there? Is it far?"

"No, it's close." He pointed to an island lined with fir trees, straight out across the water. "She said she was headed for a cove on this side of the island. From there, you can take a trail over to Wallace Island Marine Park. Takes about forty minutes of paddling to get there. Your timing's good because you'll be going with the current this time of day."

Riley had kayaked a few times around Galiano, but Marie had never been in one. Riley wasn't going to let him know that. "Sounds great. Could we rent a tandem for a half day?"

Riley smiled hopefully at Marie, who shot back an "I can't believe you're doing this" look.

Sam said, "We have a couple left. It's twenty-five dollars for four hours. Cash or credit?"

"Credit, of course," Riley said.

Sam put down the paddles and lifejackets and headed back toward the rental hut.

"Do you want that lesson?" he asked as Riley handed him her Visa card.

"Oh, no. We're experienced at this." What a lie, she thought. Hope we don't drown.

"Okay, here you go," He handed her two paddles and two bright red lifejackets. "Take number six; it's already on the dock."

"Right-o," Riley said, sounding confident. "See you later then."

Marie's expression was one of slight horror.

"What in the hell do you think you're doing?" she whispered hoarsely to Riley. "I've never been in a kayak in my life."

"How hard can it be? You get in, you paddle, you go where you want. Come on, Marie. You can do this."

"But why didn't you let him give us a lesson?"

"I don't want to take the time. What if Kit's in trouble? What if someone's kidnapped her? And we're paddling around in the shallow water, having a kayak lesson, while she's tied up somewhere and being tortured for information. That's not how a real detective does things, Marie. First, save the girl. That's my motto."

"Oh, good grief. You drive me crazy sometimes. I can only shake my head."

"Shake away." Riley headed for the dock. "You know you love me anyway." She slipped the bow of the red kayak into the water.

"I THINK WE SHOULD have asked Sam how the heck to get into this thing," Marie said as she stood contemplating the task. "Do I step into it and hope it doesn't tip over?"

"It's like getting into a canoe. I'll hold onto it, you try to stay low and not tip the thing sideways. You sit in the back. I get to be the captain, and the captain sits in front and sets the pace of the paddling." Riley pulled the kayak close to the dock, steadied it, and offered her hand to Marie. "Maybe if you sit down on the dock and swing your legs over, you can slide in that way."

Marie didn't seem convinced. "Geez, Riley. You make it sound easy, but I know it's not. Okay. Here I go." She lowered herself onto the dock and did what Riley suggested. After considerable effort and one near-spill, Marie struggled into the rear seat of the kayak.

Riley gave her a high-five. "There. That wasn't so bad, was it?"

"I'm hoping that's the hardest part. Okay. You're the captain, so I'm the princess. I hope you don't get too tired paddling."

Riley sat on the dock and pulled the bow of the kayak close. "Very funny. We both paddle, silly." Marie tried to hold onto the dock as Riley lowered herself into the front seat. The kayak wobbled but Riley managed to sit down without tipping it over.

Riley grabbed a paddle and turned to make sure Marie was settled.

"Yes, I'm ready," Marie said. "Off we go then, Captain. Hey! How come this paddle has wide things on both ends?"

Riley groaned. "It's gonna be a long trip, isn't it?"

"Uh-huh. Better get started."

Riley pushed off the dock with her paddle. "Hang on. Wallace Island, here we come."

They took a few minutes to get used to the paddles, but after a while they settled into an erratic sort of rhythm.

"Just paddle when I do, Marie, on the same side. It's not all that different from the canoes we used to go out in at Girl Scout camp." Riley had to raise her voice over the wind and the sound of paddles slicing the water. "Remember what fun we had there? What were we—about thirteen?"

"We were fourteen," Marie shouted back, "and you were in love with Miss Waterfall."

"Oh, man, was I ever." Riley remembered the starry-eyed teenage lesbian she was then. "I think I wrote in my diary that I'd die for her. Don't you think that was romantic?"

"One thing about you is you never change. You crack me up."

"What do you mean?"

"I mean you were a hopeless romantic at age fourteen, and you remain one at age thirty-five. You're consistent."

"Thank you, I think. Now, paddle!"

Riley was soon mesmerized by the slap of the water against the kayak and the low moan of the wind on the channel. As they paddled, the high cliffs grew smaller behind them. They passed over rocks as big as haystacks, submerged but close enough to the surface that Riley saw bright purple starfish clinging to them. Soon they were surrounded by splashes and circles as a school of herring passed under and around their kayak.

"Cool!" Marie hollered over the sound of the wind. "Can you eat those?"

"All I know is they make great fish bait. I guess you can eat them pickled."

"Ugh. Think I'll pass. Are we there yet?"

Riley squinted against the sun and shaded her eyes to peer down the shoreline. "Not much further." She saw a wisp of something in the distance. Was it smoke? "Check it out. Is that a campfire?"

They both strained against the wind to see down the shore.

"I think it might be," Marie said. "And look. There's a figure on the beach."

Riley's heart sped up a little.

She paddled faster.

Chapter Six

AS THE KAYAKERS DREW closer to Wallace Island and the cove where they'd spotted someone standing, the figure walked quickly toward the west end where a blue kayak was pulled up onto the sand.

"Hey, wait," Riley shouted toward the beach as they paddled hard. "We want to talk to you. Kit? Is that you?"

The figure on the beach hesitated, turned around and faced them. She didn't answer.

Close enough to make out a face now, Riley saw that it was Kit. She wore shorts, a purple T-shirt and a bright orange baseball cap, on backwards again. Her short brown hair framed her face, and Riley was struck again at how attractive Kit was. She watched them approach, and Riley felt awkward all of a sudden.

"What in the heck am I going to say to her?" she said to Marie. "What will she think of us, following her out here like this?"

Marie leaned forward in the kayak. "Great time to think about that now. I thought you had a plan!"

"Yeah, well maybe my plan isn't completely worked out." Riley gazed toward the beach where Kit was now in full view. "I just wanted to make sure she was okay."

"Guess you'd better tell her that, then, because here she comes."

Kit strode toward them with a not-too-welcoming expression on her face.

"Hi," Riley said, rather lamely, she thought. "Are you okay?"

Kit stopped about thirty feet away and frowned at them. "Why wouldn't I be?"

"We were worried about you," Riley said, searching for the right words as she used her paddle to try to stay in once place. "We found a piece of your bike up at Bluff Park. Then we asked at the Kayak School, and they didn't know where you were. Then we found your tent at the campground, and you weren't around. It looked a little fishy." Riley stopped, realizing how ridiculous it all sounded.

"My bike?" Kit asked, coming closer. "How did you know it was mine?"

"We weren't sure," Marie offered. "The bright yellow fender is like yours, and those classic bikes are rare. We got a little concerned. Was it your bike?"

Kit hesitated as though she was considering how to answer. "Could have been, I guess. Someone stole it off the back of my car a couple nights ago."

"Right after you got here?"

"Yeah. The bummer is that they got some notes and photos I had in a leather bag on the back." Kit started to say something else, then stopped. She crossed her arms as if the drawbridge on her own personal castle had suddenly closed and the door was now firmly barred.

Riley knew she'd better explain their intentions. "We were worried something had happened to you, Kit, so we went to the Kayak School. We talked to Michael, but he wasn't too concerned. Thought maybe you were off camping. That's how we found your camp, and the guy at the kayak place said you'd come over here. We decided it was worth a forty-minute paddle to come out and check on you. Besides, it's a nice day for kayaking."

Kit seemed to accept this explanation, as though women followed her all the time for no apparent reason.

"Yeah, well it's nice of you to check on me. But I'm fine. Really. Thanks for coming all the way over here."

Was this a dismissal? Not so fast, Riley thought. "So what are you doing out here on Wallace? Checking out some good kayak destinations?"

"Right, and scouting around a bit."

"For anything in particular?"

"It's kind of personal. I'm doing research. I'm going to head back in a couple of hours."

"I see," Riley said. "As long as you're okay, I guess we'll continue our excursion." She wondered if she was doing a convincing job trying to sound as though they were out on a kayak joyride.

"Great," Kit said. "Have a safe paddle back. Be careful. The tide's going to change soon, and the current gets pretty strong. You might find yourself back in Vancouver." She smiled for the first time since she'd met them on the beach. She had a warm smile and her eyes were kind.

Riley met her amused gaze.

"We'll be fine. We've done this lots of times," she lied. She thought Kit probably knew she was lying.

"Right. Maybe I'll see you back on the island."

"Yeah, maybe. Sounds like you'll be pretty busy with your classes, though."

Kit leaned over to pick up her daypack, then took a couple steps toward the water. "If you want, come by later tonight, then, before things get too crazy at the kayak school. I brought wine I plan to crack open by the fire. Both of you come. We could get better acquainted."

Riley's heart fluttered. She tried to be casual. "Oh, I don't know. We haven't talked about plans for later yet, but thanks for the invitation. I guess we might see you."

Marie didn't say a word.

"That is, if we're not too busy," Riley added importantly. "We still have a lot of Aunt Joan's things to go through."

"I'm sure you do. Be careful going back."

"We will," Marie said. "See you around."

"Yeah, see you," Riley echoed.

Kit waved and headed back up the beach.

When Kit was far enough away, Riley said, "I think that went rather well."

"I'll bet you do. I wonder what kind of wine she drinks?"

Riley splashed her with the paddle.

"Hey! Quit it!" Marie said, splashing back. "You deserve a hard time, making me labor out here to say hello to some cute dyke on the beach. Now how do we turn this thing around? I'm worried about that current Kit talked about."

"But what if she had been in trouble out here? We would have felt terrible. We had to find out."

"Uh-huh. You did."

Riley splashed her again. "Paddle hard on the right side, Marie. I'll turn us back toward Galiano."

AS THEIR BRIGHT RED kayak grew smaller on the water, Kit watched with curiosity. Why had they come? Did they suspect something? Had Michael talked about their project? Damn, she thought. I hope he didn't get too friendly and tell them more than he should. As long as Michael kept quiet, Kit knew they had a chance of making a film that could turn it all around and preserve Galiano for decades.

And besides, she thought, Michael doesn't need to know my real reason for wanting to spend the summer on Galiano. But now here are these two wanna-be-detective women, checking up on me and going to talk to him. Damn. I don't want them following me around, even if the one was pretty cute. Did I imagine it, or did the short-haired one look flustered when I mentioned the wine and the campfire? Hmmm. Could get interesting.

Life is funny. Just when you think you have it all figured out and you're ready to make your move, some cute lesbian paddles up in a kayak. Maybe they're lovers. No. The other one's probably straight. Hard to tell these days, though. Let's see who shows up tonight to drink that wine.

Kit made her way back up the trail toward the main camp area. She had stashed her supplies inside the woods next to the sheltered cove. She pulled the branches off an item she'd hidden: a metal detector. Kit had brought it to search the abandoned cabins that were once part of Wallace Island Resort. She had heard about the resort from her grandmother and then done some research to learn more about it. David Conover, who became famous as the photographer who discovered Marilyn Monroe, built it in 1946. Conover had created the place as a retreat for the rich and famous. The resort had flourished for two decades, but its isolation eventually led to its demise.

Kit's grandmother had repeatedly told her the story of the engraved charm she had left behind, hidden on Wallace Island in what she referred to as "David's prized possession." She had never explained to Kit what the "prized possession" was, so that detail remained a mystery.

The story had always intrigued Kit. Her grandmother said she had grown up on Galiano, fallen in love as a teenager, and then left the island suddenly to go live with her parents in Toronto. She never came back to the island. A romantic, tragic tale, Kit thought. She had always wanted to solve the mystery of that hidden charm. Where was it? What did it say? Why was it so important? Why did her grandmother have to leave?

As far as Kit could guess, the "prized possession" had to have been David Conover's house, which had been luxurious in its day, but abandoned for more than fifty years. The house was part of the resort, and Conover had lived there with his wife. Kit had searched it thoroughly already, checking in the usual hiding places—under cupboard shelves, inside closets, behind loose wallboards. Nothing. Of course, the truth could be that her grandmother had made up the whole thing, and what she'd described was a myth, a young woman's romantic version of what she wanted to think was real.

But, then again, her grandmother always included the same details in the story, so perhaps there was something to it. A ring box, she'd said, with the charm inside. She never told Kit why the charm was so important to her. So what did her grandmother leave behind on Wallace Island? And was it still there? Whatever it was, Kit wanted it. She wanted that piece of her grandmother's past. All that was left now that both her grandmother and mother were gone was that little bit of history. She'd never known her grandfather, who died long before she was born. Her father was killed in an auto accident when she was a teenager. She felt sad about all of it. She was too young for so much loss. Lots of her friends still had parents and grandparents. Ah, well, she thought. Life paints a picture, and we have to live in it. This was hers.

Kit missed her mother and had thought about her often in the eight months since her death. Her mom had never even been to Galiano and never showed much interest in the story about the charm. But Kit did. She was determined to find it.

Kit shouldered the daypack and tucked the metal detector under her arm. If she ran into anyone, she'd say she was checking the beach for coins. People did that all the time. She headed down the main trail toward the marine park and the guest cabins. Maybe one of them had been David Conover's prized possession.

BACK AT THE MARINA, Riley and Marie pulled up alongside the dock. Riley steadied the kayak for Marie as she put both hands on the dock and lifted herself up onto it.

"Getting out is easier than getting in," Marie said. "But not much."

Kayak Man Sam appeared from inside the rental hut as if on cue.

"Nicely done. How'd it go?" he asked, taking the line from Riley and securing it like a sailor. He offered Riley a hand as she struggled to pull herself out of the kayak. "Did you find your friend?"

"Uh, yeah, we did," Riley said, offering nothing further.

"That's good, then. The water stayed calm for you, too. That always helps."

"Sure does. Thanks again," Riley said. They waved their goodbyes and headed for the Subaru. "Geez, my arms are getting sore already'"

"Mine, too. I have a feeling they'll be a lot worse tomorrow. Can't understand why, since we're both such experienced kayakers."

"Right. We are."

As they drove home toward the Cliffhouse, Riley and Marie discussed the possibilities concerning Kit: she was digging for buried treasure; she was burying loot from a bank heist; she was an illegal alien; she was meeting drug runners at the cove; she was an American FBI agent, undercover on an important case.

None of the scenarios seemed likely, they agreed.

Arriving at the Cliffhouse, they were greeted by an enthusiastic, jumping-off-the-floor Duffy who then ran past them and down the path by the cabin.

When they returned after a few minutes, Marie announced her plan to take a short nap.

"Think I will, too," Riley said. "Come on, Duffy. Let's go rest."

"Sweet dreams," Marie said as she went into her room to lie down. "Don't let me sleep through dinner."

"Don't worry, I won't. You're cooking it."

"Oh, yeah. I forgot it's my turn. Later."

Upstairs in her aunt's bedroom, curled up with Duffy beside her, Riley felt tired but wired. Something about Kit was suspicious. Why was she here, really? Just to teach at the Kayak School? If so, what was she doing out there at Wallace Island? Too many questions and not enough answers, she thought. Gotta find some answers.

Lying back on the comfortable bed, Riley glanced at her aunt's desk and saw the pile of papers she and Marie had examined earlier. The file was there with all the notes for the mystery novel. She decided to look them over again.

As she opened the top file folder, a newspaper story fluttered out and dropped to the floor. She picked up an article dated September, 1949, and read the first paragraph of a story about the Graham family and the drowning deaths of the children. Intrigued, Riley read through to the end of the article this time.

The nanny, Katherine I. Taylor, 17, told Galiano Constable James Carver that she must have blacked out before she was pulled from the frigid water. Carver reported, "She never saw what happened to William and Emily. We are all saddened by this tragic loss." Carver said that an investigation continues, but so far only a few pieces of the boat have been found.

Memorial services for the two children will be held Sunday at the South Community Hall. Miss Taylor is recuperating and had no further comment.

Riley sighed at the tragedy of it all and dug deeper into the file to find another clipping, yellowed and paper-clipped to an old piece of lined notebook paper.

The headline read "No sign of Graham children."

The story was brief and to the point:

The Graham family reported yesterday that they have no new information from the Galiano police, and do not expect to find any more clues regarding the disappearance and apparent drowning of their children. Claude Marks, a spokesman for the family, told the Island Times *that the family wishes to put the incident behind them and would not be granting any more interviews.*

Wow, Riley thought. What a terrible loss for the family and for the island. But why did Aunt Joan keep these stories? Riley thumbed through other notes in the file and smiled at the things Aunt Joan had cut out: odd stories from the local paper, mostly, and quirky stories about island life. Maybe Aunt Joan was going to use all of this for her novel. Good idea. This stuff truly was stranger than fiction.

Chapter Seven

RILEY LET MARIE SLEEP until she was about ten minutes away from putting their dinner of pasta and fresh vegetables on the table.

"Hey, sleepy head. Dinner's on." All Riley heard was a mumbled, moaning sound. "Are you coming?" she asked again, dropping the spaghetti into the boiling water.

Marie sauntered in from the living room and the sun-drenched couch. "Goodness, how long did I sleep? What time is it?"

"It's nearly six-thirty, and you slept for almost two hours. I think the kayaking wore you out. I decided to let you snooze, and I went ahead and made dinner."

"That's great. I'll do tomorrow night's. And what about you, Oh, Buff One? Did you sleep?"

"Nope. Too much to think about. I was reading an old newspaper clipping—the one we found in Aunt Joan's things. I think she was saving it, maybe using it for her novel. We need to dig deeper around here and see what else we can find. I know she saved lots of stuff, and she probably had notes somewhere."

"You're not working on that tonight, are you? What about wine by the fire with Kit?"

Riley drained the spaghetti, set the bowl in the sink and turned to face her friend. "Now, why would I do that? Kit wasn't serious, do you think? I think she was kidding about the wine."

"Sounded like a come-on to me. And I think we're both pretty sure who she was coming on to."

In spite of herself, Riley blushed. "Geez, Marie. You're making me embarrassed. Kit's not interested in me."

"Not much."

"But I suppose it wouldn't hurt to drive out there and be friendly." Riley peered out the window toward the sunset splashing light on the water. "I mean, she is all alone here and everything."

"Not for long, I don't think."

"She wants a friend, that's all."

"Whatever you say. Let's eat, and then you go and find out, won't you? I have a good book and a bottle of Kahlua, and Duffy and I will have a relaxing evening here at the Cliffhouse. Sorry, you're not invited."

"You're sending a babe into the arms of a much more experienced, buff lesbian! Oh, dear. What shall I do?"

"Knock off the act, Riley. I know you have the hots for her," Marie said with an evil grin. "Quit pretending you don't. Just be sure to tell me all the details. Every single one."

"Ha. That's a crock. If something does happen, which it won't, I'm not telling a thing. Big secret, it will be."

"Oh, sure. Like I won't be able to tell by the look on your face. It's me, remember? I've seen you fall in love a few times. It's always fascinating to me. You're quite a study."

"Thanks, I think." Riley brought their plates of steaming pasta to the table. "Now let's eat, and don't bug me anymore about Kit. I need to relax."

"Oh, you'll relax later, with that bottle of wine and you-know-who."

THE LAST ORANGE RAYS of a beautiful sunset were fading to gray when Riley maneuvered the Subaru through the darkening campground. Parents and kids were walking the narrow one-way road back up from the beach, and wood smoke filled the still-warm evening air. Riley loved the smell of a campfire. But she was anxious about being on her way to Kit's camp.

What the hell am I doing here? What am I going to say to her? Riley laughed at herself and kept driving.

Nearing Kit's campsite, Riley was both relieved and terrified to see that she was there, sitting in a canvas chair by a flickering campfire. Her back to the road, Kit didn't see Riley coming. I could still turn around and go home, she thought. She'd never have to know. But it's a one-way road. How would I do that? No, I have to keep driving forward, and then she'd see me drive by, and that would be even more lame than if I stopped to see her. She'd think I was a nerd then, or some kind of voyeur, driving by to look at her.

Riley was so lost in thought she almost missed the turn into the campsite, but regained her composure in time. She pulled in, cut the motor, and said a prayer that she wouldn't make a fool of herself.

Kit swiveled in her chair, recognized Riley, and broke into a grin. "I didn't know if you'd come." She got up and strolled over to greet her. "Where's your friend?"

Oh, no, Riley thought. She's going to know I wanted to come alone. "Hi. Yeah, she had some work to do at home, so I thought I'd come out and say hello. She really wanted to come," Riley lied.

"Too bad. I liked her. Is she your girlfriend?"

Riley was taken aback by such a direct question, especially so soon. "Do you mean girlfriend as in girlfriend, or as in girlfriend— partner?"

"Either one, I guess. Is she?"

Riley now felt confused by the question and unsure what to answer. "We've been best friends since the first grade. She's like a sister to me, I guess, although I don't have a sister, so I'm not sure." Shut up, she thought. You sound stupid.

"Oh, I see," Kit said, taking the lead back to the campfire. Riley thought she heard a teensy bit of relief in her voice—or was she making that up?

Kit headed to the tent. "Just a minute, I'll get another chair." She brought a fold-up one. "I'll use it and you can have the queen's chair here by the fire." She gestured toward the blue camp chair.

Riley plopped into the bigger chair, and Kit pulled her seat nearby and lowered herself on to it. An awkward silence fell. Riley listened to the snap of the fire and smelled the wood smoke.

After what seemed like about five minutes to Riley, Kit said, "It's nice of you to come, I didn't think you would."

"I thought it might be nice to get acquainted. And I must admit we were worried about you last night."

"Oh, yeah, the bike thing. That was such a bummer! Whoever took my bike must have stripped it for parts and dumped the rest over the cliff up there. I can't figure why they would do that. Can you?"

"There are a few things I can't figure. "Why are you here, really?"

"To teach at the Kayak School. I thought you knew that."

"Yes, I did, but why did you take off right away, and what were you doing at Wallace Island?"

"I've only known you for twenty-four hours, and you sure ask a lot of questions."

"It's my nature, I guess. Curious. I'm a reporter. That's all."

"That makes sense. But, hey, let's not get too serious about this." Kit rose and moved toward the picnic table. "How about some wine? I hope you like Riesling because that's the house special tonight. Is that okay?"

"Sounds good. Just half a glass for me. I'm driving."

"Sure. Coming right up." She poured the wine into plastic cups and brought them back to the fire. "Sorry I don't have proper wine glasses. I always break them. Now, where were we? Oh, yeah. Wallace Island. There's not a lot to tell. I've never been to Galiano, and I heard that the marine park and some of the coves on Wallace were quite beautiful, so I kayaked over to check it out. It is. Beautiful, that is. Had you ever been there?"

"Not until today. There are lots of beautiful places around here. Trouble is, it's like the locals don't want the tourists to know how to find those places. Have you tried to get to a beach here on Galiano? Every time Marie and I set out, we end up on some narrow gravel drive marked 'No Thru Road.' Then we get to the end of it, and there's a Private Property sign there. Sometimes we can even see the water, but we can't get to it. It's crazy-making."

Kit picked up a stick and stirred the fire. "People here are pretty protective. They aren't too keen on strangers, either."

"No shit, Sherlock. Oh, sorry. That's a phrase Marie uses on me all the time. I hope I didn't offend you." Riley savored the sweet taste of cold Riesling.

Kit seemed amused. "Doesn't bother me." Long pause. "So, what do you do besides be a tourist on this mysterious island? Where are you a reporter?" Kit's warm eyes and steady gaze unnerved Riley.

"In Ashland, in Southern Oregon. It's a one-town daily. I cover schools, government and crime news. And I've started helping with our online edition."

"That must be interesting. I'll bet you meet all kinds of crazy people, too."

"No two days are the same. I love it. I'm also loving having two weeks off. And what do you do besides teach kayaking, which I'm sure can't make you a living?"

"I make films in the Seattle area. Documentaries, mostly. In fact, I'm working on one here."

This was the first Kit had said about the film project. Riley wasn't sure how to respond. Should she tell Kit that Michael had already told them about it? She decided against that. She would, however, pitch her story about writing the freelance article.

"What's the film about?" Riley asked.

"About the clash between the islanders and those money-grubbing developers. There's been a three-year controversy here about Bodega Ridge. Have you heard about it?"

"I know something about it. But why a film?"

"A guy named Michael Barsotti contacted me and asked if I'd come up here and help him. He and I met at a conference in Seattle and struck up a friendship. He said he had a project that might get kind of sticky, and would I come and help."

"Sticky?"

"Yeah, sticky, as in people don't want the story told, especially the developers. Seems there's island politics mixed in with quite a bit of greed. If their proposal goes through, people stand to make millions of dollars off those lots. If they're turned down, the developers lose it all. Stakes are high, and that means people are pretty upset on both sides of the issue."

"That's so interesting. I've been working on a freelance piece for a magazine. It's about these sorts of environmentalist versus developer struggles playing out all over the Northwest."

"Sounds like a good story."

"So why did Michael need you for the film?"

"He wants me to be here, do my teaching, and then gather information—kind of like undercover. But I don't think I'm very good at it because I've already told you way too much. Why did I do that?"

Her eyes were inquisitive and her smile was playful and inviting, and it seemed to Riley that the question was Kit's way of flirting. Riley felt embarrassed, yet delighted. She was finding Kit attractive and interesting, and the wine was helping her relax into that feeling.

"Probably because I ask so many questions. You can tell me to shut up, you know."

"I could, but I don't want to." Same warm look. Riley squirmed.

TWO HOURS LATER, THE wine was gone, and the fire was embers. We've covered at least twenty topics, Riley thought. I like this woman. She's funny and bright and mysterious, and I think she likes me.

The glowing fire and the wine were making Riley mellow.

"Wow, look how late it is, after eleven," she finally said, stretching. "I should let you get some rest. Don't you have to teach tomorrow?"

Kit gazed into the dying fire. "Yeah, but not until later. Kids come in on the six o'clock ferry. I have all day to get ready for the restless rug rats."

"Thinking about having to deal with a bunch of unruly kids gives me a stomach ache. I don't know how you do it."

"Hey, maybe I should have you as a guest speaker, since you're a professional. You could talk about your life as a reporter and give them some advice about writing. I always ask them to keep a journal during the kayak trips. What do you think? It would be a lot more interesting coming from you."

As Kit spoke, she turned toward Riley. She reached with her right hand to set her empty wine cup on the ground and then slowly raised her hand onto the arm of Riley's chair. She covered Riley's hand with hers.

No one moved.

Riley felt her heart race. She tried to sound casual. "Interesting idea," she said, not moving a muscle. "I guess I could try to teach something to a bunch of high school kids during my vacation."

Kit looked at her by the dying light of the fire. "Are your eyes brown, or deep blue?" she asked, still covering Riley's hand with her own.

"Blue." Riley didn't know what else to say, so she said nothing. The fire popped.

"Are you sure you're all right to drive?" Kit's hand felt warm. She moved her thumb up and down Riley's index finger.

"Oh, I'll be okay. It's not far to the Cliffhouse." Truth was, she could care less about the Cliffhouse. Don't ever, ever move your hand, she thought. Leave it right there for a week.

Kit hesitated, started to say something, grew quiet, then stood. She faced Riley and offered her hand. Riley took it and was pulled up and in to those dark brown eyes. The hug was warm, a little long, but not long enough. Riley stepped back, smiled, and fished in her jeans pocket for the car keys.

"Guess I'll be heading out, then. Uh, thanks for the wine."

"Oh, sure. No problem. I'm glad you came out here to share it with me."

"Me—" Riley started to say.

"Really glad," Kit interrupted.

"Yeah. Me, too." Riley moved toward her car. "Oh, one more thing," she said, not wanting to leave at all. "Where will you be at the Kayak School? How can I contact you?"

"No one's too hard to find there. Room two. That's me. On the girls' side. Can't miss it."

"Right. Room two. Got it."

"So, maybe see you soon?" The inviting expression on Kit's face gave Riley courage. "Yeah, I think you will see me soon. How about tomorrow?"

"Tomorrow's good. Before six."

"Got it. Before six, then."

Riley headed for the car, got in and backed it out. Kit was still standing by the fire. She watched as Riley drove slowly down the one-way camp lane.

Even in darkness lit only by a waning campfire, Riley could still see Kit's warm eyes.

"I TOLD YOU, NOTHING happened." Riley was brushing her teeth, and Marie was standing right outside the bathroom door, talking through it.

Marie's voice was muffled. "You didn't get home 'til late. Don't tell me you only talked all that time. And what about the wine? Did you drink some?"

Riley kept brushing, didn't answer.

Marie's voice got louder. "Either you come out here right now and tell me exactly what happened, or I'm coming in there and locking us both in until you do."

"God, Marie, you're such a snoop sometimes," Riley opened the door and shoved past her. "Nothing to tell. The end. No story."

This infuriated Marie. "Ah ha!" she said, her face brightening. "I knew it! You did the deed! Who made the first move? Was it you, Romeo oh Romeo?"

Riley turned in her tracks and pointed her finger at her friend. "Nuh-uh. You're not going to make me talk. You've got it all wrong. I told you. Nothing happened."

"Is that nothing, as in totally nothing, or is that nothing, as in something sort of happened but not enough so I'll call it nothing?"

Riley hated it when Marie knew everything.

"Okay. She did touch my hand once, and we hugged when I left."

"Ah ha! I knew it!" Marie said, victorious. "The love story is begun."

"It's not a love story. We had some wine, that's all. Wine and a hug. No big deal."

"And don't forget her hand on yours."

"Don't worry, I won't."

"I'm right, aren't I? Something has begun?" Marie's face looked hopeful.

"Oh, geez, I don't know, Marie. I think she's interesting, and maybe she likes me. Too early to tell."

"So when are you going to see her again? Later this week?"

"This afternoon."

"Ah ha! I knew it!"

"Would you stop saying that?"

"No, I don't think I will."

"You drive me crazy." Riley tossed a couch pillow at her friend.

"Thank you." Marie tossed it back. "Now, would you find some hunky guy for me on this whacked-out island?"

"Why don't you come with me later, and we'll see if Michael's there. I'm still curious about why Kit was out at Wallace Island, and I want to ask him more about that." She was thinking about how Michael had stared at Marie yesterday as if entranced.

"Too bad. Think I'm busy."

"You are not. What are you afraid of? Come with me, and we'll make a visit to the Kayak School staff. It'll be fun."

"I told you, muscular Italians aren't my type."

"Hell they aren't. He's gorgeous. You're rusty, that's all. It's been a year or so, hasn't it?"

"Since when do you keep a mental calendar of my love life? And you're wrong, anyway. It's been seventeen months."

"But who's counting?"

"Okay! I'll go. But you have to promise not to tease me. And don't say anything lame in front of Michael, or when we come back here I'll have to kill you."

"You're mean when you're falling in love."

"I am not! Falling in love, that is! Or mean, that is! Take it back."

They always used to say that when they were kids. Riley smiled, remembering how different they'd been as little girls. Marie in her foo-foo dresses, dragging a doll everywhere. Riley in her cowboy chaps and double holsters, twirling her metal cap guns and strutting around their back yard. What a pair they'd been. "Riley. Did you hear me?"

Riley came back to the present. "Huh? Uh, no. I was thinking about us as kids. We were so cute."

"We still are. Okay, let's go see those kayak people. We don't have all day, you know."

Riley threw the pillow again. It hit Marie and bounced off onto the wooden floor.

Chapter Eight

RILEY AND MARIE DECIDED on the drive over that they would skip the formality of checking in with Robert and go straight to the equipment room to see if Michael was there. They wanted to see if he would talk about the mysterious film project, and if they could get any information out of him about why Kit was poking around on Wallace Island.

They pulled up in front of the school, gave Duffy her usual instructions to stay, and headed down the stairs to Michael's subterranean hangout.

"You knock, and you talk," Riley said. "Ha! I'm a poet."

Marie was not amused. "How come I have to do the talking?"

"Because he likes you, remember? Go for the good stuff."

Michael answered after the first knock.

"Yes?" he said through the closed door.

"Oh, hi. It's Marie and Riley, again," Marie said. Riley had a wide grin on her face, and Marie rolled her eyes in response

Michael opened the door immediately. "What a nice surprise. To what do I owe the honor?"

"We were in the neighborhood," Marie said. "Just kidding."

Now it was time for Riley to roll her eyes as she knew full well that it was difficult to be "in the neighborhood" of the Kayak School, since it was at the end of a long gravel drive that went nowhere else. Michael had to know that, too.

"Whatever the reason, it's nice to see you," he said with a love-soaked smile for Marie.

"Hi. Remember me?" Riley knew that sounded snippy, but she was tired of being ignored by this handsome Italian while he caressed Marie with his eyes.

"Oh, sure." Michael extended his hand. "How's it going?"

She gave his hand the quickest shake ever. "Good. We wanted to check in with you." Riley eyed her best friend expectantly and waited.

"Right," Marie said. "We were wondering if you'd tell us more about your film project—the one about Bodega Ridge. We talked to Kit, and she shared a few things, but we're wondering if you might know why she was exploring Wallace Island, and if that had anything to do with the project."

"Can't figure why it would. That's far from the ridge. What did Kit tell you?"

"She didn't provide much detail," Riley said. "She did say that you want her to be low-key about the project, try to gather some information if she can. I understand this is a pretty emotional issue for people on the island. We talked about it because I'm working on a freelance piece about environmentalists versus developers in Oregon. I didn't put it together when you mentioned the film before, but it seems very similar to some of the situations I've run into while doing research for that."

"Calling it 'emotional' is an understatement. People are upset about the prospect of a housing development in that area, and now that it might happen, it's getting scary."

"What do you mean?" Riley asked.

"I think people are being pushed to the edge of what they'll tolerate. I hope both sides can work something out. There's a lot of money involved, though, and that's the problem."

Riley nodded slowly, delighted that he was being so forthcoming. "What will happen if the developers win?"

"We'll see anywhere from fifty to a hundred homes built over the next four years. There's already a list of buyers, mostly from the mainland. People will live here, work in Vancouver or Victoria. We'll become a commuter island, a bedroom community. The islanders are livid. Say goodbye to the peace and quiet."

Marie said, "We've been up there. It's beautiful. We walked the Bodega Ridge Trail. We saw Whistler Mountain and all of Vancouver. I understand why people would want to live on that ridge."

"Sure, so can I," said Michael. "But you have to understand that Galiano is a place of quiet beauty, and people here don't want the island population to go much over a thousand or the entire atmosphere will change. You can't serve another several hundred people with our one gas station, two grocery stores and a bakery. More people, more business, more traffic. Kiss this Galiano goodbye."

Riley said, "Sounds like you have a few feelings about it yourself."

"I've lived here most of my life. I love this island. I will do what I can to keep it."

"Is that why you're doing the film?"

"Exactly. I figure if we can capture the spirit of this place, create a documentary that tells people why Galiano should remain as it is, then I can build some public support throughout B.C. Then, when the island planning commission has to make a decision, there will be that pressure to help them make the right one."

Riley asked, "How will they go about making the decision?"

"It will come down to the recommendations of an external committee of naturalists and engineers who are studying the site. The chair is a guy named James Crawford. I think he arrives tomorrow, if you're interested in talking to him. He's going to be gathering information. He usually brings a staff of two or three people, and they talk to locals and take photos of the proposed site. I think he's staying at Driftwood Village."

"Thanks for that," Riley said. "Maybe I'll talk to him. Could be some interesting material for my story."

"Anything else I can do for you two?"

"No, I don't think so. But we'll stop by and say hi to Kit while we're here. Have you seen her around this afternoon?"

"I think she's in her room. Last I saw, she was unpacking. Her students arrive on the six o'clock ferry."

"Okay, I guess we'll go say hello. Thanks for filling us in on the political scoop of the island. It's all quite interesting."

"It is that. I hope you come by again. Where are you staying?"

"We're at the Cliffhouse," Marie said. "It was Riley's aunt's, you know."

"Of course. I forgot. What a beautiful place!"

"Thanks again," Marie said. "Maybe see you around, then. Here's where you can reach us." She wrote down her cell number and handed it to him.

"I'm counting on it." Michael gave her the sweetest Italian smile.

"TOLDJA, TOLDJA, TOLDJA," RILEY said in a sing-song voice as they headed up the stairs. "'I'm counting on it!' Oooh-whee, what a line!"

Marie looked slightly embarrassed, but she didn't say anything.

"I wonder how long it will take him to call you?" Riley said. "He's probably tapping in your number right now!"

Marie strode ahead and glanced at Riley over her shoulder. "Your turn, Smarty Pants. Let's see what your reception is like behind Door Number Two."

The side-by-side dorm rooms were in a courtyard setting with all doors facing inward and no windows on the front side. The courtyard contained scraggly grass, two madrona trees and three picnic tables with attached benches.

"Not exactly the Ritz, is it?" Riley said.

They stepped up to Kit's door, and Riley knocked loudly. The door swung open immediately.

Kit stood back and bowed low, gesturing to them to come in. "Welcome to my delightful quarters. I'd ask you both to sit, but all I have room for in here is my military-looking bunk and one lawn chair."

"That's no problem," Riley said. "You remember my friend Marie?"

"Of course. Weren't you in the kayak yesterday?"

"Uh-huh. I was the one telling Riley to be careful."

Kit laughed, glanced at Riley, and then plopped down on the lower bunk bed. She patted the comforter beside her. "Sit down on my lovely couch. Marie, you get the honor of sitting on my one chair."

"Why, thank you." Marie gave Riley a quick, knowing glance as Riley sat on the bunk next to Kit.

Damn, Riley thought. Now Marie's going to give me shit about this.

"Sweet little room," Marie said, looking around. "With an emphasis on little."

"No kidding. I don't stay in here much, though. So, what are you two up to today? Gone on any more kayak adventures, or are you sticking to land this afternoon?"

Riley felt a blush at the remark and hoped it wouldn't show in the dim light of the one thin, high window in Kit's room. "Nope, no water adventures today. We did have an interesting talk with Michael, though."

"About what?"

"Michael told us about the Bodega Ridge controversy. Sounds pretty intense. Are you sure you want to be involved in this? Michael said millions of dollars are at stake. What if these people get nasty?"

"Who—the islanders or the developers?"

"Either. People have so much to gain—or lose—and that could be dangerous. I'm worried about you being in the middle of it, that's all."

Kit smiled. "I'll be careful. No one knows I have anything to do with it, except you and Michael." Kit took stock of Marie. "And I guess you know now, also, Marie. Hope you're okay with that. But I don't plan to tell anyone else. I can be very mysterious when I need to be."

No kidding, Riley thought. Mysterious and alluring.

A long silence followed. Finally, Marie spoke. "So exactly what are you looking for?"

"Michael and I think that maybe there's a reason why this development plan has moved forward so rapidly. Maybe there's someone putting pressure on the committee chair. He's the one who will make the final recommendation to the regional planners. We're trying to find out if there's anything underhanded going on."

Riley's mid-section tightened from worry. She hardly knew Kit yet, and already she was concerned for her safety. To cover for those vulnerable feelings, she tried to express convincing concern. "Wow. Do you really think so?"

"It's possible, and it seems as though the process is moving pretty quickly, so that may mean someone is pushing it. Behind the scenes stuff, you know?"

"Behind the scenes as in illegal?"

"You got it. Illegal and potentially worth thirty or forty million."

Marie said, "What a lousy thing to do, messing with the island peacefulness and quiet. That makes me mad. Anything we can do to help?"

Riley was glad Marie asked that question because she loved the idea of working with Kit on anything. This would be a great reason to see her often.

"I'm not sure," Kit said. "I guess there might be if you two were willing to go undercover and see what you can find out."

"Undercover?" Marie drew out the word and smiled at Riley. "I think we'd love to go undercover."

I can't believe she said that, Riley thought. How embarrassing. "Uh, sure, we'd be glad to help out," she said, trying to divert attention. "What can we do?"

"I'm going to be pretty tied up here this week with my class. There's a guy coming to the island tomorrow to do some research, talk to people about the ridge."

"Yes, Michael told us. Crawford?"

"That's the guy. Do you think you could manage to get some time with him or someone on his staff? Talk to someone about what they've found out?"

"We can try," Riley said. "We love a challenge."

"Great. That would be a huge help. It will also keep Michael and me out of the picture with this guy, and I'm pretty certain he won't suspect two tourists from Oregon as being part of any island politics. It's perfect."

"We're your man," Marie said. "But I guess that's not proper grammar, is it, Oh Journalist of the Highest Order?"

"Definitely not," Riley said. "Plural pronoun, singular noun. Not to mention the gender problem."

"Thought so. I always count on you to solve grammar and gender problems. Let's get to it, then. I think we'll be off now, Kit. Thanks for the hospitality and the exciting, mysterious assignment. We're on it."

Kit stood. "I have a feeling you two will be productive. I really appreciate it."

"No problem."

"We're happy to help," Riley added. "Guess we'll go now and call you if we find out anything useful."

They exchanged cell numbers, rose to leave, and Kit extended her hand to Marie. "I think we'll make a good team."

Riley was backing toward the door. "So, see you soon?"

"Right," Kit said. "Soon."

They headed for the parking lot. Kit remained in the doorway of Room Two and gave a wave as Riley backed out the Subaru.

"Hmm," Marie said. "She seems to be lingering in the doorway. Wonder why?"

"Very funny. Maybe she wanted some fresh air."

"I don't think so, Girlfriend. I think she's smitten."

"As Aunt Joan used to say, 'You're good with fantasy.'"

"Perhaps. But I would put my money on Kit being good with reality."

Riley blushed and kept driving.

Chapter Nine

THERE THEY WERE, AGAIN. Driving down the island road like they own the place, those girls from Oregon. He watched them round the bend near the bakery. He ducked out of sight behind some blackberry bushes. He didn't want them to see him. He'd had enough of their questions and their stateside ways. Stupid tourists.

As he trudged up the hill to his house, Jonathan thought about what he needed to do next. Not much time before that government bigwig showed up at the community meeting Wednesday, and he had much to accomplish. No way were those developers going to win this one. Someone has to put them in their place, he thought. Might as well be me.

Inside his cramped kitchen, Jonathan's window view was east, out over Georgia Strait and toward Vancouver. The mountains were beautiful, and the water was a shimmering blue.

Galiano will be ruined if those people come here. Got to stop them.

Jonathan picked up the phone and dialed the number he knew by heart.

"Yes?" the solemn voice said.

"I think we need to start the plan. It's time,"

"When?"

"Tonight. The meeting is on Wednesday."

"Where?"

Jonathan said, "Start with the ferry."

"All right."

The line clicked and went dead.

SIRENS WOKE RILEY FROM a dream. The digital clock read 12:42 a.m.

"What the..." she mumbled. Duffy was sitting up, ears alert; she got worried when she heard sirens. "Come on, Duffy, let's go downstairs and see what's happening." Riley made her way carefully down to the living room.

Marie was awake, too, and peering into the dark of the island night. "I don't see any smoke or fire or anything. What do you think it could be? It sounds as though every siren on the island is blaring. It's spooky."

"No kidding." Riley shivered in her Nike nightshirt. "That's way loud. Sounds as though it's coming from the south end."

"Who could we call?"

"Try Patrick and Ruth. They live right near the ferry landing. Maybe they know what's going on."

"But it's after midnight!"

"You think they'll be sleeping through that racket? 555-3434."

Marie dialed the number.

Patrick Baird picked up on the first ring. "Hello? Who is it?" His voice sounded stressed.

"Patrick, it's Marie. Riley and I were awakened by the sirens. It sounds as though the whole island is under attack or something. What's happening down there?"

"The midnight ferry from Victoria lost control as it neared the landing. It rammed the dock. Several people on the bow were pitched into the water. They're trying to get to everybody now. It's chaos."

Riley was trying to listen, her head near the phone. She grabbed it from Marie.

"Patrick? It's Riley. How could that happen? What went wrong?"

"Don't know for sure. I went to see what I could find out. Someone said the ferry lost power as it approached. They still don't know what caused it."

"Those poor people. Should we come down there? Do they need help?"

"Don't think so. There's already a traffic jam as volunteer firefighters try to get to the boat. Lots of people on the shore and in the water. Stay put, and I'll call you if it looks like there's any way you can help."

"Okay. Please let us know."

"Will do." Patrick hung up.

Marie's face was a question. "What can we do?"

"Nothing at the moment. Patrick says we'd just be in the way while the rescuers do their jobs. People could be hurt, Marie. This is very bad."

"But why—why did the ferry crash?"

"I can't imagine. I don't think anyone knows yet."

IN THE DARK OF his kitchen, Jonathan watched as an island police car sped toward the ferry dock followed by two fire trucks. Through binoculars, he saw the damage to the ferry's bow where it had rammed the dock. Panicked foot passengers were struggling to escape and having to leap over the gap between the boat and the ramp. The pier now rested at a slight angle because when the ferry hit, one of the pilings caved in. The ramp didn't connect anymore.

His phone rang, and he picked it up in the dark.

"Well?" the male voice said.

"It's chaos, like you said. But people are in the water. They could be hurt. There could be deaths. You promised no deaths."

"What the hell, MacAlister? You think this is some kind of exact science? If you do, then *you* do the dirty work, you stupid bastard."

Jonathan was silent. He hated when this man called him names, which happened too often. He abhorred this despicable person, but he needed him.

"Never mind," Jonathan said softly. "It's done. We'll know in a few hours if any casualties occurred. You'd better hope not."

"No skin off my nose, brother. You ordered a service. I provided it. Nobody saw me. Where can I pick up the rest of the money?"

"In the post office box tomorrow morning." Jonathan hung up. He picked up his binoculars and expected a long night.

AT FIRST LIGHT, RILEY and Marie drove down the narrow island road, afraid of what they'd find at the ferry landing. As they came upon it, they saw several emergency vehicles parked near the water and people in ambulance-white uniforms sipping coffee out of Styrofoam cups. They parked near the information kiosk and walked toward the water. A young police cadet stopped them at the ferry staging area.

"Sorry, ma'am," he said to Riley. "Can't let you go down there."

"But we're worried about the people on the ferry. Is everyone all right? Do people need help?"

"All the passengers disembarked several hours ago when they finally got the ramp to connect. Only people left on the boat are police and provincial investigators."

"Investigators? What are they doing here?"

"They suspect someone tampered with the boat."

"That's terrible. Was anyone killed?"

"Doesn't look that way. We pulled eight people out of the water, though, and a couple were pretty cut up. They're at the medical clinic. Rest went home with relatives or friends, or left on the ferry that was sent over early this morning."

"Thank God no one died," Marie said.

"No kidding." Riley shook her head slowly. "What's happening on this crazy island?"

RILEY AND MARIE HEADED back to the Cliffhouse for breakfast and to make a plan. Over coffee, they discussed the incident at the ferry landing. They were interrupted by the telephone.

Riley answered. "Hello?"

"Riley, it's Kit. Can you meet me later? There's something odd about that accident at the ferry. Michael and I are worried that it's part of a bigger plan."

"What kind of plan?"

"That's what we don't know, and we need your help. Can you meet me at the Bodega Ridge trailhead at five-fifteen? My class is over at four-thirty. We need to talk."

"I'll be there."

"Of course. Thanks, friend. See you then." The phone clicked in Riley's ear.

"What's the deal?" Marie asked. "Is Kit all right?"

"Yeah, she is, but she said that she and Michael are worried about the ferry incident, and she wants to talk. I'm meeting her at the Bodega Ridge trailhead."

"Hmmm. Nice and secluded." Marie made a sound like a cat purring. How convenient."

"Come on, Marie. It's not funny. Kit needs our help. She asked me to meet her, because I think she's worried about—I don't know what she's worried about."

"I understand. I can handle it. You go alone. That's the way Kit wants it, and I'm sure it's the way you want it, also. Besides, I have my own assignment, remember? I have to get that Crawford guy alone and pump him for information. Maybe I'll work on that this afternoon. Michael said he's staying at the Driftwood Resort."

"You really think he'll talk to you?"

"Of course he will. I'm going to tell him I'm working on background for a piece for Northwest Magazine."

"But you're not a writer."

"He doesn't know that. Besides, I'm charming, and few men can resist that."

"Poor guy won't know what hit him. Good plan. Okay. You go for it, and I'll meet you here later to hear all the details."

Chapter Ten

SUNLIGHT DANCED ON DISTANT blue water as Riley pulled the Subaru into the trailhead parking lot. Kit was already there, saying goodbye to a middle-aged couple who had finished their hike.

"Hey there," Riley said as she stepped out of the car. Duffy was right behind her. "Ready for a walk?"

"I am." Kit pulled a blue daypack from the Kayak School van and headed toward Riley. She leaned toward her and gave her a hug. "How're you doing?" Kit adjusted the pack on her back. "Are you okay?"

"Yeah, just worried about that accident and about you."

"About me? Why?"

"Because if there is something going on—"

"Let's talk up the trail," Kit interrupted her. "I want to be sure we're alone."

"Sure. Okay. Come on, Duffy. Time for an adventure with our friend Kit."

Duffy bounded ahead as they started up the trail.

"Aren't you worried she'll run off?" Kit asked as Duffy raced toward whatever she thought was ahead of her in the woods.

"No. She always stops to check on me and never goes very far without turning around and racing back. She's dependable that way."

"Great dog, then."

"She's the best."

For the first several hundred yards, the path led upward through tall trees, and the surface was soft with moss. Light filtered through, casting soft sunbeams, lighting up fallen logs and moss-covered rocks. The air was heavy and moist and smelled of pine.

"This is a beautiful trail," Riley said to Kit, who was several yards ahead of her, moving quickly through the trees.

Kit glanced over her shoulder. "Yeah, I'm really loving this, also. Michael told me that the view at the top goes on forever."

They walked on, not talking, until they came to a clearing and the crest of the ridge. As they walked the forest path, the blue sky met the water below, and they could see for miles.

"Best view on the island." Kit took a graveled side-path toward a rocky point. "Come on out here, and I'll be your tour guide."

"Sounds good."

At the end of the narrow trail, a flat rock as big as a truck bed lay as though waiting for tired hikers to plop down, which is what they did. Duffy jumped up onto the rock and stretched out in the sun.

Kit pulled off her daypack and reached inside for a water bottle. "Okay, I think we're far away from anyone now, so I think we can talk." She took a long drink.

"I'm listening. What the heck is going on?"

"Here's the main thing I want to tell you, and I chose this spot on Bodega Ridge purposely. I still can't figure out why, but for some reason I trust you, and I think you need to understand what we're up against."

"We?"

"Michael and I. It could get scary."

"Now you definitely have my attention."

"Okay, here's the thing: Michael thinks that someone may be trying to push the land sale through and is doing it illegally. We don't know who yet, or why. But several incidents recently point to that possibility."

"How could anyone do that?"

"A number of ways. The land is owned by the timber company, and the execs there have a lot of power and influence."

"But isn't the decision up to that committee?"

"It is. But that committee is made up of people. And people are vulnerable, especially if money is involved, or some other kind of pressure is exerted that we aren't aware of."

"Wow. That's heavy," Riley said. "What are you going to do?"

"We're both checking out some possibilities. Michael is close to finding out who is at the center of this. He thinks that, somehow, the ferry accident this morning might be connected."

"In what way?"

"We're not sure. Maybe someone is trying to keep people away from Galiano."

"Why would they do that?"

"That's the part that doesn't make sense. If someone wants to make sure the land up here is developed, they're going to also want to make sure there are buyers for the lots. So the ferry accident is perplexing. But, somehow, there's a connection, and we're going to find it. We're also interviewing key people here—people who have been involved in saving the island since the fifties. Michael wants to use the interviews in the video and then get it on public access TV. He is convinced that if people realize what could happen to Galiano, they'll rally behind our cause and put pressure on the board to block the sale."

"What about that guy, Crawford, the chairman?"

"He seems clean, so far. But Michael is keeping an eye on him, too. There's a community meeting Wednesday night, and Crawford will be there, along with everybody else on the island, I suspect. Should be interesting."

Riley took a swig from her water bottle. "I'll be there."

"Good. That's what I wanted to ask you about. Has Marie contacted Crawford yet?"

"I think she's going to meet him later today."

"How did she manage that?"

"She told him she's doing a magazine piece about the island."

"Very clever. Maybe she'll get something out of him. It might be our best route to information."

"I know she'll try. And Marie can be very convincing."

Riley gazed out toward Vancouver. Two bright white B.C. ferries were passing each other in the blue waters. Other smaller boats dotted the waterscape. To the north of where they sat, a bald eagle rode the wind currents above the island. "This is such a beautiful place. No wonder people want to live here."

"It is, but if this area gets developed, you and I won't be sitting in this spot enjoying the view. That's the point."

"I realize that. It certainly takes a lot of effort to preserve it, though, doesn't it?"

"It does."

Kit paused, scanned the roiling water, and scooted closer to Riley. She casually took Riley's right hand in both of hers and cradled it there. "Truth is, I like this island a lot more since I've met you. All of a sudden, it's more beautiful than ever."

Riley's mouth went dry, and she said nothing. She hoped Kit couldn't hear her heart pounding.

"Are you okay?" Kit asked. She looked deep into Riley's eyes, and for a moment Riley thought she might lean in and kiss her. But Kit only continued that steady, sweet gaze.

Riley exhaled a deep, long breath. "Better than ever."

Chapter Eleven

RICHARD ELLISON PARKED HIS red Jeep Cherokee behind his place of business, got out, and unlocked the bakery's back door. A short, stocky man in his sixties, Ellison was dressed casually in light gray pants, a soft blue golf shirt and running shoes.

Even after five o'clock, there seemed to be a lot of traffic on the main road, and he wondered what was going on. Surely they'd cleaned up all the ferry mess by now, and things were getting back to normal.

Susan Collins, his main baker and the one who was best at making the famous cinnamon rolls that everyone seemed to love, was tying on her white apron as he came into the kitchen. She was forty-five, a longtime Galiano resident and had worked at the bakery for over ten years.

"Afternoon, Richard," she said as she set out the ingredients for the dough.

"Thought I'd come down and help out."

"Nice to see you. But I can manage. You really don't need to help."

"I can sort supplies and get things ready for the deliveries. I have a lot of paperwork to do, too. Buying a business makes for lots of work, you know."

"I do know. You've had a lot to do since you bought the place from the Hardins. Guess they'd had enough of island life, and it's challenging here when the kids are in high school. A ferry ride every morning just to get to school is a drag."

"So glad they accepted my offer right away," Richard said. "And I'm even more pleased you decided to stay on. I can run a business, but baking cinnamon buns is not one of my talents."

"I'm happy to do that part and to keep my job. Thanks for that."

Richard poured them each a cup of coffee, set Susan's on the counter, and headed with his cup toward his office at the rear of the kitchen. "Have fun with the cinnamon buns. Once I get all this paperwork done, I'll be out here to help you, if you're not done already."

Susan was measuring flour. "See you then." She turned around when she heard the bell on the front door, announcing the arrival of a customer.

"Hi, Michael," she said. "It's been a while since you were in. What's up? Did you have another of your cravings for baked goods?"

Michael Barsotti smiled. "That's it exactly. You know I can't go more than a couple of weeks without some of your famous scones."

"I made some this morning. You're in luck. Unless Richard ate the last of them, that is. Let me check."

"How's it going with your new boss, anyway?"

Susan glanced toward Richard's closed office door and lowered her voice. "It's going okay. It's not like working for the Hardins, though. I miss them."

"No doubt you do. I miss them, too. So how's the new guy?"

"Oh, he's fine. Have you met him yet?"

"Not officially. I've seen him at a couple of island gatherings, but never been introduced."

"Would you like to meet him now? He's in his office."

"I don't want to bother the man. I wanted to pick up some berry scones."

"Truth is, you can have both. I think he'd like to meet you. Wait right there." She headed toward the back of the bakery, knocked softly on the office door, and came back with Richard Ellison.

"I'm Richard Ellison," he said to Michael. "It's a pleasure to meet you. I've certainly heard a lot about you and your Kayak School."

Michael returned the firm grip. "Likewise. I've heard a lot about you, too. It's great that you would buy the bakery and keep my friend Susan here employed."

"She's the best. She *is* this bakery, if you ask me. I'm merely the helper, and not very good help, at that. But she puts up with me."

Susan slid the first pan of cinnamon rolls in the oven. "You're learning."

"Right. Rather slowly, though. Do you come here often?" Richard asked Michael.

"I'm a fan of the berry scones Susan makes, and of those gigantic cinnamon rolls. I like to support local business."

"We appreciate it. Thanks for coming in. By the way, where is your school, anyway? I might like to come up and visit sometime. I have a nephew in Vancouver who could benefit from some time in the wilderness."

"We're up the main road about nine miles, and then a half mile or so in toward the water. There's a green and white sign. Can't miss it."

"Maybe I'll come up and visit one day and check out your programs. If that would be all right."

"Come any time. Call ahead, and I'll give you a personal tour."

"That's very kind. Thanks. Oh, and did you get your scones?"

Michael held up the white paper bakery bag that Susan had prepared for him.

"Got 'em right here."

"Good. They're on the house today. Enjoy."

"Thanks very much."

"See you again soon. I'd better get back to work."

"Of course. Me, too. Have to meet the six o'clock ferry. I have eleven students coming in. Hope to hell there's no problem with the braking system on this one."

"No kidding. That must have been pretty scary for the people on that ferry. When I heard the sirens last night, I couldn't imagine what was wrong."

"Yeah, I know. We've never had that happen here before. Quite a freak accident, I guess."

"Let's hope it's the last one. Thanks for coming in, Michael."

"Pleasure to meet you. Bye, Susan."

Right after Richard closed his office door, his cell phone rang.

"Yes? This is Ellison." He lowered himself into his desk chair.

"Did you hear about the ferry accident?" the voice asked.

"The sirens woke me just after midnight. The lodge manager told me something went wrong as the ferry was trying to come in. It hit the dock. People were hurt."

"Shit. That's not good for business. Do they know what caused it?"

"Haven't heard that yet."

"When is the meeting?"

Richard fiddled with a paper clip on his desk. "Wednesday night at seven o'clock."

"Are you going to say anything there?"

"I don't know. I'm going to see what happens. I'm trying to keep a low profile. You and I aren't the only ones who want to see that ridge developed."

"Yeah, I know. But if things don't go our way, we're going to need another plan."

Richard said, "Perhaps. But let's not worry about that yet."

"I hope you're right."

The call ended. It should be an interesting meeting, Ellison thought.

THE SUN WAS SINKING below the tree line when Riley and Kit reached the lower part of the ridge trail. As she had the entire afternoon, Duffy led the way.

"It's getting late," Kit said. "Want to go get some dinner?"

"Good idea. How about back at the Cliffhouse? It's Marie's turn to cook, and I know she'd love to spend some time with you also."

"Sounds good to me, if you're sure she'll be okay with it."

"Let's go, then. Why don't you follow me?"

"I will."

Back at the trailhead, they got into their vehicles and drove the narrow island road toward the Cliffhouse turnoff. Riley made a right turn, smiling at the "No Thru Road" sign that marked the intersection. She routinely noticed them at different locations on the island. After all the years of visiting Galiano, she had come to believe that the islanders didn't want the tourists to find the beaches.

At the Cliffhouse, Riley once again admired the sweeping view of the water. Her aunt had always loved that.

Marie was on the deck, reading a book in the sun. She glanced up and caught sight of Riley and Kit. "Hey, hikers. How was it?"

Riley said, "The hike was nice, the view was great, and now we thought we'd pay you a visit, especially since it's your turn to cook dinner."

Marie put down her book. "That works out great for you, doesn't it, old friend?" She made a face and stuck her tongue out. With a faked sigh she said, "Sure. You're both welcome to enjoy Marie's famous cooking. Tonight it's stir-fry, followed by fresh apple cobbler."

"That sounds great, Marie." Riley turned toward Kit. "See? Told you we came to the right place."

"Do you girls want a lemonade?" Marie said as she headed into the kitchen.

"Sure," Riley said. "Okay if we hang out here on the deck a little longer?"

"Works for me. I'll bring you cold drinks, since I'm so nice."

"Thanks, Marie. And when you do, I'd like a full report on your visit with Crawford."

"You talked to Crawford?" Kit asked.

Marie stepped back out onto the deck. "I did. There's not a whole lot to tell, but he did talk some about Bodega Ridge and the conflict between the developers and the islanders. He seems pretty solid, though. I didn't get any hint that he might be up to something."

"That's my best friend, the sleuth," Riley said. "I knew you could do it."

"Thanks for the vote of confidence. I'll get the lemonades and start dinner, and then I'll tell you all about it while we eat."

"Sounds good. Kit, we'll get comfortable in the chaise lounge on the west deck, and she'll bring out the drinks."

"Excellent plan." Kit put the back of the lounge chair down a couple notches, sat heavily, and closed her eyes to soak up the last warm rays of the early evening sun. Riley, approaching with the lemonades, could not keep her eyes off her. Kit's lean frame looked relaxed in the warm light and Riley found herself fantasizing again. She's stunning, Riley thought. What am I going to do about that?

Chapter Twelve

EARLY THE NEXT MORNING, Michael was on the phone with a bed and breakfast owner who was upset because some of the kayak students had picnicked on her beach and left soda cans and other litter. Oh, God, he thought. Doesn't this woman have anything better to do?

A knock at his office door saved him. "I'm so sorry, Mrs. Tucker," he said as he tried to conclude the conversation. "I don't know who the guilty parties are, but I will send three students up later this afternoon to pick up trash on the beach. We always emphasize being mindful of the environment, but sometimes these kids get careless."

Kit opened the office door quietly and poked her head in. Michael gestured for her to sit down.

"Right," he was saying, "around four o'clock. And thanks again for bringing it to my attention." He hung up.

"Probably wasn't even our kids," he said to Kit.

"Probably not, but we have to keep up good relations with these islanders, now don't we?"

"That's for sure." Giving her his full attention, Michael realized now that Kit looked agitated. She was supposed to be off today. What was she doing in his office at nine o'clock?

"Are we ready for the community meeting tomorrow night?" she asked, picking up a pencil from the cup on Michael's desk and rolling it between her thumb and index finger. It was a nervous habit that Michael had witnessed before. Something was up.

"I guess so. It's gonna get hot, you know. Crawford, Ellison, MacAlister—there's a threesome to drive you nuts for sure. And I heard last night that one of the developers will be there, a woman named Clare Porter. She's their CEO, a 'ruthless bitch,' as someone at the pub said last night. That should be fun."

Kit didn't smile.

Michael was getting concerned. "Kit, what's wrong? Are you worried about the meeting?"

"Yes, I am."

Michael unplugged his phone, got up to close the office door and wheeled his desk chair around to the side of the desk, facing Kit. "I'm listening."

"I didn't think much of it at the time, but Riley and Marie have me convinced that whoever took my bicycle may be involved somehow with the Bodega controversy. I think maybe they're trying to scare me off."

"Why would someone want to do that?"

"I'm not sure. Maybe they realize I'm working on this video project with you and they want to squelch it."

"But who would that be? Someone from here on Galiano? I can't imagine that. I mean, I know everyone here, Kit. I think I'd be aware of that kind of opposition right here on our island."

"I know it sounds crazy. It's a gut feeling I have, and I wanted you to know."

"I'm glad you told me. It's weird, though."

"I know." Kit hesitated. "There's one other thing, Michael."

"Yes?"

"This has nothing to do with the bike incident, but I do have another connection to this island that I didn't tell you about. This is my first trip here, but my grandmother grew up on Galiano."

"Really? And did she live here as an adult?"

"No. She left and went to Toronto when she was a teenager. She never even came back to visit, as far as I know."

"I wonder if any of the old-timers here remember her."

"I doubt it. That was a long time ago. But there is a mystery about her I'm trying to unravel while I'm here. For years, as a child, she told me stories about hiding something out on Wallace Island. I still don't know if it's true or if it's just a tale she liked to tell. I was fascinated with it as a child, and she used to tell me all sorts of things about her adventures as a teenager. I don't know which parts were true and which were made up."

"What did she say she hid?"

"Some sort of an engraved charm. She told me she hid it in a ring box in 'David's prized possession' somewhere out on Wallace, in that abandoned resort. She told me the charm was given to her by her one true love, whoever that was."

"Do you know why she left it?"

"I think it was a young girl's way of being dramatic and mysterious. She told me she'd return someday and retrieve it, but she never did. Since I'm here for the summer, I decided to try to find it."

"And did you?"

"No, but I did paddle over to Wallace and snoop around. I even took a metal detector. I didn't find anything, though. I'm embarrassed to admit to you that I even looked for it. Kind of feels like a snipe hunt, if you know what I mean."

Michael laughed. "I don't think it's quite that bad. I can see why you'd be curious. Who knows what a teenager might do, anyway? It would be fun to discover what she left here. Is she still alive?"

"She died about three years ago. I guess that's why it's so important to me. My mom's gone now, too. I want to find that piece of my grandmother's past. I know it sounds kind of crazy."

"Not at all. I totally understand."

"Anyway, back to the meeting tomorrow," Kit said, changing the subject. Michael thought she seemed embarrassed.

"Yeah?"

"I think we need to be careful and listen to everybody. We can gather a lot of information there and get a sense of who's most passionate about the Bodega development."

"I agree," Michael said. "There could be fireworks."

"I asked Riley and Marie to be there. And Marie is going to meet with Crawford afterwards—have a drink. That could get us some information, too."

"Great strategy. I think we'll know a lot more about all this very soon." Michael cleared his throat, fussed with a pencil on his desk and gazed out the window.

Kit stood. "Guess I've talked enough. I'd better get back to my room and start enjoying my day off."

"I sure appreciate you telling me all this."

Kit felt uncomfortable all of a sudden and made her way to the door. "Right. I know you do."

"Have a good day away from this place."

Kit waved over her shoulder and closed the door softly behind her. Michael heard the front screen door slam and through his window, he watched Kit hasten across the courtyard to Room Two.

Something about Kit's story intrigued him, but he couldn't quite pinpoint it. He had heard that phrase, "David's prized possession," before. But where?

Michael went to the bookshelf he kept along the inner wall of his office. Something tickled at the corner of his mind, in that place where he couldn't quite get to it. He had read it somewhere, in one of the island guides. Which one? He scanned the titles: *Kayaking the B.C. Waters; 100 Best Nautical Knots; Marine Life of the Southern Gulf Islands; Once Upon an Island*. Something about that last book was familiar, and then Michael remembered that the author was David Conover. He pulled it from the shelf and sat in his rocking chair by the window. He leafed through the pages, scanning the photos of Conover, his wife Jeanne, and the cozy guest cabins he'd built out on the island. The last chapter consisted of current-day photos. He squinted at abandoned vehicles up in the meadow—an old green Jeep and a rusted-out tractor. Seeing them jogged the memory that Michael was trying to access.

Michael turned the page and saw what he was looking for, a photo of the Jeep, with a caption. "David Conover could be seen driving his precious green Jeep all over the island," it said. "He kept it in pristine shape, and often said it was his prized possession."

Bingo! Michael thought. Prized possession. The secret could be hidden in that Jeep. Maybe I can help Kit solve her grandmother's mystery.

Michael put the book back on the shelf and thought about the adventure ahead. He had grown fond of Kit in the short time he'd known her. He appreciated her willingness to help him with the film project, and now here was a way he could help her. Time to find that charm.

MICHAEL WAITED UNTIL JUST before dusk that night to make the ten-minute crossing to Wallace Island from the Spanish Hills dock in his twelve-foot Smoker Craft aluminum Jon boat. He'd decided to go before night fell because he didn't want any campers or kayakers to see him checking out the old Jeep. If there was something there, Michael wanted to be sure he was the one to find it.

The soft orange sky was melting into a deep blue. A few clouds enhanced the sunset, especially with no wind. He had good running lights and used them until the last two minutes, when he switched over to his one-horsepower electric motor. The engine was quiet enough that it wouldn't be noticed. He was on the backside of the island, away from the dock. He pulled the boat ashore at a tree-lined cove near the campground, tied it off to a scraggly pine, and stood in the growing dark to listen. He heard the usual night sounds: island crickets, the lap of the water against the rocks, and distant laughter that was probably coming from across the narrow island at Wallace Marine Park. Sailboat campers spent the night there, and Michael was certain there would be several boats moored there on a June night. The air was warm, and a clear dark sky offered up its first stars. Good camping weather. The summer crowds were arriving, more every day. The sweet aroma of wood smoke drifted up from the camping area. Someone was grilling hamburgers. Ah, summer, Michael thought.

Michael entered the trees near where he'd beached the boat and made his way toward the upper meadow. He saw the path that came up from the cove and the main camp area. Standing at the edge of the meadow, he was certain he was alone.

Michael's eyes had adjusted to the low light. There in the meadow, barely discernable now in the growing dark, were the two vehicles—a rusted-out red tractor and the remains of a 1939 Jeep pickup. The Jeep was owned by David Conover, according to Conover's book, and abandoned there in 1949, two years after the resort opened when he didn't have the money to repair the motor. The B.C. Parks people had kept the relics, and Michael guessed they'd probably been photographed by almost everyone who visited Wallace Island.

Dark enveloped the island now, but Michael still kept low as he walked the path from the trees into the meadow. The moon had not risen, and he knew he had about an hour before it did.

He headed for the Jeep. It sat on threadbare rubber tires, open to all the elements through its missing windows. Michael skipped the flashlight beam across it. Other than the faded evidence of two-tone panels, he saw mostly rust, which made it hard to tell what color the vehicle had been originally. The fender over the front tire was black, and the rest of the Jeep might have been army green.

Approaching the driver's door, Michael pulled it open and winced at the creak the rusty metal made. The door handle was worn smooth, as was the torn leather of the driver's seat, the polishing effect of hundreds of island visitors who had taken a turn behind the wheel. Michael smiled thinking of all those butts sliding in and out of that old Jeep.

Back to business, he told himself. Where would a seventeen-year-old hide something?

Michael doubted that the young woman had known much about cars, so he surmised that her hiding place would be subtle yet obvious, somewhere accessible to someone who was not a mechanic. Probably not the motor area, then. Underneath the chassis? Under the seat? Michael decided to start inside the Jeep.

Pulling the penlight from his jacket pocket, he crouched in the low grass beside the driver's seat floor and began his search. His light danced over dirty floorboards. One had a hole the size of a silver dollar, and grass sprouted through it. Flakes of rust fell as Michael moved his left hand over the worn frame of the driver's seat. Nothing unusual here. And nowhere to hide anything. He moved on.

The passenger seat floor was filthy with mud and grass, obviously the home to many tourists' feet. Brushing the dirt away, he searched with the light for anything unusual. He saw no seams or breaks in the floorboard.

Michael trained his light upward, to the dash. The glove compartment had long ago lost its door and was rusted and empty. Too obvious anyway, he thought. She wouldn't put anything there.

Or would she?

Michael tried to get inside the teenager's head. Where would she hide it? He didn't even know what size the box was, or, truthfully, if there even was a box. What had Kit called it? A snipe hunt. He was probably on a snipe hunt. He stopped to listen again, and to peer around the dark open meadow. Nothing moved, no sound except for the chorus of the crickets.

Michael stepped out of the Jeep and considered his options. The vehicle's frame was low; it had probably sunk every year for over sixty years. Great, Michael thought. I need to scoot underneath, and I'll probably get stuck under there.

Michael removed his jacket and searched with the light to see if anything visible was crawling under the Jeep. If anything was there, it was too small to see, so he laid the jacket on the moist grass and scooted beneath the vehicle. His penlight danced back and forth along the bottom of the motor, which was corroded and brushed by grass that had grown there even in low light. He pulled the grass away from the undercarriage, and dirt and grime fell onto his face and into his hair. Reaching back toward the area below the front passenger seat floorboard, Michael pulled a tuft of grass that was obscuring it. A metal brace, two inches wide, ran parallel to the ground from the passenger side to the driver's side, part of the frame of the vehicle. He shined the penlight and followed the metal support along its back side.

The light fell on a bulge on the backside of the metal strip. Grass grew around it, and Michael couldn't tell what it was. The bulge appeared different from the rest of the brace and was past the middle of the undercarriage. To see what it was, he had to scoot himself farther under to clear the grass that had grown up and around it.

Gently, Michael smoothed away the grass and trained the light on the spot. Wedged between the metal brace and the undercarriage was what looked like a jeweler's ring box—metal, smooth, a few fragments of deep purple velvet still showing, corroded shut. The box was tethered there with wire wrapped around the brace several times. The wire was rusted, but it held. That wire, and the fact that the box was only an inch and a half square, had kept it in its hiding place for over sixty years.

Michael's breath caught in his chest as he reached to remove the box. The wire crumbled in his hand when he touched it. He wrapped his fingers around the box and carefully extricated himself from beneath the Jeep.

Maybe there are snipes after all, he thought.

Michael sat on the damp grass beside the Jeep for about a minute and listened. More crickets. No more camper laughter. Nothing else. He was alone in the meadow, the answer to Kit's questions possible in his hand.

Eager to know its contents but more concerned with retreating without being seen, he rose, put the box in the pocket of his jeans, pulled his dirty jacket from under the Jeep and turned out the penlight. At the base of the trees across the meadow on the west side, Michael saw the beginning of moonlight above the horizon. No time to linger. The contents of the box would have to wait.

In the dark of the June night, Michael made his way carefully across the meadow and through the trees to his boat. He rowed for a couple minutes, then started up the gas motor and turned on his running lights. He felt excited and happy that he'd found the treasure Kit had told him about. Won't she be surprised and pleased?

Chapter Thirteen

A SILENT, STILL FIGURE sat in the dark shadow of the Spanish Hills store at the marina and waited for the sound of Michael's boat motor. Damn, he thought. He's been gone a long time. It's getting cold. What if he's spending the night somewhere? But Michael didn't take any gear with him. I would have seen it in that open boat. He didn't even see me. Not too sharp, that Michael. Talks big, though.

There. From far out. A motor noise.

He sat very still and listened as the motor came closer. He was almost positive it was Michael's boat coming toward the dock.

Sure enough. There he is.

He watched Michael float to the dock, tie the aluminum boat to the mooring post, and make his way up the ramp. With only a bare bulb to illuminate the front of the closed grocery store, Michael wouldn't be able to see him watching silently from behind the trash bins. Michael got into the Kayak School van, started the motor and headed down the island road toward the school.

He waited until Michael was out of sight to get in his own car hidden behind a storage shed.

I wonder what he was doing out there, he thought. Guess I'll know soon enough. He made the drive back to the school quickly and parked several yards off the main entrance, in the trees where the car he'd borrowed would not be seen.

Making his way up the gravel drive, he kept to the shadows of the woods until he reached the main area of the buildings. He knew he had to be careful. He crouched behind Michael's van and saw that the lights were on in the office. He crept silently and stood beneath the open window, which was low enough to see into and covered by thin beige curtains. Through the opening, he saw Michael at his desk.

Michael was unwrapping a rusty box. He strained to see what it held, but his view was blocked by a chair. He waited and watched. Michael opened the box and removed what looked like jewelry of some sort, set it on the desk, and then turned toward his computer. The man seemed to be contemplating the jewelry, as though unsure what to write. Then Michael began to type on the keyboard, interrupting his typing to pick up the object and turn it around and around in his palm. Then more typing.

Was Michael describing the item from Wallace Island? Was he interpreting what he held in his hand? Very possibly. Jackpot! He realized this was going to be worth more than he'd thought.

He watched Michael save whatever he'd typed, exit the Word program and shut down the computer. He stood perfectly still in the dark, waiting for Michael to turn out the office light and go to his room at the other end of the building, allowing himself an audible exhale after Michael closed the office door.

Slowly and quietly, he lifted the wooden window frame and pulled himself inside Michael's office. He got out his LED flashlight and used it to illuminate the computer, switched the unit on, and waited for it to boot up. With a sense of glee, he was delighted to see there was no password protection, just as he suspected.

He opened the Word program and scrolled down from "File." There it was at the top of the menu—a file Michael had called "Snipes." Hmm. Odd name for it, he thought.

Pulling a flash drive from his jacket pocket, he inserted it into the USB port and saved the file. That done, he exited the program and shut down the computer. The whole maneuver had taken under three minutes. Damn, I'm good, he thought. And I'm gonna get top dollar for this information, whatever it is. He could tell Michael was quite excited about finding that rusty box.

He slipped silently back through the open window, dropped softly to the grass beneath it, and slowly pulled the wooden window down. The bottom sash made a low creaking sound about halfway toward the sill, but he could do nothing about that. He hoped Michael couldn't hear it, but doubted he could since his living quarters were at the opposite end of the long, narrow building.

He ducked into the shadow of the building and headed for the student rooms. He saw no one, and was pretty sure everyone was in bed, or at least in their rooms, since it was after curfew. What a stupid rule, in by midnight. What did these people think they were, kids?

Safe inside Room Eight, he closed the door silently and pulled the drive from his pocket. He booted up his laptop. At least his dad had been good for something, giving him this for his birthday. He put the drive in the USB port. He opened Michael's "Snipes" document. What the hell was it, anyway? His eyes moved quickly across the lines of ten-point type, taking in what Michael had written. Midway through the short document, he found the information he'd hoped for, something Michael had written about a charm with an inscription:

I am dismayed by this find, because I like Kit and I trust her. But even though she seems to be on the up and up, the discovery of this box and the charm inside leads me to believe that she may be here for ulterior motives. Just as Kit said, the grandmother hid this charm on Wallace Island before she left Galiano for good.

The charm holds a secret that the grandmother was not willing to share with anyone—even her own daughter and granddaughter.

That was the last sentence.

He saved the document to the hard drive and on a CD, then shut down the laptop and pulled a cell phone from his jacket pocket. He punched in the number. The familiar voice said. "Yes?"

"It's me. I do have something to tell you tonight. I watched Michael, like you asked. He left at dusk. I followed him to the dock at Spanish Hills and waited there when he left in his aluminum boat. Huh? Yeah. About nine o'clock. He was gone a couple hours, so I sure as hell hope you're paying me for that time, too.

"He came back about eleven, and I waited until his car was way ahead. No, he never saw me. He came straight back here and went to his office. What? Of course he didn't see me here either. I'm not stupid.

"I saw him inside at the computer. He had a box—it was all rusty and old. No, I couldn't see what was inside, but I have something better."

He waited as the voice on the other end of the line asked questions he was so glad he had answers for.

"Yeah, I did. After he left, I slipped on in through the window, booted up the computer and saved the file. What? Yes, got it right here on my laptop. But I'll need another five hundred."

He waited, knowing he was taking a risk asking for more money, but this information was worth a lot, and he wasn't going to be pushed around anymore.

"Okay, then. Extra two-fifty. When? Tomorrow would be good. Yeah, I'm getting to that. Seems he found some kind of charm out there. For real. What? Yeah, I saved the file on a CD, too. That's the part you get."

He listened, nodding.

"I will be careful. I told you. So when do we meet?" He fidgeted a while, listening impatiently until the voice finally stopped blathering. "Why not? No one knows anything about this. Okay. I will. Where? The bookstore? I guess that would work. Who the hell is Jonathan Kellerman? Never heard of him. Mystery section? Okay. Where? Got it. I slip the CD into the first Jonathan Kellerman novel on the shelf. At ten? Right. When will you be coming to get it? And what about the money? Same place? Right. After twelve. Should work."

He paused for thirty seconds, listening. "Yeah. I got it. No one knows. And remember, with the extra two-fifty it's an even thousand. Right. I will."

He pressed the "end" button and the phone went dead. It had been a good night's work.

SAFE INSIDE HIS ROOM, Michael closed and locked the door. He pulled the window shade all the way down, turned off the overhead light, and turned on the reading light above his single bed on which he spread out a newspaper page. He pulled the corroded box from his jacket pocket and dumped the contents onto the newspaper.

The charm was about the size of a quarter and made of gold or was perhaps gold-plated. Engraved with a simple inscription, the words barely fit in the space. Only initials formed the top and bottom lines. Between them was a simple phrase: "I love you."

This time, Michael gave in to that feeling of the hair standing on the back of his neck. His palms were sweaty. The significance of the simple message and the initials engraved on the charm had begun to sink in. What disturbed him was the question that would keep him awake much of the night. Had Kit known about the secret revealed by the charm? Did she come to Galiano knowing about her grandmother's relationship?

Michael picked up the charm, wiped it with the soft fabric of his flannel shirt and put it back into its box. He dropped the corroded box into a Ziploc bag and put it under his mattress.

He changed into his sweats and slippers and headed for the front of the main office building. From there, a short walk took him across the grass to the student dorm building and the cafeteria. After such a long night, Michael was hungry. Just a bowl of Cheerios, he thought.

The dorm building was quiet, which was unusual, but it was well after midnight, and this group of students hadn't been here long enough to be up late making trouble. That would come later in the week.

Entering the darkened dining room, Michael was surprised to see light coming from under the door to the kitchen. That area was off limits to students, so there should be no one in there at this hour.

Michael tiptoed through the dark dining room. Slowly, he swung the kitchen door open. Russ Brady sat on the center metal island, a glass of soda in his hand. He was talking in low tones to two 15-year-old girls, the ones from California. They seemed mortified when they saw Michael open the door, and Russ whirled around immediately.

"You're in an off-limits area, guys," Michael said. He tried to make his voice firm, but friendly. "You need to be in your rooms. What's up, Brady?"

Russ was defiant, as usual, and he answered boldly. "Just having a little midnight snack, Michael. I bumped into the girls over in the TV room, and they wanted to sneak in here and get something to eat. That's all."

Michael thought the three looked guilty, but he decided not to fight the battle tonight. He would talk to Russ tomorrow. God, kids were stupid sometimes. Russ had been here for two weeks last summer and knew the rules. Didn't he know he'd be sent home in a flash if he got involved with drugs again? Michael hoped he didn't have to kick him out, but he would, if it came to that.

"Time to clear out. Now. Russ, come see me in the morning before the day trip. I'll be in my office."

Russ seemed offended. "Why do I have to do that? I told you, we're having a snack. It's not like a big deal or anything."

"Be there at 8:45, Brady. Girls, you need to get back to your rooms."

Russ shrugged, put down his glass and sauntered out the door, brushing Michael's shoulder as he went. The two girls followed.

"Night," one of them mumbled. Russ said nothing.

"See you in the morning," Michael said. He got his cereal, returned to his room and wondered how he would ever sleep. All he could think about was the engraving on that charm.

Chapter Fourteen

MICHAEL DID SLEEP, BUT not well. The alarm went off at 6:20 a.m. and jolted him from a dream. He was driving the old green Jeep down the middle of Wallace Island, and Kit was standing in the middle of the dirt road with a rifle. He was glad the alarm clock saved him from knowing what happened next.

Michael put on jeans and a faded blue plaid flannel shirt and headed for the cafeteria. The noise greeted him before he opened the door. It was always lively inside, so Michael's usual routine was to head straight for the coffee machine, draw a mug full and take it with him to his downstairs workroom where he could drink it in peace. After that first cup, he had more coping skills and could stand to be in the same room with forty-two teenagers.

This morning was no exception. He noticed that Kit was surrounded at her table by her advanced kayakers. She was a good teacher. Hell, she seemed like a good person, but this morning Michael felt this nagging worry that she was up to something. He couldn't tell her yet about the charm hidden in his room. He needed to know her better.

Carrying his coffee, Michael made his way back through the boisterous breakfasters and headed to the workroom. Once inside, he sat in the old maple chair, put his feet up on the scuffed oak desk and gave himself the luxury of drinking and thinking.

How would he approach Kit with this new information? Should she be told? When? Maybe soon, but first he wanted to get more information from her about why she had come to Galiano. For now, the charm and its contents had to remain his secret.

Michael felt uneasy about the situation he was in. Could he be in any danger? He didn't think so . . . but then he wondered if he should share the information about the charm with someone, just in case. What about Riley? He eliminated that idea because it seemed like she and Kit were fond of each other, and he didn't want the information to get back to Kit. Riley should know eventually, though, especially if Kit was up to something. He thought about sending her the information anonymously so someone else would have it. Might be a good idea. But who could he tell now? Michael mentally scanned the list of Galiano people he trusted, and came up with only one name—Robert. He could confide in Robert.

He trusted Robert. He'd been his office manager for nearly eight years now, and that was a long stint by Kayak School standards. Robert had come to Galiano without much. He was single, divorced, and had been living in Vancouver and working as a school bus driver. At least that's what he told Michael when he applied for the job. He didn't have any family anywhere, he said, and he wanted to make a new start. At age forty-five, he was ready to make Galiano home.

Robert had worked out extremely well. The kids liked him, he was well organized with the school files, and he hardly ever asked for any time off. Michael's kind of office manager, for sure. Yes, he would tell Robert, but not yet. Not until after the meeting. Let's wait and see what happens there, Michael thought. Maybe Kit will reveal something. Maybe I'll be able to read between the lines and figure out what she's up to. Wouldn't that be good?

Michael took the last sip of coffee and headed back up the stairs. At nearly eight-thirty, most of the kids had gone back to their rooms to get ready for the nine o'clock class. Perfect. He could eat his breakfast in peace.

Entering the warm, window-lined room, Michael noticed three students still at the breakfast table—the two girls from California, and Russ. Damn, Michael thought, I forgot about Russ. Wish I could forget about him. As he passed the trio, Michael nodded, smiled and mumbled a good morning. The three acknowledged him with their eyes, but said nothing.

"Still coming in to see me this morning, Russ?" Michael asked the teenager.

"Right. I'll be there."

"Good. We need to talk."

Michael knew the meeting with Russ would be difficult, but as director of the adventure program, all discipline problems were his to deal with. Why in the world would Russ Brady jeopardize everything he'd rectified from the past by messing up and doing something stupid again?

Russ Brady was a sixteen-year-old kid from Victoria, at the Kayak School for his second summer and on a scholarship. This time, Michael wasn't so sure letting Russ come back had been a good idea. In the kitchen the night before, Michael suspected that Russ might have been trying to sell drugs to the girls, though he hadn't searched him. Maybe he should have.

A rap on Michael's office door announced the boy's arrival.

"It's open, Russ."

"Hey," Russ said as he came in and sat in the one empty chair. He was dressed in a faded, torn red sweatshirt, blue jeans, and a Seattle Seahawks baseball cap, worn slightly off center. He said nothing more and stared at Michael to wait for him to speak.

"You know that any kind of drug activity here would be your ticket back to Victoria and probably back to detention, don't you?"

"Yeah."

"What were you doing in the kitchen after midnight?"

"I told you. I couldn't sleep. I got up to make a sandwich. Those girls were in the TV room, and they wanted to get something to eat, too.

I started talkin' to them. I didn't do nothin' wrong."

"The kitchen is off limits after midnight."

Russ shrugged. "So sue me. But I didn't have drugs, and I don't know why you think I did. I told you, man, I'm playin' it straight here."

"Yes, you did tell me. And I hope I can believe you. If I have to send you back, your father will be furious. He told me so himself."

"My old man is a freak. He hates my guts. Just wants a reason. I don't need his money anyway. "

"Maybe not," Michael said, wondering who this kid was beneath that tough exterior. "But don't you want to finish school? Make something of yourself?"

"Yeah, of course. That's why I'm playin' it clean here. Why don't you believe me?"

Michael hesitated. From past experience, he wasn't sure he could ever believe this boy. "I can start trying to trust you right now. I'll let it go, what happened last night. But I'm telling you here and now, Russ, if I ever find drugs on you, or find out that you've been dealing here on the island, you're gone. Understand? On the next ferry. No questions. Back to Victoria."

"Yeah. I understand."

Michael checked his watch and took a deep breath. "It's nearly nine, and the bus is loading. You'd better get your stuff for the day's paddle and get out there."

"I'm actually not feeling so good. Some kind of stomach thing, maybe the flu or something. Think I have a fever. I'm not going today."

"Do you want me to call Dr. Allen?" Michael asked, not believing Russ but unsure how to challenge him on it. If the kid actually was sick, he'd feel terrible about calling him a liar.

"Nah. Think I'll go back to bed for a while," Russ turned and walked out. He didn't look back.

Michael got up, closed his office door and stood at his office window. Outside, the yellow and green adventure school bus was already half-full of energetic teenagers. Michael sighed. Someday I'm going to be too old for this, he thought. Maybe sooner than later.

RUSS RUMMAGED THROUGH A desk drawer and grabbed his sunglasses; he shoved an extra pair of shorts into his daypack, pulled on a clean T-shirt and jammed his hat back on. Stupid jerk, he thought. What the hell does Michael think he's doing? The guy had better watch his back.

Russ removed a CD from his laptop and put it in his jacket pocket. He heard the bus pull out, and he hoped Michael would do what he usually did and go downstairs to the workroom. From the thin, grimy window in his room, Russ had a foggy view of the front of the main building and the steps to the outside. The workroom had only an exterior door, so he knew Michael would have to take that route.

A few minutes later, Russ waited until he heard Michael close the workroom door. He listened, but didn't hear any sounds from the dorm area. Everyone else had gone on the day trip.

Russ opened the door of his room and surveyed the courtyard. No one. He knew he could take the back route around the building and wouldn't be seen from the main office or the workroom. Still, he was cautious. No point in getting caught now.

Once behind the dorm building, Russ relaxed and started up the trail through the woods. The car would be there, right where he'd left it last night. Great of Cousin Eric to loan it to him. Good ol' Eric.

Russ pulled his set of keys from his jacket pocket, started up the old Honda, and took the back road that circled around near the beach. Once on the main road, it was only a few minutes' drive to the ferry dock area and bookstore. He parked near the ferry landing and strolled the block to the bookstore. He arrived at ten minutes to ten, right on time.

The bell on the door tinkled when Russ entered, and the woman behind the counter smiled. She didn't know him, of course. He didn't want to be acquainted with any of these weird island people.

Russ pretended to browse the shelves—the travel section, animal section, even the kid section. Acting as nonchalant as he could, he moved toward the back of the bookstore where the mysteries were shelved. This was a good choice, he realized. His boss was pretty smart. Rich, too. That was the best part. Just to be safe, Russ looked through two or three other books before settling on the Jonathan Kellerman section, whoever he was. Good thing these books were shelved alphabetically.

Several ratty hardcover Kellerman novels perched on the shelf. Which one was it? Russ stopped to think. Hadn't it been the first one on the shelf? He was sure of it. He took the CD out of his jacket pocket and slipped it into the book, between the last page and the back cover. Shouldn't have any trouble finding it, he thought.

Mission accomplished, Russ waved a goodbye and mumbled a "Thanks" to the clerk and left the store at 10:20 a.m. He was back in his room by 10:30. Eric would come and get the car by noon, and all was well.

Jesus, I do good work, he thought as he pulled the pillows out and crawled into his sleeping bag. He was tired. It had been a long night and a very busy morning.

Chapter Fifteen

"NOW TELL ME AGAIN what else you want me to ask this Crawford guy," Marie said to Riley as they cruised down the island's one road toward the Community Hall. "I want to make sure I say the right thing."

"Keep saying you're doing a profile. Get him to talk some more about the people involved. Maybe he'll slip, drop a clue. Could happen."

"Sounds easy enough. I like pretending to be the writer. I've always wanted to be a writer."

"Sure. You be the writer. I'll be your flunky. Does that make you happy?"

"Immeasurably. That means you'll have to do what I say."

"Oh, dear. Now I'm worried," Riley said.

As they walked toward the Community Hall, several people were making the short walk to the meeting from the island's best restaurant, Galiano Bistro. The parking lot at the hall was already nearly full.

"Wow, a good turnout," Marie said. "Everybody's here."

Riley searched for a parking spot. "Being here reminds me of the night my dream came true, and I got to meet Jane Rule. I had always wanted to meet her. Aunt Joan introduced me to her at a meeting in this very place."

"Must have been quite a thrill. I know you've admired her ever since you read *Desert of the Heart*."

"No kidding. And then after I got the movie *Desert Hearts* from Netflix, I was even more of a fan. That scene where the hot casino chick seduces the teacher. Every lesbian I know played it over and over!"

"Including you, as I recall."

Riley blushed. "Yeah, maybe."

"Did you talk to Jane about her writing that night?"

"Are you kidding? I was so star struck I couldn't even say 'Hello.'"

"She was pretty famous, wasn't she?"

"Yes, she was," Riley said. "I read somewhere that she once told a reporter, 'It's hard being the only out lesbian in Canada!' No kidding. She didn't like the limelight and had a reputation for being a bit of a recluse. I think it's because of her that Galiano got nicknamed 'The Gay Island' by other Canadians. But local islanders liked her, and she was always friendly with them, according to Aunt Joan."

"Wasn't there some story about her and her partner, Helen, and the kids on the island?"

"Yeah. Aunt Joan told me that every summer afternoon, Jane and Helen opened their backyard pool so island kids could come swimming. They wanted to provide a safe place so kids could have some fun without worrying about tides and undercurrents."

"Pretty nice thing for a couple of older lesbians to do, I'd say. Good for them."

Riley parked and turned off the motor. "It was. They were both respected and well-liked here. They died within a few years of each other. I bet the memorial services were well-attended events on this island. They're missed."

"But Jane's books live on. I saw lots of them at the island bookstore."

"We have those to remember her by. Long live Jane Rule."

They headed for the hall. The few empty seats were near the back on the side, so they sat there. Across the center aisle was a man in his fifties, Riley guessed, dressed neatly and expensively. Riley caught Marie's eye, raised her eyebrows, and nodded toward the man, who seemed out of place among the islanders.

"Is that Crawford?" Riley whispered.

"Uh-huh." Marie smiled and waved at Crawford, who got up greet them.

"Hello, Marie," Crawford said, extending his hand. "How nice to see you again."

"You, too, James. I'd like you to meet my friend, Riley Logan."

Riley rose and shook hands with Crawford, who towered over her. She thought he must be at least six-foot-five. Marie had neglected to tell her he could be mistaken for a professional basketball player.

"Are we still on for later?" Crawford asked Marie.

"I'm game if you are," Marie said. "Shall we go over to the Bistro?"

"Sounds good. Would you like to join us, Riley?"

Riley knew better than to get in the way of Marie's information gathering. "Oh, thanks, but I'm pretty well worn out. Think I'll head back to the Cliffhouse. That is, if you don't mind giving Marie a ride home."

"No problem. It would be my pleasure. See you then?" He smiled at Marie.

"Looking forward to it," she said. Crawford made his way back to his seat.

"Well, that part went smoothly," Marie said.

Riley smiled. "You're quoting from the movie, aren't you? The part where the cute lesbian tries to talk the cute straight teacher into getting into bed with her. The teacher says she's not sure what to do, and the cute dyke tells her that first, she should put the 'Do Not Disturb' sign on the door. She does, and then she says, 'Well, that part went smoothly.' Remember?"

"Of course I do. I love that scene."

Riley scanned the crowd for familiar faces and saw several. Michael was near the front, sitting next to a dark-haired woman and three of his local kayak students. Kit sat on the other side of the students.

"What in the world is he doing with her?" Riley said as she nodded toward Michael's row. "I didn't think they were even on speaking terms."

"Who is that?" Marie asked.

"Oh, geez, I forgot you didn't know. Kit told me. It's Michael's ex-wife, Marianne. They've been divorced for about two years, I guess."

"Interesting."

"Are you jealous?"

"Don't be ridiculous," Marie said. "That's the stupidest thing you've said in a long time."

"Stupidest isn't a word."

"I don't care."

"But I think you like him. Marie and Michael sittin' in a tree, K-I-S-S—"

"Would you stop! Give it a rest, Riley. You're making me crazy here."

"Or maybe it should be Marie and James, sittin'. . ."

Marie cut her off with a stern look that Riley knew meant shut up now. She did, but reluctantly. She was saved from more of Marie's wrath because the meeting was called to order.

A tall man, balding and somewhat overweight, stepped up to the microphone on the stage.

"Good evening everyone," he said. "Thanks for coming tonight. I'm Hank Garrison, owner of the Hamburger Hut—but most of you already know that. At least, those of you who regularly come in for coffee and a burger do, because we run the best darn café at the ferry landing. People laughed. Okay, well maybe it's the only café at the ferry landing."

"We appreciate you coming out tonight to participate. Galiano is a precious place to most of us, and I know we all have thoughts and ideas to share. As chair of the Bodega Ridge Conservation Committee, it's my job to welcome you, make some introductions and get this discussion going."

At the word "discussion," a murmur rippled through the room as people reacted to the use of such a neutral term.

"I'll begin with our island visitors. Up here at my right is Carl Brown, owner of Brown Lumber, Limited." Carl stood and gave a wave. He was sandy-haired, about forty-five, and wore khakis and a green plaid flannel shirt.

"And over here, to my left, is Dr. James Crawford, chair of the island development committee."

Crawford stood. His dark hair was neatly trimmed and he wore a blue suit with a bright red tie.

"Power tie," Riley whispered to Marie. "Guy thing."

"For sure."

Hank said, "In the front row there is Michael Barsotti, for the two or three of you who don't know him. He runs the Kayak Adventure School. Michael's working on a documentary about our beautiful island, right, Michael?"

Michael stood and turned around to address the crowd.

"I'm working on a film," he said. "I'm glad you're all here."

"And right behind him, in the red jacket, is Clare Porter of Vancouver View Homes. Miss Porter is chairman of the board for that company. Or should I say 'chairwoman'?"

"Either is fine with me," Clare said as she stood, turned and addressed the roomful of mostly islanders. "I am pleased to be here and to have this opportunity to meet you all and tell you about our wonderful plans for Bodega Ridge."

The audience was quiet. Clare stood for a moment, opened her mouth to say something, but then seemed to decide against it. She was about fifty with silver hair cropped short. Her red wool blazer and black slacks looked expensive. Riley thought she seemed capable and formidable. She wondered if the woman was really the bitch people said she was. Clare sat and turned her attention back to Hank.

"Then let's get started," Hank said. "I'll turn the floor over to Carl, who will explain the plans that the Brown Lumber trustees have for Bodega Ridge."

Riley leaned toward Marie. "Here we go," she said. "Hang on. It's going to be a wild ride."

Riley tried hard to concentrate on what everyone was saying, but she kept getting distracted by all the colorful characters in the crowd. Galiano seemed to be populated with them. She tried to bring her mind back to the present.

Clare Porter was saying, "We will make every effort to conserve the delicate beauty of Bodega. During the break, I encourage you to take a peek at the plans our landscape architect has drawn up. You'll see that many, many varieties of indigenous plants will be retained and incorporated into our neighborhood."

Neighborhood, Riley thought. I'll bet the islanders like that. Not. Bodega Ridge as a neighborhood? Wrong choice of words, oh Miss Clare.

The discussion went on, and Riley heard some of it. Michael made the point that adding a hundred homes, at an average of four persons per home, would make half again as many people as lived on the island now. "We don't have the resources to support them," he said, growing more agitated. "We have two independent groceries. One gas station. One elementary school. Do we want to change all this because some people in Vancouver like the view?"

Islanders grumbled in unison.

A loud voice came from the rear of the room. "You're stacking the deck, Michael. You know there's more to it than that."

Necks craned to see who was making the challenge. Richard Ellison, who had come in late, was standing in the back, face red and angry.

"I, for one, don't see what the big deal is," Ellison said. "I'm ready to expand my little bakery to accommodate four hundred new people. Why not? Why should we keep Galiano all to ourselves? It's beautiful here, and plenty of others, like me, would like to make a life here. What gives you the right to keep them out, Michael?"

"You have been here less than a month, Richard," Michael said slowly. "I have lived here most of my life. How dare you suggest I shouldn't want to preserve the natural beauty of this island?"

"Perhaps you're right about that. But how do you know that the development will be the big bad wolf you say it is? What if it's done tastefully and it brings people here who will love the island as you do? What about that?"

Michael hesitated. That was the wrong thing to do. Clare Porter stood and stole his thunder.

"Richard makes a good point, Michael. We're not trying to attract a bunch of wild hedonists so that they can move in and ruin what you've all worked so hard for here in Galiano. We only want to expand and make this place accessible to more people who will love it as you do. That's all we're suggesting."

"Is it?" another voice called out.

Necks craned again. This time it was Jonathan who stood. He held on to the back of the chair in front of him. His face was red and flushed.

"I am so sick of all of you pretending you're not in it for the money," he said as his dark eyes drilled right into Clare's. "How dare you come here and suggest that you care one mite about us or about our precious island? My grandfather built one of the first farmhouses here, and it still stands up at the north end of the island. He sacrificed everything to make Galiano his home. My father was born here. So was I. We have nine hundred residents year-round, and we all take care of each other. We don't want to take care of you."

The room grew quiet as everyone waited for Clare to respond. She took a deep breath and surveyed the faces. "Thank you for sharing that information, Mr..." She paused, because she didn't know Jonathan's name.

"MacAlister," he said.

"Mr. MacAlister, I appreciate your passion. It's heartening to know that people here are so devoted to this place. I'm as passionate as you are, but I don't think hours of discussion would make you believe that because you've already made up your mind about me. Is that not true?"

Eyes turned to Jonathan. He didn't answer right away, but he was still standing.

Michael cleared his throat. When Clare turned toward him, he said, "You, Ms. Porter, are wrong to compare your passion to Jonathan's. He *is* Galiano Island to many of us. He has dedicated his life to this place and to the people who live here. You have no right to insult him like that."

"And exactly what is your role in all of this, Mr. Barsotti?" Clare asked, clearly straining to keep her voice even.

"I'm trying to keep Galiano beautiful. I'm trying to make sure it's not transformed by you and your multi-million-dollar development company."

Clare considered Michael coolly, then turned to sit down. "I am..." she said to Hank, who had not spoken recently and didn't seem to know how to facilitate what had become a very personal discussion, "...quite finished."

With that, Hank saw his opportunity. "So, how about a break, folks? I think maybe we could all use some fresh air. Twenty minutes? We'll resume then, and hopefully we'll all be cooler. It's getting pretty warm in here, don't you think?" Hank smiled at his joke, but no one laughed.

Riley turned to Marie. "Ack. That got icky fast, didn't it?"

"You have such a way with words, Riley. Is that how you would describe it if you were covering this meeting for the local paper?"

"If I were covering it, I'd be dashing after Clare and Michael to get quotes during the break. I'm sure they'd be pretty juicy."

People stood, stretched, and milled about. Some headed outside for a smoke. Riley scanned the crowd for Kit, didn't see her, and headed for the women's room before a line developed. She laughed at her own joke. Lines rarely occurred anywhere on Galiano, except at the ferry terminal. Stepping out of the restroom, Riley nearly bumped into Michael, who was making his way toward the side door of the hall.

"Oh, there you are," he said. "I've been looking for you. Meet me outside, near the back, would you?"

"Sure, Michael. What's up?"

"I want to check in with you about a couple things."

"Okay. Be right there."

Riley found Marie and Kit engaged in conversation near the concession window where local island grandmas were selling home-baked cookies, tea and decaf coffee, each for a quarter. Customers were trusted to put their payment in a colorful woven basket with a handwritten sign that said, "Please pay here." Galiano was simple that way.

"Hi, Kit," Riley said. "Things are heating up here, aren't they?"

"Seem to be. I haven't heard anything from you, though. I wasn't even sure you were here, and I didn't want to turn around in my seat and scan the crowd to find you. Do you plan to get in on this debate?"

"Probably not. I'm here to listen. How about you?"

Kit dropped a quarter in the basket and picked up a cookie. "Me, too. Listen, that is. I'm taking a few notes. This is all good background info for the film project."

"I'm sure it is." Again, as the other times she'd been in the same room with her, Riley was completely taken in by Kit's presence. Something about this woman had the effect of a mild drug.

"Riley," Marie was saying. "Do you?"

"Huh?" Riley came back to present time. "Do I what?"

"Want something from the concession stand?"

"Oh, yeah, sorry," Riley mumbled, trying to cover the fact that she'd been lost in thought about Kit. "Get me a peppermint tea and a chocolate chip cookie, would you? I'll be back in a few minutes."

"Of course I would. Where are you going?"

"Outside to get some air."

Riley headed for the side door, stood outside near the edge of the dim yellow light, and pretended to be star-gazing. When she was sure no one was watching, she slowly backed into the shadows and skirted the trees to look for Michael.

She found him around back of the building in the dense dark near the trees. "Geez, Michael, I can't see a thing out here!"

"That's the idea. Shhh. Keep your voice down." He stepped back farther into the shadows.

"Right. What's up?"

"I wanted to ask you if you might be willing to help out some with our film project. I have some new information, and I'm gonna need another person on it."

"Why do you need me? I thought Kit was working with you on this."

"I really can't go into it here and now. I wanted to see if you have any time or interest and might be willing to help me out."

Michael paused. Riley thought he was straining to listen for the sounds of anyone else anywhere near them. She heard nothing but blood pounding in her ears. Something about the black of the night and Michael's furtive whispers made her shiver. Why her? Why now? She asked, "Can you give me a hint about all this?"

"This new information has to do with Kit. That's all I can tell you right now. I may need you to check some things out for me."

"About Kit?

"Maybe."

"Is she in trouble? You know Marie and I are already worried about that. We found her trashed bicycle up at Bluff Park, for God's sake. Is someone trying to get to her?"

"I don't honestly know that. And what I do know I can't tell you now, but I will say it's possible she has a connection to this island, and maybe even, in an indirect way, to your Aunt Joan."

"What? My aunt?" She wasn't sure she heard Michael correctly.

"Yes. Keep your voice down!" he whispered hoarsely. "There's something mysterious about her, and I'm unsure of her motives. Give me a little time. Meanwhile, all I'm asking is that you be willing to help out should the need arise. Are you?"

Michael started to speak again but stopped. Riley heard what had interrupted him: the sound of feet crunching on gravel. Staying in the shadows, he cautiously peeked around the side of the building.

"It's okay," Michael said. "It's my ex-wife, Marianne, on her way back from the pub with a beer."

"Probably to calm her nerves."

"No doubt. She does that a lot. Anyway, can you help me?"

"Of course. I'll do what I can. But I'm kind of mystified about what help you need."

"I know, and I'm sorry I can't be more forthright. Trust me. I will tell you more by the end of the week. I hate to leave it 'til then, but I need time to talk to Kit. She hasn't said much tonight, has she?"

"No, she's been quiet."

"I was hoping she might get involved in the discussion, but I have the feeling she's purposely holding back."

"Yeah, me too. Maybe she wants you to be the spokesman, and she's here to support you."

"I hope that's all she's here for."

"Now what the hell does that mean?" Riley asked, growing impatient with Michael's secrecy.

"Nothing," he said, sneaking a peek around the side of the building again. "People are heading back into the meeting."

"Right. We'd better get back. Guess I'll wait to hear from you."

"Thanks. I'll know more in a couple of days. Meanwhile, I want to caution you. I don't know how to say this gracefully. Be careful around Kit."

"Why? What do you mean?"

"All I can say right now is that she may be here for other reasons. I'm not sure anymore what her motivation is for coming to Galiano."

More feet on gravel, and then, from inside the Community Hall, Riley heard the sound of Hank tapping the microphone to see if it was on.

"That's all I can say. Be careful."

"Jesus, Michael, you're giving me the creeps," She peered through the darkness to see if they were being watched. She could see nothing.

Checking again for any stragglers who might still be outside, Michael motioned for Riley to follow him around the side of the building, toward the light of the porch. They headed for the side door.

"Did you hear that?" Riley whispered. "There, in the trees. I thought I heard something."

"You're just edgy. I'm sure there's no one there. Come on, the meeting is starting."

THE REMAINDER OF THE community meeting was not quite as eventful, but every person seemed to have an opinion, and by the time Hank asked for any last comments or questions, Riley was on information overload and ready to head for bed. If she wasn't worried about what people would say, she would have rested her head on Marie's shoulder and taken a little cat nap.

"Can we go home now?" she asked her friend.

"You can. I'm on another assignment, remember?"

The meeting adjourned, and the islanders and guests filed toward the front door. Marie wandered off to say goodbye to Michael, and Riley waved to Kit and motioned for her to come over.

"So, some meeting, huh?" Riley said casually. She wanted to know how Kit was feeling about it.

"Yeah," Kit said, "but I guess we knew it would get exciting, didn't we?"

"No kidding. And it did. I'm glad it's over. So, what do you have going tomorrow?"

"A half-day trip in the morning, and then some time off. Why? What's up?"

"Nothing at all. I was wondering if maybe you'd like to get together for a beer."

"Sure, I could do that. Sounds like a good idea. When?"

"How about two? At the Island Pub? No, wait, I have a better idea." Riley realized she wouldn't want anyone to overhear them. "How about if I bring the beer and we go to the beach? It's supposed to be warm tomorrow."

"Works for me. Where?"

"Montague's the best beach around."

"That's it, then. I'll bring the chips."

"You're on. See you there."

Marie joined them to say goodbye before leaving for the pub with Crawford. Riley and Kit were headed for the parking lot when they came upon Michael and Ellison in a heated argument.

"You and your damn righteousness," Ellison said. "You're not the only person on Galiano who's entitled to an opinion, you know."

"Maybe not, but I have every right to fight for the preservation of this place," Michael said. "And I'm not going to be bullied by you or anyone else."

Carl Brown strode out from behind his SUV and chimed in. "You'd better watch your back, Michael. I'm serious. We're not going to let this go without a fight."

"I'm not intimidated," Michael said, followed by the sound of his car door slamming shut.

"These people are whacked about this," Riley whispered to Kit. "I wish Michael would cool down."

Kit said, "He's fighting for what he thinks is right. He's lived here a long time, and I think he'll stay here if he can keep Galiano simple and beautiful. That's all he wants. Give the guy a break."

"You're right. And after all, he is Italian. Guess he likes a good argument."

A quick hug, and Riley said goodnight to Kit and was on her way back to the Cliffhouse.

Chapter Sixteen

WHEN RILEY AWOKE THE next morning, the first thing she thought of was Michael's worries about Kit. It was the kind of realization that comes when you wake up and remember something you really don't want to remember. Riley felt heavy, as though a bright, shiny prize she'd coveted was now tarnished. She felt disheartened.

She heard Marie rumbling around downstairs. The aroma of fresh-brewed coffee, along with a couple dog licks on her nose from Duffy, helped her wake up.

"Good morning, famous freelance writer," she called toward the steps. "How'd it go last night?"

Marie appeared at the top of the stairs with a tray and two mugs of coffee.

Riley sat up in the double bed and patted a spot on the comforter beside her. "Come sit down here and tell me all about last night."

Marie handed Riley her coffee, put the tray on the bureau and sat on the bed. "The view from up here never gets old, does it?"

"I love it every time I see that channel." This morning a catamaran with a bright orange and yellow sail skimmed past the Cliffhouse in the light wind. Riley tore her eyes away. "Okay, enough about the view. What happened with Crawford?"

"It was a pleasant enough time. Not romantic at all, so don't even go there. We talked. And drank a couple beers. By the end, Crawford did get loose-lipped."

"All right! I knew you could do it. What did he say?"

"Not much of use, unfortunately. He did make reference once to Carl, and it seemed rather familiar for someone of his position. Mostly, he referred to the others by their last names. Oh, except Clare. I guess he used her first name, too. But that could have been a gender thing."

"Do you think he's connected to either one of them in a way he shouldn't be?"

"Like I said, there wasn't that much to go on. I had a hint of a feeling when he referred to those two. Sorry, Riley. I know you were hoping for more."

"No, that's all right. It's a start. And you're on friendly terms with him, in case we need more information. You did good, Marie."

"Thanks. I tried."

"I know you did, and I appreciate it."

They sipped coffee in silence and then Riley said, "Shall we do more packing today? Lots to do, still."

"Works for me. Let's have my famous ten-grain hot cereal for breakfast and then get to it."

Marie got up and took Riley's empty coffee mug. "Be downstairs in five minutes."

"Got it."

They enjoyed breakfast on the east deck, the morning sun a welcome warmth. Duffy took up her usual position at Riley's feet.

Riley and Marie started on the packing. They spent the morning sorting out more of Aunt Joan's things. Riley was distracted from the task because she kept thinking—about Kit, about Carl Brown threatening Michael, about why Michael needed her help. What was he worried about in regard to Kit? Riley hated the idea of Kit being involved in something unsavory. That would be just my luck, she thought. I find a beautiful, smart, single woman, and she turns out to be an escaped convict. But she didn't seem like an escaped convict. Didn't seem at all sinister, actually. What was Michael talking about?

At noon, with five more boxes of Aunt Joan's dishes and collectible treasures boxed up, Marie came across a stack of letters in the bottom drawer of the desk. They were tied together with heavy string. The top one, addressed to Joan Walker, had a Toronto postmark and was dated September, 1949.

"Check this out, Riley. Your aunt saved a whole stack of mail here. Want to sort through it?"

"Seems like eavesdropping, doesn't it? But I guess we ought to take a look. If she saved the letters, maybe they're important."

Marie handed the stack to Riley who untied the string and counted twenty letters.

"Wow," Riley said, pulling the first one from its envelope. "Whoever wrote this had beautiful handwriting." She began to read.

"Who's it from?"

Riley turned to the third page and read the signature. "Oh, my gosh. It's from the nanny."

"Who?"

"The nanny. In 1949. You know—we found those clippings about the accident."

"Right. So your aunt knew the nanny?"

"I guess she did. She never said anything to me about it."

Riley sifted through the letters, one by one. They were each written about a week apart, from September 1949 to the spring of 1950. She read the first one aloud.

My Dearest Joan. I can't tell you how much I miss you and your loving support while I'm here in Toronto. No one knows me here. I am so lonely for the island, for you, for our friends.

Riley paused. "Wow. Do you think maybe my aunt was having an affair with this woman?"

"I doubt that. You never had any clue your aunt was a lesbian, did you?"

"Sure sounds as though they were close. This letter is pretty intimate."

"Intimate is one thing. Lovers is another. Read on and tell me more."

Riley did. The letter described Katherine's new life in Toronto—the house her parents rented, her work as a housekeeper in a bed and breakfast, her sadness about leaving Galiano.

"Hard to tell," Riley said when she'd finished the letter. "I guess they could have been close friends."

"Of course they were. Besides, even if they were lovers, they're not going to reveal that in a letter. It was 1949, Riley. No one talked about it back then."

"We hardly do now. Being lesbian isn't all that easy in this culture."

"Right. I know. I'm sorry. I wish I could change that."

"I know you do. Maybe in my lifetime it will get better. It's beginning to."

"We can hope. What else does the letter say? Are the other ones from Katherine, too?"

Riley picked up each envelope, studied the postmarks and found they were all from the same person.

"Wait," she said, holding two envelopes postmarked in January, 1950. "These two are empty. The letters are gone."

"Maybe your aunt mistakenly put them into envelopes with other letters."

"My aunt was meticulous. I don't think so." Riley sorted through the rest of the stack. "But I guess I won't know that until I read them all. Here I go."

She sat back on the bed, propped herself up with pillows, and began letter number two.

"I'm going downstairs to make us some lunch. Tell me if you find something interesting."

Riley was already engrossed in the second letter. "I will."

WHEN MARIE CAME UP with their sandwiches, Riley had finished skimming all eighteen letters and had found nothing more to substantiate her suspicion about Katherine and her aunt.

"What did you find?" Marie asked, handing Riley her plate and can of Diet Pepsi.

"Thanks for lunch. Not much."

"Not much what?"

"Not much more that would lead me to believe they were lovers. They were really sweet friends, and Katherine wrote often to keep Aunt Joan updated on her life. Funny thing, though. Those two letters are missing. I didn't find them anywhere."

"Your aunt must have lost them." Marie plopped herself down in the rocking chair in front of the picture window. All the blue water of Trincomali Channel stretched out before them.

"My aunt never lost anything. I think there's a reason they're not here."

"And what would that be?"

"I don't know. But she didn't keep those letters with the rest."

"Where do you think they are?"

"Good question. As she got older, my aunt sometimes kept valuables in odd places. I can check her safe deposit box, although the bank manager already told me that she had only the deed to the Cliffhouse and a few pieces of jewelry in there. At least that's what she told him."

Riley stacked the letters neatly in chronological order again and secured them with two rubber bands. She kept out two empty envelopes. "Hey, look at the time. Nearly one," she said, tucking the letters back in the hatbox. "I told Kit I'd meet her at two. And you and I have to get ready for our sunset sail later."

Marie said, "Too bad we're both not going with someone we could smooch with on the aft deck."

"No kidding. This is supposed to be one of those romantic trips. Want to pretend we're girlfriends?"

"Pretend? Knowing all the while you're thinking about the mysterious and alluring Kit? I don't think so. Thanks anyway."

"You know you'll always be number one, don't you?"

"It's what keeps me going."

JONATHAN STOOD IN HIS sunny kitchen and watched cars drive off the ferry. He knew time was running out and that he would have to act again. He dialed the number on the disposable cell phone.

"Yeah?" the familiar voice said.

"I'm ready to go forward with part two."

"When?"

"Right away. Tonight."

"Montague Harbor?"

"Yes. As we talked about."

"It's gonna cost you more."

"What do you mean?" Jonathan said. "We had a deal."

"Doesn't matter. Things are heating up on Galiano. It's getting risky. Cost you more."

"How much?"

"Thousand more."

Jonathan hesitated. Damn. Was it worth it? He knew the answer.

"All right. Six thousand then. I'll leave the cash in the same place tomorrow morning."

"Good. I'll be on the five o'clock ferry, but don't feel you have to meet me or anything." The man laughed. Jonathan did not think it was funny.

"When will you do it?"

"Tonight. Should be lots of boats in the harbor. More fun." He laughed again. It grated on Jonathan's nerves. He thoroughly despised this man, but he needed him.

"Okay. Tonight then."

"Be sure to listen for the sirens. I always love that part."

"Yes, I bet you do."

"Nice doing business with you," the man said and hung up.

Jonathan felt his insides tremble, but he was resolved. He could think of no other way to keep people off his beautiful island.

He stared out his kitchen window toward Vancouver. The afternoon sun threw diamonds on blue water. Galiano had to be one of the most beautiful places on earth, and it was up to him to make sure it stayed that way.

Chapter Seventeen

RILEY SAID GOODBYE TO Marie, let Duffy jump into the Subaru, headed for Montague campground and parked near the path to the beach. Duffy ran ahead, as always. Carrying a small cooler, just big enough for a six-pack, Riley followed the path to the first flat rocks, sat in the sun and waited. At two p.m., right on time, Kit drove up in her Volkswagen and Riley felt her heart flutter. How could it be possible that Michael suspected Kit was here for a sinister reason? She still found it hard to believe, and she wanted to give Kit the chance to explain herself.

She watched her lock the car and head toward the beach with a canvas bag slung loosely over her shoulder. Kit moved with the kind of grace one associates with a gymnast, or a dancer. She was fluid, easy in her body and her clothes. Today she wore black Nike shorts, a blue T-shirt and Keen sandals. Riley knew she was staring, then tried to pretend she wasn't.

Sensing movement coming their way, Duffy barked ferociously at the approaching figure.

"Duffy!" Riley said. "It's our friend. It's Kit! No bark!"

Duffy wasn't convinced, but she transformed the loud bark to a low growl.

Kit was smiling as she walked up. "Hi Duffy, it's me." Duffy cocked her head, the way dogs do, trying to remember and understand. "I know you want me to be terrified of you, but I'm not." Duffy wagged her stubby tail and plopped down on the sand.

Smiling broadly, Kit sat next to Riley on the flat rock. "How's it going? Did you bring the beer?"

"Got it right here. Ice cold. Did you bring the chips?"

Kit gestured toward the canvas bag. "Of course. That was my assignment, right?"

"Uh-huh. You're good at assignments. Must be because you're a teacher. It's a nice day to be at the beach, isn't it?"

"I love it when it's like this on Galiano," Kit said, gazing out across the harbor.

"For sure." She followed Kit's gaze toward the channel. The bright June sun shimmered on blue water. Overhead, a bald eagle soared in circles over the harbor, riding the wind currents. "This place is incredible. See? A bald eagle, right here at our cozy beer picnic."

"Aren't they fabulous? I never tire of seeing them soar. Makes me feel energized, seeing them. Makes me want to be one."

"Me, too. Wouldn't it be great to be able to fly like that?"

"Where would you go?" Kit asked, looking directly at Riley in a way that made her heart speed up.

"Oh, I don't know. Anywhere. Up. Over the trees."

"Sounds good. How long do I have to wait for that beer?"

"What a poor host I am," Riley said, reaching for the cooler and the bottle opener. She popped the top off a Corona and handed it to Kit.

"So, what's on your mind, friend?"

Kit's question was a little direct for Riley's style, but she knew she'd better forge ahead if she were to get any useful information. "What makes you think something's on my mind?"

"Oh, I don't know. You seemed kind of distracted last night when you asked me to come out here today. I thought maybe you had an agenda."

"That's a strong word, agenda."

"Do you? Have one, I mean?"

Kit was serious, and Riley felt unnerved, enough that she wasn't sure how to start. "No, but I am worried about you. Are you in some sort of trouble?"

Kit took a long pull on her beer, set it down and gazed at Riley. "Not really. I'm okay. It's personal. I don't feel comfortable sharing it right now."

Riley tried hard to keep her voice from sounding disappointed. "Yeah, well, that's okay. I wonder if I could help you out somehow, that's all."

"Maybe in the future, but right now there's nothing you need to do. I'm pretty busy with the classes and the film." Kit offered nothing more. Riley was quiet for a few seconds as she gazed out over the harbor. "I've felt myself getting worried since Marie and I found that piece of your bike up at Bluff Park, and I've been hoping you're not in danger."

Kit moved closer, set her beer down, and took Riley's hand in her own. "There's no trouble, but it's so sweet of you to be concerned. I'd tell you if I was in danger."

"Okay." Riley loved the feel of her hand in Kit's. "I thought I'd ask."

"Of course."

Kit looked both ways, scanning the beach and the parking lot for something—Riley didn't know what. Kit's eyes met Riley's. She pulled closer, raised a hand to Riley's face, and kissed her softly on the mouth. The kiss was brief and tender, and Riley didn't pull away.

Kit leaned back slightly. "I hope that was okay."

Riley answered with another kiss, longer this time. She forgot to care if anyone saw them.

"Please be careful, okay?" Riley finally said.

"I will. Don't worry about me. I'm fine."

"You certainly are." Riley felt excited, thrilled and confused. Who is this woman? she thought.

The warm afternoon sun was a welcome complement to the cold beer and potato chips, and after about an hour of relaxation and conversation, Kit glanced at her watch. "Hey, don't you have a sunset sail to go on with some other girl?"

"Yes, as a matter of fact I do. But I'm kind of wishing I didn't."

"Me, too. I have the rest of the afternoon and evening off."

"Bad timing on my part, isn't it?"

Duffy stood, stretched, and seemed to sense that something was happening. They rose and collected their things.

Duffy led the way as they headed toward the parking lot.

Kit paused when they reached their cars. "I want you to know how much I appreciate your concern. I really do. You're very kind to worry about me—even if it's unwarranted. It makes me feel cared for."

"You are," Riley said simply.

"Shall we check in tomorrow?" Kit asked, unlocking her door. She stepped toward Riley and pulled her into a full-body hug.

Riley let herself melt into Kit's strong, warm body. "For sure. I'll call you. When are you off?"

"Full day trip tomorrow, but I'll be back by five."

"Talk to you then."

"Right. I'll look forward to it."

"Me, too, Kit."

They got into their cars and headed out of the beach parking lot.

Oh, God, Riley thought. She didn't tell me what's going on with her, and she kissed me. This is getting more complicated every day.

Chapter Eighteen

IT HAD BEEN ANOTHER hectic day for Michael. Why do these kids have to do all their trouble-making on the same day, he thought? Is it some kind of conspiracy to force me into early retirement?

He had one more call to make and he dreaded it. He had to return a call to Edna Tucker, the bed and breakfast owner. The problem was, this time she was right. Some of his students had left a mess on her private beach, because he caught them trying to sneak in late last night. Their punishment had been another trip back to the beach for litter patrol and some yard work for Mrs. Tucker. The kids had grumbled, but they'd done the work. Too bad Edna had seen the mess before he'd managed to get the kids out there to clean it up.

"Only six-fifteen," Michael said as he pulled the school van into the parking lot. "You guys have time to wash up, eat dinner and get to the movie by seven."

"Did they save us any food?" Mark asked. Mark worried a lot about food. He was fifteen years old, two hundred pounds and always hungry.

"I phoned Robert to make sure they did," Michael said.

The five teens exited the van. No one looked back.

"Hey, Russ," Michael called after the ringleader. "Come here for a minute, would you?"

"Yeah. What?" was Russ's less than enthusiastic reply.

Michael lowered his voice. He didn't want anyone to hear this conversation.

"I hope to hell you didn't have drugs down there last night."

Russ stared blankly back at him. He didn't speak.

"Because if I find out you did, you know you're done here."

"I know that. You already told me, man."

They stared each other down until Russ looked away. "Can I go now?"

"Yes. You can. I'll expect to see you at the movie in forty-five minutes."

"Yeah. I'll be there."

MICHAEL GOT HIS OWN dinner from the kitchen and ate it in his room. He couldn't be with teenagers anymore tonight. When he was finished, he pulled the worn velvet box out from beneath his mattress and opened it. He had been checking frequently to make sure it was still there. The charm was where he had left it. He closed the box and tucked it into the pocket of his flannel shirt. He had a powerful, lighted magnifying glass in his workroom and he wanted to use it to see if he could find anything else on the charm.

Just before seven p.m., he took his dishes back to the kitchen and then stopped by the TV room. He heard boisterous laughter before he entered.

Nineteen teenagers filled the room, draping their lithe bodies all over every piece of furniture and, in some instances, on pillows on the floor. Robert was there with the DVD.

"What'll it be tonight?" Michael shouted over the din. It got quieter as the students noticed his arrival. Michael knew that many of them were aligned with Russ and that they thought Michael was, in their words, a stupid asshole. He was used to this role. Someone had to enforce the rules, after all.

"It's *Fargo* tonight," Robert said. "I took a poll, and hardly any of the kids have seen it."

"It's a good film," Michael said. "Good choice."

He scanned the room for Russ Brady, but didn't see him.

"Anyone seen Brady?" Michael asked.

Silence.

"Yeah, he was here, but I think he went to the bathroom. Any law against that?" The speaker was Angie, one of the "California girls" as Michael had come to think of them.

He smiled at their muffled giggles and said, "No. That's allowed, even here at Alcatraz, Galiano campus." More laughter.

Russ entered the room, unaware that he was the topic of conversation. He looked at Michael and surveyed the gathering. "What's so funny?" he asked.

"Nothing," Michael said. "We were just fooling around." Michael headed toward the door.

"You're not staying for the movie?" Robert asked.

"No. Not tonight. I've got a lot of repair work to do downstairs. I'm sure I'll be able to hear most of it down there anyway."

"Yeah, especially the gunshots," Angie said. "There are lots of those." She was relishing her role as the smart-mouth.

"Right. Enjoy the film, everyone."

Michael took a detour through the kitchen to see if there was any apple cobbler left and was happy to find that the cook had stashed a pan in the walk-in refrigerator. He dished up some, put ice cream on it and headed outside. He passed by the TV room on his way out the front door. Except for the sounds from the film, the room was quiet.

The night air was cool as Michael stepped out onto the covered front porch of the main building. At a little after seven there were no stars yet, and the sky was a deepening, rich blue. I love it here, Michael thought. What a beautiful island. He closed the front door to muffle the sounds of movie night.

He breathed deeply and decided to sit for a few minutes to enjoy his dessert on the porch. The air was cool but pleasantly mild for a June night. Michael heard the frog chorus that always started up about this time in the evening from the swampy area west of the Kayak School.

The frogs loved it there. Funny how frogs croak, all together, then all of a sudden they stopped, all together, Michael thought. I wonder how they know when to stop?

Checking the pocket of his flannel shirt, Michael felt the worn box with the charm inside. He was still puzzled by the charm's message and by Kit's reluctance to share the grandmother's story with him. The whole situation was a mystery.

Michael finished the cobbler and set his bowl down beside the porch swing where he sat, planning to return it to the kitchen on his way back. He descended the stairs, went around on the curved gravel path to the workroom side door and entered. Flipping on the light, he was greeted by the sight of two kayaks, elevated on sawhorses, that both needed work on their hulls. He could tell that Robert had started on some of the repairs today. One of the boats was nearly finished.

Michael repaired a dent near the stern, and stood back to admire his work. Sometimes I feel more at home here in the workroom than I do upstairs with those kids, Michael thought. Maybe it's time to think about retiring.

Having finished the kayak, Michael decided to see what he could find on the charm and sat back down at his desk. He pulled the box from his shirt pocket and carefully lifted the charm from its resting place. He examined it carefully, turning it over, and noted again that there was nothing on the back side. He ran his index finger over the engraved words, marveling again at the secret they held. Soon, he thought, it will be time to share this information and let the charm tell its story.

Michael carefully placed it back into the worn box and tucked it in his shirt pocket. Guess I ought to get a little work done while I'm down here, he thought. Paperwork wasn't his favorite, but it was time to begin the student evaluations. He leaned down, pulled a batch of student files from the bottom desk drawer and began to read the top one. He was grateful for the quiet, and for the time alone.

There was a soft knock on the workroom door. It's late, Michael thought. Who would be coming by at this hour?

Chapter Nineteen

RILEY HAD A HARD time concentrating during the sunset sail. She and Marie enjoyed the salmon dinner, the orange sky reflected in bright water all around them, and the views of the rocky cliffs along the west side of the island. But her thoughts were about Kit. By the time they arrived back at Cliffhouse, Riley was exhausted.

Riley saw Duffy's shadow under the door in the light from the kitchen as she turned the key in the lock. When the door opened, Duffy pushed off from her hind legs and leapt straight up into the air four times, bouncing off Riley's right thigh. This was their traditional celebratory greeting.

"Let's go outside," Riley said, and Duffy was out the door and disappeared into the darkness of the trees adjacent to the Cliffhouse. She was back in two minutes, looking proud of herself.

"Bedtime, little Duffy." Up the stairs she went, as if on cue, and Riley followed, pausing to lock up. "Sleep well, Marie."

"You, too," Marie called out as Riley headed up the narrow staircase.

Riley slept soundly and dreamed of Kit: They were on an island with no way to get off. But she awoke before she got to the really good part. Damn.

"I think I'll go into the *Island Times* office this morning and see if they have any more information about that nanny and the drownings," Riley said to Marie as they sat on the west deck with their coffee. "I would think they'd have a morgue."

"If I hadn't known you all these years and learned what a 'morgue' is in newspaper terms, I would think you were off your rocker right now," Marie said, waving at some morning kayakers who were passing right below the Cliffhouse.

"Don't you love being in the know? One more advantage of being best friends with Ace Reporter Riley Logan."

"Your humility is charming."

"I know. I think I'll grab breakfast at the bakery on the way in. Shall I buy you something?"

"Bring me one of those cinnamon rolls. Get yourself one, too. We'll enjoy them right here tomorrow morning."

"Always thinking of others, aren't you?" Riley rose from her chair and reached for Marie's empty coffee mug. After delivering Marie's coffee and giving her a goodbye peck on the cheek, she was out the door and into the Subaru. As she neared the main road, Riley heard sirens. Oh, no, she thought. Not again. What is it this time?

Riley headed out for the bakery and decided to try a short cut she'd seen on an island map. She made a right turn about a mile from the

Cliffhouse, and was immediately greeted by another "No Thru Road" sign. Guess this is the wrong turn for the short cut, she thought. Can't believe how many of those signs are on this island!

Back on the main road, Riley made the ten-minute drive to the bakery and parked in the one empty slot. Dorothy Reynolds, one of Aunt Joan's longtime friends, was sitting at an outside picnic table sipping coffee and eating a cinnamon roll. She was a good source for island information.

"Morning, Dorothy. Nice to see you. Hey, what are the sirens about, do you know?"

"Had a fellow stop by here on his way to catch the ten o'clock ferry. He'd been camped at Montague Park. He said there had been an oil spill during the night. The sailboats were all floating in an oil slick at daybreak. Guess it's a mess out there. Lots of people leaving the campground, too."

"What caused it, do you know?"

"Nope. No one knows yet. Kind of a mystery where it came from."

"I'll bet. Not too good for the tourism business, is it?"

"You got that right. But, then, maybe it won't be quite so busy this summer after all. It's crazy at the ferry landing this time of year, you know. My volunteer shifts in the visitor kiosk are never dull."

"I'm sure they're not. How long have you been doing that?"

"Over thirty-five years now, can you believe it? That's a lot of time in a six-by-eight booth. But I think it's important. I don't want Jonathan to be the only one greeting the tourists."

"Galiano wouldn't be the same without you there." Riley didn't know her age, but she guessed Dorothy to be near seventy-five. Would she know about the nanny? "Say, Dorothy, I wanted to ask you something. Mind if I come back with my coffee and roll and join you?"

"Fine by me," Dorothy said, opening the front section of last week's *Island Times*. "My break's up in twenty minutes."

"Be right back." Riley went inside the bakery and stood in the short line of tourists who needed that coffee fix. As she was paying, the new owner stepped out of his back office and greeted her with a welcoming smile.

"Morning. It's Riley, right?" Richard Ellison asked, and Riley was surprised he remembered her name. He had probably met lots of people at the community meeting Wednesday night.

"Is indeed. Good morning to you, Richard. Are the cinnamon rolls any good today?" She waved at the baker, Susan, who was putting another tray full into the hot oven.

"Best ever, because we have the best baker ever."

"Thanks for asking, Riley," Susan said. "I love it when the new boss tells customers how good I am."

"You're welcome. Hey, maybe you'll get a raise!"

Susan laughed and turned back to her work.

Richard poured himself a cup of coffee. "I'm sure she deserves one. Soon as we build up the business and attract some of those new homeowners, we'll all make more money. Right, Riley?"

Richard was being friendly, but Riley knew he had an agenda. Not being an islander herself, Riley hesitated to get into the Bodega Ridge controversy and decided to play it neutral.

"More people are good for business but can be bad for other things, I guess," she said in her most noncommittal voice. "Depends on how you look at it."

"Are you a politician or a lawyer? You're good."

"Neither," she said. "I'm a journalist."

"No wonder. You've made a career of being objective. Good for you. World needs more people who can see both sides of the issue."

"I'm glad you think so." Riley picked up her coffee and roll. "Nice chatting with you, Richard."

"Likewise. Stop by again."

Riley made her way out to where Dorothy was sitting. "Okay, you have sixteen minutes, and I have one question."

Dorothy looked up from her newspaper. "Shoot."

"I was going through some of Aunt Joan's things, and I found a stack of letters. They were from Katherine Taylor."

At the mention of the nanny's name, Dorothy put down her paper. "Really? I guess that doesn't surprise me. She and Joan were very good friends."

"I gathered that from the letters. I wondered if you knew her, too."

"Not as well. We were a couple of years apart. I remember her from my first year of high school. She was kind of a loner, stayed mainly with her family."

"It's funny, but my aunt never told me about her. Do you have any idea why she wouldn't tell me, since they were such good friends?"

Dorothy paused, thinking. She glanced at her watch.

"I know we're out of time," Riley said. "I thought maybe—"

Dorothy interrupted her. "It's all right. I have time to tell you that I think your aunt was heartbroken when Katherine was forced to leave the island. Joan was twenty-one then, and Katherine was seventeen. I think Joan wanted to protect her, somehow, from the way people treated her after the drownings, but of course she couldn't. When Katherine left Galiano, I never heard Joan speak of her again. I'm surprised that she got all those letters. I don't think anyone knew that."

"Would Katherine have written to anyone else?"

"I doubt it. Joan was her only friend outside the Graham family, and, of course, she couldn't communicate with them. It was too painful."

"I suppose so."

"That was a long time ago, Riley."

"Over sixty years, to be exact. Thanks, Dorothy, for the time and the answers. I appreciate it."

"Your aunt was one of the finest people who ever lived on Galiano. You can ask me about her anytime you want." With that, Dorothy picked up a bright red fanny pack off the picnic table and headed up the narrow road to the visitor kiosk. She waved over her shoulder. "See you, Riley."

Riley waved back, even though Dorothy wasn't looking.

Chapter Twenty

RILEY FINISHED HER COFFEE and gave herself the luxury of sitting in the morning sun for a few minutes before she headed out for the two-block stroll to the newspaper office. She slung her daypack over her left shoulder and meandered in the sun toward the office of the *Island Times*. As she opened the glass door, a bell that hung on the inside door handle signaled her arrival.

A fifty-ish woman with frizzy, graying hair and thick glasses stood up from her desk on the other side of the counter. She was holding a magnifying glass and had the *Island Times* open to the classified ad section.

"May I help you?" she asked politely.

"I hope so. Hi. I'm Riley Logan, Joan Walker's niece."

"Oh, my. We were all so sad to hear of Joan's passing. She was quite a spirit. I'm Alice Singleton. Very pleased to meet you."

"Likewise. I know my aunt was a dedicated fan of your newspaper her entire life. Read it cover to cover every week."

"She used to do a column for us, too, you know. In the seventies, I think it was. She called it 'Notes from the Cliff' and filled it with musings about life on the water on Galiano. Her articles were a favorite with readers."

"I remember. She saved all of them, and I always enjoyed reading those. She loved to write, didn't she?"

"She did, and she was good at it. Now, what can I do for you?"

Riley scanned the room, looking for the hard-covered, bound volumes of the newspapers that she knew must be stored somewhere nearby.

"I wanted to check your morgue for some issues from late forty-nine. Do you keep those here? Are they in bound volumes, or on microfilm?"

Alice put down the paper. "No microfilm for miles around here. Even though they weigh a ton and take up way too much room, we have all the back issues bound and shelved. Most of them are downstairs."

"Really? I didn't know there was a downstairs."

"We're one of the few buildings on the island with a basement. It's a well-guarded secret."

"Do you let anyone down there to explore, or does a person have to have some sort of important credentials?"

"You seem official enough to me. What are you searching for, if I may ask?"

Riley hesitated, but saw no reason not to be honest. "I wanted to read the accounts of the drowning of the Graham children. I found a couple clippings in my aunt's things and want to see any other stories published about the incident."

"No doubt we printed others. The tragedy remained the lead story for weeks."

"So it's okay if I go down and see what I can find?"

"Of course. Let me show you where things are stored downstairs." Alice motioned for Riley to follow her. The office was quiet except for the soft clack-clack of someone typing on a computer keyboard in the editor's office on the other side of the wall.

"That's Tony Ralls," Alice said, nodding toward the sound. "Editor-in-chief. He's working on his column for next week. He's half our news staff." She opened the door to the basement and gestured to Riley. "After you."

Riley made her way down the narrow stairs. Beneath the soft light of one overhead lamp, she saw rows of bound volumes. Each shelf was labeled with raised lettering on red plastic tape. The 1922 volume was the first.

"That's a lot of newspapers," Riley said, stating the obvious.

"Been around a long time," Alice said. "Do you need any help, or shall I leave you on your own to investigate?"

"I think I'll be fine." One oblong table, near the high-up window, afforded more light. "I'll bring a few volumes over there and see what I can see."

"Very well, then," Alice headed back up the narrow stairs. "Hope you find something useful."

Me, too, Riley thought. I wonder what I am looking for?

Scanning the shelf labeled "1949," Riley selected the volumes for September through December and lugged them back to the table. She opened the first to the newspaper dated September 12 and saw on the front page the article that she had found in her aunt's things. She marked the page with a sticky note from the tablet she'd brought with her and carefully turned each page to find other related articles. She discovered one right away, on page three, one she hadn't seen before.

"Children's father pleads for information" was the headline, with a second deck: "Matthew Graham asks islanders for any information about tragic incident." Riley read the story and felt prickles on her skin as she made her way through it:

The patriarch of the Graham family, devastated by the drowning of his two children, is asking islanders for any additional information about the tragic incident last week.

In an uncharacteristic show of emotion, Matthew Graham said that he still holds out hope that someone may have heard or seen something the night the boat capsized. He asked reporters from this newspaper and ones in Vancouver and Victoria to solicit information from anyone who might have been in the area on Sunday, either on Galiano or Wallace Islands, or in the waters between the islands. Graham is hoping that someone may have witnessed the capsizing and have information about where his children drowned. He has not given up on finding the bodies of his children, Emily, age eight, and William, age two.

"I cannot rest until they are found," Graham told the reporters and volunteers assembled at the Community Hall. "My children deserve a proper burial."

Volunteers at the meeting offered to search Galiano and Wallace Island shorelines for any trace of the children or the boat.

In one exchange, a reporter asked about the condition of the nanny, seventeen-year-old Katherine Taylor. Graham's angry response quieted the room. "She is doing as well as can be expected," he said. "Our concern now is not with her welfare. It is with the effort to find the bodies of my children." With that, Graham walked solemnly out of the room, ending the brief exchange.

Services for the two children are scheduled for this Saturday, Sept. 15, at 1 p.m. at the Community Center. The Graham family asks that remembrances be made to a memorial being created in the name of Emily and William Graham.

Riley made a few notes and turned to the next weekly *Island Times*, dated Sept. 19, 1949. The front-page story ten days after the accident summed up the events to date under the headline "Still no trace of children's bodies." Riley skimmed the story and found only one paragraph that gave her new information: "Volunteers in this effort were led by George MacAlister, who organized a fleet of fishing boats to search the waters between the two islands. MacAlister was the person who came to the aid of Katherine Taylor when he discovered her, unconscious and shivering, on the beach."

MacAlister. Jonathan's father, Riley thought. Wonder if Jonathan was there, too? If he were there, did he remember? And if he did remember, would he talk to me about it? Riley wasn't too optimistic about the answer to the last question.

Riley paged carefully through the newspapers of the next five weeks and found brief updates, mostly describing the lack of any new information. The first issue in November carried a front-page article about the establishment of the memorial fund and Matthew Graham's plans for its use under the headline "Graham family creates future out of tragedy."

Matthew Graham announced today that his estate will go to the people of Galiano upon his death. These remarks were made during a brief press conference, at which time Matthew Graham announced that the search for his children's bodies was over and, in his words, "Life must go on."

Graham told reporters that he and his wife Ella had instructed local volunteers to cease and desist their search and thanked them for their efforts. In a dramatic announcement, Graham said that he and Ella had made a decision about the disbursement of their wealth upon their deaths.

"We will never get over this loss," Graham said, "but we must do something to make sense of it. Toward that end, Ella and I are establishing the Emily and William Graham Trust Fund, to which we have allocated the gifts made in our children's memory. Our dearest hope had been that all we possess would have gone to our children upon our deaths. Since their bodies have never been found, in the absence of any heirs, we have directed that all monies in the Graham family estate be transferred to this fund and be left to the people of Galiano.

Wow, Riley thought. That's a substantial gift. She continued reading.

It is also our hope that these monies might be used to construct a new elementary school, or a medical facility, or a library, or any one of several other projects the trustees deem important—and that these facilities bear the names of Emily and William Graham.

The story concluded with a paragraph summarizing the accident and the apparent deaths of the children. No mention was made of Katherine Taylor, and Riley thought that odd. Guess she had already left the island, she thought. Out of sight, out of mind.

Riley leafed through the rest of the 1949 newspapers and found no more front-page stories, so she put the heavy volumes back on the shelf and headed back up the narrow stairs. Alice was still at her post, but the soft clicking of the computer keyboard in the newsroom could no longer be heard.

"Thanks very much, Alice."

"Did you find what you were looking for?" Alice asked, putting down the magnifying glass.

"Pretty much. But if I think of any more questions, may I come back?"

"Of course. Anytime the door's unlocked, you're welcome to visit."

"I appreciate that." Riley thanked her again, waved goodbye and headed to her car. Fishing for her keys, she heard her cell phone's familiar customized ring that told her it was Marie calling.

She fished it out of her jacket pocket.

"Hello, friend," Riley said. "What's up? Almost done here."

"Oh, God, Riley. I'm so glad you picked up," Marie said. Her voice was strained.

"What is it? What's wrong? You sound awful."

"I am. I can't believe I have to tell you this, Riley."

"Tell me what?"

"It's Michael. He's been murdered!"

Chapter Twenty-One

THE TEN-MINUTE DRIVE was one of the longest Riley had ever experienced, and when she arrived at the Cliffhouse, Marie greeted her at the front door.

Riley spoke first. "When?" she asked simply. Marie didn't answer. "How? Do they know who did it?"

Marie shook her head. "I don't think so. The Constable's office called here asking for you. They want you to go over to the school, Riley. They want to ask you some questions."

"Me? Why?" Riley said, alarmed.

"I'm not sure. It's not like you're a suspect or anything. They want some information from you."

"I can't imagine what it would be. But let's go. We have to face the reality of this sometime. Will you come with me?"

"Of course. Let me change clothes."

"I'll wait right here." Riley sat at their round kitchen table and looked out over the channel. Sailboats glided smoothly over the water in the afternoon breeze, as though nothing had happened. As though Michael, her new friend and ally, wasn't gone forever.

Marie entered the kitchen, jarring Riley from her thoughts.

"Okay," Marie said. "Let's go."

"Right. Duffy, you wait here. I don't think you should go with us."

Duffy curled up in her dog bed.

SEVERAL COUNTY VEHICLES WERE parked along the Kayak School road when Riley and Marie drove up.

Marie said, "Seems as though they have all the nearby law enforcement people out here."

"Guess so. I hope they do. I want to know who would do this to Michael. I can't believe it, still. How can Michael be dead?"

"I know, Riley. I can't believe it either."

They parked and made their way across the gravel parking lot to the school office. Robert Burrows greeted them on the front porch. He seemed distraught.

Riley went right up to him and pulled him into a hug. He didn't resist.

"I'm so sorry, Robert."

Robert stepped back and looked at Riley with sad eyes. "I can't believe this has happened. Who would want to hurt Michael?" His eyes welled up, and he said nothing more.

"I don't know, Robert. He was a gentle and kind man."

Marie, who hadn't spoken, extended her hand to Robert. "You were a good friend to him. He always knew he could depend on you."

Robert wiped his eyes with a tissue he pulled from his shirt pocket. "Why would someone do a thing like this? I don't understand."

"None of us does," Marie said. "It's a shock."

Riley heard footsteps behind her and turned to see Constable Paul Snow coming up the stairs from the downstairs workroom area of the main building. He was about forty-five, short, stocky, and graying at the temples, which showed under the hat he always wore on duty. His beige uniform was unpretentious but commanded respect. He's been in the job for as long as I can remember, Riley thought, as he walked toward her, and he knows what he's doing. She felt thankful that the investigation would be under his direction.

Paul Snow carried a notebook and a mini-recorder. He crossed the floor to the porch entrance.

"Hello, Riley," he said, offering his hand. "Thank you for coming."

Riley shook his hand. "Hello, Constable Snow. This is Marie. She said you wanted to talk to me. I'm not sure why."

"It's routine, and please call me Paul. We're trying to talk with everyone who might have had a conversation with Michael in the past forty-eight hours."

"Of course. Here?"

"No, I'd like to talk with you in private," Paul said. He directed his question to Robert. "May we use your office?"

"Sure," Robert said.

Marie said, "I can wait in the courtyard."

"Good idea," Robert said. "I'm sure some of the students might like someone to talk to. They're pretty upset about this."

"I imagine they are. I'll do that, then. Riley, just call me when you're ready to go."

"I will, Marie. Thanks."

"Shall we head in?" Paul said, ushering Riley up the front steps to Robert's office.

Once inside, Riley sat across from Paul in a straight-backed oak chair and waited for him to begin. She was unsure what he'd ask, and even more unsure what she would tell him.

Paul said, "First of all, I want to emphasize that we don't consider you a suspect."

Riley smiled in spite of the seriousness of the moment. "Well that's a relief. I didn't think you did, though, to tell you the truth."

"Good. Let's proceed now that we have that out of the way. When did you last talk to Michael?"

Riley thought for a moment. "I guess at the community meeting. Yeah, that was Wednesday night. We spoke briefly at the break, and then I told him goodbye in the parking lot. That's about it."

"Did anyone overhear your conversation during the break?"

"No, I don't think so."

"Where were you?"

This question unnerved Riley, but she knew she had to answer it truthfully. "We made a point to move out back behind the building so that no one would hear us."

"And why was that?"

Paul was still kind, but his question had an edge to it that made Riley nervous.

"We were making some plans regarding the video project he was working on. He said he might need help with some things."

"What kind of things?"

Riley hesitated. Did she need to protect Kit? What would happen if she told only part of the truth? Her mind raced. She knew she had to tell Paul everything. This was a murder investigation, for God's sake.

"Michael was suspicious of Kit," Riley said.

"Did he say why?"

"That's just, it, Paul. He didn't. He only said that he was curious about Kit's motives for being here on Galiano and that he would tell me more later."

"But he didn't get a chance to do that, did he?"

"No," Riley said simply. Her heart felt heavy.

"Did you talk to Michael yesterday?"

"I didn't. Marie and I did some more work at the Cliffhouse, and then I went out for a while in the afternoon. Marie and I went on a sunset sail last night."

"I see. So you don't have any information about where Michael was yesterday or what he did. Is that correct?"

"Yes. That's correct."

"Anything else I should know about that conversation during the break of Wednesday night's meeting?"

"I don't think so."

"Then what about afterwards, in the parking lot? I've already talked with a couple people who overheard an argument there."

"I wasn't in an argument."

"I know that. Could you tell me what you heard?"

"Sure. I'll try. Michael, Carl Brown and Richard Ellison were in a shouting match. Kit and I heard them as we left the Community Hall. The fight was so loud that I'm pretty sure lots of people did."

"What did they say?"

"Same stuff as inside at the meeting. They wanted development, Michael wanted..." Riley hesitated. "Michael wanted to preserve the island."

"Okay. Anything else?"

"Not that I recall. I headed for home after that."

"And Kit?"

"She went back to the Kayak School and her room, I assume, but I guess I don't know that for sure."

"Where was Marie? Don't you two stay together out at the Cliffhouse?"

"She was meeting someone."

"Who?"

"She went out for a beer with James Crawford."

"Are they friends?"

"I don't know. They seem to be getting acquainted, though."

"Is it a romantic acquaintance?"

Riley wondered why Paul was so interested in Marie's activities. "I don't think so, Paul. Truth is, Michael wanted us to check him out."

"For what reason?"

"Michael had a theory that someone might be putting pressure on the island committee or even on Crawford himself. He asked Marie if she would meet with him, that's all. No big deal."

"Did Marie discover anything?"

"I don't think so."

"Was there anyone else at the meeting who argued with Michael?" Paul asked, moving on from the Marie part. Riley was glad of that.

"Clare Porter," Riley said. "She got pretty hot when Jonathan joined the debate, and then Michael came to his defense. I don't think she liked that much."

"I'm sure she didn't, but do you think she was mad enough to come out here and stab him?"

"Goodness, Paul, I don't think so, but who knows what makes a person mad enough to commit murder?"

"I've been trying to figure that one out for about twenty years," he said, sighing. "And you know what? There's no answer because it's different in every situation. Human beings are complicated creatures. That's about the only thing I have figured out."

Riley felt bad for him all of a sudden, realizing how often he must have had to deal with the reality of death during his career. What a hard way to make a living.

"Paul, there's something else you should know."

"I'm listening."

"Kit told me that she and Michael thought that perhaps the ferry incident was connected somehow to the controversy about the development of Bodega Ridge."

"Very interesting. I wonder why they suspected that."

"Guess you could ask her. Kit will probably tell you all she can, now that this has happened."

"It's going to be hard to get an answer from her."

"What do you mean?" Riley asked.

"Kit's gone. She seems to have vanished."

Chapter Twenty-Two

RILEY TOOK A DEEP breath and tried not to panic.

"How do you know she's vanished?" she asked the constable, afraid for the answer.

"No one has seen her since last night. Most of her stuff is gone from her room, and she didn't show up for the day trip this morning, according to Robert. Her car's still here, though. I've got a deputy out searching the island now for any sign of her, but he hasn't found anything yet."

"So what do you think this means? Do you think it has anything to do with the murder?"

"We have to assume that. At this point, we aren't sure what to think. She could be a victim here—or she could be a suspect."

"A suspect! That's ridiculous. Kit would never kill anyone. She cared for Michael. They were partners in this video project—"

"I know that, Riley, but the fact that the murder happened and she disappeared gives us no choice but to include her on our list of suspects."

"Who else is on it?"

"You know I can't tell you that. You'll have to get that information from someone besides me. It's police business, and you have no formal role in this."

"But I'm a reporter."

"Not here."

Riley paused to think about her next question. "Have you removed the body?"

"Not yet. The medical examiner is still in there. We have to go very slowly and carefully at this point."

"He was stabbed?"

Paul gave her a frown in response. "Yes."

"I know, I know. You can't tell me anything else."

Paul said nothing.

"Okay, I'm done asking questions. Do you have any more for me?"

"Not right now, I don't, but I'll need your cell number, and for you to keep your phone on for the rest of the day and evening, in case we need to contact you."

"Right. I will." She jotted her number on the notepad Paul handed her, and turned to go.

"Oh, and one more thing," Paul said.

"Yes?"

"Be careful."

Riley looked at Paul and for a moment felt a sweep of emotion—that he would care, that Michael was dead, that Kit was missing, and that life really wasn't very good at this moment.

"Thank you, Paul."

Riley went to find Marie, and they headed for the parking lot. Riley got into the driver's seat, leaned her head on the steering wheel and let out a long, deep sigh. Marie put her hand on her friend's shoulder.

"It's so disturbing," Marie said. "All of it."

"I know. I still can't believe Michael is gone."

"Robert told me they can't seem to find Kit. Do you think she has something to do with this?"

Riley decided to tell Marie about Michael's suspicions. Why hold back, now that he was gone? "I can't believe that she would kill anyone, but I'm also worried that she's connected, somehow. Marie, what if she's been kidnapped?"

"You're kidding, right?"

"No, I mean it. What if she's been killed? What if the killer got rid of her, too?"

"But why? Why kill Kit? For that matter, why kill Michael? Is it the video project, do you think? The ridge development? Or was it a vendetta of some kind? I know there are some people on this island who are pretty mad at Michael. But mad enough to kill him?"

"Those are all good questions. And I have an idea about who might answer them. Come on," she said, getting back out of the car. "Let's go talk to Robert."

"But we told Paul we were going home."

"We will. Soon. But I can't leave here without some answers."

They circled around the back of the main building so that they wouldn't pass the door of the basement workroom, which was open. Paul, the medical examiner, and other officials were still in there. Riley didn't want to be seen.

They found Robert in the school's main office in front of his computer. He wasn't typing; he was just sitting.

"You're back," he said. "Forget something?" Robert looked tired and pale.

"We want to ask you a couple questions, Robert," Riley said. "I can't leave here without knowing more about what happened to Michael. And I think maybe you know."

"Constable Paul gave me strict orders not to talk to anyone. Especially not the media."

"According to Paul, I'm not the media here on Galiano, so that puts me more in the role of concerned friend. Come on, Robert. It's me, Riley. You know Marie and I were getting acquainted with Michael, and we're worried about Kit. Please tell us what you know."

Robert glanced toward the open door of his office. "Close it, and sit down."

Riley shut the door quietly, sat in the one chair, and Marie leaned against the bookcase.

"Who found the body?" Riley asked. "Was it you?"

"Yes," he said, near tears. "Michael didn't show up for breakfast at seven. I thought maybe he'd slept in, so I went to his room. All his gear was there from yesterday's kayak trip, and nothing seemed out of order. I couldn't tell if his bed had been slept in. He might have already made it today. Sometimes he was tidy like that. But he wasn't around, so I headed down to the workroom. I noticed an empty bowl on the porch, where someone had cobbler and left it there. I thought it must have been Michael's because I know he loves that stuff and probably had some before he went downstairs.

"Anyway, I thought I'd check for him in the workroom because sometimes he gets busy on a repair project and loses track of time down there.

"The door was ajar, and the lights were on, so I went in. That's when I saw him. He was slumped over his desk. I thought he was asleep, or that maybe he'd had a heart attack or something. I said his name, but of course, there was no response. I went over to him. I saw a wound, just inside his shoulder blade." He shuddered. "That gaping hole in him and all the blood, well, that's the worst thing I've ever experienced."

Riley and Marie waited for him to continue.

"Lots of blood. It seemed like it was everywhere. Under the body, and on the desk, and his chair. He was stabbed."

"The weapon?" Riley asked.

"I didn't see any weapon. Only the wound."

"Then what did you do?"

"I panicked. I couldn't believe it. I went upstairs and called the constable's office."

"Did you tell the kids what had happened?"

"Not right away. I didn't want to alarm them. Riley, what if the murderer is still here? What if it's one of them? I didn't know what to do, who to tell, what to say to anyone."

"Of course, Robert. That was wise. Then what happened?"

"The constable arrived, and soon after that, the medical examiner. Paul sealed off the area. About an hour later, an investigator from Vancouver showed up with a couple of men. They cordoned off the entire downstairs as a crime scene and began collecting evidence."

"Who do they think did it?" Riley asked, hoping that Robert would be forthcoming. She had to know.

"I don't know if I should say. I think that's—what do they call it? Classified information."

"Of course it is, Robert, but if I'm going to find Kit and get to the bottom of this awful event, I need all the information you have. Please. You know I'll act responsibly with it."

"I know you will. Okay. What's the use? Michael's dead. Why should I hold this back from you two?"

"Exactly," Riley said, and she waited.

"I heard Paul talking with the investigator. I was outside, in the hallway, and I think they thought I'd already come upstairs. Paul gave the guy several names, all people here on Galiano. I was shocked."

"Who does he suspect?" Riley asked. "You can tell me."

"Okay, okay. He told him to talk to Carl Brown and Clare Porter, from the development project. And also Jonathan. And Richard Ellison." Robert stopped, hesitated.

"Who else?"

"Kit."

"God. I thought so. Anyone else?"

"No, but I added someone when Paul questioned me. There's this kid here, Russ. Michael was about to kick him out and send him back to detention in Vancouver. I'm worried. I think he might have had something to do with it. He hated Michael."

"Enough to kill him? Really? I can't imagine a kid doing that. How old is he? Fourteen?"

"He's sixteen, and he's pretty sophisticated for that age. I think he's been through a lot. If he was mad enough, he might have tried to hurt Michael."

"Was he around last night?"

"Yes, he was, but I can't say for sure where he was the entire evening. It was movie night. The kids were watching *Fargo* in the main lounge."

"Isn't that right above Michael's workroom?"

"It is."

"Was Russ watching the movie?"

Robert shifted in his chair and sighed. "He was when I left, which was shortly after it started—probably about seven. He had come in late. He said he was in the bathroom. I don't know if he was in the TV room the entire time. Usually the kids go in and out, get a drink or a snack, use the restroom, things like that. We don't track their every move."

"Is that what you told Paul?"

"Pretty much."

"And what about Kit? Was she at the movie?"

Robert paused. "No, she wasn't. I don't know where she was. I haven't seen her since last night at dinner. She didn't show up for the day trip today. I had to ask another teacher to fill in for her. The kids were pretty freaked out anyway. I hope they're careful out there on the water. We certainly don't need another tragedy around here."

Riley forced herself to ask a question she didn't want to. "Do you think Kit had anything to do with this?"

"I don't know. She's been kind of mysterious, you know. She never talked much with me. I think she and Michael were pretty connected, though. I can't imagine why she would want him dead."

Riley thought about Michael's elusive comments Wednesday night out behind the Community Hall. Was there something Michael knew about Kit that he didn't share with her? Riley felt sweat form on her brow as fear settled in. Could Kit be involved with this?

Marie was asking her something.

"Huh?" Riley said, trying to pull herself back from these disturbing thoughts.

"I said, are you sure you're okay?" Marie repeated.

"Oh, yeah. I was thinking about Kit. I can't believe she would ever hurt anyone. There has to be another explanation."

"Perhaps," Robert said. "But until she shows up, how are we going to know?"

"Good point," Riley said. "How would we?"

Robert looked at her and said nothing.

Riley said, "Is there anything else you can tell us?"

Robert said, "Not that I can think of. I still can't imagine why anyone would want to kill Michael. God, it's awful. I never thought I'd have to go through anything like this. What will happen to the school? To all these kids? How am I going to explain it to them? I suppose they'll have to be sent home, won't they?" He seemed to be thinking aloud now.

"I don't think you have to decide that this afternoon," Marie said. "Give it a day or two. You can suspend the kayak trips for next week and figure out what to do. Don't rush it. You're still in shock."

"You're right. I am," he said. "Thanks for the advice. It's good."

"I think maybe we'll head out," Riley said, seeing a good place for an exit. "I appreciate what you've shared with us."

"Yeah, I know. But don't tell Paul I told you all of this, all right? Please?"

"I won't," Riley said. "You can trust me. Us. You can trust both of us," she said, glancing at Marie.

Marie said, "We won't let on we had this conversation. Are you going to be all right?"

Robert didn't seem all right. He was pale and acting scared.

"I suppose so," he said. "I hope I can sleep tonight."

"I hope so, too," Riley said. "You know, you can always call us out at the Cliffhouse if you need to. Anytime. Day or night. I mean it. In case you need it, here's my cell phone number." She wrote it on a notepad on his desk.

"Thanks, Riley. I might."

"Try to take care of yourself. Maybe you should go lie down for a while"

"Yes, I believe I will."

"We'll check in with you tomorrow," Marie added.

"Good. I'd like that."

With that, Robert got up from his desk chair and ushered them toward the door. "You be careful, too, and please tell me if you find out anything about Kit. I'm worried about her."

"So are we," Riley said. "We'll call you first thing if we find out anything."

"I'd appreciate that."

Chapter Twenty-Three

CONSTABLE PAUL SNOW KNEW that the next few hours were the crucial ones in the investigation, and he intended to make the best use of them. Kit's disappearance was weighing on his mind. Could it be true that this young woman was involved in the gruesome scene? He couldn't quite bring himself to believe it, but he'd seen stranger things in his career. Women do commit murder. Was Kit capable of that? Hard to tell. She'd made herself mysterious enough.

Paul opened the door to the downstairs workroom and surveyed the scene. The medical examiner, George Howell, was bending over the body and seemed to be in the same place he'd been when Paul left twenty minutes earlier to talk to Riley. That isn't surprising, Paul thought. Howell was a very thorough man.

"Any updates?" Paul asked as he came into the room.

"I think we can safely assume that the victim was killed right here," George said. "The blood flow is all downward, and there is a lot of it on the desk."

"And the wound?"

"Long-blade knife, I would say. The angle is down and the wound is deep. Might have gone all the way into the heart. Death would have been instant."

"What else?"

"Right-handed killer. The angle of the knife would suggest that."

Paul heard a noise behind him and saw his two detectives slip in the room and stand quietly at the back. They were followed by Gail Carter, who looked alert and ready to do her job, as always. He moved aside as the crime scene photographer came to stand by the body. She had a black camera bag over one shoulder and was making notes in a green notebook. Paul had worked with her for years and knew her to be thorough and highly professional; he was always more confident when she was part of the crime scene team. He was glad she opted to keep Galiano as part of the area she covered from her base in Vancouver.

"Hi, Gail," Paul said. "You got here pretty fast. Anything you notice right off about the body?"

"Looks to me as though the murderer plunged the knife in and then backed up and out that door. The victim slumped over right where he was sitting." Gail pulled her digital Nikon 35 mm out of the bag and attached a powerful flash. "Shouldn't take me long." She circled the desk to determine which angles she would shoot, and began recording the scene with her Nikon. "The crime scene is pretty well confined in this instance, isn't it?"

Gail examined the desk, the floor underneath it and the chair where Michael was sitting when he was killed.

"He didn't even move out of his chair," she said. "My guess is that the killer attacked from behind and stabbed him before the victim even knew what was coming. It probably happened very quickly."

"I think you're right about that," George said as he carefully examined Michael's hands for any trace of skin, blood or fiber under the nails. "There aren't any superfluous wounds on either hand, which means the victim didn't struggle with the killer. It happened too fast; he didn't see it coming."

"Anything under the nails?" Paul asked.

"Nothing telling," George said. "Just a little bit of sand under a couple of them. I see that a lot. Victim probably spends a lot of time on the water or on the beach. I would expect that."

"Anything you wouldn't expect?"

"I'm kind of perplexed that there's no sign of a struggle. Why would a strong man like Michael Barsotti sit there and let someone stab him in the back?"

"Because he knew the killer," Paul said.

"You think so?"

"I do. This island is small, George, and tensions are high over the Bodega Ridge development. Michael was a passionate and outspoken opponent of it. Chances are good that the killer is someone he knew— and maybe even someone he liked."

"Why do you say that?" Gail asked.

"Because if Michael were suspicious of this person, he probably wouldn't have remained sitting in his desk chair and let him walk behind him. His natural instinct would have been to stand up so he could defend himself. Clearly, he sensed no danger, and that's why he stayed sitting where he was."

"Makes sense," George said. "I found something else interesting."

"Show me," Paul said.

"Here, on the desk. There are some traces of purple thread, maybe from fabric? I can't tell, but we can collect them and send them over to the lab for analysis."

"Interesting. And this magnifying light? Was it in this position?"

"Far as I know, no one has moved anything," George said. "But maybe we better ask Robert about that. He found the body."

"I will. So you're sure Michael was murdered right here?"

"No question. The blood pooled below him on the desk, the chair, and all over his lap. The saliva flowed down and onto his shirt right here. He was sitting up when he was killed and then slumped over. I'm certain of that."

"I think you're right," Paul said. Turning to his two detectives, he gestured toward the workroom door. "I'd like one of you to take the area outside in the hallway, and the other to do a thorough search of the door itself and get prints off the handle, if we're lucky enough to find any. And let's have the tech do a luminol check for blood here in the workroom and outside in the hall. Probably should do that in some of the residence rooms, too."

"Why there?" Detective Adam Grant asked. "Do you suspect someone here at the school?"

"Don't know yet," Paul said. "But Robert, Michael's assistant, told me that one of the students had a beef with Michael. Name's Russ. Get the room number from Robert, would you? And check it thoroughly. While you're at it, search all the student rooms for clues. We might get lucky.

"There's another thing," Paul said as the detective headed for the door. "Check Room Two thoroughly also. It's occupied by one of the instructors, Kit Powell. Have the techs use luminol in there, too."

The detective seemed puzzled, but didn't ask any questions. "Got it. I'm on my way."

"Me, too," the photographer said as she followed them out the door. "I'll get back to you ASAP," she called over her shoulder.

Paul turned toward the medical examiner and continued to watch him work. He was carefully combing through Michael's dark, curly hair, starting with the crown of the skull and working downward. "Got something," he said. "Look at this."

He held out the comb for Paul to see. It held a delicate green piece of moss. "Did Michael go walking in the woods yesterday?"

Paul shrugged. "Don't know, but I'll find out."

"If he didn't, then it's possible our killer did. If the killer leaned over Michael to, for instance, reach into his shirt pockets or take something from the desk, it's possible the moss could have ended up there. It's an odd place for a piece of moss, don't you think? In his hair?"

"I guess it is. Let's get the crime scene tech to bag it. That's clue number one," Paul said. He let out a sigh. "Probably only about two hundred more to go."

Chapter Twenty-Four

"GOD, I'M REALLY WORRIED about Kit now," Riley said as she headed the Subaru back toward the Cliffhouse. "Why did she leave? Where do you think she might have gone?"

"Are you asking me, Riley, or are you asking yourself?" Marie said as she reached out to massage Riley's right shoulder. "You have tense muscles. Try to relax. You're going to drive us over a cliff at this rate. Slow down!"

Marie's advice sunk in as Riley rounded a curve too fast, and the station wagon skidded slightly.

"You're right. I'm more than a little upset here," Riley said. "I want to get home and sit on the deck and see what I think."

"You need to eat something. I'll fix you a sandwich when we get back. I think you're running on empty."

"No kidding. And I'm going to get emptier if this turns out badly."

"What do you mean?"

"I mean, what if Kit's involved? I like this woman, and now what will I do if it turns out she had something to do with this? Or, even worse, what if she's in danger now?"

"Do you believe she's capable of murder?"

"I haven't known her for that long. How would I know the answer to that?"

"You'd know because you have a gut feeling about it, and I want you to tell me what it is."

"You're right. I do have a gut feeling. No, I don't think she's capable of hurting anyone, let alone Michael, whom she seemed to like and respect."

"I believe you. I think we should cross her off our list of suspects."

"But where is she? Why did she disappear? I tried calling her cell, but it goes straight to voicemail, as though it's turned off. What if she's hurt somewhere? I don't know what to do first. But we can't afford to sit around and let the boys handle this. I think we should assume Kit is okay, because without that we're nowhere. Let's assume she has a reason for staying out of sight. But what in the world could that be?"

"I don't know. That's the piece of the puzzle we have to work on next."

"Let's go home. Maybe we'll get inspired."

Riley felt anxious and restless when they got back to the Cliffhouse, and wasn't sure what to do with herself, so she headed upstairs to read more of Aunt Joan's letters. She read each one carefully, beginning with the first and all the way through number twenty—with the exception, of course, of numbers fourteen and fifteen, which weren't in the empty envelopes. Each letter had news that a seventeen-year-old would think important, but it wasn't all that interesting. One made reference to another girl Riley had never heard her aunt speak of, either.

Katherine had written: "Life was so simple when you, June and I were all in school together. Oh, how I wish I could go back to those days."

Riley scanned the rest of the letter to see if the girl named June was mentioned again, but she wasn't.

The last letter in the stack was postmarked May, 1950. Katherine wrote: "I hope you did what I asked with those other two letters. If anyone knew, I would die. Really, I would, Joan. You promised. No one is to know."

Riley thought about how seventeen-year-olds are so dramatic. Everything is traumatic when you're that age.

That said, the letter went on to talk about the unusual patrons the bed and breakfast had hosted the night before and the boy Katherine met at the grocery.

Riley thought what Katherine wrote about was all pretty tame stuff—almost as though she didn't want to share anything of consequence in the letters, except for the two she referred to, the ones that weren't there. What would her Aunt Joan have done with them?

Riley bundled up the letters and bound them with the string. She put them back in the bottom drawer of the desk.

"MARIE. IT'S ALMOST EIGHT, Riley said. "Gotta get at it."

"Oh. Right," Marie said, then promptly turned over. Seconds later, she was snoring.

Riley stood beside the downstairs bed trying to awaken her sleeping friend who didn't seem to want to move. She nudged her again. "Come on, Girl Detective. I need you."

Duffy came romping in and hopped up on Marie's bed.

Marie opened both eyes but didn't look too happy. "Is the coffee ready?"

"Coffee's almost done dripping," Riley said. "I'll bring you a cup."

A few minutes later, she did, and Marie sat up to take her first sip. Then she joined Riley on the deck.

Riley said, "We need to call Paul in a few minutes, see what the new developments are. I hope they've located Kit."

Marie set down her coffee and dialed the constable's office. "Hi, Paul. It's Marie."

Riley strained to hear his voice as Marie held the phone to her own ear.

"Any news on Kit?" Marie paused while Paul talked. "Oh, God. You're kidding. When?"

"What? What!" Riley said. "Is it Kit?"

"No," Marie whispered, holding her hand over the mouthpiece. "Not Kit. Russ."

"What?!" Riley asked. This was exasperating.

"Including Wallace?" Marie was asking.

Riley wished she would hang the hell up and tell her what was going on. She glared at Marie, trying to send that message telepathically. Marie evidently received it because she started using the words one does when she's ending a conversation.

"Okay, then, we'll check back later this morning. Thanks, Paul. I know you're doing everything you can. Bye." She hung up.

"Finally!" Riley said. "What did he say? What's wrong with Russ?"

"It's not what's wrong with him. It's that he's gone. Missing. Disappeared, just like Kit."

"Jesus. Is this going to be some kind of mass exodus or something? Is everyone connected with this going undercover, or are we going to uncover a humongous kidnapping ring?"

Marie laughed. "Riley, you're funny even when you're worried and frustrated. I love that."

"Easy for you to say. I don't feel funny. What the hell happened to Russ?"

"They don't know. But he's definitely a suspect in Michael's murder, and he probably knows that, so my guess is he flew the coop."

"Is that detective talk? 'Flew the coop'? Did you hear that on some episode of *Castle*?"

"No. My mother. She used to say that about husbands who snuck out in the dead of night, never to return."

"At least they weren't murderers. Were they?"

"Definitely not. Just bad husbands."

"Right."

"OK, CARL, LET'S TAKE it from the top."

Constable Paul was seated across from Carl Brown in the windowless interrogation room at the back of his office. Just back from the crime scene, Paul's mind was busy with all the possibilities, but he had been in law enforcement long enough to know that the most obvious leads may not be the right ones. He had several suspects to interrogate, and he had started with Carl.

"Right," Carl said. "Like I told you, Thursday night I stopped by the Daystar Market to pick up a DVD. Then I went home."

"And you remained there all night?"

"Of course."

"Anyone see you there?"

"No. You know I live alone."

"I do. Who waited on you at the market?"

"Beverly did. She works the evening shift. You know that, too."

"Right. One of my detectives has already talked to her."

"Did she say I'd been there?" Carl asked.

"I can't tell you anything about what she said. Tell me about your quarrel with Michael after the meeting Wednesday night."

"It wasn't so much a quarrel. Michael got hot, that's all."

"Did you threaten him?"

"No."

"Did Ellison threaten him?"

"Ask Ellison. He was talking tough. Trading insults, stuff like that. Michael was pretty self-righteous, and that made us both mad."

"So you threatened him? Several witnesses have said you were pretty mad at him."

"Maybe. Doesn't mean I wanted to kill him, for God's sake."

"I hope not, Carl. Because if you did, we're going to find out, and it will be the end of life as you know it here on Galiano."

"I've nothing to hide. You gotta believe me."

"I hope I can."

AFTER CARL LEFT, DETECTIVE Grant knocked lightly on the interview room door.

"Come on in, Adam," Paul said. "Whatcha got?"

"Couple of lab reports. The blood on and around the victim was all his own. We didn't find any other type anywhere. We did find blood in the kid's room yesterday, though. A smudge on the lamp. I've sent it over to Vancouver for analysis."

"If Russ did it, he certainly wasn't very careful."

"He's a kid, Paul. Probably thought he could wipe it up with a paper towel. Another interesting thing is what we didn't find...his computer."

"Are you serious? His PC?"

"No, a laptop, but Robert told us he thought the kid had one, and his next-door neighbor confirmed that. There's a dusty place where it sat on the desk."

"So you figure the kid left in a kayak and took his computer? Seems kind of strange, don't you think?"

"A little, but then if he was going to blow the island and never come back, he would probably take it. That and his cell phone. It's how kids live these days, you know."

"Guess you're right. Anything else?"

"The other report is on the piece of moss we found in the victim's hair."

"Yeah?"

"It's not going to help us much. It's from the fir trees right there near the Kayak School. Probably picked it up walking to his car in the parking lot or some place like that. It's all over the place. Not much in the way of evidence."

"That's too bad," Paul said. "Anything in the woman's room?"

"Phillips didn't find anything there," Grant said. "It's clean. No blood. Now what?"

"Let's divide up the list. I talked to Carl Brown. How about you do

Ellison this afternoon, and I'll talk to Clare Porter."

"Right. Want to meet later and compare notes?"

"Yes. Couple of hours from now."

"You got it."

Paul left the interview room and went to tidy things on his desk. He picked up the phone to dial. "Ms. Porter?" he asked when there was an answer. "Is this a convenient time? I'd like to come over and talk with you."

Chapter Twenty-Five

WHILE MARIE TOOK A turn re-reading Aunt Joan's letters from Katherine, Riley busied herself with tasks that made her feel normal: she did the dishes, cleaned out the drawer with all the plastic containers in it and recycled all the ones without lids, and hauled Aunt Joan's boxes of clothes downstairs and stacked them near the front door. She tried to stay busy. In her heart, Riley knew Kit was not a killer, but she also knew that there were things that Kit wasn't telling her.

Marie came downstairs, got herself a Diet Pepsi from the fridge and sat at the kitchen table where Riley was writing in her journal.

"What are you writing?"

"I'm trying to get some thoughts down so I might be able to keep them from whirling and swirling in my mind," Riley said. "It's a calming strategy, but I'm not sure it's working."

"You're making a good effort, though. What do you say we get out of here, drive over to the school and check on Robert? I think he could use the support, and we could use the fresh air."

"That actually sounds good," Riley put the journal aside. "Should we call him first?"

"Let's just go. I'll drive."

They made the short drive, parked and knocked on the door of Robert's office.

"It's open," Robert called out.

"How are you doing, Robert?" Marie said as she and Riley entered the room. "We thought we'd check to see if you're okay today."

He looked weary and old. "I'm getting by, that's all."

Riley asked, "Have the police finished with the crime scene?"

"Yes, I think they have. It's been pretty quiet around here today."

"Any news about Russ?"

"Nothing. By now, that kid's probably long gone. He is a strong young man, and could paddle a good distance in that kayak. No telling where he headed."

Marie asked, "Do you think there's a chance that Kit is with him?"

Robert laughed. "No way."

Riley frowned. "What do you mean?"

"Russ hated Kit, too. He had it in for most of the staff. I cannot imagine him ever hooking up with Kit—or anyone in authority, for that matter—for anything. No, I don't think they're together."

"But do you think one or both of them is guilty?"

"That I don't know."

The ringing of the office phone interrupted their conversation. "Gulf Island Kayak and Adventure School," Robert said formally. "Yes, it is, Paul. All right, I guess. Thanks for asking."

Robert paused to listen, and Riley wished she could hear what Paul was saying.

"He is?" he was saying. "Yes, I'm sure we have those numbers here in the file. I'll find them and get right back to you."

Robert hung up the phone.

"Anything wrong?" Riley asked.

"I'm not sure," Robert said. "That was the constable. They still can't find the Brady kid, and his family hasn't heard from him. Paul wants me to see if there are any other emergency contacts in the kid's file. Russ certainly didn't speak very kindly about his parents. Poor kid."

"Wow. Missing," Riley said. "What is that all about, do you think? Does Paul think Russ tried to escape because he killed Michael?"

"I didn't ask that."

"No, of course you didn't. I'm sorry, Robert."

Marie said, "This seems like too much of a coincidence, don't you think?"

"I'll have to agree with that," Robert said, "but if Russ is the killer, then why did he do it? I know he was mad at Michael, but this is pretty extreme, even for a hothead like him."

"And what about Kit?" Riley said. "Where the hell is she? Does Paul consider her 'missing' also?"

Robert stared at Riley wordlessly, which made her realize she was going on about something that was pure conjecture. Riley decided to try to calm down.

"Sorry, Robert. Guess I got carried away."

"It's okay, I understand."

"All this is so upsetting. I feel like I'm in the middle of some bad movie. We'll let you get back to whatever you're doing. Marie and I'd like to check Kit's room, if you don't mind."

"Go right ahead. Don't think you'll find anything, though."

They made their way to Room Two.

"I'm not sure why you wanted to come in here," Marie said as she closed the door to Kit's dorm room. "Is there something you think you might find?"

"No, I don't think so. Paul's guys have been all over this room, and if anything was here, they would have already found it. I just wanted to sit here on this bed a minute, that's all."

"You're certainly entitled to that. What are you thinking we should do next?"

"With Russ missing, there goes one source of information about this whole mystifying series of events. Somehow, I can't fathom a sixteen-year-old boy stabbing Michael in the back. I have this feeling about it."

"So who do you think did?"

"I don't know," Riley said. "I'm praying to the Goddess that it wasn't Kit."

"No kidding."

"I did have one thought about a next step."

"I'm listening."

"I was thinking I might go back and talk to Dorothy, that woman who works in the visitor kiosk. She knew Aunt Joan and Katherine, the nanny, when they were all teenagers, you know. She goes way back on this island. Maybe Aunt Joan shared something with her about Katherine, and she hasn't felt she could tell me."

"What kind of information do you think she might have?"

Riley sighed. "I don't know. Something, anything. I have to feel as though I'm making some forward progress here." She felt exasperated. "And Michael said something to me the other night. Something I haven't told even you."

"And what exactly would that be?"

"He suspected Kit of having ulterior motives here, Marie. And he said that she has connections to the island that go way back. He thought she might even have a connection to my Aunt Joan somehow."

"How could that possibly be?"

"I don't know. I suppose there are lots of ways since Aunt Joan lived here for over sixty years. I'm thinking maybe Dorothy could fill in a gap or two."

"Of course. Let's go see her."

"I think I'd better go alone," Riley said. "It will seem more informal that way. I don't want her to think we're interrogating her. I want it to seem like a friendly visit."

"Makes sense. Guess you'd better drop me off at the Cliffhouse, then."

"Yeah. I will. Let's get out of here."

Riley closed the door to Kit's room and headed for the car with Marie. They noticed that Robert watched them drive away.

"Do you think Robert's on the up and up?" Marie asked Riley as she steered the car toward the main road.

"Robert? What do you mean? Of course, he is. Why would you even ask that?"

"I don't know. It's a gut feeling. I mean, I know he's sad and everything, and I know he and Michael were friends, but something about him bothers me. It's like he's too sad. Like maybe he's acting sad because he wants us to think he is."

"That's a disturbing thought. Are you trying to cheer me up here, or what?"

Marie laughed. "Sorry, Best Friend. I shouldn't give you anything more to worry about."

"You got that right."

"Never mind me, then. Guess I'm paranoid."

"That makes two of us," Riley said.

AT NEARLY EIGHT P.M., Paul was beginning to wonder why Adam Grant hadn't checked in when he saw him drive into the parking lot of the constable's office, get out of his car and head toward the front door. Paul greeted him in the outer office.

Paul said, "I was starting to think you'd been kidnapped, too."

"No. Had my ear talked off by Richard Ellison. That guy is a character."

"What do you mean?"

"He's an interesting guy, that's all. Upbeat, positive, and hell-bent on making Galiano a vacation destination. He's completely serious about that, Paul. Thinks his local bakery could become a real money maker."

"Any hits on whether he could be our guy?"

"Not much, other than his eagerness to see the Bodega project go through. But he's a businessman, so that makes sense."

"Where was he the night of the murder?"

"Says he took his camera and tripod and went to Shell Beach Thursday evening before sunset," Adam said. "There's a parking lot, and then a long path down to it, you know, just past Madrona Road. Said he parked, walked the half mile to the beach and took pictures. Came back after sunset."

"Anybody see him?"

"He said a family with two school-age kids wandered onto the beach while he was there. They told him they were staying at Driftwood Village. I called there and talked to the wife. She confirmed they saw him on the beach with his camera. Said they stayed until sunset, too, and that Richard was still there when they headed back up the trail. Has George established time of death?"

"I haven't heard from him yet."

"If it was during the evening, that will pretty much rule Richard out. He told me he left the beach about nine p.m. and went by the pub. Was there until nearly midnight, shooting pool with Mick Roland, the guy who runs Island Recycling. I checked that out, too. Roland confirmed it."

"Okay, but Shell Beach isn't far from the Kayak School. Isn't there a trail back in there?"

"I'm not sure, but I think they're at least a mile apart. No way could a guy walk that, kill Michael, and return in less than forty minutes. Besides, this family says they saw him, and that he was there until sunset."

"Maybe check back with them, see if he was in view the entire time, would you?"

"You sure I need to do that?"

"We need to be certain on every fact we gather," Paul said. "I'd appreciate it if you would call her back."

"Right. I will."

"What about motive for Ellison? Is there one? Did you get any sense of how he felt about the victim?"

"I asked him about the argument in the parking lot. He 'fessed up to it, said he was hot at Michael because of the way the meeting had gone. He said he didn't have anything against Michael, but felt frustrated that night because no one would listen to any of the business people there. Said it made him feel like a bad guy, and he's done nothing wrong."

"Yeah, that's kind of what Carl Brown said. Still, we'd better check Ellison out. Brown, too, in terms of any other connections they might have to the Bodega project or any of the players. Is Ellison married?"

"Divorced. Said his wife left him for a thirty-year-old musician."

Paul smiled. "Poor sucker."

"I got the name of his ex-wife. I'll call her tomorrow."

"Good. Sometimes ex-wives are excellent sources of information, especially if they're still mad. Maybe she has a Facebook page. Check that out, too. If we get the word from George about time of death, that will help narrow our list. The other question is, where are Russ Brady and Kit Powell? I think we should concentrate on that tomorrow. And until we prove otherwise, we've got to assume there could be a link."

"Did you get anything useful from Clare Porter?"

"I got a lot of indignation, mostly. She was pretty put out that I even wanted to interview her. She didn't give me much, and her alibi is tight. She took the noon ferry in to Vancouver and was at an evening business dinner from six p.m. to midnight. Says there are several witnesses. I called a couple, and they confirmed. She wasn't here when the murder happened."

"Guess that lets her out then," Adam said.

"Not totally. I asked one of her employees if I should talk to anyone else, and she hesitated long enough to let me know there was. After a bit of nudging, she shared with me that Clare and Michael have clashed before."

"Really? How?" Adam asked.

"Over another project, about ten years ago. Seems Clare was the new CEO of Vancouver View Homes then and made several trips to Galiano to gather information. While she was here, she moored a twenty-foot sailboat at Montague Harbor and lived on it during her visits. Michael was pretty rude to her then in a couple of public meetings."

"And you think that's motive for murder?"

"Wait. There's more. Seems one night while Clare was meeting with employees at the pub, her sailboat burned and sank. Arson. No one was ever arrested, but Clare believed in her heart that Michael did the deed. She's hated him ever since, this woman told me."

Adam said, "And now she's that much closer to pulling off the deal, and Michael was in her way again with this film project, right?"

"Exactly. I have one of the deputies reviewing the video he had already shot to see if there's anything incriminating about any of our cast of characters. He called and told me that in video number three there's a section of Clare ripping into Jonathan MacAlister at the community meeting."

"Michael got the meeting on video? How?"

"He had one of his students shoot it from the stage, behind the curtain just enough that it wasn't noticed. Guess they set up the camera and let it run. But with some good editing, Clare will totally look like a bitch."

"Wow. That's not good for business."

"Not at all."

"But it doesn't mean she killed him, does it?"

"Of course not," Paul said, "but we keep saying that about every suspect, don't we? Clare had motive and means, but not opportunity. But she's a rich woman, Adam. She could have hired someone to get it done."

"You think Michael's murder was a hit?"

"Anything's possible when there's millions of dollars at stake." He glanced at his watch. "Jesus, it's nearly nine o'clock. This has been a very long Saturday. Why don't we both get some rest and try again tomorrow?"

"Works for me. "I'm beat."

"See you here at seven, then?"

"You got it." Adam stood and headed for the door. "Try to sleep, Paul. We need you at your best. This is getting stranger and stranger."

"Yes, it is. I'll try."

Chapter Twenty-Six

RILEY AWOKE EARLY SUNDAY morning and felt ready to face the day. After coffee and quality time on the deck to collect her thoughts, she called Dorothy, who agreed to meet her at the Daystar Café.

Dorothy was already sitting at an outside picnic table when Riley arrived. Dorothy waved and smiled. "I'll get some coffee and join you," Riley said.

The sun was peeking over the tall madrona trees and spilled warmth on the table and its two occupants.

"Thanks for meeting me, Dorothy. I'm sure it's not exactly how you thought you'd spend your day off."

"It's no problem, Riley. It's a beautiful morning to sit out here and drink coffee. What's on your mind?"

Riley got right to the point. "You know how you told me I could always ask you questions about my Aunt Joan?"

"Of course."

"I'm very worried about my friend Kit. That's why I'm here."

"But I don't know Kit. I don't understand how you think I could help."

"I realize that. I'm so damn frustrated about all this that I'm trying everything possible to see if I can find out what happened to Kit, even looking back at old history. I think Kit's probably still here on the island."

"I see. So what can I do?"

"Did my Aunt Joan or Katherine Taylor have any other good friends here when they were kids?"

"I'm not sure. I know she and Katherine were very close, but let me think." Dorothy paused. "You know, funny as it may seem, Katherine was kind of friendly with Old Man MacAlister. He used to have her and Joan over for Sunday dinner."

"Jonathan MacAlister's father? You're kidding."

"He had only the one son, you know. I guess Jonathan would have been only five or six then. The mother died when he was very young. I think old man MacAlister always wished he'd had a daughter."

"Do you think Jonathan might remember anything about Katherine or my Aunt Joan?"

"It's possible, but he was pretty young. It's worth asking him about it, though. I think he could at least confirm my memory about them going over there for Sunday dinners."

"Okay, I guess I'll be having a conversation with him. Is there anyone else you can think of?"

"It's been a long time, Riley. Let me see. I guess the only other friend Katherine made here was an unlikely one."

"In what way?"

"Because she would only see her at school. As I recall, she never visited the girl's home. None of us did."

"What do you mean? Who?"

"I'm sure you're aware of the commune here on the island. Katherine befriended one of the commune kids." Dorothy gazed skyward as one does when she's trying to remember. "I think her name was April or June or some other month name. She was in Katherine's class, and I remember her coming to school with long, unwashed hair and wearing homemade clothes."

"Where did she live?"

"Her family was one of the originals, the creators of the commune. I think they call it Children of the Tide now. Maybe you've seen some of their dilapidated buses around the island? There must be two or three of them. In the old days, they welcomed in plenty of people with nowhere to go. Outsiders, oddballs, and the like. Some of the commune members broke off from the group and bought their own land in the sixties. They took the buses with them. I think a couple families still live in them."

"And the commune is still going?"

"Oh, yes. It's quite active, though I haven't driven out that way in years. It's tucked away on about five acres of treed land, beyond the wetlands below Bodega Ridge. They've got it all fenced and signs all over the place saying 'Private Property.'"

"Who lives there now?"

"I couldn't tell you. But sometimes you'll see some of them. They come in to buy groceries, or once in a while they take the ferry to Victoria for doctor visits and that sort of thing. I think there are several kids out there, too. Best way to spot them is to watch for tie-dyed clothing and dreadlocks."

"How would a person get in contact with someone there? Do they have a phone?"

Dorothy laughed. "Goodness no, I don't think so. Their whole emphasis is to get back to the land. Can you imagine that, here in the twenty-first century? They refuse indoor plumbing. It's a very basic life, and it seems to make them happy."

"What if I drove out there? Would they let me in? Who would I talk to?"

"I would have to say I don't know the answer to any of those questions, Riley. I'm only mentioning those people because of Katherine's friendship with that girl. Goodness, I don't even know if she's still alive, or if she's still here. Last I remember of her was at least five years ago. She and her kids and grandkids showed up for a community meeting. I didn't talk to her though. I don't think she remembered me."

"Wow. This is very interesting. I had no idea there was a commune here."

"That's the way they like it. Few off-islanders know."

"I have seen some people who, now that I think about it, probably do belong to the commune. I didn't pay them much attention."

"They keep a low profile."

"I see. I appreciate you taking the time here this morning," Riley said, realizing that perhaps she should wind up their visit. "Is there anything else you can think of that might help me out?"

Dorothy dumped cold coffee onto the ground and ate the last bite of her muffin. "I can't think of anything. But if I do, I'll call you."

"I'd appreciate that. You've given me a couple things to check out, and it's a start."

"Good luck with it. I hope you find Kit. She seems like a nice enough kid."

Riley smiled at that description. When you're over seventy, probably anyone under forty seemed like a kid.

"I'll let you know if I find out anything," Riley said.

"Be careful, won't you?"

"I will."

Riley stopped by the bakery and picked up a sandwich after she said her goodbyes to Dorothy. She saw Richard Ellison back in his office, bent over a calculator on his desk. He didn't seem to notice her.

"Thanks, Susan," Riley said as she pocketed her change and Susan handed her the wrapped sandwich. "Tell Richard I said hello."

"I will," Susan said. "He's been hunched over those spreadsheets since about seven. That's the joys of owning your own business, I guess."

"I don't envy him. It's hard work." She headed for the Subaru. As she passed Ellison's office window, he looked up.

"Morning, Riley," he said through the open window. "Nice day, huh?"

"Hi, Richard. It is that. Hope you don't have to spend all of it in your office."

"No way that could happen. Enjoy the sun."

"I will. Thanks." With each step toward her car, Riley thought about the task at hand. How was she going to convince the Children of the Tide that they could trust her, and find out if they know anything about where Kit was? And why in the world did they call themselves such a stupid-sounding name? *Reminds me of some kids' show on Saturday morning.*

Nothing to fear but fear itself, she thought. *God, where did that come from? Must be left over from U.S. History 201 at the University of Oregon. World War II? Funny how fragments of information stay in the brain and then pop out now and then. Too bad you can't control it and access them at the time you need them.*

After a short drive to the turnoff and perhaps five more minutes, Riley parked in front of a locked metal gate which seemed to be the entrance to the commune. The pavement ended at the gate, and beyond she saw a narrow gravel drive. A handmade barbed wire fence connected at either side of the gate, held by rough-hewn wooden posts. The wire was rusted. Running right below the top of the fence was another wire, metal and sleek and marked every three feet or so with a simple piece of torn white sheet. Electric fence, Riley thought. They clearly don't want anyone in there.

A simple combination padlock on the gate kept out unwanted visitors. Hanging at the center of the gate was a hand-lettered sign that said, "Children of the Tide enter here. All others, please turn around and go back to the world you know."

Riley thought about that direct order for a minute and decided it was a clever way of saying that the Children of the Tide had something others would want if they knew what it was.

She got out of the car and looked around. On either side of the gravel drive, the land was swampy and unnavigable. She wondered how the Children had succeeded in building on this marshland. Must be some part of it that is higher. She considered trying to walk the barbed wire fence line, but was certain she'd sink into the muck and very possibly never be heard from again. She decided against that.

Surveying the scene from her side of the gate, Riley noticed another sign, worn from the weather and barely discernible. Posted about twenty yards inside the gate, the sign was tacked on a leafy madrona tree. She couldn't read it at that distance and wondered why anyone would post it there. She went to the car to get her binoculars. Good thing I was a Girl Scout. Always prepared.

Riley used the glasses to read the sign and couldn't help smiling. "The Children of the Tide are vegetarian," it said, "but we make exceptions for trespassers." The double entendre amused Riley. At least these people have a sense of humor, which was more than she could say for a lot of people on Galiano.

Riley returned to her car and stowed the binoculars under the seat. She realized there wasn't even a place to turn around and figured the commune people had planned it that way to make it tough on unwanted visitors. She backed up the Subaru, hoping for a wide spot in the road. She found it about fifty yards back. As she pulled the car into the turnaround, she saw a beat-up, light blue Rambler station wagon, circa 1965, headed up the road toward the gate. Riley waited as the car sputtered by. She waved and managed a weak smile. The driver, a 20-something male with full beard and a dark blue knitted stocking cap pulled down to his ears, did not wave back. He smiled faintly and stared straight at her. Riley returned his gaze and waited for him to pass.

Pretending to be checking for something on the floor of the car, Riley bought herself a few seconds and waited for the Rambler to park at the locked gate before she sat back up. The man glanced back at her as he got out of his car, then headed for the padlock. Riley pulled out her trusty binoculars and hoped she could see something. Because she was pulled into the turnaround, the angle allowed for her to see his hands on the lock, even though the man's back was to her. She watched as he spun the dial, and she was puzzled that was all he did. No "right, left, right" like most padlocks; he gave it a spin, then pulled on the lock and it opened. The stupid thing wasn't locked! She figured the lock was only there to deter visitors who weren't enterprising enough to try to open it. He didn't touch the electric fence, though, so maybe that was the real thing. Riley didn't want to experiment to find out.

The man turned back toward his car, and Riley pulled forward and drove back down the road. She could hardly believe her good luck. She knew now that she could get into the commune and, indeed, would, as soon as it got dark. If Kit was there, or if anyone knew where she was, Riley would find out. She had to.

Chapter Twenty-Seven

"WHAT HAVE YOU DISCOVERED?" Marie asked the minute Riley walked into the Cliffhouse. "I know it's something because you've been gone too long."

"Dorothy was a big help. She steered me toward that commune over below Bodega. It's called Children of the Tide. You know, those people we see now and then in Guatemalan clothes, lots of kids?"

"Right. What about them?"

Riley repeated the conversation she'd had with Dorothy ending with, "They don't let just anyone in."

"They would have to let Constable Paul in."

"Of course, but at this point I don't think he knows its significance. I suppose they'll search it as a matter of course. They're searching the entire island. And Wallace as well. But if Kit is at the commune, those people could certainly help her hide out. Dorothy told me that for years they've been taking in people with nowhere else to go. I think they might help Kit if she asked them."

"I see what you mean. So what are you going to do?"

"I'm going out there tonight after dark, that's what. My gut tells me she's out there."

"And does your gut tell you also that she murdered Michael? Because if it does, I'm afraid I'm going to have to stop you from going out there."

"She didn't do it, Marie. She couldn't have."

"Right." Marie sounded unconvinced.

"And in the extremely unlikely occasion that she did, then there is a good reason for it, and I know she'll tell me what that is."

"I think you're going off the deep end. This woman has you all confused."

"I know."

"Okay, then off you go to see the Tide people. But guess what? I'm going with you."

"Absolutely not. Too dangerous."

"And who are you? Xena the Warrior Princess? You think you can just waltz in there and rescue the girl? Get real, Riley. There is a killer on this island, and he plays for real. I'm going. End of story."

"I hate it when you're right."

"I know."

WHEN PAUL GOT THE call from Adam Grant, he was about to chase down another lead about Kit's possible whereabouts. Grant reported that the kayak Russ had taken from the school was found partially submerged about forty yards offshore in the shallow water of Sunshine Cove. Fifteen minutes later, Paul was on the scene.

"Now we have another mystery," Adam said to Paul as he arrived at the beach.

"Tell me about it. Jesus. We're still chasing leads about Michael. Now this."

"You think it was an accident?"

"I'm hoping you'll help me figure that out," Paul said, glancing down the shoreline where a deputy was pulling the kayak out of the water. "Hey, John," he hollered. "Leave it right there, would you? I want to check it before you pull it any farther up on the sand."

The deputy did as he was directed and waited for Paul.

"What do you think he was doing up here?" Adam asked as they neared the water-logged kayak.

"Trying to get the hell off this island."

"Why? Do you think he killed Michael?"

"It's possible. We certainly haven't ruled him out. Let's load the kayak in the back of the pickup and take it to my office. Something about it bothers me."

"What do you mean?"

"The kid took off with most of his stuff. He pretty much cleaned out his room. But there's nothing in the kayak."

"Couldn't it have fallen out when the boat flipped? It could be on the bottom out there somewhere."

"I suppose. But usually kayakers attach important gear to the boat somehow. The kid took his computer with him when he left. I don't think he would have stuffed it in the bottom. Probably had it in a waterproof gear bag. It's not there. But, then, neither is he."

"Will you check the water?" Adam asked.

"We'll get a diver out here. I sure to hell hope we don't find a body."

"Do you consider this a crime scene?" Adam asked, scanning the beach. "We already talked to all three homeowners nearby. No one saw anything. They were all home last night, too."

"That's odd, isn't it? I wonder what route Russ could have taken to end up here. It seems as though he would have had to paddle right past their houses."

"Must have done so after dark,"

"Right," Paul said. "Must have. Anything else?"

"Not yet. We thought we'd check down at the marina and ask around there. Maybe someone in one of the sailboats saw the kid out on the open water."

"Good idea. Keep in contact via radio, would you? And if you find anything, call me right away."

"We will. Good luck here."

"Thanks," Paul said. "We'll need it."

Later that morning, Paul steered the aging patrol car up the narrow drive to Jonathan MacAlister's house and wondered how he was going to get him to talk. MacAlister knew something, that was for sure. Paul felt it in his bones.

He parked in front of the house and saw MacAlister pull the curtain aside to check out his visitor. Here goes nothing, Paul thought.

"Morning, Paul," Jonathan said as he opened his front door. He was dressed in a green flannel shirt and a pair of jeans. He had a coffee mug in his hand "Want some coffee?"

"That would be great. Thanks. I won't take much of your time. I have a couple questions, if you don't mind."

"Of course not," Jonathan said, ushering Paul into his kitchen. "What's on your mind?"

Paul took a seat at the kitchen table and admired the sweeping view over Georgia Strait. "Let me be clear about one thing, and that is that we don't consider you a suspect in Michael's death. I want you to know that up front."

Jonathan busied himself with the coffeepot and didn't turn around. "Right. Should I be relieved about that?"

"I suppose you should. But I've known you a long time, and I think maybe you know something. I think you may have information that would help us solve this murder. And I need you to talk to me about what you know. Now."

Turning to face the constable, Jonathan had a blank expression. "What could I possibly know? I had nothing to do with this murder. I liked Michael. You know that."

"I know. But what about the other incidents that have been happening? The ferry dock? The oil at Montague Harbor? Do you know anything about those?"

Jonathan paused and stared at the constable. "Of course not."

"I hate to say it, but I'm not sure I believe you. I've got one of my men checking to see if there's a connection between those incidents and the murder. If we find one and anything points to you, I'm afraid I would have to lock you up."

Neither man spoke for a few seconds. Jonathan set a mug of coffee in front of Paul and pulled out the chair across from him at the table.

"There's nothing to tell," he said. "I have no idea what you're talking about."

"I have to ask you where you were the night of the murder, then."

"Let's see. What night was that? Thursday?"

"Uh-huh."

"I was at Dorothy's for dinner. All evening. Call her."

"I will. And what about last week, the night the ferry hit the dock. Where were you that night?"

"Right here in my kitchen. I heard the commotion, grabbed my binoculars, and watched the whole thing. Awful scene. We're lucky someone didn't get killed."

"Indeed," Paul said. "We are."

Jonathan said nothing.

"By the way, do you have a cell phone?" Paul asked.

Jonathan hesitated. "No, I don't. Why?"

"I asked my detective to check phone records, and they're pretty easy to track with cellular phones. Just wondered."

Jonathan met his gaze and smiled. "I told you, Paul. There's nothing to find. But go ahead if you feel you must."

"Oh, I will, and I'll be in touch." He took a slug of coffee and set the brown earthenware mug back on the kitchen table. "Good coffee. Wish I could stay and enjoy it, but duty calls. Thanks for your time."

"You can come anytime to ask me anything. I've nothing to hide. Is there anything else?"

"Not right now. Goodbye, Jonathan."

JONATHAN WATCHED THE PATROL CAR go down the narrow drive. Good God, he thought. My phone records? This could be a real problem.

Jonathan pulled the curtains in the kitchen window and opened the bottom drawer of his desk. He pulled out the disposable cell phone and dialed the familiar number.

"Yeah?" the rough voice said.

"Trouble. You need to get to the phone records. Today."

"I told you that Miller said he'd take care of it," the thug said. "There are no records, you stupid bastard."

"You have to be sure. Call him, will you? And dump the phone. This is my last call from this one. You'll hear from me later today. I'll use the pay phone after dark down at Spanish Hills store."

"Good. And make sure you have the rest of the money wired to me by Wednesday."

"Yes. I will."

The line went dead. Jonathan pulled the sim card from the phone, then walked across the kitchen to the tool drawer, opened it and picked up a hammer. He stepped outside, set the card on the concrete slab and proceeded to smash the card to bits.

DETECTIVE ADAM GRANT DIALED the number for the Driftwood Village Resort. When Nancy answered, he identified himself and said, "I need to talk to that family from Seattle again. Are they there?"

"Just a minute, Detective. I'll go see if their car is parked beside cottage number six."

Adam waited, hearing her footsteps on the hardwood floors of her aging house as they faded away.

The clomping sounds got louder as they came back toward the phone.

Nancy said, "Yes, the car is there. Shall I go ask someone to come to the phone?"

"That won't be necessary, thanks. But what you could do for me is go over there and tell them I need a few more minutes of their time. And that I'm on my way. Be there in ten minutes."

"I'll certainly do that, Detective. Is something wrong?"

Adam knew that this was Nancy's way of trying to get the inside scoop before others on the island did. She was usually quite good at that.

"No, nothing's wrong," he said. "I need to ask a few more questions."

"I see. I'll go right over there."

"Thanks." Adam hung up and drove the patrol car the three miles to Driftwood Village

He got out of his vehicle at cottage number six and said hello to the two children playing badminton on the front lawn. "Your mom and dad inside?" he asked.

The boy, who looked to be about five, answered wide-eyed. "Uh-huh." He pointed to the cottage. "In there. Are my mommy and daddy gonna get arrested?"

Adam laughed. "No, they're not. Don't worry. I only want to talk to them."

The screen door opened and Lynn Evans smiled. "Hello, Detective Grant. Nancy told us you were coming. Please come in."

Adam entered the cottage and sat in the one empty chair.

Wes Evans was at the kitchen table reading this month's issue of *The Active Page*, the Galiano news-magazine. He smiled. "Morning, Detective. What more can we do for you?"

"Constable Paul asked me to come back and ask you a few more questions about Thursday night."

"Ask away then, but I think we told you everything we know." Wes gazed at his newspaper longingly.

Paul said, "Let's go over it again. I need to make sure you're positive about the timing. You arrived at the trailhead about seven-thirty, right?"

"Yes. That's right."

"And when you got there, you saw a red Jeep Cherokee in the parking lot?"

"Right."

"How long did it take you to walk down to the beach?"

Lynn jumped in and said, "With the two kids in tow it's quite an effort. I'd say eight or nine minutes."

"So you arrived about seven-forty, then?"

"Yes," she said.

"And was the bakery owner, Ellison, on the beach then?"

"He was. He had a camera and a tripod, and he was setting up on the rocks. Looked like he wanted to get some sunset shots. He waved, we waved back, and then my attention was distracted by the kids. But he was still there several minutes later."

"And about what time would that be?"

"I guess close to eight."

"Was he taking pictures?"

"I think so. The camera was all set up, but sunset wasn't for about another half an hour."

"Did you watch him the entire time?"

"Oh goodness, no," Lynn said. "I think about then Boomer found something to bark at."

"Boomer?"

"Our black lab. He was with us. Did I tell you that before?"

"You didn't."

"Oh, sorry. Guess I didn't think it mattered. Anyway, Boomer started barking at something up the beach, and the kids went off to see what it was."

"Did you follow them?"

"I did. Wes was sitting on a rock with his latest James Patterson novel, so I gave him a break and went after the kids and the dog."

"From where the dog was, was Ellison still in sight?"

"Let me see," Lynn said, thinking. "I guess not. Boomer had kind of gone around a rocky point. He found a dead fish, of course. To roll on. Why do dogs do that?"

Adam laughed. "Beats me."

Wes said, "I think he was there nearly all the time. I guess it's possible he might have been out of sight a few minutes, but he came right back. It was just after sunset. Like we told you."

Adam leafed through the pages of his college-ruled notebook. "Once the sun went down, you said Ellison came around the next rocky point and set up the tripod and camera again where he'd been the first time."

"Yeah. He did. I think he had gone up the beach a bit, around the point, to get a better view."

"And he took the camera?"

"Yes."

"So, let's see," Adam said. "He would have been gone doing sunset photographs for how long, do you think?"

Wes pondered a moment. "I'm not sure. Half an hour? Maybe less."

"That seems about right, Wes. We waved goodbye and headed back to the parking lot."

"After you waved, did you see him again? Did he come up to the parking lot when you did?"

"No, he didn't," Wes said. "The kids ran on ahead, and when we got to the lot the red Jeep was still there."

"I see," Adam said, making another note. "Anything else you can think of that we should know?"

"I can't imagine what it would be," Lynn said. "We've told you everything we can remember."

"And you've been most helpful. Thank you again for your time."

"No problem," Wes said. "Glad to help—although I'm not sure how much help we were."

"That remains to be seen. I'll be in touch if there's anything else we need."

"Okay. We'll be here until Thursday."

Adam said his goodbyes, returned to his car and headed out the gravel drive from cottage number six. Guess Paul is going to be kind of disappointed, he thought. Not much here to point toward Ellison doing anything he shouldn't. The guy likes to take pictures of sunsets. That's no crime, now is it?

Chapter Twenty-Eight

AT NEARLY NINE O'CLOCK, the last rays of the Galiano sun were filtering through the trees as Riley and Marie drove slowly toward the faux-locked gate that separated the Children of the Tide from everyone else on earth.

"This is almost as creepy as Bluff Park," Marie said as she squinted to make out shapes in the shadows. "Are you sure this is a good idea?"

"It's the only idea right now, Marie, and we have to go with it. What if Kit's there? Or at least has been there? The only way we're going to find out is to sneak in and snoop around."

"Sneak and snoop. That would be a good name for your detective agency one day. Maybe I'll be your first employee."

"And who do you think we'd sneak and snoop on in this new business?"

"Oh, I don't know. Petty criminals, deadbeat dads, stuff like that. Nothing dangerous, that's for sure. And certainly not murder suspects." Marie turned in her seat to make sure no one followed them on the narrow gravel road. On either side, the land disappeared into a marshy muck, and the few trees near the road grew at odd angles, as though the ground were not firm enough to support them. Marie resettled face forward. "Reminds me of that swamp tour we did in New Orleans, remember? On that humongous jet boat with those tourists from Vermont? That one woman kept screaming every time the guide pointed out an alligator. Why go on a tour, for God's sake, if you're going to spend the whole time screaming? Not very relaxing for her or the rest of us."

"Yeah, and we paid good money for it, too. I felt like whacking that woman with her purse and sending her overboard."

"Good thing you don't act on those impulses. I think you'll live longer because of that."

"And remember the Gray Line bus tour? When he stopped at the cemetery and we got all spooked out because the graves were above ground? Creepy."

"Especially when you kept poking your nose through all the holes in the crypts. God, Riley. Your curiosity gets to me sometimes."

"Like now?"

"Good point. We could be home watching that one channel that comes in on Aunt Joan's TV at the Cliffhouse. Maybe *Wheel of Fortune* is on. But, no. We're out here in some quasi-swamp searching for a possible murder suspect. Good thing we didn't bring Duffy. She'd be sure to bark and give away our secret location."

"She wasn't too happy about staying home, though. Hang on. It's gonna be an adventure!" Riley sped up toward the gate, which was now in view at the end of the gravel drive. "I wonder where I should park the Subaru. I'm not sure if we should get off to the side of the road or not."

"Duh," Marie said. "I can see the headline now: 'Tourists disappear when car sucked into muck.' That's the fifteen minutes of fame I don't need."

"Hey, what's that?" Riley asked, pointing to a wide area to the north of the road. "Does that go anywhere?"

Up and to the right was a two-rutted side road built on gravel. After about fifty yards it disappeared into a grove of oak and fir trees.

"We'll park in there," Riley said. "Out of sight. I doubt there'll be much traffic tonight, anyway."

"Who else would be stupid enough to be out here trying to find a murderer?"

"She's not a murderer! I told you." Riley steered the Subaru carefully down the rutted road. She parked it in the one wide spot. "Come on. Duty calls."

"How far do we have to walk?" Marie asked as they headed toward the gate.

"How should I know?"

"You mean you didn't ask Dorothy how far in the commune is? Geez, Riley. It could be miles!"

"Don't think so, Princess. The island is only seventeen miles long, remember? And we're way up at the north end, so that's in our favor."

Marie gave her a dirty look and kept moving.

The gate lock was as Riley hoped—unlocked, but positioned in such a way as to appear as though it were. She carefully moved the lock out of the way, swung the gate open, and closed it behind them. They moved forward in the growing darkness. Riley had brought a penlight, but didn't want to use it unless she had to.

Marie seemed especially happy to see lights ahead after they'd walked only about ten minutes. "There, up and to the right," she whispered. "Lights."

"Come on. No sounds now, right, Tonto?"

"Right."

They crept toward the lights, which they could now see came from a circle of five platform tents, all facing inward. A campfire burned near the center, and people were gathered around it. Darting in and out in the firelight were four children who seemed oblivious to the adults. They were playing tag, laughing and hollering after each other. One tripped over a tree root, let out a wail, and a woman got up off her campstool to assess his injuries.

"Over here," Riley said, beckoning Marie toward a fir on the perimeter of the circled tents. "We can watch from here."

Crouching in the darkness, they watched and listened.

"You mean you didn't even call him yet?" a woman's voice said.

Riley couldn't make out any faces. The figures were silhouettes in the firelight.

"And say what?" came a man's voice in response.

"That we think we saw him," she said.

"We can't say that," the man said. "We don't even know for sure it was him."

Marie leaned in close and whispered in Riley's ear. "Who do you think they're talking about?"

"I have no idea," Riley said softly.

The woman got up from the fire circle and headed toward the tent nearest where Riley and Marie crouched. They both froze, afraid any movement might attract her attention.

The voice was louder because she must be facing them.

"We're going to have to report it, even though she doesn't want us to," the woman said. "I don't care what Grandmother says. This is serious, Steve. We're talking about murder here."

Riley and Marie both stifled their audible reactions and looked at each other knowingly.

"You don't know that," another man said. His voice was deeper, gruffer than the first man's.

"She said he could have done it, he was mad enough," the woman said. "Grandmother says we should believe her, but she's basing that on nothing, really. She doesn't know Kit."

At the mention of Kit's name, Riley's mouth dropped open and Marie put her hand over it.

The one named Steve said, "I know that, but the other thing is that she could be making it all up. And if that's the case, then we'll be handing Constable Paul a big fat nothing."

As she reentered the fire area, the woman said, "The kayak was on the beach, and we could describe it and say what he was wearing. I'm telling you, it was Russ. He was certainly trying to get away from something."

"Or someone," Steve said. "What if she's lying?"

"Have to take that chance," the woman said.

"Where did she go?" the other man asked.

"Same place," she said. "I told her we'd give her one more day. It's too risky, guys. We can't take the chance. It's bad enough, what the people here think of us. We can't keep her here."

"I know," Steve said, "but what if Paul doesn't find anything in one more day?"

"Then we come forward and she's on her own," the woman said. "We've done our part."

"Doesn't seem quite right," the man said, getting up to put another chunk of wood on the fire.

"That's life." The woman disappeared into the tent.

Riley glanced at Marie, barely visible in the darkness. She nodded toward the road they'd come on and silently backed away from their tree hiding place. Marie followed. When she felt they were out of earshot, Riley whispered, "She's here somewhere. I told you!"

"Yes, and they don't know whether to believe her, either."

"At least we know she's alive."

"But why is she hiding?"

"Because Paul thinks she killed Michael, of course. What would you do?"

"If I were innocent, I'd turn myself in."

"Right. Well, maybe you're a better person."

"Maybe."

They stayed in the shadows of the trees near the tent circle and made their way carefully toward the gravel road and back to the gate. Neither spoke.

Safely back to the car, Riley let out a sigh as she got in the driver's seat. "Oh, my God. This sleuthing is hard work. Aren't you tired?"

"Way," Marie said. "I can't believe you dragged me out here to spy on some aging hippies."

"You wanted to come, remember?"

"Oh, yeah. I did. But now I don't."

"Too late."

"Let's go home."

"Good idea."

Back at the Cliffhouse, Riley hardly had any time to think about her next move because Duffy greeted her in her usual, rambunctious way. Riley took her outside for her nightly walk and then headed for bed. Marie was already snoring downstairs. Once Riley's head hit the pillow she was asleep in three minutes.

In her dream, Riley was swinging on a smooth, thick vine toward a tent hidden deep in the jungle. Kit was inside, waving a lavender hankie and calling her name. She felt the wind on her face as she clung to the vine and flew through the hot air toward her love.

Thunk. The noise woke Riley up. Did she hit a tree, or what? Where was she? The night was pitch black around her. In their haste to get to bed, they'd forgotten to leave the bathroom light on.

Again, a soft thunk, coming from downstairs. Riley was wide awake now and realized she was trembling. Duffy sat up on the foot of the bed, ears alert. She started to make her low, menacing growl.

Someone was in the house. Riley strained to hear any other noises. Marie was still snoring, so it wasn't her moving around. She squinted at her digital clock: 3:15 a.m. She didn't think she'd been asleep that long. Quick. Think of a way to protect ourselves. Pepper spray.

Damn! She'd left her pepper spray in her daypack, which she tossed at the bottom of the stairs when they'd come back from the commune. Lot of good it does me there, she thought.

Her mind raced. What to do? If she got out of the bed, the floor would squeak and the intruder would know she was awake, not to mention the fact that Duffy was going to break into a full-throttle bark at any moment.

But she couldn't lie there defenseless. She forced herself to see in her mind what potential weapons were around her there in the bedroom. A book? No, they were all paperbacks. Candle? That's it. The candle holder, like in Clue. She had a silver one by the bed. It would have to do. She groped for it in the dark. Her hand felt the cool metal. She picked it up, took out the tapered candle and clutched the holder in her right hand. She stepped out of bed onto the cool floor. No squeaks yet.

Riley stood by the bed and listened. No sounds. Duffy was looking at her quizzically, as she did when she did something out of the ordinary. But she wasn't barking. "Good girl," Riley whispered. "It's okay. No bark."

Either the intruder was waiting, listening, too, or he was gone. Riley hoped with all her life it was the latter.

Hearing nothing, she took a small step toward the staircase. Duffy started growling because she knew Riley was worried and on the move. But she didn't bark.

The staircase was narrow and steep and every stair creaked, so Riley had no intention of going down there; she only wanted to listen. As she got closer, she heard a rustling sound coming from downstairs. Someone was at the desk. She heard shuffling paper. What could he want? Or she? Was it a burglar? The one phone was downstairs. Damn. That's stupid. Why didn't I bring the cell up to bed with me? Too bad I didn't think of that before.

Had they locked the door? Riley couldn't remember. Oh, great. Make it easy for him to steal everything they owned.

Silently, she strained to listen. Footsteps on the kitchen floor, then the soft click of the door handle turning. He was leaving.

Duffy heard the door close and evidently took that as her cue to bark.

Riley stood motionless. "It's okay, Duffy. He's gone. Good girl." She stopped barking and looked at her, expecting her next instructions.

Riley listened. Nothing. Then, from outside and up the hill near where the Subaru was parked, an engine started up. The unmistakable crunch of tires on gravel told her their intruder was leaving.

God, who would have the nerve to come on in while they were asleep?

Riley heard Marie's bedroom door open as she descended the narrow staircase.

"What's Duffy barking at?" a sleepy Marie asked as she and Riley both came into the living room. "That dog woke me up!"

Riley didn't want to scare her, but Marie needed to know. "I heard something. Downstairs. Someone was in the house."

"Jesus, Mary and Joseph! Are you trying to scare the crap out of me?"

"Possibly, but I can't worry about that now. Someone was in the house. We have to call the police."

"How do you know he's gone?" Marie whispered.

"I heard him leave and then a car started up."

"What did he want?"

"How should I know?"

"What will we do?"

"Why do you ask so many questions?"

Riley knew she sounded cranky and exasperated but she was glad that for once Marie kept quiet.

"Come on," Riley said. "We'll investigate the house together."

They did. Not much was different, except the desk area. The computer was on, the soothing underwater screensaver lighting up the room.

"Did we leave the computer on?" Marie asked, walking toward it gingerly as though it might self-combust.

"I'm sure we did not. And look at this. All the paper files are messed up. Aunt Joan's stuff has been gone through."

"What was he trying to find?"

"I don't know," Riley said.

They checked out the rest of the house. Nothing was missing, and nothing else seemed out of place.

"You have to call Paul."

"At three in the morning?!"

"Don't you think he's used to that, Riley? It's a crime, for heaven's sake. We could have been injured, or worse."

"You think it's the killer who was here? In the Cliffhouse? Jesus, Marie, you are totally freaking me out!"

"Good. Call Paul."

Riley did. He answered after four rings.

"Paul, I'm sorry to wake you but someone broke into the Cliffhouse and rummaged around down here. No, we're okay. Just a bit scared, that's all. Yeah. I heard him drive off."

She saw Marie listening to her listen.

"No, maybe it's not necessary. We'll be all right. But do you think you could come at first light?"

Marie was gesturing wildly.

"What!" Riley put her hand over the mouthpiece. "What do you want?"

"Tell him we think it might have been the murderer. Maybe he should come now."

"I'm not telling him that. We don't know," Riley whispered. "He'll come at dawn."

Marie made a harrumph noise and shuffled away in her pink slippers.

"What? Oh, yes, Paul. I'm here. I was talking to Marie. No, dawn will be fine. We'll try to go back to sleep."

"Fat chance of that," Marie muttered as she headed across the living room to her bedroom.

"Thanks, Paul. We appreciate it. See you then."

She hung up, locked the front door and pushed a kitchen chair in front of it, with the chair leaning in under the doorknob. She'd learned that trick watching *Law and Order.*

"Marie? Are you okay?"

She opened the bedroom door. Marie wasn't there. Riley heard some movement above, in her room. She grabbed her pack and her cell phone, climbed the narrow stairs and saw Marie in her bed, with the covers pulled over her face.

"What are you doing in my bed?"

"Like you don't know. You think I'm going to sleep with a murderer in our house? I don't think so."

"Marie, there's no one in our house but us. And we don't know if the intruder was a murderer."

"I'm not taking any chances. If he comes back, he'll have to kill you first and by then I'll be outta here."

"That's comforting. Just what I want to hear from my best friend."

"Survival of the fittest. At least I'll hear him if I'm in here with you and it will buy me some time."

Riley crawled in beside her and pulled the covers over her head, too. "We are pathetic," she said. And then she lay there awake, listening to Marie snore. Would dawn ever come?

RILEY WAS DRAGGED FROM a good dream by the sound of someone knocking. This time in the dream, she had already landed successfully right near the tropical tree where Kit sat waiting for her. Then the knocking was louder, and the dream was gone.

"Get up, Riley," Marie had been awake for a while and heard a car drive up. "It must be Paul."

Duffy started barking in her usual, ferocious way.

The clock read 6:42.

"He's awfully early, isn't he?" Riley whined.

"You asked him to come, remember?"

"Oh, yeah."

Riley went down the steep stairs to let Paul in, Duffy right behind her. As soon as Riley opened the door, Duffy was quiet. She liked Paul.

"I was beginning to think you'd left," Paul said. "Had me worried there for a minute."

"Or maybe you thought he got us both, and that would look bad for you, wouldn't it?"

Paul hesitated, then smiled when he realized she was joking. "Right. Funny. Shall I get started?"

"Please do. Is there anything we can do to help?"

"I don't think so. Just give me time to check around here and outside."

"I'll put on some coffee. I'll let you know when it's ready."

Paul proceeded to move carefully through the kitchen and study area. Then he headed outside, and Riley sat in the kitchen window and gazed out at the channel.

He was back in less than five minutes.

"Anything interesting out there?" she asked as she handed him a mug of steaming black coffee.

"Thanks. Yes, as a matter of fact there is. But I need to know first if you or Marie have been walking around on the back side of the house recently."

"Back? As in where the house meets the rocks? No, we haven't. There's no reason to go back there. Why?"

"Found some footprints," Paul paused.

Riley waited.

"Yes?" she said, finally. "Is there more?"

"Either of you have big feet? A size ten, maybe?"

"Let's see. I know Marie has pretty small feet. I'm always teasing her about it. Size six, I think. And mine are about eight, women's sizes, of course."

"This is definitely bigger. The prints are along the back, and then lead right up to the kitchen door. Last night was damp, and the footprints are still fresh."

"You think this is related to the murder?"

"I don't know. We can't rule that out, though."

"You think that the murderer broke in here? Why?"

"I was hoping you could tell me. By the way, what size shoe does Kit wear?"

"I have no idea, Paul. I hardly know her. I didn't notice the size of her feet."

"Since we have no idea who this was, I think it's best if you and Marie go somewhere else for a couple days. I can't guarantee your safety here."

"You're kidding, right?"

"I'm dead serious, if you'll pardon the pun."

"Marie!" Riley yelled up the stairs. "I think you'd better come down here." They had some confessing to do about their activities the previous night.

Chapter Twenty-Nine

AS SOON AS HE got back to his car, Paul dialed Adam Grant's cell phone number to tell him to report in right away. Grant answered on the first ring and said he'd be at the office in ten minutes.

"What's going on, Paul?" Adam asked as he came into the front door and headed directly for the coffee maker.

"Had a break-in out at the Cliffhouse," Paul said.

"The gals are all right, aren't they?"

"Yup."

"Any idea who it was?"

"I don't know, but it's too much of a coincidence to think it's not related to our murder. I told those two girls they need to get out of there. Something's up, that's for sure. We need to keep digging."

"Where do you want me to start?"

"I think you'd better go with Deputy Clark out to the commune and see what those people know. Riley told me she thinks they may be harboring Kit."

"Why would they do that?"

"Beats me, but Riley and Marie went snooping around there last night and overheard a conversation. They think Kit may be there, or was there, anyway. Track down that blonde woman, the one with the three young kids. Riley said she's the one who was doing the talking last night."

"Got it. And what about Carl Brown? Did you talk to him again last night?"

"I did. He swears he told us everything and that he was home Thursday night by eight. No way to confirm that, so we're at a dead end there, and frankly I don't want to take Brown off our list. Something about him isn't quite right. I can't put my finger on it, but I'm hesitant to say he's not our man. Not yet. How about your interview with the beach people? The ones who saw Ellison?"

Grant poured his coffee. "Not much new, except for one thing. I think there's a chance they didn't see Ellison the entire time. He could have ducked out of sight around the bend there. There's some time missing."

"What do you mean?"

"They were all distracted because their dog got into something. Maybe Ellison disappeared for a while."

"For long enough to hike to the Kayak School and stab Michael and hike back?"

"I don't know. Doesn't seem likely, does it? That leaves us back with our short list of suspects: Russ, Jonathan and Kit."

"Don't forget Brown."

"Right—and then assuming there aren't others we haven't thought to put on the list."

"God, that's a depressing thought," Grant said.

"No kidding."

"Now what?"

"You go to the commune. I'm going to pay a quick visit to Clare, and then I'll call George to see if he's got anything on the body yet. Something's got to break in our favor soon, don't you think?"

"Hope so. Maybe those Tide people can shed some light where we need it."

"Remember, Adam, if you find Kit, be careful. We have to assume she's armed and dangerous."

Grant patted the gun he always kept in a holster on his right hip. "Got it covered, Chief."

"Call me if you get anything."

"I will. Good luck with Clare."

"I'll need it."

Grant headed for his unmarked patrol car and Paul dialed Clare's number, which he now knew by heart. "Good morning, Clare," he said in a most pleasant voice. "Could I have a few minutes of your time?"

Chapter Thirty

"HEY, MARIE," RILEY YELLED down the stairs. "Do you have your stuff packed? We need to get going."

Riley picked up her overnight bag and poured another cup of coffee, to go. Marie appeared in the kitchen, her pillow in one hand and a suitcase in the other.

"What the heck are you bringing?" Riley asked. "We're only going to Dorothy's for a couple days."

"I know, but I may as well be comfortable. You know I always take my pillow."

Riley smiled at her friend, remembering the trip to Europe when they were nineteen, the time Marie dragged her pillow onto every train in Italy, Germany and Switzerland. Riley had been embarrassed, but Marie didn't care then and she didn't care now.

"Come on," Riley said. "I packed some dry food for Duffy—not that she'll eat it—and her cozy bed. She may as well be comfortable, too."

Duffy stood near the door, anticipating another fun adventure.

They got in the car and headed for Dorothy's house, which was up from the ferry dock. "I think I'll stop and check the mail on the way," Riley said. "We haven't picked it up in a couple days, and there may be letters there in regard to the settlement of Aunt Joan's estate. The attorney was supposed to send me something here."

"I thought you got that already."

"No, that was something else that came last week. A list of Aunt Joan's assets."

"Okay. Let's stop, then. I'm sure Dorothy will be glad for more free time."

Riley pulled into the parking lot in front of the Daystar Market and post office. Marie opted to wait in the car.

"Morning," Riley said to the postmistress as she entered. "I wanted to check Aunt Joan's mail this morning."

This time, the woman turned to face Riley and even seemed to manage a weak smile. "That's good, because I think there's a letter there. Came in last night through the local mail."

"Really? For Aunt Joan?"

"No. For you."

Riley gave her a puzzled look and went to unlock the box. She loved those tiny, old-fashioned doors on the post office boxes. They reminded her of her childhood, walking with her grandpa to the post office. She had always been enchanted with those doors, as though she could go through one into some magical land of elves who came and went by them.

She had to boost herself out of that fantasy to tend to the task at hand. Peeking through the glass window in P.O. Box 77, she saw an envelope there addressed to her. No return address, though. Riley opened the door, extracted the letter, and went back out to the car.

"Something for Aunt Joan?" Marie asked when she saw the letter.

"No, for me."

"Do you recognize the writing?"

"No. I have no idea whose it is. I'll open it at Dorothy's."

Marie shrugged and drove up the hill to Dorothy's house. With Dorothy's two German shepherds in the fenced yard and an alarm system monitored by a company in Vancouver, the house was the safest one Paul had thought of for the women's temporary lodging. They could either stay there or in the jail on Salt Spring, and Riley hadn't been too thrilled with that idea.

As Marie pulled into the parking area to the side of the house, Dorothy came to the front door to greet them. Over the barking of the two dogs, she said, "Welcome to Dorothy's Waterview Bed and Breakfast. Do you have a reservation?"

"Duffy does," Riley said, grinning. She hoped that Dorothy's giant dogs wouldn't go gonzo and scare the hell out of Duffy.

Riley and Marie followed Dorothy inside, settled in to a room containing twin beds, and then went out to sit on the deck. Duffy plodded after them.

"Guess we'd better check out this letter," Riley said, settling into a deck chair. She tore open the envelope. Her heart tugged and her eyes filled up when she saw the signature at the bottom and realized that the note had been sent by Michael. "Oh, God," she said aloud.

She read out loud. "I'm sending this to you, Riley, so that there will be one other person who knows about my discovery. I am very concerned about Kit, and although I know you have begun a friendship with her, I think you should have this information. Even though she seems to be trustworthy, I've discovered something on Wallace Island that leads me to believe Kit may be here with ulterior motives."

Riley stared at the letter and braced herself for whatever came next.

Michael's note continued. "I have some information about Kit's past that's troubling. I don't want to involve you yet, and for that reason I can't say what it is I've found. Just know that I'm trying to get to the bottom of this, and until I do, I want you to be wary of Kit. She may not be who she says she is. I'm sorry, Riley, to have to tell you this. Please be careful.

"Of course, it's possible Kit has already confided in you and told you about her family's past here. There's no way for me to know if she has.

"As soon as I find out more, I will tell you. I thought I should send this along to alert you that something's up with Kit.

"Best Wishes, Michael."

Riley got up from her chair and went straight to Dorothy's phone to dial Constable Paul. She got the voice mail. "Paul, call me here at Dorothy's right away. I got a very strange letter from Michael."

Only twenty minutes later the constable pulled up in the driveway. After looking at the letter, Paul said, "I can't decide what to think about this. Do you believe this is on the up and up?"

"I've got no clue." Riley hadn't considered that the letter might be a fraud—or that it was possible someone else had sent it. She used Dorothy's printer to make a copy and gave Paul the original.

"What now, Constable?" she asked.

"Until we figure out what Michael discovered about Kit, we aren't much further along in this investigation, but we have to zero in on finding Kit. When we do, either we'll have the killer, or we'll have information that will help us find the killer. I think she's a key element here, Riley."

"Yeah. I think you're right." She felt dispirited and vaguely sick about the whole situation. Had she really misjudged Kit so completely?

"I'll call you here if anything comes up," Paul said. "And for God's sake, don't go anywhere or do any more snooping around. I realize you're trying to help, but until we get this figured out, I have to be sure you and Marie are safe. It's possible that the killer thinks you know something important—did you ever think of that?"

"How could that be?"

"It's a small island. Things are overheard. Or read on a computer. Or whispered over a cup of coffee at the deli. Somebody here knows something about the murder, and they could also think that you have key information if you and Michael were seen talking at the community meeting. Also, someone may have noticed you got chummy with Kit. I'm going to assign a deputy to drive up here once an hour."

When Riley began to protest, he silenced her by raising his hand. "Don't want to hear it. You and Marie need protection and even though Dorothy's place is better than the Cliffhouse, you are still vulnerable. Once an hour. Stay put, okay?"

"We will, Paul. Thanks for your concern."

"It's my job, you know." Then he smiled. "Besides, I like you guys."

Riley watched Paul drive away and turned to Marie and Dorothy, who were sitting in the kitchen drinking tea. "Well, what do you say, companions? Anyone up for a game of Scrabble?"

"I'll get the board," Dorothy said. "Sounds like a lovely way to spend an anxious afternoon."

PAUL'S CELL PHONE RANG as he headed downhill toward the ferry landing.

"Constable Paul here." The call was from his deputy, Dan Clark, the one he'd put on watching Jonathan MacAlister.

"There's something going on," Clark said. "I think you'd better get over here."

"What's up"

"You know how you told me to park above and keep a watch on MacAlister's house?"

"Yes."

"Not much happened at first. No one in or out. But then about five minutes ago he came out in the back yard with a bunch of crumpled up newspaper. Started a fire in his burn barrel."

"I'm listening."

"He dropped in a bunch of garbage first, then a particularly interesting item."

"Which was?"

"His cell phone. The guy incinerated it."

"I'll be right there. Go to the house, knock on the door and keep him occupied. Won't take me more than two minutes."

Chapter Thirty-One

ROBERT BURROWS TURNED THE lock on the Kayak School office door and pocketed his keys. He made his way down the front steps and around the side of the building to Michael's workroom. I guess I'll have to call it something else now, he thought. It surely isn't Michael's space anymore.

The constable had ordered the crime scene tape taken down late the day before and told Robert he could resume normal activities at the school. Ha. Normal. That was a laugh. Nothing was normal anymore, least of all the use of that terrible place where Michael had died.

Robert went in, stood by Michael's desk and glanced around the room. Things had been put back in place, but the air smelled of chemicals and death. He could hardly stand to be in there. He wanted to check the desk drawers again, even though the police had been through them. He needed to see for himself. Pulling out the bottom drawer, Robert leafed through some old notebooks Michael had stashed there. They were filled with notes about the Kayak School's programs and participants. Robert leafed through the most recent one and found nothing out of the ordinary. He pulled another, dated 2015, and read some of Michael's notes about that summer's activities. Near the back, an underlined passage caught his eye. "Check on Russ B," it said. "Vancouver juvenile court records. Sentence commuted?"

Robert stared at the words. Had Russ been arrested? Did Michael have that information when he arranged for him to be here this summer? Michael was forever advocating for kids in trouble, but this time the consequences had been deadly. Maybe he had pushed Russ too hard and the kid had snapped.

Robert took the notebook with him, turned off the lights and locked the door to the workroom. He never wanted to see it again.

"TIME'S UP, JONATHAN," PAUL said as he sat across from Jonathan at his kitchen table. "Tell me what you know. Now. This is serious stuff. We know you destroyed the cell phone. We have it on video from the surveillance Deputy Clark did from up above your house."

Dan Clark leaned against the wall behind Jonathan, arms folded over his chest.

Paul said, "We also have a report that you did a money-drop recently at a location here on the island. We picked up your pal from Vancouver about half an hour ago when he tried to retrieve it."

Jonathan's face remained impassive.

"Either you tell me now what you know, or you'll be joining him for a boat ride to the lockup on Salt Spring."

Jonathan stared at Paul and said nothing.

"Okay, have it your way," Paul said. "Dan, get your cuffs out, would you?"

"Wait," Jonathan said. "That won't be necessary."

"I'm listening," Paul said.

"I don't know anything about why Michael was killed. You have to believe me."

"What about the rest? The ferry? The oil slick? And the chemicals we found in your hit man's car."

"Hit man? He's not a hit man. He's a two-bit thug."

"Whatever. He had toxic chemicals and an institutional-sized sprayer in his car, along with a local island map with four or five areas circled. We checked them out. They all have high concentrations of blackberries. We figure he was going to spray them, make people sick. Is that what you figure?"

Jonathan let out a breath and sagged as if defeated. "Yes, I suppose that's what he was going to do."

"Why are you messed up in this? Are you trying to create a diversion, get people's attention away from the murders? Hoping against hope you won't be found out? It's a pretty clever way to spread our resources thin. I don't have enough help as it is."

"No. That's not it," Jonathan said simply. "But there's no reason for me to tell you anything because all you have is that video and the word of a two-bit drug addict."

"You can think that if you wish. But the truth is, we have physical evidence to connect you to him and to these incidents." Paul paused, waiting to see if Jonathan would take the bait. He had no physical evidence, but he had a gut feeling Jonathan would break down and talk. He still couldn't figure out what these incidents had to do with the murder, but he was sure Jonathan knew.

"I don't believe you," Jonathan said.

"Suit yourself. You'll believe me at your trial. It's a lot to give up. Are you protecting someone? Is that it? Michael's killer?"

"If I knew who killed Michael I'd certainly be telling you. Of course I'm not protecting anyone. I'm only protecting what I love the most, which is this island. You think that's a crime?"

Bingo! Paul thought. Now we're getting somewhere. At times, Jonathan didn't seem quite stable, quite rational. He had a feeling this was another of those times.

"I've lived here all my life," Jonathan said, much in the same way he had at the community meeting. "All we hear around here lately is about development, expansion, the brilliant future of Galiano. More homes. More ferries. And for what? So a bunch of mainlanders can call Galiano their weekend retreat? At our expense? Do you think the bald eagles will still soar overhead if their nests start getting disturbed by overzealous contractors?"

Jonathan paused. He seemed to realize that he was pontificating, but couldn't quite stop himself. "They're the criminals, not me," he went on. "I'm only trying to convince people they don't want to come to Galiano. Who wants to sail in an oil slick? Ride on a ferry that's unsafe? I figured the bad publicity would keep people away and might affect the decision about the ridge. That's all. I never meant to hurt anyone."

"But people on the ferry were hurt. They could have been killed."

"I know. I'm so sorry about that. It isn't how he told me it would happen."

"He?"

"Jacobson, the mean bastard. He told me no one would get hurt."

"But you paid him, didn't you? You paid him to alter the ferry's braking mechanism and to dump the oil in Montague Harbor." Paul waited for an answer which was several seconds in coming.

"Yes. I did."

"You paid him to kill Michael. And now with Russ missing, maybe you paid to have him killed, too. Did you think that was a good diversion? I guess people aren't going to be too excited about vacationing on an island where there's a double homicide. Good strategy on your part. Problem is, you and Jacobson got caught."

"My God, Paul. Do you think I would do that? Kill Michael? Of course I didn't pay to have him killed."

"But the timing is too coincidental. I think you know why Michael had to die. Tell us why."

"I swear. I don't know anything about that."

"I think you know I have to lock you up on charges related to the ferry and harbor incidents. You need to come with me now."

Jonathan lowered his head, closed his eyes and sat silently for several seconds. Then he gazed out the window toward the Georgia Strait, over the water that sparkled in the morning sun. "I know," he said. "I understand."

"Dan," Paul said. "Help Mr. MacAlister to the patrol car, would you?"

"Should I cuff him?" Dan asked.

"No. I don't think so." To Jonathan, he said, "We're taking you in on charges of menacing and suspicion of murder. You need to get a lawyer."

"Don't know one."

"Then the province will provide you one."

"Let's go, MacAlister," Dan said as he put his hand under Jonathan's right elbow. "You're under arrest."

Paul watched the two men make their way to the patrol car. Dan opened the back door and Jonathan got in. When the car pulled out, Jonathan had his head down and his eyes closed.

Poor bastard, Paul thought. I hope he didn't pay to have Michael and Russ killed because if he did, life as he knows it is over.

NEWS ABOUT JONATHAN'S ARREST spread quickly. Alice, from the *Island Times*, phoned Dorothy to let her know her friend Jonathan was facing serious charges, and Dorothy shared the information. She and Riley and Marie spent much of the afternoon speculating about Jonathan's arrest and what it meant in relationship to Kit. Riley was relieved, and Dorothy was perplexed.

"Jonathan doesn't seem like the type," Dorothy said. "I know he's eccentric, but I've always cared about him and I can't believe he would be involved in a murder."

Marie agreed that the arrest was a mistake. "I mean, come on. Jonathan? A killer? You've got to be kidding me. He wouldn't hurt a slug if it showed up on his kitchen floor. The man's a pacifist."

Riley shook her head slowly. "You think a pacifist would hire someone to spray the wild blackberries so we all get sick? He wasn't as innocent as you think, Marie. I think he could have done it."

"But what's the motive? Why? You and I have both read enough mystery novels to know that the man needed a motive."

"He wants to scare people away from Galiano," Riley said. "Jonathan is trying to protect what he loves best, this island."

"That may be true," Dorothy said. "But I've known Jonathan a long time. He loves Galiano, but as odd as he seems, he has a good heart. He didn't do this."

"I hope you're right," Riley said. "For his sake."

Chapter Thirty-Two

DETECTIVE ADAM GRANT AND Deputy Dan Clark stood at the metal gate at the entrance to the Tide People's land.

"Riley said the gate isn't locked," Adam said. "We can go on through."

He nudged the patrol car within a few feet, and Dan got out to swing the gate open.

Dan muttered, "Why the hell do they have a lockable gate and then keep it unlocked? I don't understand hippies."

"Something wrong?" Adam asked as Dan slid into the passenger seat. "This assignment make you uncomfortable?"

"No. Sorry. I've never been out here and I'm not sure what to expect."

"Whatever," Adam said. "Let's get ourselves mentally prepared for these Tide People."

Adam drove the patrol car into the commune area and parked behind the first tent. An old school bus, faded yellow, sat there. "Vancouver Public" was barely visible along the side of the bus. Someone had painted over the word "Schools."

"You think they live in that thing?" Dan said. "Strange."

"Maybe they did at one time, but it looks empty." He was beginning to wonder about the wisdom of bringing Dan along on this trip.

They walked toward the center of the tents and were greeted by a man with his hair pulled back into a ponytail. He wore faded jeans and a blue sweatshirt.

"I'm Steve Daly," he said as he extended his hand to Adam.

"Detective Adam Grant, and this is Deputy Clark. Thanks for taking the time."

"It's important," Steve said. "Come on in. Constable Paul phoned to say you were on your way. My partner and her mother are waiting to see you."

Steve led the way toward a canvas tent set back from the fire circle. The tent sat on a wooden platform with two steps up to it. The front flaps were tied open, and Adam saw electric lamps were on inside. The delicious aroma of vegetable soup filled the tent. Near the back, an old Kenmore stove had a kettle simmering on it.

"You folks have electric out here?" Adam asked as Steve stepped inside.

Steve laughed. "Yeah. Can you believe it? All the modern conveniences." He smiled at Adam. "Are you surprised?"

Adam felt a little embarrassed at his question and realized Steve was mocking him.

"Sorry," he mumbled. "I don't know much about the Tide People."

"That's the way we like it."

Adam and Clark followed him inside the tent which was comfortably furnished with a faded green futon on one side and a double bed on the other. A kitchen area held the stove, a water tank, and wooden shelves with cooking utensils. At the center was a wood-burning stove. The chimney pipe extended up and through the top of the canvas. All the comforts of home, Adam thought. Not bad.

Steve said, "Fay, June, this is Detective Grant. And this is Deputy Clark."

They exchanged polite greetings with the two women. Steve pulled up two straight-back chairs, and the policemen sat near the stove.

"What is it you want from us?" the older woman asked. "Why are you here?"

"We have reason to believe you might have information about the whereabouts of a young woman," Adam began, choosing his words carefully. He did not want to alienate this woman, as he was getting the idea that she was the decision maker in this group. It felt almost like a Native American scene with the powerful matriarch ready to impart her wisdom. Adam realized he was lost in thought and that Steve was addressing him.

"Detective?" Steve was saying. "Why do you think so?"

"I can't divulge that information. It's part of our ongoing investigation. We received a report that you may have seen or spoken with Kit Powell, and Constable Paul sent us out here to confirm that. Have you seen her?"

At that question, the older woman, Fay, said, "We are very private people. We bother no one out here, and we live our lives simply. Who we speak to or who we invite into our circle is no concern of yours."

"I'm sorry, ma'am, but that isn't so in this instance," Adam said, holding his voice steady. "This young woman we're looking for is a suspect in a murder."

Fay didn't flinch. "I know. She told us so."

"Then you have spoken to her?"

"Of course. We offered her safe haven here."

"Why would you do that?" Adam asked.

"She is welcome here because she asked us to help keep her safe. We believe in the inherent goodness of people, and Kit needed our help. She will always have a place here."

"Ma'am, you need to tell me where she is," Adam said, growing frustrated with the smoke and mirrors. "She may be armed and dangerous."

At that, Steve laughed. "Come on, Detective. You can't be serious."

"I am serious. It's possible that she murdered Michael Barsotti."

"She told us she didn't." Fay stood as she spoke. "She left something here. It's addressed to Constable Paul. She told us that under no circumstances should we open it or should we allow anyone else to open it." Fay reached under the mattress on the double bed and pulled out an envelope. "Can we trust you with this, Detective? Will you deliver it to the constable?"

"Of course," Adam said. "I will. But I must ask you again: where is she?"

"That is for us to know and you to find out," Fay said, smiling. "See? We did learn a few things when we were a part of your society."

Her dark eyes sparkled, and Adam knew she was toying with him. Patiently he said, "Do you realize that you could be charged with aiding and abetting a criminal?"

The younger of the two women, June, spoke for the first time. "Of course we won't be charged because Kit did nothing wrong. She has gone into hiding because she fears you will find a way to make it look as though she's guilty. She told us she didn't trust the people of Galiano, including you and your constable."

"Have you considered that she might be lying?" Adam asked.

Steve answered this time. "Have you considered that she might be innocent?"

Adam said nothing. Dan began to speak, but Adam cut him off. "Okay, I get the picture. We'll move on. I'll take the letter to Constable Paul. But I must remind you that we don't know how Kit is involved, and there may be two people dead."

"Two?" Steve responded. "What do you mean, two?" The women seemed perplexed.

"We found the kayak Russ took off in submerged near Sunshine Cove yesterday."

"And you suspect Kit has something to do with his disappearance?" Steve asked. "Why?"

"We saw him," Fay said. "Yesterday, near our land. He was loading things into his kayak."

"That doesn't surprise me," Adam said. "We've had a few sightings. Most say he seemed to be paddling at a good speed and was intent on covering some distance. But he didn't get far."

No one spoke as the three commune members took in this disturbing information.

Adam finally said, "Knowing that, would you like to change your minds about telling us where you think Kit is?"

All was quiet for a few seconds, until Fay responded. "No, we would not," she said simply. "We have given you what you came here for, and we do not want to be involved any further."

"All right, then," Adam said, standing. "Thank you all for your time." He handed a card to Fay. "If there's anything else you would like to share, please call me."

Fay accepted the card and handed it over to Steve. "Oh, we will," she said.

Adam knew she had no intention of calling.

"Great," he said. "Thanks, then."

He turned to exit the tent, Dan following.

"Detective," Fay said as he stepped outside. "Kit is not a murderer."

"I hope you're right about that," Adam said. "It's not looking good for her."

Chapter Thirty-Three

ADAM GRANT PACED NERVOUSLY in his office as he waited for Paul to arrive. Dan had gone home to have supper with his family, but Adam stayed behind. He wanted to know what the letter said. He held the envelope in his hand and hoped it would give them some answers.

Paul was flustered as he came through the front door of the office. "Got here as quickly as I could," he told the detective. "Even after you called, I had a hard time getting Clare to shut up. That woman irritates the hell out of me."

"Any new information?" Adam asked.

"Not much. She did show her true colors about Michael, though, when I asked her about the incident with her boat down at Montague. She hated him, all right, but I don't see how she could have orchestrated his murder, or for that matter, why. I mean, if she's had a grudge all these years, why act on it now? Doesn't make sense. But enough about her. Let's see what is in that letter."

Adam handed it to him and sat. Paul opened the envelope and read the letter aloud.

I am leaving this with my friends at the commune because I don't know where else to turn. I did not kill Michael. I asked him to help me find some answers about my family, and perhaps Jonathan's. I think Michael made an important discovery out at Wallace the night before he was killed—something to do with "David's prized possession."

You must believe me when I say I am innocent, and that the killer is still out there. I fear for my life. Michael never got to tell me what he found at Wallace Island, but I know it's connected to this murder.

Paul paused, letting the words fill the office. "It's signed, 'Kit.' That's all it says."

"Jesus, what was Michael mixed up in?" Adam asked. "Some kind of mystery involving Wallace Island? What does that have to do with anything? And who is this Kit? Do you know anything about her having ties to the island? What is that about?"

Paul shook his head and sounded weary. "I don't, and I still don't feel certain we can trust Kit. And if she has left the island and, most likely, British Columbia, then who was it out there at the Cliffhouse last night?"

"Do you think there's someone else involved here?"

"That's a big possibility. I'd better phone Riley and Marie. Then let's take a boat trip out to Wallace and check around. I think I know what she means by 'David's prized possession.' Rings a bell. We'll talk to some campers. Maybe somebody saw something out there last week. It's worth a shot."

RILEY HUNG UP THE phone as Marie came into the guestroom.

"Who was that?" Marie asked.

"Constable Paul. He has a note from Kit proclaiming her innocence, but he still thinks she was involved in Michael's murder."

"Oh, shit. Why does he think that? What did the note say? Where did it come from?"

"Paul said Kit left the note with the Tide People. She said she knows he suspects her of Michael's murder, but she had nothing to do with it. And that Michael discovered something out at Wallace Island. Information involving her family. Kit thinks that's why he was killed."

Marie let this information sink in. "What information?"

"Don't know. Nobody does, except Michael and maybe Kit. I guess that's just Kit now."

"This gets stranger and stranger. Now what? Do you have a plan of some sort?"

Riley smiled at the question and realized that even in the middle of a crisis like this, she loved it when Marie depended on her for a plan. It made her feel like the president of a secret club, the one everyone counted on for ideas and answers.

"Paul said that he and Detective Grant were going out to Wallace to poke around and see if they can come up with any new clues. I think we should do the same thing."

"That's scary. What if the killer is out there? Or what if Constable Paul is right, and Kit is involved in Michael's death? We don't even know what this is all about. Don't you think that's risky?"

"Of course it is. And Paul told me specifically to stay away from Wallace."

"And...?" Marie stopped mid-sentence as Riley interrupted her.

"And that's exactly why we're going. I have to know if and how Kit is involved."

"All right, then. I'm with you, Kemosabe."

"What a great sidekick you are."

Marie beamed at her. "One of my best qualities."

"And one of your most endearing ones. Saddle up."

"HOW ABOUT IF WE go by the bakery and get some real coffee?" Adam Grant said as he and Paul pulled out of the parking lot. "That stuff we have here isn't so good."

"Works for me," Paul said.

Adam parked in front of the bakery, and Paul got out and headed inside. Carl Brown, Richard Ellison and Clare Porter were seated at a corner table, studying a map of Bodega Ridge.

"Afternoon, Constable," Ellison said. "Nice to see you. Any news on the investigation?"

"Not much so far. Still trying to piece it all together."

"Any idea yet who could be involved? We heard you arrested Jonathan. Do you think he did it? Crazy old guy. And did you locate the girl? Kit?"

Paul smiled. "You ask a lot of questions, Ellison. Still don't know much. We're heading to Wallace Island later to check things out. May be for nothing, but we've covered Galiano pretty thoroughly so decided to expand the search."

Richard nodded. "Hope it turns up something. Everyone's a little edgy around here. Not good for business."

"Murder seldom is," Paul said.

"Good point, Constable. Hope you find something."

Paul glanced at Clare Porter and Carl Brown, neither of whom had said anything. They seemed to be avoiding his gaze. "Just stopped in for some good coffee, Richard."

"For you, no charge today. Good luck out there."

"That's very kind. Thanks." Paul poured two cups and headed for the door.

"Let us know if anything turns up?" Ellison said.

"Will do."

Chapter Thirty-Four

EARLY THAT EVENING, CONSTABLE Paul nudged the island police boat into the sheltered harbor that served Wallace Island Marine Park. Several sailboats were moored there for the night, and the smell of hamburgers on a grill reminded him that he'd forgotten to eat supper before they left.

"Jesus, that smells good," he said to Adam. "Wonder if they'd share with a couple of law enforcement officers?"

"Maybe we could cite them for some obscure infraction and confiscate the meat. Most American tourists don't have a clue about B.C. laws." He smiled.

"I'm hungry enough that I might entertain the idea. I guess our other option is the more appropriate one. Here." He dug around in his daypack and came up with two high-protein energy bars, ones he had gotten from the health food store on Salt Spring. He tossed one to Adam.

"Right. Wish to hell it tasted like a hamburger, though."

"Me, too," Paul said.

After tying the boat to the dock, the two men hiked up the main trail toward the center of Wallace Island. A congregation of colorful tents dotted the grassy field above the harbor, and Paul and Adam headed toward the two pitched closest to the trail where a young man was stirring a pan of pork and beans on a Coleman stove. It smelled smoky and delicious.

"Evening. Could I ask you a couple questions?" Paul pulled his constable badge from his breast pocket and flashed it. "I'm Constable Paul Snow from Galiano. This is my detective, Adam Grant."

"Sure," the young man said. "Is there something wrong?"

"No, not necessarily. We're trying to get to the bottom of a situation we have over on Galiano."

"What kind of situation?" the man asked.

"Just a bit of trouble," Paul said, realizing that the man probably knew nothing about the murder. "We're trying to locate someone we think may have been here on Wallace Island in the past couple days."

"I got here this afternoon. I'm kayaking up the west side of Galiano, and I decided to check out this island. Beautiful, isn't it?"

"Indeed, it is," Paul said. "We love it here."

"Me, too. But who are you searching for, and why?"

Paul answered the first question and ignored the second. "A woman, early thirties, short dark hair. She's a kayak teacher on Galiano. We think maybe she's been out here in the past couple days."

The kayaker was silent for a few seconds, then said,

"Can't say as I've seen anyone matching that description. Not today. Are you sure she's out here?"

"Well, no—we aren't sure. I have a hunch."

"Good luck, then. Hope you find her."

"Thanks. So do we."

After six similar conversations with other campers, Paul and Adam headed up the main trail toward the upper meadow. Light was fading as the sun made a brilliant exit behind Salt Spring Island to the southwest. "It's so beautiful here," Adam said as they hiked the gravel trail. "I need to come out here when I'm off duty."

"Yeah, for sure. I guess old David was quite a shrewd guy, claiming this island for himself and his family and creating that resort out here. For an American, he was smart."

"Indeed. He must have been a clever person. Did you know him?"

Paul said, "No. He died in the eighties. But I remember my dad talking about him. The guy discovered Marilyn Monroe, you know."

"Yeah. I read about that. I wonder why he settled up here, though."

"Because he could. He had a boatload of money, and he liked to spend it. He also liked to hobnob with Hollywood types, and they came here in droves."

"Wow," Adam said. "Who would have thought?"

"I know. Strange, isn't it?"

They were silent for a couple minutes as they inched their way through the growing dark toward the meadow. Several campfires flickered below them near backpack tents pitched along the shore. The air was cooler and damper as they got to the meadow, and the low moan of an owl's call broke the stillness of the night.

"There's no other sound like that, is there?" Paul said.

"Absolutely none." They walked on in silence. Up ahead, the meadow was soft green in the fading light, and Paul could barely make out the silhouette of David's old cars that were left there, a testament to richer and more glorious times on Wallace Island.

"I've never been here at dusk," Adam said in a hushed tone. "Damn if it isn't kinda spooky. I half expect David to step out of that old Jeep."

"Knock it off. You're going to scare the hell out of me, and I won't be much of a law enforcement officer if you do that. By the way, that's it: David's prized possession."

"That old Jeep?"

"Yup. He loved that thing. I read about it in his biography. Wouldn't let anyone haul it out of here, even after it broke down. So, there it sits."

"Wow," Adam said. "So, what's your game plan?"

"I figure we ought to do some thorough searching near and around those vehicles."

"I'm right with you."

"KEEP LOW," RILEY WHISPERED to Marie as they made their way from the rented motorboat up and over the rocks onto the soft earth of Wallace Island. Even motoring with the four-horse Johnson, the crossing had taken longer than they'd planned, and the evening twilight was fading fast.

"How come we came ashore all the way down here?" Marie asked as they hiked toward a grove of cottonwood trees that would shelter them from view. "This is the south end of the island!"

"Shh!" Riley said. "I know. But if we landed any closer to the overnighters we'd surely be seen, and if Paul finds out we're out here he'll lay into me about it. I don't want anyone to know we're here."

"Okay. But what if the murderer finds out?"

"That's not going to happen."

"Right. So now we have to walk all the way to the meadow in the dark? Excellent. I hope I don't break an ankle."

Riley was not amused. "Come on, Marie. Cut it out. You know this is the only way we can get away with this."

"Humph" was her reply. "I hope the killer didn't choose this same dark and scary route."

"Thanks for boosting my confidence. Now will you try to be quiet and follow me?"

Marie made no reply but fell into step behind Riley as she headed deeper into the trees. The smell of wood smoke and grilled hamburgers filled the cool evening air as they crept as silently as they could through the woods.

After about two minutes, Riley stopped suddenly. She motioned for Marie to be still, also. "Did you hear that?" she whispered.

"Hear what?"

"Never mind. Thought I heard something. Probably a deer. But let's stay here a minute anyway."

They crouched low and listened. A faint crackle, which sounded like a footstep, made them both open their eyes wide.

They waited.

Another crackle, this time a little closer.

Marie started to tremble. Riley knew they needed to keep moving or she was going to lose her faithful companion to a bad case of the heebie-jeebies.

She motioned to get up, and Marie did. They moved away from the sound, slowly and silently. Marie looked relieved.

Riley kept low and in the trees until the little harbor was visible in the distance. Colorful tents dotted the camping area—red, purple, bright green—but few people were outside as night had fallen and the dew had presented itself, making the grassy area too damp to sit out on. Lots of the tents had lantern light coming from within, making them appear like so many paper lanterns on a soft green globe of grass.

Riley spotted Constable Paul's law enforcement motorboat moored at the far of the end of the dock, but she saw no sign of Paul or Detective Grant. "Come on," she whispered to Marie, "I think they've already headed up to the meadow."

Marie nodded and followed her trusted leader.

Riley was not as worried about being spotted by campers because they were probably all tourists and would have no idea who she and Marie were or what they were doing there.

Skirting the edge of the camping area, Riley and Marie took the gravel trail that led north into the meadow. Even in the growing darkness, the trail was easy to follow. Riley and Marie kept moving and quickly covered the short distance to the meadow. Ahead, they saw lights near an abandoned Jeep. Riley stopped again and motioned for Marie to follow her into the cover of a grove of trees at the meadow's edge where they wouldn't be seen, but could still hear the men's conversation.

Riley pulled a pair of binoculars from her jacket pocket and honed in on the Jeep.

"What are they doing?" Marie whispered.

"Hard to tell," Riley whispered back. "Looks as though Paul is inside the Jeep, and Grant is trying to scoot underneath it. Let's watch and listen."

"See anything?" they heard Paul say. "I'm not finding much in here."

Grant's answer was muffled.

"Okay," Paul said. "Give it a few more minutes."

Marie moved closer to Riley and crouched beside her. "You're gonna kill me, but I have to pee."

"Oh, geez, Marie. Now?"

Marie looked chagrined. "Uh-huh."

"Then do it right here," Riley said, her eyes still glued to the binoculars.

"I can't! You know that. I have to have a little privacy, or I can't go."

Riley breathed an audible, lengthy sigh. "You are a piece of work. Go, then. But not very far. I need to hear you."

"I can't go if I know you can hear me."

Exasperated, Riley said, "Good grief, Marie. We're on a stakeout here!"

"Just stake by yourself for a minute. I'll be right back." With that, Marie backed silently away from her friend. Riley heard a little rustling, though she was pleasantly surprised at how quiet Marie could be when she had to be. She could still hear her, but the noises were slight and Riley felt confident that Paul and Grant wouldn't notice.

At that moment, Riley was distracted by the commotion that Adam Grant was making.

"What is it?" she heard Paul say. "Did you find something?"

Grant scooted out from under the old Jeep, stood and brushed himself off. From the glow of Paul's Coleman lantern, Riley could see the whole scene.

"There is definitely a place underneath where someone has removed something. It's a spot about three inches square."

"How can you tell?"

"It's rusted all the way around the place. Something was attached there—a box, maybe, or something else square. The undercarriage is much cleaner in that spot, as though something kept it from the weather and the elements all these years."

"Jesus. Maybe Michael did find something out here. And maybe the killer wanted whatever it was."

"We're not gonna know until we discover whoever that is, are we?" Adam shined his powerful flashlight on the ground and in a wide arc around the Jeep. Riley ducked behind a tree in case Grant decided to aim the beam her way. She hoped Marie wouldn't let herself get caught in the light, either.

Marie! Damn, Riley thought. In the excitement of Grant's discovery, she had forgotten to listen for her friend. She turned toward where Marie had gone and listened. No sounds. Way to go, Marie. Way to be quiet! She listened some more, but nothing. Riley knew she had to risk being heard to find her. "Marie!" she whispered. "Get back over here! I don't like it that you're where I can't see you."

No response.

Riley felt her heart rate rise. She waited. Nothing. Keeping her eye on the two men, who were illuminated by the lantern light and were now both underneath the Jeep, Riley backed up slowly, taking the same route Marie had toward the old stump. Drawing near enough to touch it, Riley felt her way around it and whispered Marie's name again.

Nothing.

Riley felt scared now and didn't care if Paul and Adam Grant saw or heard her. She turned on her flashlight and scanned the area behind and around the stump.

Marie was gone.

"Paul! Adam! Over here!" Riley yelled into the night and flashed her light toward the two men.

Startled, Paul called back, "Riley. Is that you? What the hell are you doing out here?"

Riley ran toward them and was out of breath when she arrived.

"I know. I know. I was supposed to stay on Galiano. But I thought I might learn something out here tonight, so Marie and I brought the boat over. But she's gone, Paul. Gone!"

"Slow down, Riley. Marie? Marie's gone? Gone where?"

"I don't know that! She went behind a stump to pee and disappeared. Just now. Come on. I need your help to find her."

"Wait a minute," Paul said. "Slow down a little."

"There are no minutes to wait. Something bad has happened to

Marie and it's my fault because I convinced her to come out here tonight. What if it's the killer? What if she's victim number three? I could never live with myself if something happens to her."

With that, Riley turned and headed back toward the woods. Over her shoulder she said, "Either you're coming now or I'm going without you. We're not going to find her by standing around arguing about it."

"I'm coming," Paul said. "You, too, Adam. Come on. We'd better find out what the hell happened here. Jesus. When will this all end?"

"Good question." Adam pulled his service revolver from its holster. The two men followed Riley into the grove of trees.

"Wait, Riley," Paul called out. "Stop right there, and let's come up with a plan. I don't want you going into the woods hell-bent on righting whatever's wrong here. This could be nothing, or it could be a very dangerous situation. We don't know yet, and so I want you somewhere safe."

"I'm safe if I'm with you. I can't leave her out here, Paul."

"Okay. But stay right here behind me, and Adam will follow close behind you. Let's see what we can see."

The dark night was thicker now, and Riley saw no trace of Marie during nearly an hour of thrashing through underbrush calling her name.

Paul tried to convince Riley they should return to the central area of the island and alert the campers there about Marie's disappearance. "I don't want to alarm you or anybody else here, Riley, but we have to face the truth that Marie is missing, and we don't know why. It's still possible that she got disoriented in the dark and wandered away, but we all know that the chances of that are slim. The other possibility is sobering, and we have to address it. Someone wanted Marie to disappear."

Riley, tired and distraught, found words hard to come up with. "I want to find her now. I'll do whatever you think is best, Paul, but I'm not leaving until we find Marie."

"We're not quitting, but it won't be daylight for a couple more hours. Let's all three head back to the campground. You can stay there at the day shelter while Adam and I organize a search to start at first light."

Alarmed, Riley asked, "We have to wait 'til daybreak?"

Paul said, "It's too risky to send others out here in the dark. You know that. We can't be effective at all until morning."

"Right. But two hours is a long time. Marie could be anywhere by then."

"Maybe so, but this is a small island, and no one goes anywhere except by boat. Either we'll find her in the morning, or we'll find someone who saw her. I have to believe that."

"I hope you're right," Riley said. "I don't like it, but okay, let's head back."

Chapter Thirty-Five

WAITING UNTIL DAYLIGHT WAS anxious agony for Riley, but she knew Paul was right and that they had no choice. She passed the two hours until dawn fretting about Marie, trying to imagine what she could have done differently. She felt relief when she saw the first sign of the sunrise.

The constables had created a temporary command center in the three-sided, covered day shelter which featured a stone fireplace on one end. Several kayakers had already gathered, recruited by the two officers to help search for Marie. One, a woman about thirty years old, came to sit by Riley and offered her coffee in a tin cup.

"It's strong and hot," she said. "I'm Karen. I'm so sorry about your friend."

For an instant, Riley thought the woman knew something she didn't, and she felt the panic rise.

"You must be frantic with worry," Karen added.

"That's for sure," Riley said. "Thank you for the coffee." She realized the woman was offering comfort because Marie was missing and not because she had any new information. Riley felt her heartbeat calm the slightest bit.

"I'm Riley Logan. Thank you so much for offering to help out."

"No need for thanks," Karen said. "Of course we'll help. My partner is down there getting our stuff in the kayaks. The constable said we can head out in about ten minutes."

Riley felt a bit of relief at hearing the term "partner" and suddenly felt like crying. The tears began to well up. "Your partner?" she said.

"Her name's Peg. She's an excellent kayaker, and she taught me all I know. I'm still not so good at it, but Peg can cover a lot of water in a short amount of time."

"That's great." She was silent a few seconds. "I'm so worried about Marie."

"How long have you two been together?" Karen asked.

Riley realized the assumption being made. "We're not partners. We're best friends. A long, long time ago, Marie and I went to elementary school together, if you can believe that. I love her like a sister."

"I see. How fortunate you both are to have that relationship."

"I know we are," Riley said, and she felt the tears trying to rise again. "I am so sorry I brought her out here."

"Sounds to me as though she wanted to come. Constable Paul said you two are looking for some woman from Galiano. He didn't explain much more, but said there's some concern that your friend might be in danger. He also said there had been a murder on Galiano and encouraged us to get out of here. Peg insisted we stay and help. I think there are three or four other kayakers who volunteered, also."

"God, what a mess this is."

"But it's going to get sorted out. Hang in there. You've got a lot of people on your side. And Paul told us he'd radioed for help from the officers on Salt Spring and Gabriola. They're on their way. We'll find her."

Riley felt comforted, ever so slightly. She sighed. "I hope you're right."

Paul came over, sat on the picnic bench next to Riley and offered his hand to Karen. "Thanks for helping. It's time to head out. I'm going to have you and your partner stick with Adam Grant and head up the west side of the island. He's armed, so I want you to stick close to him at all times. If the three of you kayak near shore, maybe you'll spot something or someone. It should take you about three hours to go all the way around.

Karen said, "We're on it."

"Whatever you do, stay together," Paul added. "And if you see something, let Adam know, and he'll radio back to me. We're not going to take any action without backup. It's possible there's a very dangerous person on this island."

"Got it," Karen said. "I understand."

Riley thought that Karen looked resolute. Determined. She felt a rush of gratitude to this woman she'd only known for five minutes.

Paul turned to Riley. "Guess we'd better get at it, then. Riley, you know what you have to do. Stay here in the shelter. I've left a radio here, and one of the campers will stay with you. His name's Craig—an American from Seattle. He's a city policeman there, so he's familiar with this kind of trouble. He's not armed, though, so it's essential you both stay here and be ready to receive any information that comes in. The constables from Salt Spring and Denman are on their way. When they arrive, one of them will take over, and Craig can be support."

Riley nodded. "I understand, Paul. It's going to be very hard, but I'll stay put."

"All right, then. Karen, let's get going."

Karen smiled at Riley and then pulled her into an awkward hug. "We'll find her. Try not to worry."

Riley muttered a muffled, "Thanks" and tried very hard to keep the tears in. She wasn't successful.

As the first rays of sun broke over the water, Paul walked with Karen to where Adam was waiting with the kayaks.

"I THINK OUR BEST bet is to paddle slowly along the shoreline," Adam Grant said to Peg and Karen as they nudged their kayaks away from the sandy beach. "With three of us, we ought to be able to notice anything irregular. Mostly, I guess we're watching for any evidence of someone either going ashore or launching—broken branches, scuff marks, left behind gear, any kind of sign that someone's been there."

"But don't a lot of people come ashore here on Wallace?" Karen asked as she dug her paddle into the bright blue water. "What about that? Maybe it'll just be another kayaker."

"That's possible, but it's the only thing we can look for at this point. If someone is hiding out here and has taken Marie, we have to start somewhere. Watch carefully for anything out of the ordinary."

Adam knew the entire effort was a long shot, but he also knew that Constable Paul was not going to rest until they found some sign of Marie. He paddled away from the beach and gently turned the kayak left, northward, toward the far end of the island. The two women were close behind.

God, I hope we find something, he thought. Anything.

ON SHORE, CONSTABLE PAUL was finishing up his instructions to the volunteer searchers. Riley stood by silently and listened.

"That will work," he said to two young American men. "If you two take the aluminum motorboat and head south, along the shoreline, then eventually you'll meet up with Adam and the other two searchers."

"And if we see something?" the dark-haired one, Andy, asked. "What then?"

"I'm sending along a radio. All you have to do is notify me, and let me know where you are. If you find something, stay put and use the radio. I don't want anyone to take unnecessary risks."

"Right. Got it."

His companion, Vince, a wiry athlete with a blond stubble of a beard, nodded agreement. "We'll be careful," Vince said. "We want to help."

"And I appreciate that," Paul said. "The more of us, the better. If someone is hiding out here, he or she is going to be less likely to try anything if they know there are lots of us beating the bushes and the shoreline trying to find them."

"He or she?" Andy said. "We could be looking for a woman? You suspect a woman is behind Marie's disappearance?"

Constable Paul glanced at Riley before answering. "It could be. We're not sure who is to blame, that's all. We have a lot of unanswered questions."

That's for sure, Riley thought. Way too many.

PEG LOVED THE FEEL of warm sun on her back as she dipped and pulled the kayak paddle. She experienced another feeling, too: fear, which left a metallic taste in her mouth and perspiration on her hands. What or who was out there? She wanted to help, but she didn't like knowing that Karen, a few strokes behind her, could be in danger, and she knew they could both be as well. Looking for Marie was the right thing to do, though. She would want someone to do the same for her.

"Let's slow down a bit," Adam was saying, turning in his kayak so that his words could be heard above the breeze and the slap of the water on the side of the boat. "We don't want to miss anything."

Peg focused her full attention on the shoreline. No beach was in view now, only rocks that were sandy-colored and full of holes and tiny caves. She'd find it difficult to pull a kayak or any other kind of boat up along here, but it could be done. Who knows what someone might do if he's desperate, she thought.

The three kayakers paddled slowly along the shoreline. Karen called "Wait a minute" once when she noticed a broken branch on the side of a rocky outcrop. Upon closer inspection, she saw that the break was weathered, not new. They paddled on.

At the other end of the island, the two Americans were doing the same thing. Andy had slowed the motor to its minimum, and they stared at the shoreline as they motored by. Vince pointed toward a stand of trees above the rocky shoreline. "Did you see that?"

"See what?" Andy said. "I didn't see anything."

"Up the hill, by the crooked tree. Ya see something?"

Andy stared for several seconds. "I don't see a dang thing. I think you're spooked by the constable's story."

"I hope to hell you're right."

CONSTABLE TOM WILSON, THE chief on Salt Spring Island, greeted Paul while stepping off his patrol craft. "Jesus, Paul, what gives with Galiano, anyway? You're getting way more than your share of trouble."

Tom had been Paul's best friend for nearly twenty years, ever since they both started their careers. They'd been through many, many stressful times together and had always relied on each other for support.

"I don't know," Paul said. "I'm in over my head here."

"What about Michael Barsotti's murder? Do you know any more about that? Is this somehow connected?"

"I've been in law enforcement too long to think anything is merely coincidence, and I know you know what I mean."

"Was thinking the same thing myself. But how do you think it's connected?"

"I have to admit that I don't know," Paul said. "But I can't even worry about that now until I locate this woman from the States. We've got ourselves quite a mess here."

"That's for sure. Let's get at it, then. What's your plan?"

"I'm thinking that you and I should split up, each take a couple volunteer searchers, and head opposite ways down the island. Let's talk to anyone we encounter. Certainly someone would have seen something if Marie really has been kidnapped."

"Hope you're right. Let's do it."

Chapter Thirty-Six

ANDY GOT A GLIMPSE, a brief movement.

There.

On the shoreline, above the old oak tree. "Did you see that?" Andy said, leaning forward to nudge Vince to get his attention. His voice could barely be heard above the low purr of the motor.

"What?"

"There. To the right of the old oak. In the underbrush. I saw movement."

"Didn't see it," Vince said. "Do you want to pull in? Should we radio Paul?"

"I don't want to radio him yet. What if it's nothing? I don't want to sound foolish."

"What shall we do then?"

"Let's pull in and check around. We'll stay together."

"Yeah. Good idea."

Andy killed the motor as Vince grabbed the oars and guided the motorboat to the sandy shoreline. He nudged it onto the beach and put one foot out into the shallow water. Ashore, he pulled the aluminum boat, with Andy still in it, up a couple feet.

"Come on. Let's check this out," Vince said. "Maybe we can be heroes and find this missing girl."

PAUL AND HIS GROUP of four camper volunteers had just left the dock area when the sound of a motorboat drew his attention back to the harbor. He watched as the boat pulled in to dock.

"Hang on a minute," he told his volunteers. "Let's see who this is. I hope it's more help."

"Hey Paul," someone shouted above the motor noise. "What's the latest?"

Carl Brown was at the wheel of a cabin cruiser. Paul saw that the others on board were Richard Ellison, Robert from the Kayak School, and a woman he didn't recognize.

"Hey, Carl," Paul said. He made his way toward the cabin cruiser. "Stay put," he called out to his volunteers. "I'll be right back."

"We thought we'd see if there's something we could do," Carl said as Richard stepped onto the dock to tie the boat. "It's all over Galiano what happened. Do you have any trace of Marie yet?"

"Not yet," Paul said. "But we've got lots of people looking for her."

Ellison said, "Now you'll have us, too. Tell us what you want us to do."

Robert stepped from the boat. "God, Paul, what's happening

around here? It's one thing after another."

"I know, Robert. It makes me afraid to get up in the morning."

The woman exited the boat last. Paul nodded a greeting to her. He knew he'd seen her in town, but he had no idea who she was.

"Oh, sorry," Robert said. "This is Anne Myers, from our school. She's on our summer staff. She's a friend of Kit's."

"I see," Paul said. "Thanks for coming, Anne."

"No need for thanks. I needed to do something to help."

"I know what you mean," Paul said. "We all feel that way, I think."

"Where can we help?" Ellison asked as he pulled a daypack from the boat and slung it over his shoulder. "What's not being covered?"

"I guess you could assist us with the search on foot," Paul said. "My group is heading south from here, and Tom Wilson took a group north from the campground. How about if you four split up into pairs and hunt along the western shoreline, where most of the kayakers come onto the island? We have a search group in kayaks, but they can see only what's visible from the water. Maybe you could explore inside the tree line. It might pay off."

"Sounds good," Carl said. "Robert, why don't you come with me? Ellison and Anne can go the other way."

"Okay. Paul, anything else we can do?" Robert asked.

"I think that's it for now." Paul turned back toward his searchers. "Let's pray one of us finds something, and that Marie is all right."

"I'm with you on that one," Carl said.

The searchers fanned out as the early morning sun began to warm the island paths.

ANDY TUCKED THE RADIO in the pocket of his windbreaker as he stepped out of the boat and onto the sandy shore.

"Let's stay close together," he whispered to Vince as they made their way toward the tree line. "It may be nothing, but if it's something, it's going to take both of us to deal with it, I'm sure."

Carefully, quietly, they headed for the trees.

No movement.

They kept sneaking along, and Andy looked behind them every few steps to make sure they were still alone.

As they stood under the oak tree, they heard nothing but the breeze and the occasional call of a hawk making its morning sweep of the island.

Vince whispered, "Where did you think you saw movement?"

"There, beyond those bushes." Andy pointed about twenty yards beyond where they stood.

The snap of a twig under a boot was their only warning that they were not alone. Vince whirled around first and found himself at the end of the barrel of a .22 pistol. Close behind him, Andy made a move toward his jacket pocket and heard the click of the hammer being pulled back.

A harsh, raspy voice said, "Bad idea. Take off the jacket, very slowly."

"Okay! Okay!" Andy said, raising his hands. "For God's sake, don't shoot!" He knew he was trembling, and he didn't want that to show, but he couldn't help it. Vince raised his hands, too, and said nothing.

Slowly, carefully, their adversary stepped toward the two men, the gun aimed directly at Andy.

"I have no reason to hurt either of you unless you do something stupid. Now, keep your hands raised, and take three steps backward from the jacket. Please don't give me a reason to shoot."

Vince finally raised his eyes from the gun barrel to look at their assailant. "Jesus, you're a girl!"

"Good observation," she said. "What are you, some kind of detective?"

Feeling foolish, Vince did not reply.

"He means you're not what we expected," Andy said, by way of explanation.

"I know what he means. But I'd like it if you'd stay quiet. I talk, you listen. Okay?"

"Whatever you say," Andy said.

"That's for sure," She picked up the jacket and retrieved the radio from inside the pocket. "Looks like you were hoping to communicate with someone here, huh? Who? Constable Paul, maybe?"

Andy nodded silently.

"I think poor Paul is going to be disappointed not to hear from you. But he's a grown-up. He'll get over his disappointment."

With that, she opened the back of the radio, removed the batteries and flung them into the woods. She tossed the radio thirty feet the other direction. "Darn, I think it's broken. Too bad." She kept the gun trained on them. "Who else is out here with you two amateur detectives? And what is it you think you're doing?"

Andy said, "There are several others, but I don't know any of them. We're here on a kayak trip, and we volunteered to help search for her."

"For who?"

"As if you don't know." Andy thought Kit's blank stare was almost convincing. "Who are you? Maybe we're supposed to find you."

"Are you looking for someone named Kit?"

"No."

She snorted. "I thought not. You just made all that up."

Andy said, "No! No, I didn't."

"Then who are you supposedly looking for?"

"Marie, of course. I don't know her last name."

"What happened to Marie?" Kit asked. She sounded anxious for the first time since they'd encountered her.

"Good cover," Andy said. "What did you take? Acting classes?"

"This inane banter sure is fun, but I think I've had enough." Kit motioned with the gun toward the grove of fir trees. "How about we three take a stroll? You two lead, and I'll follow. Keep your hands where I can see them. This awesomely effective .22 isn't all that loud, but it's deadly at close range. But I suppose you know that."

Arms raised, Andy and Vince trudged toward the trees. Once under cover of the tall firs and low underbrush, Kit ordered them to stop. She opened her daypack and pulled out rope and duct tape.

"Always prepared, that's the Girl Scout motto. Okay, you first. Step over to that fir. Keep your hands raised." She motioned to Vince, who did exactly what she said. "Now, hug that tree." Vince gave her a quizzical look, then put his arms around the fir. "Okay," she said to Andy, "now you take this hunk of rope and tie it around his wrist.

Once Andy did as he was told, Kit said, "Now pull the rope around the tree and tie his other wrist. She kept the gun pointed in their general direction. When Andy finished the second knot, Kit said, "Step back." She made sure the rope was taut around the tree, and then cut off a six-inch length of duct tape and put it over Vince's mouth.

"Your turn," she said to Andy, motioning with the pistol. "There's your tree. I'm waiting."

Andy did what he'd seen Vince do and wrapped his arms around the fir. Kit tucked the gun in her jacket pocket so she could tie Andy's wrists and slap a piece of duct tape over his mouth, and he was soon in the same quiet predicament.

"That should hold you for a while," Kit said. "You'll be fine, except for the cougars. I wonder if they're out this early? Can't remember if they're morning hunters or nighttime hunters. Ah, well, I guess we'll find out. Main thing is, if they can't hear you, they probably won't find you. Unless they smell you. But I think the wind's blowing the wrong way for that. Not sure though."

Vince and Andy watched her with wide eyes as she returned the unused rope and tape to the daypack.

"Probably your best bet is to stay quiet. I'm figuring that those other searchers should find you by at least tomorrow morning."

With that, Kit slowly let down the hammer of the pistol, shoved the gun into her belt and hoisted the daypack. She waved over her shoulder as she headed for their boat.

"Thanks for the ride," she called out smugly. "It sure beats swimming. Tell everyone hi from Kit."

With that, she nudged the bow of the boat off the sand, hopped in and used an oar to propel the boat into deeper water. The motor started on the first pull, and she turned the boat toward Galiano Island.

From where he was tied, Andy couldn't see the boat as it moved, full throttle, through the choppy water. He was still trembling. Oh, God, he thought. At least she didn't kill us, too.

Chapter Thirty-Seven

THE RADIO CALL WAS crackly yet understandable. Paul stopped and reached for the volume control to hear over the sound of the ever-increasing wind that had sprung up and blew through the trees. His fellow searchers stopped and waited.

"Say again?" he said.

"It's Adam," came the voice over the black hand-held walkie-talkie. "We're at the tip of the island and turning 'round to head south again. Nothing suspicious yet."

"Copy that," Paul said. "No news here, either."

"Have you heard from the guys in the rowboat? They oughta be about to the other end by now."

"Not yet, but I'll give them a call right away. We also have several more searchers out on foot, including a group that came over from Galiano about an hour ago. Carl Brown, Ellison, Robert and Anne, who helps out in the kayak school office. I sent them toward you guys."

"Curious group, that is. News travels fast, doesn't it?"

"Indeed. Thanks for checking in. Over and out for now."

"Roger. Over and out here."

The radio was quiet until Paul sent a message. "Calling Station Three, come in please. You there?"

No one answered.

"Station Three, it's Central. Calling Station Three."

Paul thought it curious that the two men didn't pick up. Probably forgot to turn up the volume, he thought. He tried one more time, then gave up and put the radio back in the pocket of his vest.

"Let's keep going, then," he said to his searchers, who had taken a rest break while he talked to Adam. "Onward."

AT THE OTHER END of the island, two young kayakers from Vancouver were nearing the tip of Wallace when they passed a motorboat heading full throttle the other way. They waved a hello, but the woman ignored them.

"Not so friendly out here, are they?" one said as he dug his paddle deep. Near the shore now, he motioned for his friend to follow and nosed the kayak up onto a sandy beach.

"Gotta get out for a minute," he said over his shoulder. "Nature calls."

"Right. Me, too," the other man said. He gave a last deep paddle and thrust the bright yellow sea kayak onto the sand, scrambled out, and headed up the hill toward the trees.

"Doesn't seem to be anyone around, but I suppose we should at least get out of sight of the beach," one said.

About sixty seconds later, they were face-to-face with two men, each tied to a tree, mouths taped shut.

"What the hell?" the first kayaker said. His pal scurried over to one tree as he reached the first guy. He said, "Jesus. This might hurt." He pulled the duct tape gently from the guy's face.

The man looked scared and grateful. "Oh, thank God. Are we ever happy to see you!"

"Yeah," said the other man. "Glad you got here before the cougars came out."

The first kayaker set to work untying the rope. "What happened here? Who did this to you?"

"We were brought here at gunpoint," the man said, "by a woman."

The rescuers seemed surprised. "A woman?" one asked. "Did she leave here in a motorboat?"

"Yeah, our boat," the second man said, having had his tape and rope removed. He was rubbing his wrists. "Did you see her?"

"We paddled right by her."

"You're lucky she didn't turn on you," the first man said. "She's already killed two people."

THE RADIO CALL CAME as Constable Paul and his group of hikers were about to reach the southern tip of the island.

"Station One. Station One. Do you copy?"

"I'm here," Paul said.

It was Adam, sounding excited. "We've got her! We have Marie! She's okay."

Paul broke into a grin. "Oh, thank God," he said. "Where are you? What happened?"

"We noticed some breaking of the underbrush way up north of here near an old maintenance shed. One of the women put ashore and determined that they were fresh breaks. So we came ashore and started poking around. I'd forgotten this shed was even here."

"And Marie? Is she all right?"

"She's fine, just scared. She said someone came up behind her in the woods last night, put a hand over her mouth, a gun in her ribs, and a pillowcase over her head, then pushed her through the forest. Whoever it was disguised his voice and spoke only one word, 'Quiet.' The gun in her ribs convinced her he was serious. When we found her, she was in the shed, bound and gagged."

"Does she know who it was?"

"Afraid not. Said she was about to head back to where Riley was last night when all of a sudden this person surprised her from behind. She never saw whoever it was, and the person never spoke any other words."

"At least she's alive, and that's what matters. I'll send a boat up to meet you at the harbor."

"Roger that. We're at the north tip."

"Got it. I'll send up Carl Brown. Stay put and tell Marie she's gonna be okay. I'll head back to the harbor now, too."

"Roger."

"Thanks, Adam. This is welcome news."

"Sure is, Paul. See you in a few."

"Over and out."

Paul was quick to radio his central station. "Station Two. Station Two. Come in."

"We're here," a voice said.

"Is Riley nearby?"

"She's here in the shelter."

"Put her on." Paul waited.

"Riley here," crackled the radio. "What's going on, Paul?"

"We found her. Marie's okay.

"Oh, what a relief. Is she hurt?"

"Adam says she's just fine."

"Thank God. Where is she now? Can I see her?"

"Yes. You stay put. We're sending Carl Brown up to bring her back."

"I'm going nowhere."

"Over and out." Paul returned the radio to his pocket and was about to gather his searchers for the walk back when one of them called out.

"Paul, over here! It's Andy and Vince!"

What now? Paul thought. "Coming," he yelled.

Andy and Vince were sitting on a downed tree sucking down bottles of water and surrounded by Paul's searchers and two other men he'd never seen. "What's this all about?" he asked.

"You'll never believe it," Andy said. "We've been tied to the trees over there. We were held at gunpoint, Paul, by a woman!"

A woman? Paul felt sick as he realized what this meant. Kit was behind all this after all, and things were looking very, very bad for her.

"I see," he said, trying to keep his voice even and calm. "I think that was probably Kit. Early thirties, dark hair?"

"She did say something about her name being Kit. That's her," Andy said. "And these two discovered us, or we'd still be tied up for who knows how long. We could have been cougar food."

Paul frowned. "Cougar? What do you mean?"

"That's what she said, that woman with the gun. The cougars would feed on us."

Cougars? Paul smiled in spite of himself. "Biggest thing on this island is jack rabbits, fellas. I think Kit was trying to scare you."

The men looked embarrassed and tried to compensate. "Oh, we knew that," Vince offered. "Andy's just kidding."

"Right," Paul said, letting the two men have their bit of dignity back. "At least you weren't harmed. What did she say? Where did she go?"

"She tied us up and took the boat," Andy said. "These guys say they passed her."

Paul fixed his gaze on the two unknowns. One said, "Looked like she was headed for Galiano."

Paul said, "Guess our work out here is done, then. Let's all head back toward the harbor. Guys," he added, speaking to the kayakers, "I'll need to ask you to come with us so we can get your statement. Maybe you should get back in the kayaks and come around the south end and up to the harbor. I'll meet you there."

"Will do," one said.

"Let's get cranking, then," Paul said to the rest of the group. "Time to go sort things out."

Chapter Thirty-Eight

MARIE'S REUNION WITH RILEY and all the searchers was tearful and joyous, but there wasn't much time to celebrate because Paul ordered everyone off the island and back to Galiano.

"I think we may be closing in on some answers here," he told the group that had gathered in the day shelter to welcome Marie back. "This incident and the murder of Michael Barsotti and the possible death of Russ Brady are very likely related, and we're determined to get to the bottom of all of it.

"I want to thank all of you for your help here on Wallace. I know we're all grateful to have Marie back unharmed. I think the best thing now is for everyone to get off Wallace Island and head back to Galiano, because we don't know what dangers are still here."

One volunteer asked, "But didn't Andy say that Kit took their boat and headed out across the channel? What's the danger, then? Why can't we stay here?"

"Yes, that is what he said," Paul said. "But we can't be certain that this is all Kit's doing, even though it's more and more likely that's true. It's possible she has an accomplice, someone else who's involved in all this. We can't take the risk of having anybody out here right now. You'll need to pack up and head out. I've asked Constable Tom to stay behind until everyone clears out. He'll escort you back to Galiano. Any questions? Good. And thank you again for all your help."

"I'd like to second that," Riley said. "I want to thank you for helping find Marie."

Marie, standing next to Riley, was close to tears again. "I am so grateful to all of you."

"Good, then," Paul said, in an effort to move things along. "We'll see you all back on Galiano. I'd appreciate it if you stayed on Galiano at least one more day, until we get more of this straightened out. You can camp at Montague if necessary. Check in with Detective Grant or me in the morning, and we'll let you know if it's okay to leave the island."

The group began to disperse. Marie and Riley were escorted to Carl's boat for the short trip to Galiano.

"Get me out of here," Marie said to Riley. "Enough adventure for me."

"Ditto," Riley said.

They boarded the boat and sat silently as Richard, Robert, Anne and Carl climbed on.

"We're off, then," Carl said. "Galiano's going to be a welcome sight now, isn't it?"

"SO WHAT DO YOU make of all this, Chief?" Adam Grant asked as he and Constable Paul headed for their island patrol boat.

"What do we know for sure?" Paul said. "Let's see. It seems to me that whatever was hidden in—and retrieved from—that old Jeep of David's holds the key to everything here. Michael had that box in his possession, and I think that's why he was killed. What secrets did it reveal? Who would care so much that they would take his life to protect those secrets? There are answers, Adam, and we have to find them."

"What now, then?"

"We have to find the box. Michael had it for only a couple days. Maybe he hid it somewhere, and the killer was unsuccessful in his attempt to get it. Or maybe he wrote something down in his room, on his computer. Maybe he told someone else about it. We have to retrace our steps. We've got to go over everything again. Maybe we missed something."

"Where would you like me to start?"

"I think you should go back to the Kayak School and talk to the kids again. Maybe one of them talked to Michael about it. Or maybe Robert knows something he hasn't told us. Talk to anyone and everyone, Adam. You might turn up something."

"Right. I'll head straight over there. And how about you?"

"I'm going to concentrate on finding Kit. She's armed and dangerous. We know she's a kidnapper, and she may be a killer. We have to find her."

AFTER A QUICK STOP at Dorothy's to pick up Duffy, Riley and Marie drove back down the main island road toward the Cliffhouse.

"Are you sure we should be doing this?" Marie asked as they unloaded a few of their things from the car and unlocked the front door. "What if Paul finds out? He's going to be furious!"

"He won't find out, Marie, because Dorothy agreed to cover for us tonight. I want to be at home. If Kit is behind all this, then I need to know that. I don't think she would ever harm us. Do you?"

"You weren't the one who was jumped in the woods, gagged, and tied up inside a damp old shed."

"We don't know for sure that it was Kit who did that."

"Who the hell else do you think it was? Those guys saw her leave in their boat, and she was armed. Doesn't that concern you?"

Riley was quiet for a few seconds. "Yeah, you're right. It concerns me. So I'll lock the door, put a chair under the door handle and sleep next to my rifle. Will that help?"

"But I'll be the person downstairs, and that's where the killer will come first. To me."

"But we established that he or she won't be able to get in, didn't we?"

"So you say. I'm not so sure."

"Okay, then let's trade beds for tonight, and you go upstairs. You can even take Duffy if you want to. I'll stay down. Feel better?"

"Some. But not that much. And you know Duffy won't sleep up there with me if you're down here."

"Maybe not, but at least she'll be on guard if we need her. Let's unpack a bit, and if you want me to, I'll even call Constable Paul and tell him we're out here. Would that make you feel better?"

"Immensely."

"Right. I'll do it, then. I hope he doesn't make us leave. I'll tell him it's only for one night."

"And tell me again why this is so important to you?"

"I want to go through Aunt Joan's things again. What if we missed something? We know now that Michael discovered something with some important information in it. We know that Kit has history, somehow, with this island. We know that the nanny wrote all those letters to Aunt Joan, and that two are still missing. These are all puzzle pieces that I think are somehow connected. I have to find those two letters. It's possible they could help us figure this all out, don't you think?"

As apprehensive as she was, Marie agreed that Riley was right about that. "Okay, you win. We have some work to do here, but let's make it snappy so we can get out of here first thing tomorrow. I would sleep a lot better anywhere else."

"Yeah, me too, but sleep isn't the most important thing right now."

Once inside, they settled in to their various tasks. Marie went about making some lunch, and Riley went upstairs to begin the search process through her aunt's things.

Riley turned her attention to Aunt Joan's closet as a first step. She removed articles of clothing, one by one, and folded them and put them in a cardboard box. As mundane as the task was at one level, at another it was very personal and painful. She saw Aunt Joan's cranberry red sweater, the one she always wore during the Christmas season. Checking the pockets, Riley found two pieces of peppermint candy, individually wrapped. Aunt Joan loved sweets. Riley felt the tears rising, and she let them spill over. She felt too much, thinking about Joan and Kit and Michael. Why did life have to get hard sometimes?

She allowed herself some time to let the sadness in, and then tried to go on with the task at hand. She knew of a women's shelter in Vancouver that could always use donations, and Riley thought that's where Aunt Joan would want her things to go. She put them carefully into the three produce boxes she'd picked up at the Daystar Market.

Once she'd stowed the few dresses and the many blouses and pants that Aunt Joan had hanging in her closet, Riley noticed a hatbox tucked in the back with a stack of books on top of it. She boxed up the books—mystery paperbacks, mostly, she noted—but none that Aunt Joan would want her to keep. The important books, many by Jane Rule, had been in a special glass bookcase downstairs, and her aunt had displayed them proudly. They were Riley's now.

She pulled the hatbox out to check its contents. Probably one of Aunt Joan's old frilly church hats. She had been intrigued with her aunt's hats as a kid. She loved the ones with the delicate lace that came down in front of Aunt Joan's face. What were the hat designers thinking? How could Aunt Joan see out?

She opened the light blue box and was surprised to find not hats inside, but Aunt Joan's family Bible. Riley knew it immediately, for it was the one Aunt Joan had always carried with her to church since Riley was a little girl. The white leather was worn from years of handling. The case closed with a zipper, and Aunt Joan always kept it zipped, except when she was in church. Riley could still hear the sound of that zipper opening, ever so slowly and quietly, as she and Aunt Joan sat in the balcony of the Portland First Christian Church. Aunt Joan had lived with them for a year or so when Riley was ten, and she always insisted Riley go to church with her. Riley had sometimes resisted back then, but now she was glad she had the memory. She never thought she would lose both her parents by age thirty-five, but she had. And now she had lost her one remaining aunt, and any memories she could hang onto were precious.

Riley lifted the Bible out of the box and ran her hand over its soft leather cover. The spine was worn from so many openings and closings, but the pages themselves were in excellent condition, of course. Aunt Joan always took good care of her things.

She unzipped it and turned to the first page.

"To Joan with all our love, Mother and Dad. May, 1945." She'd never seen that inscription. That would have been her grandmother's writing. Riley wondered if Aunt Joan would have wanted her to have her Bible, and she supposed she would, since Aunt Joan had left everything else to her. This seemed like a very important piece of Aunt Joan's life, though. Riley knew she would take good care of it.

She leafed through the pages and smiled at the tiny notes Aunt Joan had written in the margins. Some passages were underlined, in blue fountain pen ink, and Riley recognized many of them because her aunt had taught them to her. As a ten-year-old, Riley's favorite had been the Bible's shortest verse: "Jesus wept." She always wanted to choose that one when it came to memorizing Bible verses for Sunday School, but Aunt Joan only let her use it once. For never having kids of her own, Aunt Joan had been pretty savvy when it came to understanding them.

Riley was about to zip up her Sunday school memories when a soft pink envelope peeked out of the back of the worn white book. She was surprised to see her name on it in Aunt Joan's neat handwriting.

Riley opened the envelope cautiously. Why would Aunt Joan write something to me and then leave it in here? She unfolded the page. It was written on a page of thin stationery, which was paper clipped to four or five more pages of writing.

> *My Dear Niece,*
> *I will leave these letters here in my Bible because I know that you would never part with the Bible, and these words will be for your eyes only, whenever you may discover them after I'm gone.*

Riley read on, her heartbeat quickening.

> *Attached here are two letters I've kept since 1949. They are from my oldest and dearest friend, Katherine Taylor.*

Oh, my God, Riley thought. The missing letters!

> *Katherine left Galiano that year, shamed and humiliated. We were the dearest of friends, and it broke my heart to see the way people treated her. I cried every night for a month, missing her so and wanting her to return. But she never could. You'll see why when you read what she wrote.*
> *Here is what I want you to do with these. Never disclose their contents to anyone. Keep the letters with my things, just in case there is ever any situation which would make them valuable. I cannot imagine what it would be, but neither can I bring myself to burn them. They and the others she wrote are all I have left of my Katherine.*
> *This I ask of you, my dear and only niece. I trust you above all others, and I know you will do the right thing.*
> *Lovingly,*
> *Aunt Joan.*

The note was dated July, 1996.

Riley smiled at Aunt Joan's cleverness in putting the letters where she did. It made sense: Aunt Joan knew Riley well, and knew that some day after her death her niece would find the Bible, hold it lovingly and unzip that familiar, worn zipper. And when she did, she would find the letters.

Your plan worked, Aunt Joan. I only wish you were here so I could ask you all the questions that are flying around in my head.

Riley removed the paper clip and began to read the first letter, dated September, 1949.

> *My Dearest Joan,*
> *It is the hardest thing I ever did, leaving Galiano. I only wish I could turn back the clock and bring those children home. But we both know I can't, and we both know I must go.*
> *He will never admit that he loved me, and there is no way I can ever prove it. But that doesn't matter, anyway, because I'll*

never see him again.

The letter went on, describing Katherine's new home and the people she was living with, but making no more mention of "him." Riley skipped over most of it and got to the end.

I will write again in a month or so.
I love you.
Your Katherine.

Reading what Katherine had written, Riley realized that she and Aunt Joan were such sweet, dear friends, much like she and Marie were. It made her feel closer to them, somehow.

She put the first letter aside and began the second, dated December, 1949.

My Dear Joan,
I don't know if I can even tell you this, my closest and dearest friend in the world. Please, Joan, you must swear to tell no one, ever.
I'm afraid my worst fears are come true. The doctor confirmed it, Joan. Oh, God, I don't know what I'll do. I'm going to have a baby.

Riley stopped reading and let the news sink in: Katherine was pregnant when she left Galiano. She thought for a moment about what this news must have meant to her aunt, who could tell no one. What a burden, all those years.

She read on.

I feared this, Joan, but I was hoping it wouldn't be so. He told me it wouldn't happen. He told me he loved me, too. We had such a wonderful connection, and he told me that someday we could be together. I believed him, Joan. I did. But now because of the accident I can't be with him because I can never come back to Galiano, and he can't come here to be with me. He must never know. Please, Joan. Don't tell him. I only tell you because I am about to burst with it, and I can't handle this alone.

I will never write another word about it, though. You must burn this letter, Joan. Please. I don't want to run the risk of anyone else ever finding out.

If he knew, he would probably follow me and want me to be with him. That can't happen. He has a life there, don't you see? I must do this alone.

The letter ended with another plea.

I have told the people here that the father is a boy I met on the ferry. I told them he's a musician, from the States, and I'll never see him again. Please, Joan. You must say that too, if anyone ever asks. But I don't suppose they will because I can never come back.

I have left something there. On Wallace. It's a charm, Joan. He gave it to me. It's in David's prized possession. That's all I'll say, because I know you know what I mean. Someday, when the time is right, maybe you can retrieve it.

I love you. You are my dearest friend in the world.

It was signed, again, "Your Katherine." Riley folded the letter and put it back into the envelope that Aunt Joan had written her name on. Aunt Joan had wanted her to have these letters, but Riley wasn't sure she understood why. She was sure, however, that the story had something to do with Michael's murder. What did he find on Wallace Island? Was it information crucial enough to lose his life over? Riley shuddered. Please, God, don't let Kit be a murderer.

Chapter Thirty-Nine

"I'VE FOUND SOMETHING ELSE," Riley yelled down to Marie. "I think it's significant."

Marie came upstairs and read the two letters. When she was finished, she looked up at Riley and sighed. "Now what?" This is very disturbing. We have to tell Constable Paul."

"I know. We will. Right now."

Riley phoned for the constable, and Detective Grant said Paul was out at the Kayak School re-interviewing several people about Michael's murder. He would call him on his cell and tell him they needed to talk to him.

"Is there something I can do?" Adam asked.

Riley hesitated, but she wanted Paul to hear about this new information first.

"No, thanks, Detective Grant. Have the constable call me, okay?"

He said he would. A few minutes later, Paul called, and Riley was explaining the letters' contents to him. Paul told her to put them in a safe place. His plan was to interview two others, and then come by the Cliffhouse later that evening.

"That information can wait for now, don't you think?" he asked Riley. "I mean, it happened over sixty years ago, and whatever clues those letters hold will still be there when I arrive tonight. And by the way, Riley, what the hell are you doing at the Cliffhouse, anyway? I thought you were staying with Dorothy."

"I know, Paul. We are. I was going to call you to let you know we're here for a few hours. I wanted to see if I'd missed anything in my aunt's effects, and indeed, I had."

"Well, you're okay there for a few hours, but when I come out later tonight I want you to collect your things and follow me back to Dorothy's."

"But—"

"No arguments, Riley. I'm the law here, remember?"

"Right, Paul. We'll see you later tonight, then."

"Good. And don't go anywhere."

Riley agreed to that simple request, hung up the phone and wondered when this all would end.

They passed the afternoon doing more sorting and packing, which Riley found therapeutic. She didn't expect Paul until after nine, so she had plenty of time to keep digging around the Cliffhouse for whatever clues might be hidden there. So far, nothing had presented itself, but Riley wouldn't give up.

"What exactly do you think you might find now?" Marie asked her after they'd stopped for a bite of dinner and took a break out on the deck. The sun was beginning to set, sending orange sparkles across the dark green water. Three sailboats moved slowly down the channel, and a couple of kayakers were exploring the rocky outcroppings far below them.

"I'm not sure, Marie. Maybe nothing."

"Then why keep looking?"

"What if Aunt Joan knew the answers? What if we can turn up something to show Kit isn't involved with these murders? Wouldn't that be worth any amount of searching?"

"Yes, it would."

"Okay, then. Back up I go." Riley headed inside to go upstairs to her aunt's bedroom.

"Do you think it's cold tonight?" Marie asked, reaching for her sweatshirt.

"Yeah, it is kind of chilly. Shall we make a fire in the wood stove?"

"Good plan. You know how quickly the place warms up. It will be toasty upstairs very soon. Clever the way they left the stovepipe exposed in the bedroom when they built this place."

"Clever and funky, but it does serve a purpose."

"I'll light a fire and do these few dishes. Holler if you need me."

The sunlight was fading fast, and Riley had to turn on the bedside lamp to see enough to sort through the drawers of the desk. It was a tedious process because Aunt Joan seemed to have been one who never threw anything away.

After forty-five minutes of sorting through stubby pencils, paper clips, old grocery receipts, and miscellaneous books of matches from all over everywhere, Riley realized it was getting late, and they hadn't heard from Paul.

"What time is it, Marie?" she yelled down the steps.

"Nearly nine-thirty."

"Paul's late. I wonder if he forgot us."

As Riley posed that question, the crunch of tires sounded on the gravel driveway.

"I think he's here now," Marie said. "I heard a car pull up."

"About time. What if we'd needed the law here? Guess he doesn't consider us too high a priority, after all."

"He's got a lot to do, Riley, remember? Be nice."

Riley heard the knock and walked into the kitchen as Marie opened the door. Duffy was barking madly, as she always did when anyone knocked.

"Glad to see you, Pa—" Marie began to say.

But it wasn't Paul at the door.

"Richard. What a surprise! Come on in. We thought you were Paul. He's coming by tonight to pick up some things."

"Oh, yeah, I know," Ellison said, glancing around the room and then nodding a greeting to Riley. "He asked me to come by and let you know he's going to be late. Got held up."

"That's kind of you," Riley said, "but you could have called. You didn't have to drive all the way out here."

"It's no trouble. I was coming this direction anyway. So what are you gals up to? Find some more tantalizing clues?"

Riley liked Ellison, but she didn't feel she knew him well enough to share any real information with him. "No, not at all. I was looking at a few old things of Aunt Joan's—some letters and notes she was keeping for a novel, that's all."

"I see," Ellison said.

"We're hoping that Paul can solve this case," Marie said. "It has everyone on the island feeling edgy."

"Sure has," Ellison said. "I'm surprised you two are even staying out here, all alone at the Cliffhouse."

"We're not alone," Riley said. "We have Duffy."

"Good watchdog," Marie added.

"Sure is." He laughed. "She watched me walk right in."

Riley didn't like it when people made fun of her dog, so she said nothing.

"Gals, I'm going to say goodnight, and I'm glad you're okay. I'm sure Paul will be here in the next hour or so. He told me to ask you to stay put."

"We will, Richard," Riley said. "Thank you for coming by."

"No problem. Maybe see you two again soon back in town." With that, he headed for the front door. "You keep your door locked now, okay?"

"We will," Marie said. "Goodnight."

Riley went to stand by the window and watch as his headlights came on, then panned across the grove of madrona trees next to the Cliffhouse. The car made its way slowly down the narrow gravel lane.

"Did that seem odd to you?" Marie asked as Riley turned away from the window.

"Yeah, it did. Can't quite put my finger on why, though."

"I must say there's something a bit strange about him. But it was nice of him to come by."

"Uh-huh, it was. Wish I knew if he was up to something."

"Shall we let it be and move on now?" Marie asked. She was always good about trying to put closure on things. "No need to start worrying about something new, is there?"

Riley knew she was right. "Okay, then back upstairs I go. Call me if you need me for anything."

Riley went up to tackle another desk drawer. An hour later, she was still sorting and Paul still hadn't shown up.

"Marie, what time is it now?" she yelled. I should get a watch, she thought. They have them at Thrifty Drug for $4.99.

"It's almost 10:30, Friend. It's getting late. I'm going to take Duffy out for her evening business. Back in a minute."

"Do you want me to come with you?" Riley called down the stairs.

"No, I'm okay. I'll take a flashlight. And of course, I have Duffy to protect me."

"Okay, be careful out there."

Riley heard the door close behind Marie. From the upstairs window, she saw Duffy and Marie go down the path, just out of the light from the porch.

A couple minutes later, Riley heard the front door open. It had a distinctive squeak. "Hey, Marie. Back already?"

Marie didn't answer, but Riley heard some thumping around.

"Hey, Night Owl," Riley hollered. "Did Duffy do what Duffy was supposed to do?"

Marie's thumping turned into Marie's footsteps on the staircase as she made her way up the seven steep steps to the bedroom.

"I think you'd better get a new battery for that hearing aid," Riley teased as she turned around to greet Marie. "It's not working very..."

Kit stood at the top of the stairs holding a .22 pistol.

"Please, don't say anything," Kit said. The gun, in her right hand, was pointed toward the floor. She had a green daypack over her left shoulder. "I'll talk for now."

Riley was silent and stunned at the sight of this person who had become both intriguing and dangerous. She hoped Kit couldn't hear the thumping of her heart because it sounded very loud from where she was standing.

"There's a lot you need to know, Riley, and I don't have much time. I guess you know I took a huge risk in coming here."

"How? Why?" Riley began to form another question. Kit cut her off.

"Don't talk, Riley. Please listen. I'm here because you're the only person on this island I feel I can trust, and I need your help."

Riley examined Kit as she waited for her to go on. Kit was disheveled. Agitated, unkempt. Like she was a fugitive, which, Riley realized, she was.

"I know it looks bad, Riley, but you've got to believe me. I didn't kill Michael. I wish I knew who did. I wasn't anywhere near the Kayak School the night he was murdered. I don't even know why someone wanted him dead."

As Kit spoke those words, the front door of the Cliffhouse opened, and Riley heard the jingle of Duffy's collar as she and Marie came into the kitchen. Kit put a finger to her lips in a "Shhhh" gesture and whispered "Call her up here."

Riley didn't want Marie within range of Kit's gun, but didn't think she had much choice.

"That you, Marie?" she called down the stairs. "Come on up here for a minute, would you?"

"Of course it's me, Dearie. Who else would come waltzing through our front door at this time of night? Any word from Paul?" Marie came the stairs, still talking. Duffy followed her. "I can't believe he's not here yet. I wonder if something came—" She stopped when she saw Kit, who was now standing on the far side of the bedroom where she could keep both women in her sight at all times.

"Hello, Marie," Kit said. "Sit down, won't you?" She gestured toward the rocking chair in the corner of the bedroom. Marie sat. Duffy, seemingly unaware of the unfolding drama, plopped down by the bed and closed her eyes.

"Marie," Riley began slowly in a forced-calm voice, "Kit was beginning to tell me why she's here."

Marie's face was pale. "Right."

Kit continued. "As I said to Riley, you have to believe me. I didn't kill Michael. Why would I?"

Riley desperately hoped that Marie would not try to answer that question. "What do you want with us?"

"I want you to talk to the constable for me. I want you to convince him I'm innocent so that I can come out into the open, and we can all find the real killer."

"And how do you expect me to do that?" Riley asked. "After what you did to Marie out on Wallace? Come on, Kit. Do you think I'm stupid? I mean, we—"

"No, I don't think you're stupid. But what are you talking about? On Wallace? I never even saw Marie out there."

Riley laughed. "You are one hell of a trip. How can you stand there and tell me that, when just last night, you grabbed her in the woods and left her tied up in some old shed? How can I trust you about anything, knowing you did that?"

"I suppose you can't, *if I had actually done that!*" Kit spoke the last six words slowly and loudly. Then she turned to Marie. "Do you think I did that? Why do you think it was me?"

"I couldn't see who it was," Marie said. "Constable Paul says it was you because then you tied up those two guys and took their boat."

"I will admit to the boat heist, but that's the only thing I wish I hadn't had to do. I had to get out of there, didn't I? From the way I hear it, Constable Paul has me already tried and convicted for Michael's murder. I was out at Wallace hiding because I can't, under any circumstance, let him take me into custody. I managed to stay out of sight there, but when all the commotion started, I knew I had to disappear. I didn't even know what it was all about."

"So, it wasn't you? Who kidnapped Marie?" Riley asked, still skeptical.

"Of course not. Why would I? What purpose would that serve? I don't know who kidnapped her, or why."

Riley hadn't thought about it that way. "I don't know, but after everything else they say you've done, it didn't seem out of character."

"See? That's what I mean! They have convinced even you that I'm evil. Jesus, Riley. I felt like maybe we had something together. What about that kiss on the beach? How could you think those things about me?"

Of course, Riley had had the same thoughts, but she was determined not to let Kit know that. She said nothing.

"Okay, I guess that's not a question I expected you to answer. I have some other things to tell both of you, and then I'm gone. By morning, I will be far from here, and you can bet you'll never see me again.

"Here's the thing," Kit said. "I think Michael was killed because he found out something at Wallace Island, and whatever he found has to do with my grandmother. I didn't tell you, Riley, because I wanted to wait until I had more information. I asked Michael to get it for me. He did, but when I asked him what he found, he wouldn't tell me. Whatever it was, I think that's why he was killed. I don't think I can ever forgive myself because if it weren't for me, he would never have gone out there." Kit paused, apparently contemplating her next sentence.

Riley started to say something, but decided to wait and see what else Kit might divulge.

"My grandmother left this island as a teenager. She moved to Toronto, and she never came back. She told me she left something here. An old charm of some kind, on Wallace Island, in what she called 'David's prized possession.' I've been out there searching, and yesterday I think I discovered where it had been. But the charm is gone, Riley. I think Michael beat me to it."

Riley's face paled. That *was* it, the connection! The enormity of the truth almost knocked her over. This mysterious, alluring, dangerous, beautiful woman was the granddaughter of Katherine Taylor, Aunt Joan's best friend.

Riley shot a glance at Marie, and she could tell by the look on her friend's face that Marie understood, too.

"What was significant about the charm?" Riley asked.

"I honestly don't know." Kit paused. "You have to believe that."

"If you don't know, then who does?" Marie asked.

"Whoever killed Michael knows. And that person is still out there."

"And you want me to go to Paul with this story?" Riley asked. "Do you actually think he'll believe it?"

"I have to try."

Riley, still standing beside the bed, shifted her weight. "Do you want to sit down?" Kit asked. "Go ahead. It's okay"

Riley sat at the foot of the bed. She sneaked a peek at Marie, who was still pale and scared. Riley opened her mouth to ask another question, but stopped when she heard another thump from downstairs. It was a soft sound. She glanced quickly at Kit to see if she'd heard it, too, but it didn't seem she had. Thank God, Riley thought. It's Paul. But

I have to warn him she's here! She desperately wanted to do something, but she heard him walking across the kitchen floor and toward the stairs, which gave her no time to formulate a plan.

By now, Kit heard him, too. She did another "Shhh" gesture and kept the pistol trained on the top of the stairs.

The visitor was silent. His form slowly emerged as he came up the stairs. Riley let out an involuntary gasp when she first got a glimpse of his face.

Richard Ellison.

He had a gun.

He quickly rounded the newel post at the top of the stairs and pointed his weapon directly at Kit.

Chapter Forty

"WHAT THE—?" RILEY BEGAN to say.

Ellison cut her off. "It's what I thought. That's why I came back, ladies," he said, the pistol still aimed at Kit. He stood at the top of the stairs in the doorway of the bedroom. "I was worried about you two, so I parked down at the end of your lane, out of sight, and waited. I saw her come this way on foot.

"You can shoot me, Kit," he said, "but when you do, I'll shoot back. No telling which of us will be successful, is there?"

Kit did not drop her gun. She stood, silent, for a few moments. Riley so wanted to know what was going through her head.

"It's over, Kit," Ellison said. "You've done enough damage. How many more do you think you have to kill to protect your terrible secret?"

"I don't know what you're talking about, Ellison," Kit said. "You're a liar. Riley, Marie—don't believe him. It's not true!"

"It's not, huh?"

He seems pretty sure of himself, Riley thought. Actually, she didn't know what to think, so right then and there she made a promise to herself not to come to any conclusions in the next few minutes. Whatever was going down here was dangerous, and she needed to concentrate on getting Marie and herself out safely. How they would manage that, she had no idea. But she knew she'd better come up with a plan.

"Come on, you two," Riley said. "Let's—"

"Riley, I think this is a good time for you to be quiet," Marie said, surprising everyone by demonstrating she still had a voice.

"Good idea, Marie," Kit said. Then, to Ellison, "Why is it you think I did all these terrible things, anyway? What possible motive could I have for killing Michael?"

"I'm not sure, but I have an idea about that, and I think I can prove it."

Riley's mind raced with what to do.

"Let's settle this debate once and for all," he said. "If you're innocent, you'll go free, Kit. We have a good justice system here in B.C. But if you killed Michael and Russ you know you have to pay."

Kit said nothing, and she didn't put down the gun.

"I'd like you to empty your pockets and turn them inside out," Ellison said. "Do it slowly, so all three of us can see what's in them."

"My pockets? Are you nuts?"

"Why no, I don't believe I am," Ellison said coolly. "Do it, Kit."

"Right. So I'll put down the gun, and you can control this whole scene, right? I don't think so."

"So hang on to the gun if you want. All I want is to see what's in your pockets."

Kit sighed, looked first at Riley and then at Marie, and shifted the gun to her left hand. With her right, she pulled a book of matches from her jeans pocket. "There. Satisfied?"

"Turn it inside out, and then do the others. Your jacket, too," he said.

Kit emptied them, one by one. Some Chapstick, a two-dollar coin, a stubby pencil. "That's it. Can we stop playing this game now?"

"Not quite. Riley, get her daypack."

No one moved.

Kit asked, "What do you want with it?"

"I think you know."

Flustered, Kit fumbled at the strap, pulled the pack closer to her body, and stared at Ellison.

Ellison narrowed his eyes into an evil grimace. "Are you going to give up the daypack, or do you want to go three against one? Your choices here aren't all that good, are they, Kit? If you've nothing to hide, then why's it such a big deal?"

Riley thought Kit was about to relent. Good. At least if there's nothing in there, maybe Ellison would back off, call Paul, take her into custody and get to the bottom of this. No bloodshed, please, God.

Kit shrugged, kept the gun pointed at Ellison, slipped the daypack off her shoulder and tossed it to Riley who began to unzip it.

"Hold it right there," Ellison said. "Bring it over here. How do I know you're not in cahoots with her? Jesus, you can't tell who to trust anymore on Galiano. It's like the entire island is filled with liars, murderers and thieves."

"Hey," Riley said. "I'm none of the above, so leave me off that list."

"Just toss it over here," he said. "I'll do the honors."

Riley turned to Marie for advice, got a nod, then tossed the daypack across the room.

"Okay, then, let's see what we have here." He rifled through the items in the outer zippered pockets. Another Chapstick, keys, a pencil, and a few receipts. He put it all on the nightstand.

"Told you," Kit said. "There's nothing in there."

"I'm not done. Not so fast." He continued his search. When he got to Kit's wallet, he removed the bills—about $60 in Canadian currency—and then unzipped a coin purse. He spilled out eight coins of varying amounts onto the table. Nothing unusual there, either.

"Satisfied?" Kit asked.

"Not quite." He dug deeper into the daypack. "There's a separate pocket here, closed with Velcro. Let's check that."

It was quiet in the room, except for the sound of Ellison rifling through Kit's things. Yep, there's the sound of the Velcro opening, Riley thought. Come on, Ellison, let's get this over with.

"Feels like there are other coins in here. Special hiding place, Kit?" She glared at him. He didn't let up. "Let's see what's in here, then." He pulled his hand from the bag and dropped three more coins onto the nightstand.

Except one of them was not a coin. Even from across the room, Riley could tell that it was a charm. It still had the metal loop attached where it had been fastened to a necklace or a bracelet.

Kit stared at what Ellison dropped on the table. She was speechless, it seemed, momentarily.

"Where did that come from? That wasn't in my bag! It's a lie, Riley! It's all a lie!"

Ellison used a pencil tip to pick up the charm by the loop so that Marie and Riley could see clearly what it was. It was about the size of a quarter, tarnished, but the inscription seemed legible.

"Would you all like to know what is inscribed here?" Ellison asked. His voice was starting to give Riley the creeps. "I'm sure Kit would like to know. But then, she already does. Don't you, Kit?"

Kit managed to keep her gun on Ellison, but Riley could tell that she was reeling from the sight of that charm.

"As a matter of fact, I don't," Kit said. "I guess you're going to have to read it to all of us."

If she's faking it, Riley thought, she's an amazing actress. She seems totally surprised.

"Before I do, why don't you put down the gun, Kit? It's over. You've been found out. You may as well turn yourself in."

Kit looked agitated, almost desperate, Riley thought. Please, please don't do anything stupid.

"I don't think that's such a good idea," Kit said, tightening her grip and keeping the pistol aimed right at Ellison. "At least not until I hear what you're about to read."

He shrugged. "Have it your way, then. Let's check it out." He held the charm closer to the bedside lamp. "It's a silver 'I love you' charm. It's pretty ordinary, except for the initials. 'I love you' it says in the middle. At the top are the initials 'KIT.' Underneath are more initials. And would you all like to know what those are? Would you believe 'MWG'?"

Chapter Forty-One

THE ROOM WAS SILENT as everyone contemplated the meaning of those words and letters. Riley's mouth fell open, and she quickly shut it.

Kit looked pale, flustered, and upset. "That can't be! Those are my grandmother's initials, all right. But that charm can't be real. He planted it there, Riley. I never saw it before."

"Of course she'd say that," Ellison said, "because Kit knows already what we all found out just now. Ladies, meet the granddaughter of none other than Matthew William Graham."

A stunned silence permeated every inch of the room. It lingered, until Kit couldn't stand it any longer.

"That can't be true," she said. "I knew nothing about this, I swear!"

"You'd better be saying that to Constable Paul when he gets here because it's the only way you may get out of hanging for Michael's murder."

Unfortunately for her, Riley was beginning to understand. "Okay, let me see if I get what you're saying. Kit asked for Michael's help. Michael found the charm, and in doing so, he found out Kit's identity. Right? But why kill him?"

"It's quite obvious," Ellison said, still keeping his gun aimed directly at Kit. "As his grandchild, Kit is heir to the Graham family fortune. She didn't want that known until the time came to collect her inheritance—and that time isn't here yet because old man Graham is still alive. When he dies, she'll be ready to make her move and claim the money. A simple blood test would prove who she is, and she'd inherit millions of dollars and the Bodega Ridge property."

"Makes a good story," Kit said. "But that's all it is, a story. I never saw that charm before in my life."

"Right," he said. "Tell it to Paul. Thing is, I bet forensics can prove that it came from that ring box the detective found in Michael's room. The box was empty, Kit, because Michael had the charm with him when he was killed. I'm thinking they'll find two sets of fingerprints on it: Michael's and yours." He looked away from Kit and at Riley. "You know, ladies, it may be that poor Kit here never intended to kill Michael. Maybe she wanted to get the charm from him, and he wouldn't hand it over. Greed. It's a terrible thing."

Kit continued to glare at Ellison and shake her head. "How did you get it in there?" she asked. "Ha. Very clever."

Riley and Marie exchanged glances, and Riley thought that Marie looked as totally confused and befuddled as she was. What was the truth here? How could they possibly know who to believe? Something had to give, and Riley was still praying furiously that no one would get hurt. She decided to try reasoning with Kit.

"Listen, Kit, maybe this is true, and maybe it's not, but you have to realize that you're in a tight spot here, and Ellison's not going to let you walk away. Please. Don't endanger your life, or Marie's or mine. Is it worth that? If you're innocent, the constable will get to the bottom of this."

"And what if he doesn't? What if I'm convicted for something I didn't do? What then, Riley?"

"We have to let justice take its course." She knew that sounded stupid, like something she'd seen on a television crime show. She felt foolish and helpless and was beginning to think something very bad was about to happen.

"Tell you what, Kit," Ellison said. "I'll make you a deal. You put down the gun first, and then I'll put mine down. Then we sit and wait for the constable to show up. Fair?"

Kit sighed. "I hope to hell that there is justice here on Galiano, but I have a sick feeling I won't experience it."

Riley realized now that perhaps Kit didn't actually know who her grandmother was, or that she had been the nanny to Graham's children. Crazy as it seemed, she thought it was time to tell her. "Kit, there's something else."

"What, Riley? Are you going to tell me you think I murdered Michael now? What does it take for you to believe me?"

"That's not what I'm going to tell you. It's something else about your grandmother. As it turns out, she and my Aunt Joan were best friends when they were girls."

Kit looked surprised and confused. "How could you possibly know that?"

"I have letters your grandmother wrote to Aunt Joan," Riley said. "Twenty of them, to be exact. Written in late 1949 and early 1950."

"And? What was in these letters?"

"There's more you need to know. Your grandmother worked for Matthew and Ella Graham as their nanny. She was charged with the care of their children, William and Emily. A terrible boating accident happened here on Galiano in 1949. Your grandmother survived the accident but was unable to save the children. William and Emily were presumed drowned, and their bodies were never found. Nearly everyone on the island blamed your grandmother for the deaths, and she was forced to leave. She never came back."

"Oh, my God," Kit said. "She never told me that. I had no idea. No wonder she went to Toronto when she was a young woman."

Kit paused, and Riley thought she must be trying to process this new information.

"There's more," Riley said. "Your grandmother fell in love and had an affair with Matthew Graham, and when she left Galiano, she was pregnant."

Kit looked stunned. When she finally spoke, she said, "What a sad, sad thing. To think that my seventeen-year-old grandmother—banished from Galiano—was pregnant with the child of the wealthiest and most powerful man on the island, and he never helped her."

Riley said, "According to your grandmother's letters, Matthew Graham never knew she was pregnant. She didn't want him to know."

Kit said nothing, but Ellison did. "What a great act, Kit. You expect us to believe you never knew all of this? That you didn't come here specifically to find that charm and prove your bloodline? You must take us for a bunch of fools. Even your pal Riley, here. That's pretty low. You have to face up to what you've done. Michael got in your way. His death is on your conscience now. It's over. Give it up."

"So you say, Ellison." Kit gritted her teeth and said, "I'm still trying to find out what your real interest is in all of this. And believe me, Riley and Marie, he has one."

Ellison said, "Until you figure out this creative, made-up scenario of yours, Kit, what say we put the guns down, like I said, and wait for Paul?"

Angry as she was, Kit set the gun softly on the nightstand. And what would happen next, Riley never would have guessed in a thousand years.

Chapter Forty-Two

SEEMINGLY UNAWARE OF THE tense situation she was in the middle of, Duffy stood, stretched and sauntered over to lie next to Riley. All the humans in the room watched her, as though she were suddenly the star player in the drama unfolding. Five seconds later, Duffy stood again, took several tiny-dog steps over to where Kit's daypack lay on the floor, and began to growl at it.

"Duffy! No!" Riley admonished, to no avail. Duffy's growl got louder.

"You see?" Ellison said. "Even the dog realizes there's something sinister about that daypack and the woman who owns it. Good dog, Duffy."

As he finished his sentence, Duffy turned her fifteen-pound body full of guard dog spirit toward Ellison and growled at him.

"Duffy, shush!" Marie said, with an apologetic glance at Ellison. "Sorry, Richard. I'll pick her up."

Ellison still had his gun trained on Kit as Marie rose from the rocking chair to fetch and silence Duffy. No one else moved.

Duffy's low growl was the only sound in the room. Then she stopped. From outside, through the open window, came the sound of footsteps crunching on the gravel path.

Ellison turned toward the window, distracted by the sound. Duffy started barking at Ellison's feet, and Marie stooped as if to pick her up. But instead of lifting the dog, Marie used the low angle of her body to thrust all her weight into Ellison, knocking him backwards, and right into the hot stovepipe.

He screamed with pain as the hot pipe burned through his light cotton shirt to his skin. Ellison dropped to the floor. The gun skittered from his hand.

"Marie!" Riley yelled. "What the hell?"

"Get the gun!" Marie yelled back.

"You stupid bitch!" Ellison snarled.

Riley dove to retrieve Ellison's gun, but once she had it she wasn't sure what to do with it. "Marie, what were you thinking?" she hollered.

"I'm thinking there are two loaded guns here and I don't want it to end badly. I had to decide which of them to trust, so I chose Kit."

Kit looked confused, but relieved.

"I knew he wouldn't be too badly hurt. I just wanted him to drop the gun."

"Good point." Riley said. "Now what?"

Ellison was still on the floor but made a move to stand up.

"I think we'd prefer it if you stayed right there, Ellison,"

Marie took a few steps back from him and stood beside Riley. "Riley, keep the gun on him. Now we wait for the constable. He's the one who has to sort this out."

"But what if was Kit who murdered Michael?" Riley asked, making a point not to look in Kit's direction. "How can we be sure?"

"We can't," Marie said. "But I didn't think you'd want me shoving Kit into the stovepipe. You two were getting to be friends, after all. Besides, he was the one Duffy growled at, and I trust her judgment. She has a sense about people."

"Yes, she does. And I am glad you chose not to hurt Kit."

"No kidding," Kit muttered. She had picked up her own gun, but aimed it at the floor.

"How would you feel about putting that down, now that Ellison isn't threatening you?" Marie asked

Kit hesitated, sat on the edge of the bed and put the gun, within reach, back on the nightstand. "Okay, but let's keep it right here in case he decides to try something."

"Works for me," Riley said. She felt bad about having suggested Kit could be the murderer, but, really—who knew the truth?

The unmistakable sound of the front door opening downstairs filled Riley's mind with hope. Please, God, let it be Paul.

Footsteps. Toward the stairs.

"Paul, is that you?" Riley called down.

No response.

"We're all up here," Marie said.

The visitor made his way toward the steps. Two seconds later, the top of his head appeared.

Riley thought that everyone in the room let out a gasp.

"Hello, Ellison." Ignoring the guns, the women, the dog, Russ Brady moved across the creaky floor to stand over Ellison. "Surprised to see me?"

Ellison went pale. "What the hell?" he muttered, looking like he might pass out, and all of a sudden, Riley was hoping he would.

"Think you're seeing a ghost?" Russ said. "Maybe you are. Maybe you're already in hell, which is where you're going when this is all over."

The three women stared at Russ. No one spoke.

Duffy started to growl again. At Russ.

"Duffy! Shhhh!" Marie said, picking her up and holding her tightly.

"We thought you were dead," Kit said, stating the obvious.

"Yeah, I know," Russ said. "So did Ellison, because he's the one who tried to kill me."

Kit shot Riley a "told you so" glance and then directed her question to Russ. "Kill you?"

"Yeah. If I hadn't come to in time, he would have succeeded."

Kit eyed her gun, which was still within reach. "Go on, please, Russ. I think we all need to know what you have to say."

"He hired me, and then he tried to get rid of me," Russ said. "I knew too much. Just like Michael."

Riley's eyes opened wide at the mention of Michael's name, and she felt a shiver run up her spine.

"Go on," Kit said. "This is getting very interesting."

Ellison was on his side on the floor, shivering uncontrollably from shock and the pain of the burn on his back. "He's a liar!" he growled.

"Shut up, Richard," Russ said. "It's not your show anymore."

"Tell us what you know," Riley said. She stared at Kit, trying to discern any change in her expression. There was none.

Russ stepped back from Ellison. "He hired me to watch Michael and find out what he was planning for the environmental film. I knew Ellison back in the States. It was his idea for me to come back to the Kayak School and get all the dirt I could on Michael. Things went pretty well for a while, but I found out about the charm, and that was enough to worry Ellison. He didn't want anyone to know."

"And Michael knew, too?" Riley asked. She felt a balloon of hope, and she didn't want it to burst.

"I think he must have," Russ said. "He had the charm."

"Then how in the world did it end up in Kit's daypack?" Marie asked.

"Good question," Kit said. "But the thing is, it didn't."

"We all saw Ellison pull it out of your bag," Marie said.

Ellison groaned.

"I'm telling you, he planted it there," Kit said. "I never saw that charm before in my life."

"But you knew what it said, didn't you?" Russ asked, scowling at Kit. "That's why all this had to happen."

"No! It's not true. I had no idea!"

"Then who did?" Riley asked.

Russ gestured toward Ellison. "He did. He knew, and he killed Michael to get the charm."

"But why would he do that?" Marie asked.

"I'm not sure," Russ said. "But he has an interest in all this, and when we figure out what it is, I think we'll know why he wanted that charm so badly."

The sound of the downstairs door opening alerted Duffy, who jumped from Marie's arms, barking ferociously. "Riley? Marie? You up there?"

THIS TIME IT WAS Constable Paul who appeared on the stairs.

"Good God!" he exclaimed as he reached the top of the steps and came face to face with the five people in the Cliffhouse bedroom. "What the hell is happening here?" He drew his gun and for a moment seemed perplexed as to where to point it.

"What happened to you?!" he asked Ellison, who was still on the floor, his knees drawn up to his chest now as he grimaced with the pain of the burn.

"He had an accident," Marie said. "He kind of got burned, so to speak."

The pun made Riley raise her eyebrows, but only for a split second. Leave it to Marie!

Paul surveyed the room for the first time and saw Russ standing in the corner.

Paul suddenly looked like he'd just seen a ghost, too. "What the—?"

"Russ survived the 'accident,'" Riley said. "He didn't drown, but, according to him, Ellison tried to make sure he did."

"Thank God we're dealing with only one murder now, not two," Paul said. "That's the only good news I've gotten since all this started."

Kit said, "And are you going to tell us what you mean by 'all this?'"

"I think you already know most of it, Kit," Paul said, "because you're right in the middle of the whole story."

She smiled. "I'm beginning to understand that now, but as I told Riley and Marie, I didn't know anything about 'all this' until now, Paul. You have to believe me."

"I would like to. Maybe now we'll getting closer to the truth." He turned to Russ. "And how in the world did you end up here, Brady? We all thought you were dead. We found your kayak."

"I nearly was," Russ said. "After Michael was killed, I was afraid I'd be blamed, being the bad boy student and all. I decided I'd better get away. I packed my stuff and called Ellison because he still owed me some money."

Everyone listened, but nobody spoke.

"I headed out in my kayak and pulled ashore where Ellison told me he'd meet me. He was there, at the cove. He had the money, just like he promised. He gave it to me, I turned to get back into my kayak, and that's all I remember."

"What do you mean?" Paul asked.

"It's all I remember because he whacked me from behind. He put me into the kayak, tied me in and then submerged it."

"Jesus," Riley muttered under her breath.

"Yeah, no kidding," Russ said. "Nice guy, huh? I guess Jesus was nearby because somehow I sputtered to life and was able to get out of there. I knew if he found out I was alive, he'd try again, so I hid out not too far from here. Today when I saw his car turn down the Cliffhouse driveway, I thought I'd come and pay him a visit."

Ellison groaned again.

Paul holstered his pistol and moved to put handcuffs on Ellison. "Seems you're in a bit of trouble, Richard."

That's an understatement, Riley thought.

Chapter Forty-Three

PAUL PULLED HIS CELL phone from his vest pocket and called Adam. "Hey, I'm here at the Cliffhouse with quite a cast of characters. You won't believe it, but I'll tell you anyway. Riley, Marie, Kit, Ellison. And Russ."

Adam's response was so loud that Riley could hear squawking from Paul's phone.

"Yeah," Paul said "He's alive! What a relief. I need an ambulance out here right away, though. Ellison's been hurt. What? No. Nothing like that. No shots fired as far as I know." Paul looked up at Riley, as if for confirmation.

Riley shook her head.

"No shots, but I think Ellison's injured. Huh? No, I'm not sure how. Send a medic. And one other thing. Get over to Ellison's right away and start a search. Yeah. Russ says that Ellison tried to drown him, so I guess that gives us cause to search his place. What? I don't know. No, there's nothing yet to connect him to Michael, but I think we're getting closer. Thanks, Adam."

Paul punched a button and put the phone on the dresser. "So, would someone like to explain exactly what happened here? And, Kit, would you kindly put down that revolver?"

Kit studied the gun in her hand like she had forgotten it was there.

"Oh, yeah, I guess I can let it go now."

Riley sat back down on the bed. "Paul, is there something else you can tell us about what's been going on?"

Kit said, "I hope to God he can."

Paul paused before he spoke. "Kit, the situation is better as far as you're concerned. We found some evidence that might link Richard to the murder."

Kit and Riley's sighs were spontaneous and in stereo.

"What kind of evidence?" Kit asked.

"Detective Grant has been working the angle that it was possible for Ellison to make his way to the Kayak School through the woods and up from the beach. We found some tire tracks off-road in the forest, and they match a vehicle that's owned by an acquaintance of Ellison—Carl Brown. Isn't that right, Ellison? You had Brown doing your dirty work, too?"

Ellison scowled at Paul and said nothing.

"There are still several questions to be answered, Kit, and I need you to be very clear and straight with me. You, too, Russ," Paul added.

"What do you want to know?" Russ asked. "I got nothin' to hide."

"What did Ellison hire you to do, and why?" Paul asked.

Ellison said, "I don't have to speak to you. I have rights."

"I don't need you to tell me," Paul said. "I don't think you've been telling the truth for a long time."

Russ said, "He wanted me to spy on Michael and find out what plans he had for his film."

Ellison glared at him. He muttered, "Shut the hell up."

Russ ignored him and spoke louder. "He told me he didn't want some liberal bastard fouling up the plan to sell off the land on Bodega Ridge, and he wanted to make sure Michael wasn't going to create a film that would persuade people that way."

"And he hired you to tail him?"

"Yeah, that's it, basically. I was supposed to check in every other day or so and tell him what Michael had been doing."

"And did you know that Michael had gone out to Wallace Island that night?" Kit asked. Paul shot her a glance that said "I'm asking the questions here," but Kit ignored him. "Did you, Russ?"

"Yeah, I knew. I followed him to Spanish Hills store and then waited while he went off in his boat. I could tell he was headed for Wallace."

"And when he returned?" Paul asked.

"I followed him back to the Kayak School, watched him through his office window, and then broke in and fired up his computer. I found something interesting there."

Everyone waited.

"We're listening," Paul said.

"He wrote about a charm with a surprising piece of information on it. That's all I know."

"And you told Ellison this?"

"Yeah. He paid extra for the information."

"And exactly what was on the charm, Russ?" Paul asked.

"I don't know. I never saw it."

"But didn't Michael write about it?"

"Yeah, but only that it had information on it about Kit and that he was worried she might be here for ulterior motives. And something about sharing the information with Riley."

Paul said, "Why would Ellison care what was on that charm?" Then, turning his attention to Ellison, he added "Why did you, Richard?"

"Fuck you," Ellison muttered.

Kit said, "I guess he's not going to be too forthcoming on that topic."

"But we have the charm, Paul," Riley said. "Richard found it in Kit's backpack."

This news seemed to knock Paul off course. "He what?" Paul asked, astonished.

"The charm. It's here." On the bedside table, the charm lay next to the coins. Riley carefully picked it up with the pencil. "Here," she said as she handed the charm to Paul. "Now could you please tell us why this is so damned important?"

Paul held the charm up to the light of the bedside lamp and read the inscription. He paled. "KIT. Katherine Irene Taylor, right?" he asked, looking at Kit.

"Yes, I believe so."

"Your grandmother?"

"Yes."

"And you knew she was in love with Matthew Graham?"

"No, I didn't know. My grandmother never told us anything about him. I swear. I just found out about this ten minutes ago, right here, when Riley told me."

"But isn't that why you're here?"

"I'm here to find out what my grandmother left behind," Kit said slowly and deliberately. "I had no idea she was connected to Graham."

"Then who did know?" Riley asked.

Paul's cell phone gave two short, loud rings. He grabbed it from the dresser. "Yeah. This is Paul. You did? Where? Now? Jesus Christ, Adam. You've got to be kidding me. This gets stranger and stranger."

Everyone else was quiet as Paul wound up his conversation.

"What is it, Paul?" Kit asked.

Ellison groaned again and cursed "Fuck!" under his breath.

"Kit," Paul said, "I think you might be interested to know what Adam found in Ellison's safe."

THE SOUND OF AN ambulance siren broke the silence in the bedroom, and Riley was the first to speak. "What the hell are you talking about, Paul?" She noticed that Ellison's expression had changed from a grimace of pain to one of defeat.

"Adam and his deputy have finished a search of Ellison's house. They found an envelope of old newspaper clippings and some photographs."

"Huh?" Kit asked. "What kind of clippings?"

"About the boat accident and the drownings here on Galiano back in 1949."

Riley said, "We found those same ones in Aunt Joan's stuff. So what?"

"So Ellison had them in a locked portable safe at his home. Adam had to shoot the damn lock off to get into it. But the clippings aren't the most interesting part."

"Okay, you have our attention," Marie said. "Please go on."

"Anybody up there?" someone shouted up the stairs. "We have a stretcher here. Where's the injured party?"

"Up here, Keith," Paul said. "We're all up here."

Keith Reynolds appeared on the stairway, his EMT partner, Chris Bolton, right behind him. "Jesus, it's crowded up here," Keith said.

"Sure is getting that way," Paul said. "Glad to see you both."

Riley, upset at the interruption, said, "Come on, Paul, don't leave us hanging!"

"Wait a minute," Paul said. "We need to get Ellison out of here."

"Fine," Riley said. "But tell us what you know."

The EMTs did a quick examination while everyone waited impatiently. Keith said, "He's got a nasty burn there on his back. How'd he do that, anyway?"

"Long story," Marie said. "Let's just say he had an unfortunate accident."

"I guess so," Chris said. "When did this happen?"

"A few minutes ago," Marie said. "I kind of bumped into him and he fell against the woodstove pipe."

Chris raised her eyebrows and scanned the room for reaction or comments from any of the others assembled there, but got none.

"Get him out of here, would you?" Paul said. Then, to Ellison: "But before you go, Richard, would you like to tell all of us here why you returned to Galiano Island?"

Ellison glared at Paul and said nothing.

"Well, then, I guess I'll have to tell them."

Paul walked across the room, took Kit by the hand, and led her to stand next to Ellison. "Kit, I would like you to meet your uncle, William Graham."

Chapter Forty-Four

KIT STARED AT PAUL, then at Richard, then back at Paul. But it was Riley who spoke.

"What in the world are you saying? How can that be? William drowned when he was two years old! Is this some kind of hoax?"

"I suppose that's possible," Paul said, "but I don't think so. Along with those clippings, Adam also found several family photographs dated Christmas, 1949. Writing on the back identifies 'Theodore, Clara and Richard.' Other photos stored with those were taken in and around Victoria."

"I'm not sure I understand," Kit said.

Paul said, "Maybe Ellison would like to explain it to us before he goes."

"I'm not telling you anything, you stupid small-town cop. You're making this all up."

"I guess you can always hope so," Paul said, "but you and I both know I'm not."

"Whatever," Ellison muttered. "Screw you."

"I guess we'll take that as a goodbye," Paul said. "Get him out of here, would you?"

"Right, Paul," Keith said. "You can catch up with him at the medical lockup on Salt Spring."

"You know I will," Paul said.

Riley, meanwhile, was looking at Kit in what some would say was a whole new light.

THE DOOR CLOSED downstairs, and the siren wailed again. This time, it was Russ who was first to speak. "You mean I was doing all this for Ellison because I thought he wanted to push through the development, and all the time he had a whole different reason? Christ!"

"It looks that way," Paul said.

"But why kill Michael?" Riley asked. "What did Michael do to deserve that?"

"Michael figured out who I am and how my grandmother was connected to Graham," Kit said, finally realizing the truth. "He is the only other person who knew that I'm Graham's granddaughter."

"And legal heir," Paul added. "You stand to inherit the Graham fortune. We know that Ellison tried to befriend Michael, and maybe the two men talked about what Michael found out on Wallace Island. Maybe Michael even showed him the charm. Ellison must have gone to see Michael to get his hands on it. He wanted to stop Michael from telling that secret and stop you from knowing it. We won't ever know what really happened that night, but Ellison was desperate to get his hands on that charm. With it out of the picture, Ellison would be the legal heir."

"And inherit the estate and Bodega Ridge," Kit said. "All of it."

"That's right," Paul said. "Ellison and Carl Brown were working together. Initially, I think, to find out about Michael's film project on Bodega and stop it if they could."

"Why Carl Brown?" Riley asked. "Is he responsible for Michael's murder, too?"

"I don't think so," Paul said. "Carl's not a murderer. His interest was only in the development of Bodega Ridge. He wanted that project to go through. I suspect, though, that Carl may have been the one who stole your bike, Kit."

"Why would he do that?"

"Did you have some notes in a leather bag?"

"Geez. Yes, I did. I forgot about that."

"Adam found your notebook in Ellison's safe. Pages had been ripped out. We think it was Carl who took it and gave it to Ellison because he was working with some thug who was on the same ferry you were on when you arrived on the island."

"How would Carl know that?" Kit asked. "Why would these guys be following me?"

"We're not sure, but somehow Ellison had you pegged as a collaborator on the film project. He knew you were here to work with Michael. He was watching both of you. And I think it was either Ellison or Brown who broke into the Cliffhouse that night."

Riley said, "Why would they do that?"

"Maybe Ellison was worried about your connection with Kit, or with Michael. I think he was checking out your computer to see if you had any correspondence that would provide important information."

"Good God," Riley said, feeling miffed. "I had no idea. But I still don't get it. How could Ellison prove his relationship to Graham? Graham has Alzheimer's. He's not going to recognize even his own son."

"Simple blood testing would prove paternity," Paul said. "By the same token, we can test Kit and get that same result. It will show that she's Graham's blood relative."

"So Michael was murdered because he had the charm, and because he knew about Kit?"

"Exactly," Paul said. "But Michael wouldn't have suspected Ellison of anything. Just Kit. Michael probably thought that Kit was here with ulterior motives and planned to reveal her family connection in time to inherit all the Bodega Ridge money."

"So when Richard came to see him in his studio that night, Michael had no reason to be alarmed, did he?"

"No, he didn't," Paul said. "Probably thought it was a social visit. They talked, maybe even looked at the charm, and Michael put it back in his pocket. Ellison made his move when Michael wasn't paying attention and attacked him from behind."

Kit said, "God, I wish he'd said something to me about the charm right away. Maybe he'd still be alive."

"No way to know that, Kit," Paul said. "You can't blame yourself. Besides, if Michael had given you the charm, you both would have been in jeopardy. Ellison took it, and was probably just waiting for an opportunity to plant it on Kit. Make her look guilty."

Riley felt the tears well up—of relief, of sadness, of joy. She took a step toward Kit. "I'm so sorry I didn't trust you."

There was an awkward silence.

"How would you know?" Kit said. "You had to be careful."

Riley pulled her into a long-awaited embrace.

Chapter Forty-Five

"ALL RIGHT, EVERYBODY. IT'S getting late," Paul said, breaking the awkward silence. "I think we should say this is enough for one night and reconvene in the morning."

"Fine by me," Marie said. "I would like to get the heck out of this bedroom. I'm afraid I'll never see it quite the same way."

Paul said, "I would still like you and Riley to stay with Dorothy tonight. I'm pretty sure we have the bad guy locked up, but then again, with all that's happened, I don't want to assume even that."

"That's not a problem," Riley said. "I think a break from the Cliffhouse is an excellent idea. Kit, would you come with us?"

"I'd like that very much. That is, unless you have other plans for me, Paul. Am I free to go?"

"You are, indeed. And I'm sorry that you had to go through all this. I think you understand that I was only doing my job."

"Of course I do," Kit said, "and I still can't believe all that's been revealed tonight. It's going to take some time to sink in."

"By the way, Kit, let me ask you one other thing. Was it you who snatched Marie out on Wallace Island?"

"No, it wasn't."

"Then it was Ellison who did that, too," Paul said. "Or Carl Brown. Russ, did you know about that?"

Russ said, "I don't know what you're talking about."

Paul sighed. "Someone grabbed Marie and hauled her off to an old shed at the north end of the island. I'm thinking it was Ellison."

"But why would he do that?" Riley said.

"Probably to scare you guys and to muddy the already murky waters of the investigation. To throw us off."

Marie said, "I'd have to say that stunt was pretty successful in that regard, wasn't it? Scared the pants off me, I don't mind admitting."

"Me, too," Riley said. "I'm so sorry that happened to you."

"Wasn't your fault," Marie said. "Ellison is a creep."

Kit's eyes twinkled. "You're just lucky you're not the one who's related to him."

IN HER DREAM, RILEY was saving Kit from a sinister baker in a white apron and chef's hat. The sound of Dorothy's voice didn't fit in the scene.

"Huh?" she mumbled, turning over in her single bed.

"It's Paul," Dorothy said. "He called on my cell for you. Shall I tell him you're still asleep?"

"No, I'll talk to him."

Dorothy handed her the phone.

"Morning, Paul."

"Hi, Riley. Did you gals get any sleep over there?"

"We did, but it was a pretty late night. I would say we were all rather wound up."

"No kidding. Me, too."

"What's up this morning?"

"I'm headed over to Salt Spring to interrogate Ellison. I wanted to check in with you all before I go and make sure everyone's okay. Did Kit stay there, too?"

"She did. I think she slept out on Dorothy's couch."

"Good," Paul said. "I'd like to talk with all three of you later today, maybe around two o'clock or so. Could we do that?"

"Sure. Shall we come to your office?"

"That would be great."

"By the way, have you figured out how Jonathan fits into all this?" Riley asked. "Is he still in custody?"

"He is, and I'm afraid he's going to be there for a while. I don't think he had anything to do with Ellison or with Michael's murder, but he was involved in the ferry accident and will face charges for that."

"That's pretty sad. Poor Jonathan. He got overzealous, didn't he?"

"That he did. I think he let his passion for the island interfere with his ability to reason and do the right thing."

"Will he go to prison?"

"Don't know yet about that," Paul said. "Time will tell."

"Okay. Good luck with Ellison, and thanks for the call."

"See you this afternoon."

"We'll be there."

As she ended the call, Kit appeared in the doorway of the guest bedroom.

"Hey there, sleepyhead," she said as she came and sat on the edge of Riley's bed. "Did you rest?"

"Eventually. It was a short night, wasn't it?"

"Sure was. Kind of hard to go to sleep."

"Everything is different this morning," Riley said. "You don't have to hide anymore, and I don't have to worry about you. I'm so relieved you're safe."

"And that I'm not a murderer?" Kit said, smiling.

"Well, yeah, that too."

"There's something I've been wanting to do now for several days," Kit said. "I think now's a good time."

Kit put her hand on Riley's cheek, then bent down and kissed her gently on the lips. "Let's start over."

"I'd like that," Riley said. "Nice to meet you."

Chapter Forty-Six

"DID PAUL TELL YOU anything else about Ellison?" Marie asked as Riley pulled the car out of Dorothy's driveway.

"We didn't talk about much. I'm sure he'll tell us what he knows this afternoon."

Kit, in the back seat of the Subaru, was quiet.

"I wonder if he got Ellison to confess," Marie mused. "God, I still can't believe he's actually William Graham."

"Me, neither," Kit said.

Riley glanced in the rearview mirror. Kit saw her and smiled.

Marie asked, "What are you going to do now about all this, Kit?"

"Geez, Marie," Riley said, "you sure ask a lot of questions."

"It's okay," Kit said. "Those are all excellent questions, but I'm afraid I'm pretty short on answers today."

"Sorry," Marie said. "Sometimes my mind zooms forward, and I get ahead of myself. I know you'll need time to sort things out."

"I will. There's a lot to think about."

It was quiet for the rest of the three-minute drive to Paul's office. He greeted the women at the door. "Thanks for coming, everyone. I appreciate your willingness to help me figure all this out."

Kit said, "I, for one, am happy to help you do that."

"I imagine you are. It's been quite an ordeal for you."

Paul motioned toward the conference room, and the three women sat down. He closed the door and joined them.

"First, let me say again that I am truly sorry for all the angst this whole situation has caused the three of you, and especially you, Kit. But I think you understand that my detectives and I had to follow every lead, and some of them seemed to lead to you."

"I know that. You were doing your job. It got complicated."

"Indeed, it did. At times I wished it would all go away. Maybe soon it will. I spent two hours with Ellison this morning, and although he wasn't all that cooperative, I think we've got enough evidence now to charge him with Michael's murder and with attempted murder in regard to the incident with Russ."

"My God," Kit said. "What kind of a monster is this man?"

"We had no idea," Paul said.

"Why did Ellison show up on Galiano, anyway?" Riley asked. "Where the hell did he come from?"

"Detective Grant has been doing some investigation into Ellison's background and the picture is a lot clearer."

"How did he survive that boating accident?" Riley asked.

"Adam tried to contact the people in the photograph and found that they are both deceased and evidently have no surviving relatives, either. He did some digging and was able to determine where they lived, and he found an elderly neighbor who knew the couple when they first came to Victoria in 1949.

"Evidently the Ellisons moved from Vancouver with their two-year-old son, Richard. The neighbor said that the family seemed to be starting over. The father explained that his business in Vancouver had burned to the ground, and he and his wife wanted to make a fresh start. They bought a bakery and made quite a success of it."

"But how did Richard—or should I say William?—end up with these people?"

"Ellison says he has no memory of anything that happened, and I believe him. He was only two. We were unsuccessful in trying to locate any mention of the Ellisons here on Galiano during that time period, so the only other possibility is that they were here the day of that storm and pulled the child out of the water."

"But why didn't they tell anyone? Why didn't they bring him to shore and find his parents? And what about the other child?"

"That we can only speculate about," Paul said. "It's likely the sister drowned that night. Adam is going into Vancouver tomorrow to see what he can find out about the Ellisons' life there. The couple was childless, which in 1949, at the height of the baby boom, was unusual. We're going to try to see if there are any public records that mention their births, deaths, even a business license. That would give us more information and might provide some answers."

"What do you think happened?" Kit asked.

"Gut feeling?" Paul asked. "Or official constable information?"

"The former, please."

"I think that fate put Clara and Theodore in the right place at the right time. They had no children, but maybe they wanted children. Maybe they were unable to conceive. We'll never know that. But they must have been in a boat during that storm and plucked William from the water. Once they had him aboard, they certainly could have left the area unnoticed."

"My God," Riley said. "How could someone do that to the child's parents?"

"We'll never know the answer to that," Paul said. "Maybe they thought they were supposed to save and raise this child. Maybe they were religious and thought God sent him to them. There are so many possibilities."

"I suppose there are."

"It's always difficult to try to understand a person's motives, isn't it?" Kit said. "It's easy to judge these people, but we weren't there, and we don't know what they were thinking."

"You're right about that," Riley said. "But I still can't imagine someone taking off with another couple's child."

"I realize it's a pretty strange scenario," Paul said, "but I think it's what happened."

"And why do you think Ellison came back here?"

"Greed, pure and simple. I think he was monitoring what was going on with the Bodega Ridge controversy and keeping track of Matthew Graham's health. He was waiting for the right time to reveal his identity and claim his inheritance."

"And then Kit showed up," Marie said, "and all of a sudden his master plan was in trouble."

"Exactly," Paul said. "He was not interested in sharing the Graham estate with another heir."

"So why didn't he come after me, then?" Kit said.

"We don't know that he wouldn't have," Paul said. "I think he killed Michael to keep that secret, and if he thought you knew about it, he might have tried to eliminate you, too. That scene in the Cliffhouse bedroom could have turned out very differently if you'd given Ellison any reason to shoot."

Riley felt sick. She experienced that familiar racing of her heart. Good God, she thought. Kit could have been killed. We all could have been.

She forced herself to speak. "But he didn't get that chance, and for that we are all very, very grateful. Paul, your hard work and determination may have saved Kit's life."

"Thank you for that," he said. "I'm so relieved that we have Ellison in custody."

"I'll have to second that," Kit said. "Thank you, Paul."

"Know what? You're welcome," Paul said, smiling.

It's good to see him smile, finally, Riley thought. Really good.

Chapter Forty-Seven

"WHAT TIME DID YOU say our ferry leaves tomorrow morning?" Marie asked as she packed up the canned goods from the Cliffhouse kitchen cupboard.

"I think it's at nine-thirty," Riley said. She was carrying the last box of Aunt Joan's clothing.

"Are we going to have room for all that in the car?"

"I don't think so. I'll take it over to the Galiano Community School. The woman in charge there said she'll make the clothes available to women on the island who might need them."

"I think your aunt would like that."

"Me, too," Riley said.

"And when are you seeing Kit tonight?"

"We're having dinner at the pub around seven. Are you sure you don't want to join us?"

Marie smiled at her best friend. "I think we both know that you and Kit need some time alone. Don't you think it's going to be hard to say goodbye?"

"Love 'em and leave 'em, that's my motto," Riley said, trying to sound chipper.

"You're such a faker. But I've known you too long, Miss Riley Logan. You can't fake me out that easily."

"Are you sure? I mean, I could keep trying."

"No need, Dear One. I know you're bummed."

"Yeah, I guess I am," Riley said, "but I'm hoping it's a temporary goodbye."

"I'm thinking there's no doubt about that," Marie said. "No doubt at all."

"THANKS FOR DINNER, BUT you don't have to pay that," Kit said as the waiter left with the check and Riley's credit card.

"I know, but I want to. You're welcome."

They were in the very back booth at the pub, and the only other diners were at the other end, near the door. Riley was grateful for the privacy. Kit was playing with the plastic red straw from her Perrier.

Riley reached across the table and took Kit's hands into her own. "What are we going to do about this?" she asked, letting herself get drawn into those delicious dark eyes again.

"I'm not sure. But definitely something. We're going to do something."

"Yes. We are."

"Can I visit you in Ashland?"

"Would you?"

"Yes."

"When?" Riley asked.

"How about Sunday?"

"That's two days from now."

"Right. Are you thinking maybe that's too soon?"

"Absolutely not." Riley felt a rush—of warmth, of relief, of excitement, and of gratitude—for the presence of this bright, funny, tender-hearted woman seated across from her. "It's only a ten-hour drive down I-5 from the border, you know."

"No problem, then," Kit said.

Riley sat, holding Kit's hands, letting the silence wrap around them.

"And by the way," Riley said, "unlike the ones here on Galiano, that's a road that does go through...all the way to my house."

Kit smiled and her eyes sparkled. "Then that," she said, "is the one I'll be on."

Linda M. Vogt, a retired college educator, is a mystery writer who lives near Portland, Oregon, in the company of fine friends and a devoted terrier-poodle named Scout (who greatly resembles the character of Duffy in the book.) Her debut novel, **No Thru Road,** was a 2015 Rainbow Awards Runner-up for Best Lesbian Mystery/Thriller. She also has a short story in **Lesbians on the Loose: Crime Writers on the Lam**, a Goldie Award-winning mystery/crime anthology edited by Lori L. Lake and Jessie Chandler.

Linda produces concerts for a four-woman band, Motherlode, and teaches mandolin and ukulele at women's music camps. She is also a coordinator of the annual Northwest Women's Music Celebration, held near Portland, Oregon: www.nwmusiccelebration.com.

When she's not busy writing the second book in the Riley Logan mystery series, Linda enjoys camping, taking road trips, fishing, and watching Oregon Duck football.

Visit Linda online at www.lindamvogt.com

LAUNCHPOINT PRESS

CPSIA information can be obtained
at www.ICGtesting.com
Printed in the USA
FSHW021729190719
60191FS